Learning to Speak American

A Londoner by birth, Colette Dartford went to university in Bath and made it her home. A scholarship to undertake a doctorate led to a career in health and social research, before she moved to California's Napa Valley. Here she studied Viticulture and Enology and wrote her debut novel.

Read what people are already saying about

Learning to Speak American

'**A heartrending story, well-told**, about coping with unimaginable loss. Dartford evokes strong, sympathetic characters while writing fluently and from the heart. I raced through it.'
Hilary Boyd, author of Thursdays in the Park

'**A moving and engaging debut novel** . . . shortens the dark nights.'
Santa Montefiore

'A beautiful read, lyrically written, **poignant and emotional**.'
Nicola Cornick, author of House of Shadows

'Does everything a good book should do; **it made me smile, it made me cry**, it taught me lessons about life and love I didn't know before.'
Claire Dyer, author of The Moment

'**Sensitively written**, the characters are both believable and likeable.'

Fab after Fifty

'Lovely writing throughout captures the changes to their fragile relationship perfectly, and it's **wonderfully done**.'

Little Bookness Lane

'This is a beautifully written book, with engaging characters and **a powerfully emotional storyline**.'

The Book World of Anne

'Colette Dartford takes the reader on **an emotional roller-coaster**.'

The Book Corner

'**An incredibly emotional book**.'

Annie's Book Corner

'*Learning to Speak American* is a **beautifully written** novel.'

Rea Book Reviews

'**Engaging, well-written** . . . held my attention throughout.'

A Spoonful of Happy Endings

'*Learning to Speak American* is Colette Dartford's debut novel, but to me, it seems like she has been **a very experienced author** for a long time!'

Inked Brownies

'**An emotional story**.'

Chicklit Club

Learning to Speak American

Colette Dartford

twenty7

First published in Great Britain in 2015 by Twenty7 Books

This paperback edition published in 2016 by

Twenty7 Books
80–81 Wimpole St, London W1G 9RE
www.twenty7books.com

A CIP catalogue record for this book is available from the British Library.

Paperback ISBN: 978 1 78577 002 9
Ebook ISBN: 978 1 78577 001 2

1 3 5 7 9 10 8 6 4 2

Printed and bound by Clays Ltd, St Ives Plc

Twenty7 Books is and imprint of Bonnier Zaffre,
a Bonnier Publishing company
www.bonnierzaffre.co.uk
www.bonnierpublishing.com

For my husband, Trevor, and our children Charlotte, Matthew and Nicholas.

Marriage is a very secret place.

Iris Murdoch, *The Black Prince*

Prologue

The first time you feel the earth shudder and shake, you instinctively reach for something solid to grab on to, but everything is moving and you hold your breath in case this isn't just another tremor, but the quake that's long overdue – the one you tell yourself will never happen.

Americans talk about disaster preparedness, an expression Lola had never heard before she visited California. She was sceptical, firmly of the belief that disaster would strike in the time and place of its own choosing, and preparedness was a myth people took comfort in, one that offered the illusion of control.

She admired them, though, all those Americans busily preparing for disaster. England was brought to a standstill by a bit of snow or a heavier than usual downpour. She was often asked if she missed it. It was difficult to explain that she had willingly relinquished her world of mud and manners. She had relinquished much more too, but what choice did she have?

One

Lola remembered how only Darcy had enjoyed that foray into the Mendips, bounding along rutted paths, scampering through swampy fields, rolling joyously in cowpats. She should have told him off – bad boy Darcy, bad dog – but she was grateful to have him there, a welcome buffer between her and Duncan.

It had been almost a year since Clarissa's accident and Darcy would still lie outside her bedroom door and whimper, unable to understand why she wasn't there. Lola didn't understand either.

As Duncan had consulted an Ordnance Survey map, Lola felt it best not to mention that she and Clarissa used to hack over the myriad of bridleways that criss-crossed the Mendip hills, rendering the map somewhat redundant. If she had mentioned it, Duncan would have got that dark, brooding look she had become all too familiar with, followed by a punitive silence – the price she paid for saying their daughter's name out loud. But as they picked their way along the muddy tracks, memories of those precious times had flooded back; one so vivid Lola couldn't hold it inside.

'Polo spooked along here,' she blurted, pointing to a bend in the bridleway. 'A pair of terriers appeared out of nowhere, barking and getting under his hooves, then he took off.' Grief stabbed at her chest. So painful to talk about her little girl, but more painful not to. She swallowed hard. 'Clarissa didn't have time to gather up her reins, but she managed to grab a handful of mane and cling on until I could get past and pull him up.'

Lola relived the scene in her head, eyes closed, face tilted to the milky sky. Clarissa had let out a shrill cry when Polo bolted. Lola listened hard, trying to hear something, anything that might pull her further back into that moment, but the only sound was the wild October wind cavorting among the trees.

When she opened her eyes Duncan was gone. She called his name but he didn't answer. Darcy headed along the track at a jog and Lola followed. She spotted Duncan ahead, his back to her. He ignored her when she reached him.

'I didn't mean to upset you,' she said. 'It just reminded me ...' Her voice trailed off when he quickened his pace. Darcy dropped a stick at his feet, tail wagging, but Duncan ignored him too. Lola resigned herself to the inevitable silence, but Duncan stopped abruptly and turned.

'I don't need to be reminded we had a daughter,' he said. 'Nor do I need to be reminded why we lost her – '

Was that what he had taken from her recollection? That she had saved Clarissa from danger and he hadn't? He turned his back to her again. She wanted to touch him but he looked rigid, unyielding. A string of riders appeared, galloping towards them. Duncan and Lola retreated to the edge of the path and when the riders had thundered past Duncan muttered something about rain and that they should probably head home.

*　*　*　*　*

3

How bizarre that memory should intrude here, now, in a smart San Francisco hotel room, a world away from the windswept Mendips. But how much had really changed? Any mention of Clarissa was still taboo and Duncan's strategy was still to distract her, keep her busy, not give her time to think. Moping he called it. She called it missing Clarissa.

Duncan didn't say why he chose San Francisco for their anniversary and Lola didn't ask. She feigned delight, all the time thinking how exhausting it would be to have a whole two weeks of his undivided attention. At home they had mastered the art of avoidance – Duncan ensconced in his study, Lola busy with the horses – but such enforced proximity would quickly deplete their arsenal of small talk.

The hotel room was a shrine to French antiques. While Duncan dealt with the luggage, Lola wandered over to the tall arched windows. A glassy cyan ocean glistened beneath a blood orange sun. Swirls of pink and peach washed through the dusk sky. Parallel to the water a long, wide street pulsed with traffic and pedestrians. Lola stared unblinking, mesmerised by the unfamiliar scene. She was used to sky that teetered between various shades of grey and narrow muddy lanes that convoluted through the English countryside, as if to go anywhere directly was to miss the point of the journey. The contrast surprised her, sparked a flicker of interest she hadn't expected.

'Do you like it?' asked Duncan.

'I do,' said Lola, and not just because that was what he wanted to hear.

Nothing shone a spotlight on unhappiness like the pressure of a happy occasion, but she knew how much trouble he had gone to and that it wasn't just about their anniversary. He was trying to make recompense for Clarissa, as if such a thing were possible. Lola didn't believe it was possible to get over the loss of a child, but Duncan was determined they should move on with their lives, put it all behind them. He never said as much – that would have meant talking about Clarissa – but he offered all sorts of diversions, his way of saying, see, life goes on, without actually having to say it. He planned weekend trips that Lola would cancel, or offered a litany of hobbies in which she had no interest: tennis, bridge, a little golf perhaps.

'I've planned a pretty full itinerary,' he said, unpacking his suitcase.

'Of course you have,' said Lola quietly.

He disappeared into the bathroom saying something about an exhibition that Lola didn't quite catch. She looked at her own suitcase but couldn't summon up the enthusiasm to unpack. Instead, she went back to the window and pressed her forehead against the cool glass. They had been married twenty years. Clarissa had been dead for two. Lola wondered quite what they had to celebrate.

Duncan was brisk and full of purpose the following morning, already showered and dressed before Lola had finished her first cup of tea. His shirt – cornflower blue with a faint white stripe – had sharp creases, as though just removed from its packaging. Only the very top button was undone.

'New shirt?' asked Lola.

He adjusted the starched collar and nodded. She noticed he was wearing cufflinks: square, gold and shiny. Distinguished – it described him perfectly. No hint of the paunch that afflicted most men in middle age, or the 'scourge of alopecia', as he called it. Duncan was mystified by the fashion among young men to shave their head, as if baldness was something to aspire to. His own hair was thick and dark but for liberal glints of gunmetal grey. Lola saw the way women looked at him and remembered that she used to look at him that way too.

'Come on,' he cajoled. 'Why don't you get up?'

'I didn't sleep very well,' she said. 'Jetlag I suppose.'

He sat on the end of the bed and offered an indulgent smile.

'It's a beautiful day,' he said. 'A walk will do you good. You'll feel much better when you're up and about and doing something.'

Lola wasn't convinced, but she stifled a yawn and asked what he had in mind.

'There's an exhibition at MOMA I thought you might enjoy,' he said, on the move again. He fetched a colourful flyer from the desk and handed it to her. 'Matisse as Sculptor.'

His pleased-with-himself smile reminded her how hard he was trying and the least she could do was play along.

'Sounds great,' she said, draining her cup and pouring another tea.

* * * * *

The sun was warm and a cool breeze fluttered off the ocean. Lola looked at the ferries, the trams, the giant double-decker bridge, and thought how foreign it all seemed. The vibrancy of the city, its barefaced vitality, flooded her fragile senses, reminding her how insular her life had become. She tried to compare it to London, but San Francisco felt different – younger and more rebellious. And besides, Lola couldn't remember the last time she had visited London – nowadays she rarely ventured beyond the Somerset village they moved to six months after they were married, let alone made the hundred-mile journey to the capital. Duncan encouraged her to meet him there, tempting her with museums, galleries, the theatre – all the things she once loved. Maybe next week, she would say.

Yet he'd got her to San Francisco, and it did seem to seep through the veil of sadness that shrouded her from the world. It unsettled her, though, this reminder that there was so much in life that she used to take pleasure in.

Their timing could not have been worse. They arrived at the museum just as a party of schoolgirls filed in, and suddenly all Lola could see was her daughter. Their blazers were like the one Clarissa used to wear, navy blue with a white crest on the right breast pocket. A couple of the girls had the same long glossy hair. Lola willed them to turn around so she could see their faces. Even now, part of her couldn't quite believe she would never see her child again. The girls' excited chatter echoed in the huge marble hall, and Lola watched how they moved, laughed, spoke, longing to see some mannerism or gesture that reminded her of Clarissa – something physical to flesh out her memories, give them shape and form, right there in front of her eyes. One of the glossy-haired girls turned and looked straight at her. She was nothing like Clarissa.

'Darling?' said Duncan.

He was holding two exhibition guides that she hadn't noticed him buy.

'Yes?'

'Where would you like to start? I thought we might go straight to the Matisse?'

Lola couldn't have cared less. She longed to say, look at what we've lost, but she saw the set of his mouth, the tightness in his jaw, and realised Duncan was thinking about Clarissa too. Lola took one of the guides.

'Yes,' she said. 'Let's start with the Matisse.'

She let Duncan take the lead, even though art was her field, not his. He asked what she thought, what she knew about Matisse, why he took up sculpting so late in his career, but her monosyllabic responses must have worn him down because he said that if she wasn't interested they could leave. She wanted to say yes, but that would have spoiled the whole day, and what then? They'd go back to the hotel, be polite to each other while avoiding eye contact and any mention of the one subject Lola wanted to talk about. No. She racked her brains to remember what she knew about Matisse, what fragments of knowledge she could piece together to reward Duncan for having thought of the exhibition in the first place.

'He sculpted throughout his career,' she said, 'but his sculptures were overshadowed by his paintings. It's his painting people recognise.'

Duncan looked at her, his head tilted slightly to one side. 'Really? I didn't know that.'

'Yes. He often sculpted and painted the same figures, like this one,' she said, pointing to Large Seated Nude.

'Is it me,' asked Duncan, studying the sculpture, 'or is it ugly?'

'He liked to challenge idealised notions of gender, represent women as thin and muscular at the same time, blend elements of masculine and feminine.'

Duncan nodded. 'Impressive,' he said.

'You like it?'

'Not particularly. I meant you – your knowledge of Matisse.'

Lola smiled, said she'd forgotten most of it.

'Maybe you should take a course, brush up on your art history.'

'Maybe,' said Lola, although she knew she wouldn't.

It was later, back at the hotel, when Duncan phoned room service and ordered a bottle of champagne, that Lola was on her guard. What better opportunity to resurrect their dormant sex-life than in a five-star hotel on their wedding anniversary? It wasn't that she didn't want him, more that they had lost the rhythm of being a couple – intimacy nurtured through small, everyday gestures of love and affection. Their intimacy had been so violently disrupted that it had never recovered. Lola no longer undressed in front of him. They didn't talk about that either.

'I'm going to have a bath,' she said, shutting the bathroom door behind her.

When Duncan knocked ten minutes later, she quickly arranged the foamy bubbles so that only her head and shoulders were visible.

'Yes?' she said.

He came in holding two flutes of champagne, perched on the side of the bath tub and handed her one of the flutes. She rarely drank champagne anymore, but instantly recalled the sweet sherbet taste, the way the bubbles danced on her tongue.

'It's Schramsberg,' said Duncan, holding up his glass.

'Pardon?'

'The champagne – it's Schramsberg, produced in the Napa Valley. Official wine of the White House. We could do a tour of the caves if you like.'

'Could we?'

There it was again – that pleased-with-himself look. 'I didn't think you'd want to spend too long in the city so I found a hotel right in the heart of wine country.'

'Clever you,' said Lola, although she now realised she was coming to enjoy the novelty of the city.

He grazed her shoulder with his hand and offered to wash her back.

'Already done,' she said too brightly.

She willed him to leave but he sat there in his thick white robe, sweat beading on his face and neck. It was easier at home – so many rooms that avoiding each other hardly seemed like avoiding each other at all. Here there was nowhere to hide.

'I won't be long,' said Lola when the silence became unbearable. 'Why don't you see what's on TV…?'

He never watched television, but got the message and left. She closed her eyes and slid under the water.

Duncan hired a sleek red convertible for the drive to the Napa Valley and insisted on having the roof down, even in the chilly morning air. Lola tilted her face to the sun and breathed deeply, detecting a faint tang of salt. She could see him out of the corner of her eye, watching her, monitoring her mood. It felt strange to be sitting next to him in an open-top car – not like them at all. Over breakfast he had mentioned something about pushing her out of her comfort zone, an expression Lola thought was very un-Duncan-like, one she'd expect him to dismiss as psychobabble.

'You worry about me too much,' she said.

He kept his eyes on the road.

'It's a while since you've been more than ten miles outside of Piliton,' he said. 'I don't want you to feel' – he seemed to struggle for the right word – 'overwhelmed.'

Lola was surprised. Had Duncan just alluded to the fragility he carefully tiptoed around without ever mentioning by name?

'I don't,' she said. 'Actually, I've rather enjoyed the strangeness of it – the fact that it's so different to home.'

The tightness in his jaw relaxed.

'I'm doing my best,' she said.

He patted her leg.

'I know you are.'

Duncan's uncanny ability to find his way around foreign cities had always impressed Lola. It reminded her of a time before Clarissa was born, when she sometimes accompanied him on business trips. He travelled to alien, exotic places and she was flattered he wanted her with him. She assumed men used these occasions for extra-marital sex, a sort of adultery amnesty, so far from home that it didn't count. During the day she'd busy herself sightseeing and at night Duncan would ravish her, aroused by some hotel-room fantasy she willingly fulfilled.

'Look,' Duncan said, jolting her back to the present. 'The Golden Gate Bridge.'

Lola pushed her sunglasses onto her head, wanting to see the bridge in all its glory, illuminated by the dazzling yellow sun. The way it spanned the ocean, disappearing into what remained of the Pacific fog, endowed it with an almost mystical quality. Its colour seemed to change from one moment to the next – reddish orange, then brown, then more of a brick red. The sailing boats bobbing below looked like toys. Everything sparkled: the bridge, the white sails, the infinite expanse of water. She was gripped with the same feeling she'd had when she looked out of the tall arched window – that momentary sense of awe.

When Duncan had announced they were going to California, Lola thought of vast arid landscapes and endless sandy beaches, yet just forty minutes out of San Francisco, they were in lush, verdant wine country. She liked how the breeze whipped through her hair, the way the air smelled sweet and clean. Duncan fiddled with the radio and found a station called Vine. He sang along to the Eagles like he didn't have a care in the world. Lola sat back and tried to imagine what that would be like.

Hotel Auberge clung to a hillside above the Silverado Trail that ran between Yountville and St Helena. It mimicked the style of a Tuscan villa, with terracotta walls and tall shuttered windows. Duncan pulled up outside and two young men in polo shirts and Bermuda shorts opened the car doors for them.

Honeysuckle, jasmine and sage: as the bellboy led them through the luxuriant gardens, Lola marvelled at how intense even familiar scents became with the kiss of warm air.

'Here we are.'

The bellboy stopped outside a whitewashed cabin framed with vivid pink bougainvillea.

'This is a cottage?' said Lola.

'Uh-huh,' he said. 'You have cottages in Britain, right?'

Lola thought how 'Britain' was something only a foreigner would say in that context.

Inside it was cool and surprisingly spacious. A huge bed stood in the centre of the room, an oak armoire and dressing table to one side, a chaise longue and coffee table to the other.

'The bathroom is through here,' said the bellboy, opening a door at the far end of the room. 'Is there anything else I can help you with?'

'No, thank you,' said Duncan, pressing a ten-dollar bill into his hand.

'Have a great day.'

'Such an effusive expression,' said Lola when the bellboy had left.

'It's their way of being polite.'

'I suppose.'

'Welcome to America,' he said.

Lola wasn't sure if it was because she had resolved to try harder, or if it was the intoxicating effect of the wines, but over dinner that evening she relaxed, found herself enjoying Duncan's company, even flirting a little. She wore a black silk dress and high heels, her hair arranged in an elegant chignon. Duncan kept refilling her glass and when she asked if he was trying to get her drunk, he said *absolutely*. She wanted to reward him for not giving up on her. The odds were against them – that's what it warned in one of the bereavement counsellor's booklets, although not in so many words. The loss of a child, an only child, was more than most couples could bear. But their marriage had survived – if that was what this was. Lola wasn't sure anymore, but she was a little drunk and they hadn't made love in such a long time. He must have read her mind because he asked for the bill as the waitress cleared their dinner plates.

They made their way back through the garden, the high-pitched frenzy of a thousand crickets ringing in their ears, and when Duncan opened the door to the cottage and reached for the light switch, Lola put her hand over his.

'Leave it,' she said softly, removing the clip from her hair.

In the thin shard of moonlight that sliced through the shutters, he looked so grateful that Lola ached with regret for all the times she had rebuffed him, turned away when he had reached for her in the night. She cupped his face in her hands and tried to banish thoughts of Clarissa. Duncan unzipped her dress and let it fall to the floor. As she stood there in a puddle of black silk, she struggled to remember what it felt like before they were damaged, and wondered if it would ever feel like that again. She closed her eyes and willed herself back to those hot, passionate nights in far-flung hotels, when she yielded to his fantasies and thrilled him with her own. He moved her hair aside and kissed the soft, warm skin on her neck. Shivers of pleasure radiated from his touch, rousing some sensual memory, long forgotten. She undressed him quickly, fearful the memory would vanish into the darkness, and when he whispered – what's the hurry? – she didn't answer. Instead, she lay down on the bed and opened herself to him, knowing that if they lost this too, there might be nothing of their marriage left to save.

When Lola woke in the unfamiliar room, it took a few moments to remember where she was. Her head hurt and her mouth was parched. She needed water but there was none on the bedside table. Then she remembered: anniversary, wine, sex. She covered her face with her hands. What had seemed so natural last night felt faintly embarrassing now. They had got out of the habit of having sex, of being intimate. Duncan opened his eyes and stretched.

'Do we have any water?' she asked.

He got out of bed and fetched a bottle of Pellegrino and two tumblers from the coffee table. It seemed strange watching him walk across the room naked. At home he wore pyjamas in bed and as soon as he got up, he put on a dressing gown and slippers. He filled one of the tumblers and handed it to Lola.

'How are you feeling?' he asked.

'Hung over,' she said.

Duncan poured some water for himself and got back into bed. When she had finished drinking he took the tumbler and pulled her into an embrace. His body felt warm and strong – familiar, yet unfamiliar at the same time. He ran his fingers along the length of her spine, kissing her neck and shoulder. Lola closed her eyes and tried to relax, but the pressure in her head and the sour taste in her mouth were too much.

'I need the bathroom,' she said, freeing herself from his long limbs. 'Do we have any aspirin?'

'In my toilet bag.'

Lola could hear the disappointment in his voice but sex was the last thing she wanted. After five minutes in a hot shower, the pain in her head subsided. Duncan came in as she was drying herself, lifted the toilet seat and peed. She unhooked a robe from the bathroom door and as she was putting it on, he suggested she come back to bed.

'I'm hungry,' she said, though she wasn't at all.

'I'll order room service,' he said.

A romantic breakfast in bed would make it more difficult to fend off his advances.

'Let's wander over to the restaurant,' she said.

He turned to face her.

'Last night was wonderful,' he said.

Lola unhooked the other robe and handed it to him. She knew his nakedness shouldn't bother her, but it implied an intimacy she didn't feel. He took the robe but didn't put it on.

'Did you hear what I said?' he asked.

She nodded. He put down the robe, opened Lola's and slid his hands around her waist. She rested her forehead on his shoulder and tried to find the right words. His skin was smooth and smelled of her.

'It was wonderful,' she said. 'But be patient with me, give me time.'

He said nothing at first, just held her. She worried that she'd spoiled things – said too much, or not enough.

'Does this mean I have to get you drunk every time we have sex?' he asked.

'Not every time,' she said and he laughed.

Wine tasting was top of Duncan's agenda, but Lola couldn't face alcohol and suggested they go for a walk around town instead, get to know the place a bit. She thought he might be disappointed but he seemed pleased that she was taking the initiative, not just going along with whatever he wanted because she didn't care one way or another.

'Good idea,' he said, picking up the car keys and handing them to her. 'Why don't you drive?'

Her heart quickened at the thought of it; driving on the right, on unfamiliar roads with unfamiliar rules. They had played out variations of this scenario many times since Clarissa died. Lola wanted to be left alone, surprised that he expected anything of her when simply getting through the day took all her strength. Yet he set her tasks and tests to prove she was fine – they both were fine.

'Come on, darling,' he said, opening the driver's door. 'It's easy.'

It would take more effort to protest than to drive a few miles, so even though her head still felt fuzzy, she got in, adjusted the seat and turned on the ignition. And he was right – it was easy.

'Brilliant,' he said as she negotiated a crossroads and turned onto St Helena's tree-lined Main Street. 'I knew you could do it.'

When she reversed smoothly into a parking space and positioned the convertible in perfect parallel to the kerb, Duncan beamed with satisfaction.

'That's my girl,' he said and Lola had to look away, remembering how he used to say exactly the same thing to Clarissa.

As they strolled along Main Street, Duncan took her hand. Focus on the positive – that was his philosophy. He would be thinking about the rare closeness of last night's lovemaking, not her unwillingness to repeat it this morning. He seemed relaxed, almost content. She wondered if he faked it like she did. It was hard to tell with Duncan.

'I'm glad you suggested this,' he said. 'It's a glorious afternoon.'

'Have you noticed how everyone here smiles at you?' asked Lola.

'Can you imagine in London if everyone you walked past offered a cheery smile? We'd think them insane; hardly dare to make eye contact. I must say, I find it rather odd, all this unfettered friendliness.'

'Maybe it's the sunshine.'

'Or the wine.'

Their easy rapport made it seem as though they had stepped back in time, reconnected with an earlier version of themselves. It was Duncan's idea to stop by the estate agents. In the window were photographs of everything from hundred-acre estates to small wooden houses squeezed onto tiny scraps of land.

'See anything you like?'

A young, fair-haired man stood behind them – styrofoam cup in one hand, mobile phone in the other. The logo on his T-shirt looked like a fish and his faded jeans had the beginnings of a tear over the knee. His smile revealed dazzlingly white teeth, straight and perfectly spaced. Perhaps it was the artist in Lola, but a face like his, defined by predictably symmetrical features, seemed to lack character. Imperfections and irregularities were what made faces interesting.

'Sorry,' he said as Duncan spun around. 'Didn't mean to startle you.' He slipped the phone into his pocket and held out his hand. 'Cain McCann. I work here.'

His air of casual confidence, the ease with which he inhabited the world, struck Lola as very American. Duncan wore his confidence on the inside, strong but private. This man's confidence was of a different vintage and calibre, displayed for all to see. Duncan shook his hand.

'Duncan Drummond. This is my wife, Lola.'

'Great to meet you,' said McCann. 'Where are you guys from?'

'England,' said Duncan. 'We're staying at the Auberge.'

'Good choice,' said McCann. He took a sip from the styrofoam cup. 'You thinking of investing in some property? A vacation home, maybe?'

All they had done was look in the window. To Lola he seemed pushy, although Duncan didn't appear to mind.

'It's all rather expensive,' he said.

'Yeah,' said McCann, 'St Helena is pretty pricey. Still, if you want to come in out of the heat, I'll see what I can tempt you with.' He opened the door and waited.

Lola stayed put, reluctant to be subjected to the inevitable sales pitch, but Duncan gave her one of his encouraging smiles and led the way.

The air-conditioner hummed while a pair of ceiling fans whirred frenetically. Lola's eyes took a moment to adjust to the relative lack of brightness. Next to McCann, Duncan looked very formal – his dress code made no concessions to the heat. He wouldn't dream of wearing a T-shirt anywhere but the gym. Weekends he swapped expensive Savile Row suits for pale corduroy trousers and casual shirts. He didn't even own a pair of jeans. She knew she was being stuffy but McCann looked like he was going to a rock concert, not to work.

'Here's my card,' he said, handing them one each.

'That's odd,' said Lola, reading the card. ' "Realtor" isn't a word we use in England.'

'Really?' said McCann.

'We say "estate agent".'

'Thanks for the English lesson,' he said, treating her to another full-frontal smile. It was impossible not to smile back but just as Lola began to warm to his eager exuberance, he turned away and addressed himself to Duncan.

'So, if you were thinking of investing in a vacation property, what kind of budget would we be talking about?'

This was not how Lola wanted to spend her time. She was usually more tolerant but the dull pain of her hangover still lingered and she craved coffee and carbs. It wasn't as if they had any intention of buying a property – vacation or otherwise. She was about to make light of the idea when Duncan spoke.

'Four hundred thousand,' he said, casually. 'Dollars.'

Lola stared at him, eyebrows raised. What was going on here? Why was Duncan humouring him? If he noticed her consternation, he didn't let on. Perhaps he was missing work and wanted a distraction. McCann put his hands in his pockets and shook his head.

'I don't have anything in that price range.'

'Nothing at all?' said Duncan.

'Don't think so,' said McCann.

He sat down at one of the desks and peered at a computer screen.

'No,' he said. 'Only thing is a little fixer-upper at the bottom of Spring Mountain. Been empty for a couple of years. Before that it was rented.'

'How much is it?' asked Duncan.

McCann hit the keyboard with a decisive click.

'They're asking four-fifty but it's been listed for a while so they'll probably take an offer.'

A printer at the far end of the office sprang into life.

'Great location,' said McCann, picking up the details. 'Just a mile from town.'

He handed a set to Duncan and then, as an after-thought, printed another set for Lola. As he leaned over her she noticed a slight bump on the bridge of his nose and the faintest hint of a scar. It blurred the bland perfection of his face.

'It needs remodelling,' he said, 'but for that price, you really can't go wrong.'

Lola looked at the picture – a square wooden structure on four wooden stilts – and immediately thought of a treehouse. She had one as a child – a precarious lopsided thing her father built before he absconded with a woman half his age. When Lola wanted to escape her mother's lugubrious presence, or the many reminders of her father's absence, she retreated to the quiet solitude of her treehouse.

'It looks interesting,' she said, studying the picture. 'Unusual.'

Now it was Duncan who raised his eyebrows.

'It's a beautiful spot,' said McCann. 'We could take a drive over there if you want.'

Despite her pique at having been railroaded into it, Lola was curious to see this odd little house. The setting looked gorgeous, and he did say it was close to town. They could have a quick look around and then find somewhere to eat.

At the very least it would give them an interesting topic of conversation over lunch.

She turned to Duncan. 'Why not?'

It was the sweet, comforting smell of warm wood that first struck her. The house, made entirely of timber, stood nestled among a cordon of tall, spindly pines and shorter, thicker firs. There appeared to be just a single room – a fireplace at one end, the shell of a kitchen at the other – with a ceiling that sloped upwards to a height of maybe twenty feet. Fiery June sunshine bombarded the filthy windows, imbuing the air with a soft amber glow. A mesh of silvery cobwebs fanned out from every crevice. Dust sat thick and languid, disturbed only by resident vermin as they scurried about their business.

'Is this it?' asked Duncan.

'There are two bedrooms at the back,' said McCann. He pointed to an opening – a doorframe, but no door. 'And a small bathroom.'

Lola touched Duncan's arm, signalling that she wanted to explore. He appeared surprised but followed anyway. McCann said he had to make a phone call, that he'd be right outside if they needed him. Duncan pulled a pristine white handkerchief from his pocket and wiped a film of sweat from his brow.

'No wonder the particulars only showed a picture of the outside,' he said, looking around. 'You don't get much for your money.'

Lola peered into the tiny bathroom that led off the tiny bedroom and decided not to venture further.

'How much is it in sterling?' she asked.

Duncan thought for a moment.

'Around three hundred thousand,' he said. 'Why? You don't actually like it do you?'

It made no sense at all, but she did. Something about the neglected house defied her grief-soaked indifference. It was as though those few momentary flashes of pleasure – the view from the window, the taste of champagne, the magnificent Golden Gate – had gathered momentum and released something inside of her, allowed it to break free.

She took Duncan's arm and led him onto the rickety wooden deck. A canopy of leaves offered shade from the sun and a soft breeze carried the scent of cut grass and rosemary. She looked out at the trees and vineyards, birds she'd never seen before, butterflies as big as her hand.

'You seem enthralled,' he said.

'I am,' she said, 'but don't ask me to explain why.'

How could she explain the ludicrous notion that bringing this house back to life might somehow bring her back to life?

Two

Duncan woke to the faint peal of church bells, calling the faithful to worship. For a moment he thought he was back home in Piliton, but as his eyes adjusted to the shuttered darkness he remembered he was five thousand miles away, and that he had stopped believing in God when he lost Clarissa. Only a cruel and vengeful deity could allow the death of a child. When Father Michael had come to talk about the funeral service, he sat at the kitchen table, weathered hands clasped together as though in prayer, and spoke solemnly about the mystery of God's purpose and how it wasn't man's place to question it. He said it was a test, to which Duncan had replied, 'Well, it's a test I've failed.' Clarissa's funeral was the last time Duncan had set foot inside a church, but as he lay listening to the bells and bracing himself to face another day, his chest was heavy with nostalgia that he doubted would ever fade.

He looked at Lola, asleep beside him, and inhaled the musky scent of her skin. Such a sensual smell, uniquely Lola. It carried memories of passion and lust, of a time when they couldn't get enough of each other. She would be in his head all day when he was trying to work, and on the long train journey home he'd close his eyes and allow her to saturate his thoughts. Once she picked him up from the station wearing nothing but underwear beneath her coat, pulled off the road just outside the village and they made love, right there in the Land Rover. God, he missed that. Not just the physical act – the heat between them, the intensity.

It was a risk, bringing her to California. He had thought about Europe – Provence maybe, where they'd spent their honeymoon – but changed his mind in favour of somewhere she hadn't been before, somewhere fresh and colourful enough to penetrate her apathy, reveal some glimmer of the person she used to be. That first night, when she had watched the sun setting over the Pacific, he held his breath and waited. If that couldn't move her, maybe nothing could. Where the ramshackle little house fitted in, he wasn't sure, but that definitely stirred something in her. It made him hopeful they might finally put the tragedy behind them – start a fresh chapter in their lives, one not mired in ghosts and mourning.

After the accident, Lola had slept in Clarissa's bed, clutching her teddy bear, her pink striped pyjamas, anything that carried her scent. Often Lola didn't sleep and for days on end she didn't eat, dress or speak either. It was as if she had wanted to fade from the world. One night Duncan found her wandering through the house whispering Clarissa's name, like some macabre game of hide and seek. He knew she was lost to him, that she had slipped beyond his reach. That's when he got professional help, paid a counsellor to do what he couldn't. Emotional outsourcing – wasn't that what it was? Abdicating his responsibility. *But I want to talk to you, not a stranger. She didn't even know Clarissa.* Duncan didn't want to talk at all, but he had to do something. *Can she bring Clarissa back?* asked Lola. Duncan answered with a long sigh.

The counsellor had come to the house once a week. Duncan tried to anaesthetise himself with Scotch for those sessions, but no amount of alcohol could deaden the pain of talking about his daughter or the accident that had happened on his watch.

They would sit in the drawing room, Duncan on one sofa, Lola on another, the counsellor between them in a fancy leather wing chair. She reminded him of an English teacher he had at prep school, pale grey hair loosely pinned into a bun, sad eyes of the same colour. He was at a loss to understand why anyone would choose to wade through the murky swamp of other people's tragedy, or what words of comfort they could possibly hope to pluck from the detritus.

Tell me about Clarissa, she would say, as if it was the easiest thing in the world. Duncan remembered shooting Lola a pleading look, willing her to speak, but she had stared blindly ahead, leaving him to fill the silence. *What would you like to know?* The counsellor offered an encouraging smile. *Whatever you would like to tell me.* They waited. A grandfather clock ticked loudly, counting down every excruciating second until he could bolt back to his study and drown himself in Scotch. He took a deep breath. *She liked to draw, and play with the dog, and have cereal for breakfast, except at the weekend. I always cook a full English at the weekend.* Lola pulled a tissue from her sleeve and dabbed at her bloodshot eyes. Duncan hung his head. Had this whole counselling idea only made things worse? All he wanted was to bring Lola back to him, to establish a post-Clarissa life that was at least bearable. He understood that things would never be the same but he had to try.

He was still trying, filling the trip with things he thought Lola would find interesting. He had been particularly pleased about the Matisse exhibition until they got there and found it swarming with Clarissa lookalikes. God, the expression on Lola's face, that futile longing. He had almost given up on the whole trip, but things turned around when they got to the Napa Valley. Happening upon the estate agent's was pure good fortune. Duncan had only wanted to get out of the sun for a while – he had no intention of actually looking at property. But as soon as Lola saw a picture of that run-down wooden shack, he sensed it was the beginning of something – he didn't know what – but something. The way she looked in that hot, dusty room, the sun streaming through the grimy windows, reminded him of the way she looked when they first saw Piliton Grange, just months after they were married.

Lola's lonely childhood created a ravenous hunger that only family could sate. When she told Duncan she wanted lots of children he said, hang on a minute – how many is lots? She laughed that throaty, sexy laugh of hers and said at least a dozen. Duncan wasn't sure he wanted children but he was sure he wanted Lola, so every weekend they drove to the countryside in search of somewhere to raise their brood.

She said she was looking for the perfect village: a green with a duck pond, an old church, a village hall of course, farmhouses and thatched cottages, animals grazing lazily in a neat patchwork of fields. They found all of those things in Piliton, and a run-down seventeenth-century house too. Lola said she knew immediately it would be their home, that it was like looking into a crystal ball and glimpsing flashes of their future. It's the hope and promise of that future you're really buying. The building is just a shell until you fill it with your life, your love, your memories, and then it becomes a home. He remembered her saying it, eyes wide, voice breathy with excitement. Destiny, she called it. *Can we buy it?* He should have said it was outrageously impractical, far too large and expensive, not to mention a hundred miles from his office, but the joy on her face, the happiness he could induce with one small word, overrode all of those things.

He said yes.

She was only twenty-two, but with her history she could have been bitter, cynical about life and love. When she should have been learning about boys and French kissing, she was looking after her mother; searching for bottles, hiding the car keys, making sure the house didn't burn down because Mummy liked a cigarette with her gin and tonic. Just after her eighteenth birthday, Lola had come home from a riding lesson and found her mother unconscious on the bathroom floor, bleeding from a deep gash to her head, an empty bottle of gin still clutched in her hand. Hendricks, Lola told him. Mummy's favourite.

Her mother died three days later. She never recovered consciousness, never said she was sorry. Duncan had put his arms around Lola when she told him, said it must have been awful, but Lola said no, living with her was awful – her death was a merciful release. Lola wasn't being cruel, merely honest. It disarmed him, that degree of honesty. With Lola, things were as they seemed. No manipulation, no second-guessing. This is me, this is what you get. Is it what you want?

He said yes.

When the church bells stopped ringing, Duncan reached over to the bedside table and checked his watch. Six o'clock – half an hour later than he usually slept. Maybe the break was doing him good too. He had deliberately not called the office, not even checked his emails. He wanted to give Lola his full attention, get her to engage with life again, not merely endure it. So far so good.

'I'm going for a swim,' he whispered, not sure whether she had heard. He didn't want to wake her if she really was asleep. He knew that sometimes she just pretended.

The early-morning sun felt good on his back and when he dived into the cold water, he thought of baptism, the belief that sin could be washed away, the soul purified. He swam fifty-seven laps, one for each year of his life. His limbs felt weak as he climbed out of the pool: the good kind of fatigue that comes from physical exertion, not the bad kind that comes from lying awake at night, desperate for sleep but terrified of the nightmares it might hold. He dried himself, put on his robe and walked back to the cottage, hoping Lola hadn't lapsed into the despondency that was her default position. In many ways he blamed himself for that too. He had colluded in her prolonged mourning by allowing it to go unchallenged. He arranged the counselling sessions so Lola would have someone to talk to, but she had drifted through them in a state of trance. At first he almost envied her, the way she grieved so wantonly, so utterly without inhibition. His own grief was gagged and bound and buried in a deep dark place he couldn't reach. Sometimes it tried to wrestle free and it took all his power to hold it down. But Lola's grief had gone on too long. It had become part of who she was, who they were. He needed to put a stop to it.

'How was your swim?' she asked, rubbing the sleep from her eyes.

'Good,' said Duncan. 'Do you mind if I open the shutters?'

'Must you?' she said, stretching.

He sat on the bed and brushed her hair back from her face. It was the first thing he had noticed about her all those years ago, the luxurious auburn hair. It was longer then, halfway down her back, and she wore it in complicated styles: French plaits, chignons, things he'd never heard of. He preferred it loose and dishevelled, like it was now. She turned on her side to face him.

'I've been thinking,' she said.

'Oh?'

'About that house.'

Duncan stroked her hair. It slipped through his fingers like fine silk.

'Can we go and see it again?'

'Of course, if you want to.'

'I do. I'm not sure why, but I do.'

Seeing her lie there under the cool white sheets, he thought again about their anniversary night, how for the first time in a long time, he felt she had wanted him. It aroused him, the feeling of being wanted. He leaned over and kissed her mouth, his hand still stroking her hair. The kiss lingered between them like a question. She guided his hand to her breast. It was the answer he wanted.

McCann sounded surprised when Duncan called and asked if they could meet him at the house.

'Sure,' he said. 'No problem. How does ten-thirty sound?'

'Perfect,' said Duncan.

He put down the phone and turned to Lola.

'I don't think he expected to hear from us again.'

She finished applying sunscreen and offered Duncan the tube. He shook his head.

'So it must have been a nice surprise,' said Lola.

'Like you driving,' said Duncan and threw her the car keys.

She caught them without protest.

All the neat, tree-lined streets looked the same to Duncan.

'Do you remember the way?' he asked.

'I think so. It's somewhere along here on the left.'

Duncan sat back and relaxed, content to enjoy the sunshine and the scenery and hum along to West Coast music. The Mamas and Papas singing 'California Dreamin'' got

Lola humming along too. At first it was just a hum, then she mouthed the words, then Duncan was sure he heard her actually sing.

The house was on Falcon Drive, a wide country lane with a few single-storey houses on one side and a vineyard on the other. There was no pavement, and olive trees grew along the verge between the lane and the vines. In the distance were hills and densely forested mountains. Tucked away at the end of the lane was the house. McCann's Prius was already in the driveway and when Lola pulled up beside it, McCann jumped out and opened the door for her.

'Thank you,' she said, adjusting her sunhat. Duncan had run back to the cottage to fetch it for her when she'd left it behind.

'Beautiful morning,' said McCann, shaking Duncan's hand.

'Certainly is,' said Duncan.

He looked around, trying to fathom what Lola saw that he didn't. It did have a sort of rustic charm, and the location was certainly enchanting, but so was Piliton. Maybe it was the sunshine that seduced her, the promise of long hot days and warm clear nights. And he had to admit he'd never seen such a flawless, powder-blue sky.

'So glad you guys decided to have another look around,' said McCann. 'We could start outside if you like.'

'Good idea,' said Duncan. 'Remind me how much land there is?'

'Around an acre. It's not landscaped or fenced so it kind of blends into the hillside. There's a seasonal creek too,' he said, pointing to a clearing among the trees.

'Seasonal?' said Lola.

'It only has water a few months of the year,' said McCann. 'Rest of the time it's dry.'

'When does it rain?' asked Duncan.

'We don't get much rain,' said McCann, 'but what we do get falls in the winter. November to March usually.'

'It rains all the time in England,' said Lola, and Duncan knew instantly that the spell had been broken, that she had been sucked back to that wet November day when they lost their little girl.

'Let's go inside,' he said, taking her arm.

McCann's phone rang and he excused himself. Duncan led Lola into the house, hoping its strange magic would chase away their daughter's ghost. He looked around the empty room – at the broken window, the light bulb dangling from a piece of flex, the stained concrete floor, the doors on the kitchen cabinets hanging off their hinges. 'Tell me again why you like this place?'

Lola gave a small shrug of her shoulders. 'It's hard to explain. I feel cocooned somehow, just like when I was a child and I'd sneak off to my treehouse. It was as if none of the bad stuff could follow me there – crazy, I know.'

'So much of life is.'

'Maybe it's the climate,' she said. 'Back home is so grey. We never get a proper summer. Just to see the sun every day, smell the warm air – it feels, I don't know, energising.'

McCann joined them, said that was the office – another couple wanted to view the property. Nothing for months, now two viewings in as many days. He slipped the phone into his pocket. Duncan suspected it was a sales ploy, that there was no other couple, but he didn't want to risk it. He asked McCann to give them a moment.

'Sure,' he said. 'Take all the time you need. I'll be right outside.'

Duncan put his hands on Lola's shoulders and looked her in the eye. He knew what he had to do and the fact that he had the means, the power to do it, gave him an almost sexual thrill.

'I want to give you something – an anniversary present.'

'There's no need. This whole trip—'

'How about a little wine country bolthole? Somewhere to escape the so-called English summer.'

Lola covered her mouth with her hand, her eyes fixed on his.

'Are you serious?'

'Perfectly.'

She giggled – a light, sweet sound that dissolved in his chest. All he wanted was to fix what he had broken. It was a work in progress, he knew that, but here was a chance to prise her away from the place where their daughter had lived and died, get her to think about the future, not the past.

'Can we afford it?' she said.

'Let me worry about that.'

'But it's not even habitable. What about all the work that needs doing? How will we manage that from so far away?'

'Let me worry about that too.'

'But –'

'Look, all those things can be sorted out later. For now, you just have to decide whether you think you could be happy here.'

Lola walked over to the fireplace and lightly touched the panelling above it. With her index finger, she traced a dark knot in the amber wood. It was a few moments before she turned back to Duncan and said, 'I think maybe I could.'

Outside, McCann was talking to an older couple while a rangy black dog sniffed his leg. The dog barked when it saw Duncan and Lola. Duncan wondered if McCann had been telling the truth after all and these were the other prospective buyers.

'Hey,' called McCann. 'Duncan, Lola – come meet the Curtellas.'

Duncan knew it was old-fashioned – uncool, as McCann might say – but he thought it impolite to address them by their Christian names.

'Mike and Joanne Curtella,' said McCann, 'this is Duncan and Lola Drummond.'

What caught Duncan's attention was Mike Curtella's leg – a shiny metal prosthetic that looked like a pole with a trainer on the end.

'Good to meet you,' he said, taking Mike's outstretched hand.

'Mike and Joanne live on the other side of the creek,' said McCann.

'Oh?' said Duncan. 'I didn't realise there was a house over there.'

'We're pretty much hidden by all these trees,' said Mike, the smile on his face so big it seemed to swallow up his other features. Duncan put him at around seventy. A halo of frizzy white hair stood out at right angles from his head. His scalp was pink and shiny.

'Been there thirty-five years,' said Joanne.

'And who's this?' asked Lola, crouching down to make a fuss of the dog.

'Oh, this is Riley,' said Joanne.

The Curtellas struck Duncan as one of those couples that looked like each other: same stout build, same weather-beaten complexion, even the same wide, fleshy mouth. He was curious as to whether the likeness evolved gradually over time, a by-product of familiarity, or if it was the reason they were attracted to each other in the first place. He and Lola were both tall and slim but that was where their physical similarity ended. Her eyes and skin were pale, and in the sunlight her hair had glints of red, copper, gold. Clarissa had his dark hair and eyes, although her skin was pale like Lola's and in the summer, her face had a light dusting of toffee-coloured freckles.

'Hello, Riley,' said Lola, ruffling his floppy ears. 'We have a black Lab,' she said. 'Darcy – he's three.'

'Riley's about the same,' said Joanne. 'He's Lab crossed with something – not sure what. We rescued him from the shelter when he was a puppy. Isn't your dog travelling with you?'

'No,' said Lola. 'We left him at home.'

'Where's home?' asked Mike.

'England,' said Duncan, aware of the crispness of his accent and the fact he was the only one not wearing shorts. McCann's and the Curtellas' were loose fitting – the type that came down to the knee. McCann's had large pockets down the side of each leg. Lola wore shorts too, though hers were more tailored.

'Never been to England,' said Mike.

'Are you thinking of buying the old Treehouse?' asked Joanne.

'Did you say "Treehouse"?' said Lola.

'Well, that's what we've always called it,' said Joanne.

'How funny,' said Lola. 'When I first saw it, that's exactly what it reminded me of.'

She stopped fussing over Riley and looked back at the house. The dog sauntered off, sniffed a few trees and chose one to pee against. Duncan was impatient to talk business with McCann and asked him what time the other couple were looking at the house.

'Three-thirty,' he said.

'Another viewing?' said Joanne.

'Yeah,' said McCann. 'Maybe the old place will finally sell.'

'I hope so,' said Joanne. 'It would be nice to have some new neighbours. And it looks so sad standing there all empty and unloved.'

'That's what I thought,' said Lola.

'So you guys are interested?' said Mike.

Duncan looked at Lola and said, 'We are.'

'Seriously?' said McCann.

'Seriously,' said Duncan.

The Curtellas exchanged a glance and Mike said, 'Well, I guess you have plenty to talk about. It was great meeting you both – and Cain, say hi to Roger for me.'

'Sure.'

'Drop by anytime,' said Joanne as she took hold of Riley's collar and headed back towards the creek. 'I mean that.'

'She does,' said McCann.

'They seemed terribly nice,' said Lola, and Duncan smiled, thinking that was such an English thing to say. She looked elegant and refined in her white sunhat and sunglasses. Anyone looking at her would think how lucky she was, how privileged. They wouldn't see a mother grieving for her child. Sometimes that was all he saw, and it crucified him. At least now he had something to work on; something tangible, something solid.

He looked at McCann. 'We'd like to make an offer.'

On the drive back to the hotel – Lola at the wheel – Duncan couldn't help but feel pleased with himself. It was more than he could have hoped for – a project for Lola, something to absorb her, kick-start her life again. He was pretty sure their offer would be accepted and if it wasn't, he would offer more.

'What do you think happened to Mike's leg?' said Lola.

'Don't know,' said Duncan. 'He's the right age for Vietnam. Maybe he lost it in the war.'

'Mmm,' she said. 'It didn't seem to bother him, though – he barely had a limp.'

'Seemed very pally with McCann.'

'Well, they're all so friendly, don't you think? Joanne was sweet, asking us to drop by anytime. They'll make wonderful neighbours.'

That she was already thinking in terms of neighbours encouraged Duncan even more. It meant she had pictured herself living there, popping across the creek to the Curtellas, making a fuss of that scruffy old dog of theirs. Duncan noticed she was mouthing the words to a song again – something by The Beach Boys. She probably didn't even realise she was doing it. He sensed a rare lightness between them, a frisson of expectation. And over an alfresco lunch back at the Auberge, when McCann rang to say their offer had been accepted, Duncan dragged out the call, savouring Lola's suspense. She leaned forward and tried to listen. When Duncan hung up, put his phone on the table and took a leisurely sip of wine, Lola told him to stop teasing and just tell her what McCann had said. Did they get it?

'We did,' said Duncan. 'We did.'

She sat back, a look of astonishment on her face.

'I don't believe it,' she said.

'Cheers,' Duncan said, picking up his wine glass.

Lola didn't pick up her glass. Her expression was difficult to read.

'I don't believe it,' she said again. 'We've just bought a house.'

Duncan nodded.

'In California.'

Her wide-eyed astonishment gave way to a frown. Was she was having second thoughts? No, he wouldn't let that happen.

'Destiny,' he said, evoking the memory of Piliton Grange.

As soon as he said the word, he regretted it. Had he just reminded her of the one thing he was trying to help her forget? A big house for a big family that it turned out they couldn't have? One child they waited ten years for, who only lived for eight? Jesus. What the hell was wrong with him?

'We should celebrate,' he said, his voice artificially jolly. 'Champagne?'

Lola looked at the wine she had barely touched and said she didn't want to drink any more. Duncan felt suddenly weary.

'What do you want, Lola?'

He wished it wasn't all so difficult. Just for once he'd like to let down his guard, not have to think about every word, every subtext, worry that everything led back to Clarissa. Lola looked at him without speaking and when he didn't rush to fill the silence she said, 'I want to go back to the Treehouse.'

It was mid-afternoon when they got to Falcon Drive, the scorching sun ablaze above them. Lola pulled into the driveway and switched off the engine. Duncan opted for silence, fearing that whatever he said it would be the wrong thing. He told himself he'd done as much as any man could reasonably do, that it was up to her now. Too restless to just sit there, he got out of the car and walked towards the creek. He was startled when the black dog appeared from the trees and barked at him.

'It's Riley,' called Lola, heading over to join him. 'Good boy, Riley,' she said, holding her hand out for the dog to sniff. 'Good boy.'

The shape of the dog's head – wide with a long muzzle – was not unlike Darcy's, but its lean body and gangly legs were more greyhound than Labrador.

'He's an ugly mutt,' said Duncan, and Lola laughed.

'Don't be mean,' she said, patting Riley's back. 'He just needs a bath.'

'Hey,' called Mike Curtella, 'I see you met the welcoming party.'

'Hello again,' said Duncan.

'Couldn't keep away?' said Mike.

'Afraid not,' said Lola, still stroking the dog. 'Actually, we're going to be neighbours. Well, summertime neighbours.'

'No kidding,' said Mike. 'That's great news.'

It was great news for Duncan too, confirmation that Lola hadn't changed her mind.

'Say, why don't you come over for a glass of wine? Joanne would love to see you.'

'Are you sure it's not inconvenient?' asked Lola.

'Not at all,' said Mike. 'We're pretty relaxed around here.'

Duncan took Lola's hand as they followed Mike and Riley through the clearing and over the narrow wooden bridge that straddled the dry creek. Beyond the bridge was a paved path and a low, ranch-style house, dwarfed by the redwoods and oaks that towered over it. A dusty wooden deck wrapped around the house. In the corner stood a stainless-steel barbecue that looked like it got a lot of use. A wicker dining table and eight mismatched chairs were laid out to face the creek.

'Joanne,' Mike called. 'We got company.'

Joanne came out of the house, a magazine in her hand.

'Well, hi there!' she said. 'Great to see you again.'

'They bought the old Treehouse,' said Mike.

'That's wonderful,' said Joanne, throwing her arms around Lola.

Duncan offered Mike his hand and they shook. When Joanne released Lola and headed straight for Duncan, he offered his hand to her too, uncomfortable with the faux intimacy of an embrace. Riley picked up on the excitement and started barking again, his tail swishing back and forth like it was swatting flies.

'You'll stay for a glass of wine,' said Mike, heading into the house.

'Of course they will,' said Joanne, pulling out a chair for Lola. 'I want to hear all about your plans for the old place.'

Lola took off her hat and sat down. Duncan was surprised how cool the air was under the shade of all those trees.

'I'm not sure we have any yet,' she said, looking at Duncan. 'Yesterday was the first time we'd seen it.'

'Wow,' said Joanne.

'We knew straightaway' said Lola.

Duncan didn't correct her use of the plural. Joanne nodded.

'Well, that's just how it should be,' she said.

Mike appeared with a bottle of red wine and four glasses. He put them on the table and pulled a corkscrew from his pocket.

'Cabernet from Spring Mountain,' he said, nodding towards the vineyard just visible through the thicket of redwoods.

He uncorked the wine and poured four glasses.

'Should really let it breathe a while,' he said, 'but what the heck.' He picked up a glass and said, 'A toast to our new neighbours, Duncan and Lola.'

'Wait,' said Joanne. 'What did you say your dog was called?'

'Darcy,' said Lola, reaching for her wine.

'Duncan, Lola and Darcy,' said Joanne, her glass held high.

They sipped in unison, Duncan savouring the intensity of flavours that erupted in his mouth.

'Excellent Cab,' he said. 'Just the right balance of fruit and oak.'

'You a wine man?' asked Mike.

Duncan shook his head.

'It's a hobby,' he said. 'I keep a small cellar at home.'

'I'd be glad to show you around mine sometime,' said Mike.

'How long did you say you've been here?' asked Lola.

'Thirty-five years,' said Mike. 'The house was smaller then but it grew with the family. Four kids.'

'Four?' said Lola.

'Twins from Mike's first marriage,' said Joanne. 'Carla's a doctor up in Seattle and Tony and his wife are teachers. They moved to Pasadena last year. Then there's Luke – he's a sports physio, and Sandy, our youngest. She just left home last year to go work in the city – something to do with commercial property management. Riley's her dog but she's in a condo with a "no pets" rule, so we got to keep him. What about you – you got any kids?'

The question they dreaded. Duncan saw a flicker of pain flash across Lola's face.

'No,' he said in a tone that was polite, but firm enough to shut down that particular line of enquiry. 'So, what should we know about the Treehouse?'

Lola would have realised he wanted to move the conversation in a different direction but the Curtellas didn't seem to notice. Joanne said the house had been built in the sixties by a writer from Los Angeles, who visited three or four times a year and kept himself to himself.

'Strange guy,' Mike said. 'We'd see him wandering around talking to himself. Argued with himself sometimes.'

'Creative types can be a bit quirky,' said Joanne, 'but he was okay. He sold it to a local winemaker – nice guy by the name of Josh. Worked for a little boutique winery over in Calistoga. When he got married he moved into his wife's place downtown. She didn't want to be in the country. He rented it out for a couple of years but the last tenant – great guy, real friendly – moved out Christmas before last and it's been empty ever since.'

'Would you like something else, Lola?' asked Mike, looking at her full glass of wine.

'No, thank you,' she said. 'I'm driving.'

'Can I get you some coffee,' asked Joanne, 'or some water, maybe?'

'Water would be nice,' she said. 'Thank you.'

Duncan was grateful for Joanne's persistence, the way she kept pulling Lola into the conversation, asking her questions about Piliton, about how long they'd been married and what life was like in England. Mike went into the house again and came out with a plate of cheese and biscuits and a glass of iced water for Lola.

Duncan couldn't help but compare the Curtellas' easy friendliness to the cool reception they had received when they first moved to Piliton. The locals called them 'townies', a despicable breed that used London money to buy second homes in the country, pushing up property prices in the process and spoiling the whole character of the village. It didn't matter that they'd sold their London house to make Piliton their home; they were treated as outsiders, regarded with suspicion. Duncan wasn't a beer drinker, but Lola used to send him off to the pub while she prepared Sunday lunch. She said it would be good for him, help him to get to know some of the other men. They acknowledged him – a half-hearted smile, a quick nod of the head – but never joined him or asked him to join them. He appeared to be the only person in the village who commuted to London and was often away on business, leaving Lola in a house that didn't feel like home and a village where she had no friends. It was only because they kept on the old caretaker, Mr Snook, and allowed him to live rent-free in the cottage by the stable yard, that attitudes towards them softened. Mr Snook was fiercely loyal. He refused to hear a word against them. Still, it had taken a long time before they were accepted, and even now Duncan thought of the villagers as acquaintances rather than friends.

There was a time when Lola was part of a community of mothers but when Clarissa died, they had kept their distance. They sent flowers, notes of condolence, but Lola stopped getting invited to their gatherings. He was sure they didn't mean to be hurtful; they just didn't know what to say, how to be around her. He knew how they felt.

It was over an hour before Duncan thanked the Curtellas for their hospitality and said they really should be making tracks. He stood up, and Lola did the same.

'Yes, thanks so much,' she said.

'Anything you need, just let us know,' said Joanne, hugging Lola like she really meant it. Mike shook Duncan's hand then put his arm around Lola's shoulder.

'Next time let your husband drive,' he said and she nodded, said that was an excellent idea.

Lola didn't bother with her hat on the way back to the Auberge. It was after five and the heat of the day had abated. They drove in silence, Lola staring intently at the road.

'Nice people,' said Duncan, thinking how tedious to have to break the ice for the millionth time.

Lola wouldn't have forgiven him yet for the 'no kids' comment, but what choice did he have? Say yes, we had a daughter, she had a fatal accident when I was supposed to be looking after her? Great afternoon that would have turned out to be. Wonderful introduction to the neighbours. It was too much effort, and if she wanted to brood she could. He was resigned to being punished, being frozen out. God, it was wearing, being around her day and night. They spent so little time together in Piliton he'd forgotten how bad she made him feel. A single withering look could annihilate him. Did she ever think how he felt, what it was like for him?

They didn't speak again until they got back to the cottage, when Duncan said he was going for a swim. He pounded up and down the pool, trying to wash away the sin of denying the existence of his only child to the Curtellas. The water was cold and smelled of chlorine. When he was too exhausted to swim anymore he floated on his back for a while, putting off having to face his wife. In the distance he heard the church bells again, reminding him of yet another thing he'd lost. The mortifying memory of a pious neighbour offering to pray for him on hearing of Clarissa's death, made Duncan grimace. His fury at God had been a grenade inside of him – hard, cold, waiting to explode. He was blind to the woman's sincerity, to her belief that such words could bring comfort. The only thing Duncan had hated more than himself was God, and here was this devout woman, so smug in her faith and certainty, offering to pray to him. Duncan spat out his reply with ill-concealed contempt – *don't trouble yourself on my behalf.* These days he missed God more than he hated him, but he knew he could never trust in him again.

He walked back to the cottage and was surprised to see Lola sitting at the round metal table on their little slab of patio. There was an ice bucket on the table, and two glasses. Lola's was already half empty. She looked up at him – a tinge of sunburn across her nose and cheeks.

'I thought we should celebrate,' she said. She took a bottle of champagne out of the ice bucket and poured him a glass. 'After all, it's not every day we buy a house.'

Such swift absolution was more than he could have hoped for. He sat down and raised his glass.

'To the Treehouse,' he said.

'The Treehouse,' said Lola.

Three

There wasn't much traffic on the Pacific Coast Highway – unusual for Saturday. Cain McCann drove a steady seventy in his old white pick-up, singing along to the music on Vine. To his left was the ocean, its huge breakers a reminder of all the good surf he'd missed that morning because he'd had to go into the office first thing. When he had told Roger Williamson he'd made a sale, that a British couple were buying the house on Falcon Drive, his colleague said, 'Seriously? That falling-down wooden thing?'

Cain shrugged.

'I know. Crazy, huh?'

Then Roger had made some joke about going out of town more often if it meant that Cain cleared his backlog of old listings. Cain smiled politely. He had no idea why the Drummonds wanted that house, but he was pretty sure it wasn't because of anything he'd said.

'What did they offer?' Roger had asked.

'Four hundred,' said Cain.

Roger jiggled the loose change in his pocket – a habit when he was trying to figure something out.

'It's a fair price for the lot,' he said. 'They'll probably tear down the house, build something else.'

Cain shrugged and said they really seemed into it, especially the wife.

'What are they like?' Roger asked.

When Cain had seen them looking in the window he knew they were tourists. Locals didn't dress so formal. He wondered if the wife was a model, but when she took off her sunglasses he saw she wasn't as young as he thought. Thirty-five? Maybe forty? Still in great shape, though. The husband was older. Cain felt like he should call him 'sir'. They had probably had enough of wine tasting, were doing a little window-shopping instead. Cain was just being friendly, inviting them in out of the heat. He hadn't expected them to actually be interested in real estate.

'They seemed okay,' said Cain. 'I introduced them to the Curtellas. They say hi, by the way.'

Roger nodded. Cain knew he was waiting for some shrewd realtor insight, some evidence that he understood how to match buyers with their perfect property, how to make a sale, close a deal.

'I guess they just liked it,' he said.

Roger had jiggled his change again and walked over to his desk.

'They're coming in tomorrow morning to do the paperwork,' said Cain, following him. 'Will you be around?'

'Sure,' said Roger. 'I'd be happy to walk you through it, seeing as it's your first contract.'

They had arrived at exactly nine-thirty. Cain introduced them to Roger as Mr and Mrs Drummond because when he introduced them to the Curtellas by their Christian names, the husband had shot him a disapproving look.

But then the wife shook Roger's hand, told him to call her Lola and the husband chilled out a bit – said to call him Duncan.

Roger didn't usually open the office at weekends and if he did, it was just for a couple of hours. He said weekends were for golf. Cain agreed with the sentiment, if not about golf. Real estate had been his dad's idea. He considered it an aberration that Cain was thirty-three and had never had a proper job. A proper job meant an office, a desk, a computer and a company car. Roger did let him use his wife's Prius for viewings – can't let you show clients around in that old pick-up – and he did go to an office, sit at a desk and use a computer, so at least his dad was happy. Cain, not so much. He had worked for Roger for five months and the best thing about it was his parents' relief at having solved the problem of what to do with Cain. All that money on education and he'd barely made it through prep school. The fifth grade diagnosis of dyslexia should have let him off the hook but instead it made him feel even more guilty, like he'd let them down on a genetic level. His inability to learn seemed to worry them more than his brother's habit of bringing home trouble, or not coming home at all. That was just a phase – teenage rebellion. Cain's problems were more enduring. He wouldn't wake up one morning an academic success, off to an Ivy League college like the other McCann men. The fact that it never bothered him only added to their worry. Cain was happy to drift from one casual job to the next, as long as he made enough money to do the things he loved. He worked construction, tended bars, waited tables – anything that meant he could surf in the summer, ski in the winter and hang out with his friends. In his parents' eyes, this represented failure. Cain couldn't imagine a better life.

Today he was glad Roger had stuck around to help with the contract; page after page of real-estate jargon that would have taken him hours to figure out on his own. And Duncan Drummond didn't strike him as a patient man. He seemed to hit it off with Roger, though. They talked about golf, the economy, and how the heck Bush and Blair were ever going sort out that mess in the Middle East. Lola Drummond didn't say much. She smiled and nodded in all the right places, but she didn't seem any more interested in contracts or politics than Cain was. Her mind had seemed somewhere else too. Cain's was on Stinson Beach, and the great ocean surf that was waiting for him. He pictured Lola Drummond in a wetsuit. She looked pretty hot.

'So I think we're done here,' said Roger, finally.

Cain glanced at his watch. Ten-thirty. With any luck he'd make Stinson by midday.

Clusters of sunbathers dotted the long yellow beach, bringing to mind a Robert Frost poem Cain had learned by heart at school.

> The people along the sand
> All turn to look one way.
> They turn their back on the land.
> They look at the sea all day.

His mother made him recite it over and over until he had it word perfect. She didn't believe in dyslexia.

Cain spotted his buddies taking a break from the waves, hanging out in their own ocean-facing cluster. He put on his wetsuit in the parking lot, tossed his clothes into the cab, then jogged over to join them, surfboard tucked under his arm.

'Hey!' called Pete. 'You made it.'

'You bet,' said Cain, sitting down next to him. 'How's the surf?'

'Awesome,' said Summer.

Cain thought how cute she looked with her pixie hair-cut and dolphin tattoo. He worried things might be weird between them after they'd spent the night together, but she seemed cool. Megan raised a hand to acknowledge him but didn't speak.

'You okay, Meg?' he asked.

'She had a major wipe-out,' said Summer.

'Too bad,' said Cain. 'You hurt?'

'Only my pride,' said Megan.

She hugged her knees to her chest and stared out at the ocean. Pete slipped his arm around her shoulder, said it happened to everyone.

'You ready to go again?' asked Cain, impatient to get into the water.

'Five minutes,' said Pete.

'Summer?' said Cain.

She shook her head.

'I want to sit for a while,' she said. 'You go.'

Cain picked up his surfboard and ran into the white foam. He lay on the board and paddled out, his eyes fixed on the huge wall of water ahead. He watched the wave curl, anticipated the thunderous boom as it crashed. Adrenalin shot through his veins, tightening every muscle, every sinew. His heart pounded in sync with the pounding of the ocean. When he caught the first wave he knew he had made a mistake. His timing was off, his balance too. He swirled helplessly in the powerful undercurrent until he managed to swim back to the surface and gulp a lungful of air, angry at having got it so wrong. The wave had sucked him in, tossed him around, spat him out. Come on, man, you can do better than that. He climbed back on his board and when the next wave came he was ready. He sprang to his feet, knees bent, caught it just right. There was no rush like the rush of riding a wave, knowing you're at its fickle mercy, that it could be the best or worst moment of your life. Surfing wasn't a sport for Cain, it was a spiritual experience. In the ocean he understood how insignificant he was, how easily he could be wiped out. Being close to the possibility of death made him feel fiercely alive. He lost a friend a few years back – disappeared into a wave and didn't come out again. His neck had been snapped. Cain spoke at the guy's funeral, said he died doing something he truly loved. He didn't know if that helped his family come to terms with losing their son, but it sure helped Cain.

With the sun large and low over the darkening ocean, Cain and his friends walked to the restaurant along the shore. They ordered beer and lobster, cracked crab and fries. Talk was easy; silence was okay too. Cain got home just after ten and slept for eight hours straight.

'How was your weekend?' asked Roger.

'Good,' said Cain. 'Did some surfing at Stinson. How about you?'

'Played some golf,' said Roger. 'I got a call from Mike Curtella, said he wanted to invite the British couple over, asked if you were free tonight.'

'Sure. I think so. They want me there too?'

'Yeah, and me. A kind of "welcome to the neighbourhood" thing. You know, grill some steaks, drink some wine, get to know them a bit.'

'Sounds cool,' said Cain. 'What time?'

'Around six,' said Roger.

Mondays always dragged. When Cain thought of the week ahead, a whole five days playing realtor, it seemed such a waste. There were better ways to earn a living than hanging around an office waiting for the phone to ring. He felt confined. Roger gave him the job because his dad had asked him to, not because Cain had any aptitude for selling real estate – or any interest in it, for that matter. And it wasn't like he made a lot of money. One sale in five months didn't bring in much commission. He had made more working construction, and at least then he wasn't cooped up all day. He'd give it another month so his dad could see he'd tried. After that he'd tell Roger thanks, he appreciated the opportunity, but real estate wasn't for him.

* * * * *

The evening was warmer than usual, even on the Curtellas' shaded deck. A heat wave had been forecast; triple-digit temperatures for the rest of the week. Mike wore a red baseball cap and a Hawaiian shirt with green and yellow palm trees. He was over by the barbecue, poking around at the coals.

'Hey, Cain. Glad you could make it,' he said.

'Well, thanks for the invite,' said Cain, handing him a bottle of Pinot Noir. 'I don't think I've tried this,' said Mike, studying the label.

'It's good,' said Cain. 'My buddy Pete is the winemaker.'

Joanne appeared a moment later, wearing an apron with 'I kiss better than I cook' written across the front. Her hair was scraped back into a ponytail, short and stubby like a shaving brush. She handed Cain a beer and hugged him.

'Good to see you,' she said.

She smelled of flour and soap.

'You changed your hair,' said Cain.

Joanne put her hand to her head.

'Sweet of you to notice.' She looked around. 'You didn't bring a date?'

'She's trying to find out if you're seeing anyone right now,' said Mike.

'Not really,' said Cain. 'Why?'

'Take no notice of him,' said Joanne. 'Sandy's home next weekend, that's all.'

Cain tried to picture Sandy Curtella. Short, like her mother. Dark hair. Cute in a girl-next-door sort of way.

'I usually head to the beach on the weekend but sure, if I'm around, I'll drop by.'

Roger and the Drummonds arrived at the same time. Duncan Drummond wore a jacket and tie despite the heat. His wife wore a black silk dress and heels. Next to them, everyone looked like they were dressed to clear out the garage. Mike took off his baseball hat and smoothed his wiry white curls.

'Welcome,' he said, and to Lola, 'You look great.'

The way she accepted the compliment with a gracious smile told Cain that she was used to getting them. While the men shook hands, Joanne and Lola hugged. Cain thought how funny they looked – the refined British woman, nearly six feet in those heels, and the small American in sneakers and an apron.

Joanne asked everybody what they wanted to drink. Cain was the only one having beer. Mike opened the Pinot Noir, poured a glass for Duncan and one for himself. Roger and the women had Chardonnay. Lola caught Cain looking at her and confided that she felt rather overdressed.

'You ever heard the expression "wine country casual"?' he said, looking down at his Levis and Birkenstocks. It was supposed to be a joke, but Lola didn't seem like she got it. Cain backtracked.

'You look beautiful,' he said, then realised he'd overshot. 'Nice. You look very nice. You and your husband. Kind of make the rest of us look bad.'

He took a long drink of beer and wondered why he was babbling like an idiot. There was something about Lola Drummond that unnerved him. He didn't know any

British people, only their reputation for being uptight and reserved.

'Did I imagine it,' he said, 'or did we get off on the wrong foot?'

She gave him a long cool look, as though trying to decide whether to politely brush off the question, or give a straight answer.

'You didn't imagine it. I'm embarrassed to say I was rather hung over when we first met.'

'No need to be embarrassed. They call it wine country for a reason.'

'And you'll have to fill me in on the dress code. At home I spend most of my time in jeans or jodhpurs.'

'Jodhpurs?'

'I have a livery yard, which means a lot of time spent mucking out stables.'

Everything about her was flawless: long lustrous hair, clear, sun-kissed skin, neat, pale pink nails. He couldn't imagine her shovelling manure.

'Only one of the horses is mine – a retired polo pony, rather unoriginally called Polo. The others have own-ers that come and ride them when they can, usually weekends.' She smiled and held up her hands. 'Sorry. Occupational hazard. If I start talking about horses I'll witter on all evening.'

She leaned over to pat Riley, even though Mike called out for her to ignore him if she didn't want him pestering her all night.

'And this chap reminds me how much I miss my own dog, Darcy.'

Cain saw that a small leaf had fallen onto her head and as he removed it, his fingers grazed her hair. It felt as good as it looked. She glanced up and he showed her the leaf. Her hand touched her hair where his fingers had touched it a second before.

'Steak's just about ready,' called Mike.

Joanne put a pitcher of iced water on the table. When Duncan asked where he should sit, she told him to sit anywhere he wanted. Mike piled the steaks onto a platter while Joanne passed around a bowl of potato salad and a plate of grilled vegetables. The Drummonds sat side by side, Duncan next to Roger and Lola next to Joanne. Cain took the chair next to Mike.

'Medium rare okay for everyone?' asked Mike.

He stabbed each piece of meat with a fork. Watery blood oozed onto the platter.

'Goodness,' said Lola. 'Those steaks are huge.'

'New York Strip,' said Mike. 'You don't have these in England?'

'Don't think so,' said Lola.

'How about we share?' said Joanne.

She cut one of the steaks down the middle and put half on Lola's plate, half on her own.

'These are perfect,' said Duncan, helping himself. 'Watching you cook really whet my appetite.'

'Haven't heard that expression in a while,' said Mike. 'Glad you're hungry, though.'

Cain helped himself to a slab of meat.

'Lola was telling me she keeps horses,' he said.

'Really?' said Roger.

Lola finished chewing.

'Just eight at the moment,' she said.

'Sounds like a lot of work,' said Joanne.

'I have a girl who helps me,' said Lola. 'Kathy – she's taking care of everything while I'm away. And we have a caretaker, Mr Snook. He's quite elderly now but he likes to help out when he can.'

'What do you do, Duncan?' asked Roger.

'Sales director for a global water-recycling company. I work out of the head office in London but I travel quite a bit,' said Duncan. 'AquaEco. You may have heard of it.'

'Can't say that I have,' said Roger.

Cain excused himself and went to the bathroom while Roger and Mike asked Duncan about his work. They were still talking about it when he came back.

'Water's a real problem in this state,' said Mike. 'Reservoirs haven't been full since 2002 – a year after I retired. I'm pretty sure that was the last wet winter.'

'What did you do?' asked Lola. 'Before you retired?'

'Well, I planned a career in the military, but a landmine kinda changed all that.'

He tapped the metal prosthesis with his fork, making a tinny sound.

'Vietnam?' asked Duncan.

Mike nodded.

'I was twenty-six – just a kid. At the time it seemed like the end of the world, but at least I came home. Not in one piece, but still, I was luckier than all those guys who never made it. So I came back here, to my first wife and our infant twins, and didn't have time to sit round feeling sorry for myself. A journalist from the local paper asked if he could do an interview and when we got talking, I said I'd really like to write something in my own words, you know – a first-hand account. Anyway, the editor loved it – got a lot of letters about it too – and it sort of became a regular thing. That's how I ended up being a journalist for forty years. Not something I planned, just something that happened. Funny how life works out.'

Cain had heard the story before, but the way it made him think about his own life bothered him a little. He was thirty-three years old – single, no kids that he knew of, no college degree and no career. It wasn't like he wanted those things, but when he heard what Mike had been through and what he'd made of his life Cain couldn't help feel like a bit of a loser. He hadn't figured out what he wanted, where he fitted in. Sure, he loved to ski and surf and hang out with his buddies, but he was the only one who had nothing else besides. Pete and Megan were respected winemakers. Summer made jewellery and sold it to high-end stores. When he checked out his old school friends on Facebook, they were doctors, teachers, lawyers. Cain had never saved a life or changed one. He'd never kept an innocent man out of prison or put a guilty man away. All he had done was sold one run-down old house.

'How long have you been in real estate?' asked Duncan.

Roger looked at Cain and said, 'I'm pretty sure that's to you.'

'Oh, just a few months,' said Cain. 'Actually, the Treehouse was my first sale.'

'Really?' said Lola.

Cain poured himself a glass of Pinot Noir and nodded.

'Uh-huh,' he said. 'Lucky I got back to the office when I did.'

'Destiny,' said Joanne, raising her glass for a toast.

Everyone picked up their glasses and toasted destiny. Cain saw Duncan glance at his wife, like he was trying to read her mood.

'Skip McCann, Cain's dad, was my roommate at Stanford,' said Roger. 'Our wives were roommates too. We double-dated all through college – got married as soon as we graduated. 1970. Thirty-eight years ago. Mona and I weren't blessed with children but we're godparents to Skip and Helen's boys. Cain's like family to me.'

He couldn't say why, but Roger calling him family knotted Cain's insides, made him feel like he hadn't just let his parents down, but Roger and Mona too. Roger would have been a great dad. Never forgot a birthday. When Cain was a kid, he looked forward all year to their fishing trips on Lake Tahoe. Boys only: Roger, Skip, Cain and Josh. Mona and his mom went to New York for the weekend, did girl stuff. Everything seemed to fit back then.

'What a lovely story,' said Lola. 'Could your wife not make it tonight?'

Cain felt bad for Lola. She didn't know Mona had died, that Roger was lost without her. Joanne squeezed Roger's hand.

'She passed last year,' said Roger. 'Cancer.'

Lola laid down her knife and fork and said she was so very sorry. Cain could see that she meant it.

'Thank you,' said Roger. 'She was a great gal.'

'She sure was,' said Joanne, still holding Roger's hand.

'To Mona,' said Mike, raising his glass.

Cain raised his glass for the second toast of the evening. 'To Mona.'

It was around eight-thirty when Joanne cleared the table and suggested they go inside to finish their wine. Cain had always liked the Curtellas' house, the simple clutter of it. The kitchen and the living room seemed to merge into one big comfortable space. Untidy shelves overflowed with books crammed together in no particular order. Newspapers and magazines were stacked next to the overstuffed sofa opposite the fireplace. Family photographs and Joanne's watercolours covered the walls: beach scenes, vineyard views, a field of tall red poppies bending in the breeze.

'You still painting?' Cain asked her.

'When I get the chance,' said Joanne.

'Oh, do you paint?' said Lola.

In her hand was the empty meat platter. She looked around for somewhere to put it.

'Here, give that to me,' said Joanne. She took the platter and set it down on the counter by the sink. 'I dabble in watercolour,' said Joanne. 'It's just a hobby.'

'They're good,' said Lola, studying the poppy field. 'Bold use of colour.'

'You an artist?' asked Joanne.

Lola shook her head. Cain saw how much more relaxed she was now that she'd had a few drinks. A flush of colour warmed her cheeks.

'No,' said Lola. 'I studied Art History at university but no, I don't paint anymore.'

Mike and Duncan came into the kitchen holding the last of the glasses.

'So this is where the party is,' said Mike, carefully placing the glasses into the already crowded sink. 'You guys thought how you're going to remodel?'

Lola looked at her husband.

'Well, it needs the basics,' said Duncan. 'New kitchen, bathroom and so on, but it might be interesting to get an architect to look at it.'

'I know just the gal,' said Roger. 'Birdie Johnson. Done quite a bit of work around here over the years.'

Duncan nodded.

'And she's good is she?'

'Oh yeah. Birdie's great. I could give her a call if you wanted to meet her.'

'Well, if you're sure it's no trouble,' said Duncan.

'No trouble at all,' said Mike.

Lola tried to stifle a yawn, and apologised.

'You want some coffee?' asked Joanne.

'No, thank you,' said Lola. 'Dinner was delightful. I'm so glad to have had the chance to get to know you all a little better.'

'Well, don't be strangers,' said Joanne. 'Drop by whenever you want. I mean that.'

'She does,' said Mike. 'And watch out, Duncan, she's a hugger. Don't think you're going to escape every time.'

Duncan chuckled awkwardly, looking down at his shoes. Cain glanced down at his Birkenstocks, remembering that he hadn't worn anything more formal since Mona's funeral last year.

Joanne flung her arms around Lola, who leaned over to minimise the height difference. Duncan shook hands and thanked everyone for a wonderful evening.

Once Roger and the Drummonds had left, Cain hung out in the kitchen with the Curtellas. He rinsed a stack of plates and handed them to Joanne to load into the dishwasher.

'So what do you think of the enigmatic Mrs Drummond?' Cain asked.

'Other than she's a knockout?' said Mike.

'Other than she's a knockout,' said Cain.

Joanne stopped what she was doing and wiped her hands.

'She certainly is beautiful,' she said. 'And she seems to have a nice life in England. Big house, live-in help.'

'Oh, you mean the caretaker?' said Cain. 'I think he's pretty old.'

'There's something, though,' said Joanne. 'Something I can't quite put my finger on. A kind of loneliness...'

'Did you get that too?' said Cain.

They looked at Mike but he shrugged, said she seemed okay to him.

'I just can't figure out what's missing,' said Joanne, 'or why they think they'll find it here.'

'Do they have kids?' asked Cain.

'No,' said Joanne. 'No kids.'

'Well, maybe that's it,' said Cain. 'Maybe they wanted kids and couldn't have them. You know, like Roger and Mona.'

'Maybe,' said Joanne. 'Anyway, honey, I can take it from here. You get off home now, and thanks for helping with the dishes.'

Cain put his arm around her shoulder and gave it a firm squeeze.

'Good to see you, son,' said Mike, with a wave. 'Say hi to your folks from me.'

It was just before ten when Cain got back to the shabby house he rented on the other side of town. He turned on the TV, flicked through the channels but couldn't find anything he wanted to watch. He felt kind of restless – thought of calling Summer but called Pete instead.

'Hey, man, what's up?' said Pete.

'Not much. Took a bottle of your Pinot Noir over to the Curtellas this evening.'

'What'd you think?'

'Good.'

'Come on, man. You didn't call to tell me you like my wine. What's going on?'

'I was thinking of asking Summer to come over.'

'You guys hooked up a few weeks back, right?'

'Right. I just don't want things to get, you know, weird.'

'Things are weird?'

'No. She seems pretty cool, actually.'

'So what's the problem?'

* * * * *

Summer was in Cain's bed forty minutes later, naked and showing off her new tattoo – a peace sign just above her pubic bone.

'Does it hurt?' asked Cain.

'A little.'

'Can I kiss it better?'

'If you promise to be gentle.'

She came quickly and breathlessly. When he kissed her mouth she said he tasted of her. She took hold of him, guided him inside her. He moved deep and slow, wanting her to come again before he did. She moaned and rocked, her hands gripping the headboard. He concentrated on her face, on her long, shuddering orgasm, but when he surrendered to his own orgasm, it was Lola Drummond's face he saw.

Four

Duncan glanced at Lola dozing peacefully in the passenger seat. The three glasses of wine she'd had at dinner would have made her sleepy. Duncan had drunk at least that much himself, but he drove anyway. After the Pinot Noir, Mike Curtella had opened a very good Cabernet. He certainly knew his wine. They all did, even McCann. Duncan wasn't sure why that surprised him.

What also surprised him was how uneasy he had felt talking about work. There was no reason to feel like that, except he hadn't been in touch with the office the whole time he'd been away. He wanted to show Lola that she was what mattered, that she came first. Still, it made him nervous to think of all the unread messages on his BlackBerry. He could picture it sitting on the desk in his study, between his laptop and the Montblanc writing set he never used. He pressed his fingertips into his temples and took a slow breath. It would be fine – everything would be fine. Anyway, what was the point of having assistants if he didn't allow them to assist? Alison was the most efficient secretary he had ever had. The bossy woman from Human Resources told him that 'secretary' was a pejorative term these days – 'Personal Assistant' was more politically correct. However he described her, Alison had been with him long enough to know how he liked things done. William Hilliard was another matter. He had only been in the job three months and Duncan hadn't quite got the measure of him yet. Duncan wasn't even convinced he needed a second in command (Hilliard's term – not his), but the other directors each had a deputy and it might look odd if Duncan didn't.

Hilliard's predecessor had quit because Duncan insisted on doing everything himself. He overheard him telling Alison that the boss was a control freak. He didn't hear Alison's reply. When Duncan asked the Human Resources woman to advertise for a replacement, she made some comment about his department's high staff turnover – a comment that Duncan chose to ignore. He was inundated with applicants. Most had sales experience and several had experience in the water industry, but only a handful had both. Hilliard was the best of the bunch. He worked for AquaEco's main competitor and certainly interviewed well. Duncan couldn't think of a good reason not to hire him. But there was something about the man that irked Duncan. He was too confident, too sure of himself. He reminded Duncan of how he used to be before Clarissa died.

A month after the accident, Duncan went back to work. He didn't know what else to do. AquaEco wouldn't keep his job open indefinitely, bills still had to be paid and God knows he was useless to Lola. He thought it best to carry on as normal – part of his *life must go on* charade. Then he had his first panic attack. He was on his usual train – the seven-fifteen from Bristol to Paddington – a copy of the *Financial Times* and a cup of coffee on the table in front of him, and out of nowhere came the sensation that his heart had burst. Blood gushed through his body at a ferocious pace. He couldn't breathe. It was as though he had a tourniquet around his chest. He tried to stand but couldn't feel his legs. He needed help but didn't have the breath to ask for it. Then it was over. The tourniquet loosened, his heart rate slowed. He gulped air like a drowning man. When he could trust his legs, he made his way to the toilet and splashed cold water onto his face. He steadied himself on the sink and tried to understand what the hell had just happened. He thought it was some sort of episode, something his doctor and an ECG could sort out. But when his doctor gave him a clean bill of health, explained that anxiety was the most likely cause of his symptoms, it was the worst diagnosis Duncan could have imagined. A physical illness he could understand, but an emotional one? Not possible. The doctor delivered a patronising pep talk about anxiety being a perfectly natural response to bereavement but Duncan stopped listening when he suggested counselling and Diazepam. He had already been down the counselling route and had no desire to revisit it. And drugs? Absurd. He went from the surgery to a bar and self-medicated with Scotch. Three drinks later he had convinced himself that if he told no one it would be like it had never happened. He almost believed it too.

A hare darted across the lane and Duncan braked. Lola opened her eyes and sat forward.

'Everything alright?' she asked.

'Fine,' said Duncan. 'Go back to sleep.'

'I wasn't asleep. I was thinking with my eyes closed.'

'Thinking about what?'

'Oh, about how friendly everyone was.' When Duncan didn't comment she continued. 'A little too friendly for you maybe?'

'Mmm,' he said. 'Roger seems a decent sort.'

'What's wrong with the others?'

'Nothing.'

Duncan didn't want to say anything negative about the Curtellas and McCann because he could see how Lola's blossoming affection for them seemed to be part of what attracted her to this place. It didn't appear to be just about the Treehouse for her, but everything that came with it.

'Oh come on,' she said. 'Don't you like them?'

'No, of course I do,' he said. 'It's just –'

He hesitated.

'What?'

Best keep it light-hearted, show her he was just being stuffy.

'Okay. Well, take Mike, for example. I don't understand why a grown man would choose to wear a baseball cap at dinner, and that ghastly Hawaiian shirt.'

'He took off the baseball cap when we sat down to eat. And Cain called it "wine country casual". I think we were the ones out of place. Radically overdressed.'

'Nonsense. Imagine a guest at a one of our dinner parties turning up in shorts or some hideously loud shirt. We'd think he'd lost his mind.'

'It's different in England. People are more easy-going here. They don't stand on ceremony.'

'So you didn't mind Joanne Curtella clucking over you like a mother hen?'

'Not at all. I like her.'

'What about McCann?'

'What about him?'

'I think you have an admirer there.'

Lola smiled. 'Don't be ridiculous.'

'I'm not being ridiculous. He couldn't take his eyes off you. Swooned over you like a lovesick puppy.'

Lola threw her head back and laughed. Duncan laughed too, not because he thought he was wrong about McCann, but because Lola was happy. And he knew exactly how McCann felt. When Duncan first saw Lola, he hadn't been able to take his eyes off her either. She was twenty-one and breathtaking – so sleek and long-legged that she put him in mind of a thoroughbred. There was nothing equine about her face, though. It was heart shaped, with high cheek-bones and a full, sensuous mouth. He noticed how she bit her bottom lip. He had wanted to bite it too. They chatted, flirted a little, smiled a lot. He invited her to dinner and a year later they were married. Twenty years later they were still married and Duncan still desired her. It wasn't that he was jealous of McCann – that had never been an issue with Lola. She was honest and straightforward, utterly incapable of infidelity. But one of their fantasies, all those years ago, was that some virile younger man was intent on seducing her. She would tease him with explicit details of imaginary encounters, thrilled at how easily she could arouse and excite her husband. It made Duncan want to dominate her sexually, show her that she was his. It was out of character, but wasn't that the point of fantasies?

* * * * *

He put his arm around her as they walked back through the gardens to the cottage. The air inside smelled of her perfume. He kissed her mouth, her neck, her bare shoulder. When he unzipped her dress she raised her arms so he could pull it off. Her underwear was black lace. He traced the contour of her breasts with his hands. When she was pregnant, he hated how her body stretched and swelled, how everything he loved about it became unfamiliar to him. He knew it was selfish. After three miscarriages he wanted to give up trying to have a child but Lola wouldn't hear of it. She said she wanted a child more than anything. What did that say about their marriage? That he wasn't enough for her, that without a child something would always be missing? Not for him.

Lola unhooked her bra and slipped it off. She started to take off her high heels but Duncan said no, leave them on. He undid his shirt, his belt, his fly, and told her to lie down. She gasped when he entered her. He gripped her arms, almost pinning her to the bed. It wasn't how he usually made love to his wife, but when he thought how McCann had looked at her – had touched her hair for Christ's sake – he couldn't help himself. He cried out when he came, a deep, guttural sound. Afterwards, he lay still and waited for his heart to stop hammering. Lola stroked his back with her fingernails. He wanted to make her come but she said she was tired; it didn't matter.

Duncan lay awake in the darkness, listening to Lola breathe. The more he wished for sleep, the more elusive it became. He tried to distract himself by mentally listing each of the wineries he wanted to visit. Opus One was top of the list. He would take Lola there tomorrow – see if he could wean her off Chardonnay and interest her in some serious reds. But when he closed his eyes he saw his BlackBerry on his meticulously organised desk and wondered why the hell he hadn't just slipped the damn thing into his pocket. Lola wouldn't have noticed and if she had, she probably wouldn't have cared. At four-thirty he decided it wouldn't hurt if he quickly checked his emails after his morning swim, and at last drifted into a restless sleep.

When he got back from the pool, his hair dripping onto the collar of his white towelling robe, Lola was already dressed in navy Bermuda shorts and a cream cotton T-shirt that fitted snugly over her breasts. He had hoped she might still be in bed, that he could finish what he hadn't the night before.

'Roger called,' she said. 'He wants to meet at the Treehouse around eleven. The architect is going to be there. Birdie somebody.'

'I thought we could do some wine tasting,' said Duncan.

'This morning?'

'Lunchtime.'

'Oh, well, that's alright,' she said. 'We'll probably be finished by then.'

Her usual apathy seemed to have given way to a sense of purpose. She applied sunscreen with brisk efficiency, dabbed something shiny onto her lips, brushed her hair with long, firm strokes and pulled it back into a ponytail that swished from side to side when she moved her head.

'Have you seen my sandals?' she asked.

Duncan glanced around the room and saw them poking out from under the bed. He bent down and picked them up.

'These?' he said.

'Thanks,' she said, taking them from him. She sat on the side of the bed and slipped the sandals onto her bare feet.

'Have you had breakfast?' asked Duncan.

'No. I was waiting for you.'

She stood to attention in front of him, clearly eager to get on with the day. The lack of sleep made him suddenly weary.

'I need to shower, and I thought I might pop into the business centre for five minutes. You go – I'll see you over there.'

The business centre was a small drab room with four laptops and a printer. The only other person was a teenage boy playing some sort of computer game. Duncan took a seat in the corner, put on his reading glasses and logged onto his email. He drummed his fingers on the desk while his emails downloaded, trying to ignore the tightness in his gut. Twenty-three messages. Alison would have deleted the rubbish and William Hilliard would have weeded out those that didn't need Duncan's personal attention. He clicked open each one in order, relieved that there was nothing urgent. He gave Alison a quick call just to check in. When he got her voicemail he remembered – nine-thirty in California was five-thirty in London. Alison would have gone home.

'Here you are,' said Lola.

She sat down next to him and put a styrofoam cup and a plate of pastries on the desk. 'I brought you breakfast.'

'Thanks,' he said. 'I'm finished here anyway.'

He logged out and took a sip of coffee.

'Everything okay?' she asked.

Duncan nodded. Even if it weren't, he wouldn't tell Lola.

Roger Williamson and McCann stood in front of the house talking to a petite redhead. The Curtellas' dog barked as the convertible approached, so Duncan assumed they weren't far away either.

'Morning,' called Roger. 'Come and meet Birdie.'

Lola stopped to pet the dog, who wagged his tail and made an appreciative whining sound.

'Duncan Drummond,' said Roger. 'This is Birdie Johnson.'

Duncan shook Birdie's hand and felt the thin little bones that ran from her fingers to her wrist. Her skin was even paler than Lola's. Flame red curls framed her narrow face and Duncan thought her pretty in a curious sort of way.

'I've been hoping somebody would buy this place,' she said.

Lola and the dog joined them and when Duncan saw how casually she and McCann greeted each other, he felt embarrassed about the previous night, about letting himself get carried away with the idea that McCann had designs on her.

'Lola Drummond,' said Roger. 'Birdie Johnson. She was just saying how great it was that someone has finally rescued this place.'

'I think we're the ones who've been rescued,' said Lola.

Duncan was surprised. Was she actually going to confide in these people – explain about Clarissa, about the chronic depression that for some inexplicable reason this ruin of a house seemed to have soothed? It wasn't a conversation he wanted to have.

'I don't follow,' said Birdie.

'Tell me about your practice,' said Duncan. 'Do you have partners or do you work alone?'

Birdie raised an eyebrow at the quick change of subject, but went along with it. She said there were two other architects, as well as a draftsman and an administrator.

'And are you based here, in St Helena?'

'Yes. My office is on Main.'

Duncan nodded. He couldn't think what to ask next but then Mike Curtella appeared through the clearing in the trees, wearing the same baseball cap and Hawaiian shirt he'd worn at dinner. Duncan realised Lola was right – he barely limped at all. If it was the dog Curtella was after, he'd have to coax it away from Lola. It was by her side, panting and wagging its tail.

'Thanks for a great evening last night' said Roger.

'Yeah, that was a lot of fun,' said Mike. 'Birdie, haven't seen you in a while.'

'I've been around,' she said. 'Pretty busy, though. How's Joanne?'

'Great. Why don't you stop by for coffee when you've finished?'

Birdie checked her watch and said sure, if she had time – she had another appointment at one.

'Why don't you all come?' said Mike. 'Joanne's baked cookies.'

When he called Riley, the dog looked at him but stayed put. Lola patted its head and said sorry, it was her fault for making such a fuss of him.

'Guess you must be missing your own,' said Mike. 'What did you say he was called?'

'Darcy,' said Lola. 'Yes, I do miss him. He'd love it here. I can't wait for him to meet Riley.'

'But this will be a vacation home, right?' said Birdie.

'Absolutely,' said Duncan. 'I imagine we'll visit in July or August. Possibly both. We haven't worked out the logistics yet.'

'Will you be able to take that much time off work?' asked Roger.

'No,' said Duncan. 'But I travel a lot anyway, so rather than flying back to London, I suppose I'll fly to San Francisco instead.'

'What about you Lola?' asked Roger. 'Last night you said something about a livery yard?'

Lola nodded. 'Mmm … I'm not sure how long I'll be able to get away for.'

Duncan didn't like where this was heading. They hadn't discussed any of the practicalities and he didn't want her to start fretting about them, finding reasons why it was insane to buy a house on the west coast of America.

'Anyway,' he said to Birdie, 'I'm interested to hear your ideas.'

Mike took hold of Riley's collar and turned back towards the clearing.

'I'll get the coffee on,' he called.

'Later,' called McCann.

'So,' said Duncan, looking at Birdie. 'The house?'

She talked about remodelling on a contemporary theme, creating a wood and glass structure that blurred the distinction between inside and outside space, opened the house to all the natural beauty that surrounded it.

'That sounds wonderful,' said Lola. 'Could we really do that?'

'Sure,' said Birdie. 'Why not?'

Because it sounded like it would cost a bloody fortune, thought Duncan.

'What about planning permission?' he asked.

'Well, the city would have to agree the plans but I can't see that being a problem,' said Birdie. 'It's just one idea. If you wanted to go with a more traditional –'

'No,' said Lola. 'I love your idea.'

Duncan looked at her, surprised at how adamant she was.

'Great,' said Birdie, pulling a notepad and pen out of her bag, and jotting something down. 'What about accommodation? It's two-bed right now – are you thinking of maybe a third bedroom?'

'No,' said Duncan. 'Two is fine.'

'And what about a den, or maybe a home office?'

Duncan nodded. 'That would be useful.'

'In which case we might be talking about a small addition,' said Birdie, still scribbling.

'Isn't it funny,' said Lola, 'how we speak the same language differently?'

'What do you mean?' said Birdie.

'You say addition – we say extension. We have a study, rather than a home office, and I'm not sure we even have an equivalent to a den.'

'Lola gave me an English lesson too,' said McCann. 'What did you say you call realtors?'

'Estate agents,' said Lola.

'What do you call swimming pools?' asked Birdie.

'Expensive,' said Duncan, dryly.

He wondered if he'd given the impression that money was no object.

'Perhaps you could put together some preliminary figures,' he said. 'Give me some idea what all this might cost.'

'Sure,' said Birdie. 'I could have something on paper by tomorrow afternoon. It would be pretty rough – a starting point – but we could take it from there.'

She made another note and gave Duncan her business card.

'Why don't you give me a call tomorrow morning?' she said.

Duncan slipped the card in his pocket.

'You stopping by the Curtellas'?' asked Roger.

'I'll just say hi,' said Birdie, checking her watch again. 'Don't think I've got time for coffee.'

Roger looked at Duncan.

'You guys?'

'Of course,' said Lola. 'I want to thank them again for dinner.'

Duncan was just about to remind her about wine tasting but she was already heading towards the clearing with Birdie. He could hear them chatting about the perils of the Californian sun, how with their colouring, they had to be extra careful. Birdie said something about dipping herself in sun block before she left the house and Lola laughed, said she would have to get into the habit of doing that too.

Duncan couldn't believe how far she'd come in such a short space of time. It was as if her world had shifted on its axis. She had just slotted into place, like she'd known these people for years. And it wasn't as if she made friends easily. As a child, she'd told him she was too ashamed of her drunken mother to invite friends to her house. When she was invited to their houses, she had to make excuses why she couldn't go – the truth was that she had to dash home from school every day to make sure her mother wasn't passed out on the floor. After a while her friends made new friends and Lola was ostracised. It wasn't the sniggering or name-calling that hurt the most, she'd said, it was being an outsider, being excluded from everything. In some ways it made her self-sufficient, more independent than her peers. It also made her lonely. Duncan watched her chatting happily with Joanne and Birdie, and felt glad she didn't seem lonely now.

After two cups of strong black coffee, Duncan needed to use the bathroom. Mike Curtella directed him.

'Through the kitchen, along the hall, first door on the right.'

There was barely an inch of free space on the kitchen work surfaces. Dishes, pans, books, a huge bowl of fruit, framed photographs, vulgar ornaments. Untidiness mystified Duncan. Why would the Curtellas – why would anyone – choose to live in such disarray? Duncan preferred order. Everything in its place and a place for everything – that's what his mother used to say. Not that his mother actually did any housework. She left that to the cleaning ladies that came and went over the years.

He was eager to get going – have lunch and do some wine tasting – but as he headed back from the bathroom, he opened the wrong door and found himself in what he assumed was Mike's study. It was just as untidy as the kitchen, with newspapers and magazines stacked in precarious piles on the floor. Bookshelves overflowed and a large, half-finished jigsaw puzzle covered a low round coffee table. A scratched mahogany desk and a leather swivel chair dominated the room. On the wall above the desk hung a crucifix with a tortured, dying Jesus, wearing a loincloth and a crown of thorns. It looked just like the one that had hung above his parents' bed. Duncan had had a smaller version in his own bedroom. As a child, he would kneel in front of it to say his prayers. It made him feel safe, knowing he could talk to God and that God would listen. Understanding God's rules had helped him understand the world – the difference between right and wrong, good and evil. A simple, uncomplicated dichotomy. He yearned for that simplicity – the certainty that faith had brought. Like so many things in his life, he had taken it entirely for granted.

'I wondered where you'd gotten to,' said Mike.

Duncan spun around, said sorry, he took a wrong turn. He hoped Curtella hadn't seen him studying the crucifix, but he must have done.

'You Catholic?' Mike said.

That such a personal question could be posed in such a casual way, summed up for Duncan just how different the Americans were.

'Lapsed,' he said.

Duncan hated that word. Once the Catholic Church had you, they wouldn't let you go. There was no such thing as an ex-Catholic, only a lapsed one. Even if you never went to Mass, never took communion, you were still a Catholic, just a bad one. Curtella nodded.

'Yeah, Joanne and I don't get to church as often as we should.'

Duncan realised it was his turn to say something but he was reluctant to get into an ecclesiastical discussion, or, worse still, be asked why he had turned his back on God.

'Lola and I really should get going,' he said. 'We have lunch reservations.'

It was a sin to lie. Duncan added it to the list.

'Sure,' said Mike. 'Well, it was great to see you. And Duncan?'

'Yes?'

'We're real glad you and Lola bought the house.'

That comment played on Duncan's mind for the rest of the day. It was such a kind thing to say. When he thought of how he'd judged the Curtellas, sneered at their clothes, their lack of finesse, he felt ashamed. Who the hell was he to judge others? What did he have to feel so bloody smug about? He had failed in the most profound way a man could fail. He had failed his family.

When Duncan had finally managed to prise Lola away from the Curtellas and talked his way into a tasting at Opus One (he hadn't realised it was by appointment only), the effort of it all had dulled his palate and he found it hard to muster up any enthusiasm for the wines. Even the bold design of the winery – oddly space age but with grass on the steeply sloping walls – failed to arouse much interest.

'Is everything alright?' asked Lola. 'Only I expected you to wax lyrical about the balance of fruit and oak – that sort of thing.'

'Sorry,' he said. 'I didn't sleep very well.'

'Would you like to go back to the hotel?' said Lola.

'We're here now,' he said. 'Let's make the most of it.'

Lola took a sip of wine and put down her glass.

'Is it the house?' she said.

The last thing he wanted was for Lola to start worrying. Yes, it was an impetuous decision and he would need to sit down and work out the numbers, but that was his problem, not hers. A deal he had been working on for nearly a year was about to be signed. His bonus would pay for the renovations, providing Birdie didn't get too carried away.

'Not at all,' he said.

'If we can't afford it –'

'We can. Now, what about this wine?'

He tipped his glass sideways and held it to the light.

'Dark ruby with a violet edge.'

He swirled the glass a few times then put it to his nose and inhaled.

'Oak, spice, black cherry, cassis.'

Lola sniffed her wine.

'I get oak and spice. Not cherry or cassis.'

Duncan washed the wine around his mouth.

'The tannins are just about right – not too soft, not too overpowering. It's complex but well balanced.'

Lola sipped from her glass and agreed with his analysis.

'Maybe we could take a wine appreciation course,' she said. 'It might be fun.'

Duncan could hardly believe it. Had Lola just suggested they take up a hobby together? Astounding.

Instead of going out to dinner, they had room service and watched a film – a light-hearted romantic comedy that required no thought or effort. Lola seemed relaxed. She sat cross-legged on the king-sized bed wearing one of the hotel's white fluffy robes. Duncan relaxed too after three large glasses of the Cabernet he'd bought at the tasting. When Lola suggested they take a bath together Duncan thought back to that night in the San Francisco hotel, when she wouldn't even let him wash her back.

The tub was deep and wide but still too small for their long legs. Their knees poked out of the bubbles like a snowy mountain range. Duncan reached for his glass and took a long drink of wine. He looked at Lola's shapely breasts, at her pale, round nipples, and felt something very like joy.

The wine, the long hot soak and the sex that followed, led Duncan into a better night's sleep. He rose at six and went to the business centre before his swim. There were no new emails, but he made a quick call to the office anyway. He waited for Alison to answer and distracted himself from the abdominal knot by calculating how long she had been his secretary. Five years, maybe six? Perhaps he should bring her back a gift. He would ask Lola to choose something.

'Duncan Drummond's office. Alison Davey speaking.'

'Alison. Hello. It's Duncan.'

'Duncan,' she said, her voice suddenly high. 'I wasn't expecting to hear from you. How's your holiday?'

'Wonderful, thank you. I just thought I should check in'

'Of course.'

'Perhaps you could put me through to Hilliard.'

'Certainly.'

The line went quiet and Duncan imagined Alison at her neat and tidy desk, the water cooler in the corner of her office gurgling away, the well-tended parlour palm pert and shiny.

'This is a surprise,' said William Hilliard. He sounded slightly out of breath. 'How's the holiday?'

'Good, thank you. It's just a quick call – making sure there's nothing I need to know about.'

Something about the way Hilliard said *nothing*, made Duncan think there was something. He was too emphatic, too eager to bring the conversation to a close. Only one deal was at a crucial stage. The fact that Hilliard didn't mention it seemed odd.

'Any news from Vasquez?' asked Duncan.

'Umm, not really.'

'What does that mean?'

'It's nothing to worry about. He just wanted clarification on a couple of things.'

The knot in Duncan's gut twisted a little tighter.

'What exactly did he say?'

'Look, I'm sure it can wait.'

'What did he say?'

Hilliard paused before replying.

'He's asked for a bit more technical info and a break-down of some of the costs.'

Duncan's heart kicked hard against his chest.

'That doesn't make any sense. I've spent months going through this with Vasquez. We've covered everything. I would never have even considered going away if I wasn't sure. Give me his number.'

'Certainly,' said Hilliard. 'But he's not in his office for the next few days. I know because I offered to fly out to Spain to see him, iron out any little glitches in the contract.'

'What glitches?'

Hilliard cleared his throat.

'There are no glitches. It was a figure of speech. I just thought if I could sit down with him, face to face, then any last-minute concerns could be addressed. Anyway, he told me he's going to Madrid, to his son's graduation ceremony, apparently. He won't be back in the office until Monday.'

Duncan massaged his temples and tried to process this information. Was Vasquez getting cold feet? Christ. The contract was worth five million euros – his commission, two per cent of that. It had taken Duncan a year to negotiate. If Hilliard had screwed things up in some way –

'Duncan?'

'I'm still here. Do we have a mobile number for Vasquez?'

'Not sure. I would need to check the file.'

'Then check the file.'

Duncan waited.

'Afraid not,' said Hilliard, eventually. 'Only his office number.'

Shit. He had the mobile number on his BlackBerry.

'I'm sure it will wait until Monday,' said Hilliard.

It was a few moments before Duncan said, 'I sincerely hope you're right.'

There was only one other person in the pool. Duncan started to pound out his fifty-seven laps but only got to ten. It wasn't just his stomach that hurt now, it was his head too. He climbed out of the pool and slumped down on one of the loungers. He kept going over the Vasquez deal, trying to understand what the hell might have gone wrong. It was all but signed up when he had left.

'Sir?'

A teenage attendant offered Duncan a *San Francisco Chronicle* and a towel. Duncan dried his hands and flipped through the newspaper. On the front page was a story about a politician who had been caught using public money to pay for call girls. The man had two young children and a wife with breast cancer. He'd received hate mail and death threats. Someone smeared his car with excrement and wrote SHIT on the windscreen. Duncan shook his head. He couldn't garner much sympathy for the man but reminded himself it wasn't his place to judge. Let he who has not sinned cast the first stone. Duncan made a moral distinction between having an extramarital affair and using prostitutes for sex. An affair was an emotional betrayal – much more serious, he believed, than paying to satisfy a physical need. He also believed using prostitutes wasn't necessarily about sex. Sometimes it was about control. Not the need to control a woman, but the need to restore some sense of control in one's own life.

Clarissa's death had opened up a vast, jagged fault line in Duncan's dichotomous view of the world – his naive belief that there was right and wrong, and a clear, identifiable difference between the two. Had he really been so sure of everything back then? That first panic attack was his wake-up call, a preview of how things would be from now on. Some days were worse than others. When things went well at work, the panic would curl up inside him and sleep for a while. But when things weren't going well, when Duncan needed all the confidence he could muster, the panic stirred and threatened to unleash its malevolence. Full-blown attacks were mercifully rare, but the fear of an attack haunted him. That he didn't understand why it happened only made it worse. It was by accident that he discovered an antidote. Not a cure, but something that brought temporary relief.

It was a few months after Clarissa's death. Duncan couldn't face going home, seeing in Lola's grief-stricken face the terrible thing he had allowed to happen, so he crossed the street from his office and went to the Carfax Hotel instead. He sat at the bar and sought solace in a string of martinis. He hadn't noticed the woman until she came and sat next to him – told him he looked like he'd had a hard day. She was Asian – petite with brown, almond-shaped eyes. Young, but not obscenely young. In her twenties. He didn't encourage her but he didn't tell her to go away either. The barman asked what she wanted to drink and she pointed to Duncan's martini, said she'd have the same. She didn't ask questions. He liked that. Her voice was high and accented – Chinese or Korean perhaps. He liked that as well. It was too late to go home so he went to reception and booked a room. The woman followed, asked if he wanted some company. He said he didn't know what he wanted. When he stepped out into the street – quiet now, empty except for a cab waiting for a fare – it was because he needed time to think. Sleet fell in wet, icy sheets and turned to sludge on the pavement. Could he do really this? He pulled his phone out of his jacket pocket and called Lola. When she answered he could tell she was crying. A fresh surge of guilt engulfed him. He said he was still at the office – would she mind if he stayed at Carfax, save him the journey home? She said no and hung up before he had the chance to say goodnight. He slipped his phone back into his pocket and took out his wallet.

Seventy pounds in cash. He had no idea how much the woman would charge. There was a cashpoint just along the street. He withdrew two hundred pounds and walked back to the hotel.

The woman was still standing in the lobby. He looked at her and she followed him to the lift. Neither of them spoke. They didn't speak in the room either, except when she told him it would be two hundred for an hour. He counted out the cash and handed it to her. She put it in her bag and put her bag on the table. They stood opposite each other in the semi-darkness. She took off her dress, her shoes, her underwear. He liked that she was a stranger, that her breasts were small, her nipples dark. What he liked the most was that she was nothing like Lola. She removed his tie, undid the top three buttons of his shirt and slipped off his suit jacket. He was passive, curious to see how he would respond. She unbuttoned the rest of his shirt and slid her hand along his chest. He felt himself become hard. She moved her hand down to his belt, undid the buckle, then his fly. He was conscious of his breathing, of her flesh pressed against his flesh. When she kissed him her mouth felt warm and forgiving. He looked at her for a moment, trying to understand what it was he felt. It wasn't guilt. The guilt he felt over Clarissa was all consuming – there wasn't space for more. It wasn't even lust. The woman was naked and sexy but it wasn't about the sex – that was just the catalyst for something more important. In that room, with that woman, he felt in control again. It made no sense but he had stopped trying to make sense of things. As she knelt in front of him, the guilt and anxiety melted away. Afterwards he felt calm. When she left he took a bath and managed to get five hours unbroken sleep.

The conversation Duncan had just had with Hilliard made him crave that calm, that sense of control. He could feel panic flexing its muscles, getting ready to overpower him. It stalked him for the rest of the day – through breakfast with Lola, at the mountain winery they visited, and during their romantic dinner overlooking the Napa River. It festered inside him like a canker. When Lola asked if anything was the matter he mumbled something about a headache.

'Should you be drinking?' she asked gently.

He topped up his glass in reply.

Later, as he sat on the edge of the bed undressing, Lola kneeled behind him and massaged his shoulders. When she remarked how tense they felt and whispered in his ear that she knew a magic cure for that, he stood up. Sex with Lola was about love and tenderness and what he needed was to disconnect – rid himself of emotion, not drown in it. He apologised, said he had probably had too much red wine, that he would feel better in the morning.

He didn't. The sense that something bad was brewing wouldn't let go. During their meeting with Birdie Johnson Duncan struggled to concentrate. Lola, on the other hand, was animated with enthusiasm. He went along with it all – tried not to think about the major contract he may have lost, the commission he might not get, the crippling anxiety he was unable to fend off because he was on holiday with his wife and sex with a stranger wasn't really an option. Birdie's ballpark figure for the renovations – and a plunge pool – was a hundred thousand dollars.

The Curtellas threw them a small leaving party. Duncan didn't want any fuss and would have preferred a quiet meal with Lola, but she was so touched by the gesture that he went along with it. He began to see that the reason she found things so much easier here was because no one knew about Clarissa. There was no awkwardness, no pity. People took them at face value.

McCann brought a pretty, elfin-like girl with short black hair and a small dolphin tattoo on the side of her neck. Roger and Birdie seemed like a good match, although when he said that to Lola, she insisted they were just friends. Mike Curtella clearly enjoyed being the host and Duncan had never known anyone as tactile as Joanne Curtella. She clucked around Lola, rubbed her arm, squeezed her hand, treated her like a long-lost friend. Lola looked happy enough, though. Duncan reminded himself that had been the whole point of the holiday: objective achieved.

On the drive to the airport Lola was quiet. When Duncan asked if she was okay she said she was sad to leave, that she would miss them all. She put her hand on his leg.

'It's been surprisingly wonderful,' she said. 'Thank you.'

He patted her hand and said she didn't have to thank him, that seeing her happy was thanks enough.

'It's a long time since I've felt hopeful,' she said. 'Felt as though there was something to look forward to.'

She brought his hand to her lips and kissed it. That was when he decided that whatever it took, he would find the money to transform the Treehouse into everything Lola wanted it to be. He wouldn't let her down again.

Five

The damp, slightly acrid smell of the city hit Lola as soon as they arrived at Heathrow. The air in San Francisco had been so fresh – washed clean by the salty Pacific breeze. Compared to the sunshine and brightness she had got used to, everything looked dreary and dull.

Duncan drove in silence. He stared straight ahead, expressionless, lost in his own thoughts. Lola was glad he didn't try to make conversation. She closed her eyes and must have dozed off because when she opened them again they had left the motorway and were on the country lane that led into Piliton. Dense green hedgerows pressed in from either side. Rain spat down from a rumbling sky. Lola looked away when they passed the turning to Clarissa's school. A weeping willow had been planted in her memory, but Lola had never seen it. It wasn't the tree she couldn't bear to see, it was the children.

A painted roadside sign welcomed them to Piliton, every inch of the village imprinted on Lola's mind: the hall where Clarissa went to playgroup, the shop where she counted out her pocket money to buy pony magazines, the church where Father Michael poured water over her small newborn head and eight years later prayed over her small white coffin.

Rosebushes bordered the curved gravel drive that led up to the Grange. Its Georgian symmetry contrasted with the other houses in the village: cottages of various shapes and sizes, the odd barn conversion, and a row of modern, box-like semis hidden behind the churchyard. A tangle of ivy and Virginia creeper had begun to colonise the Grange's proud facade. In a month or two the honey-coloured stone would be almost obscured by the vines. Lola liked it best in the autumn, when the leaves changed from green to red.

Duncan pulled up in front of the house and turned off the engine. He exhaled loudly, like he'd been holding his breath, got out of the car and began to unload the luggage. Lola asked if she could help and he handed her the bag of duty-free, said he could manage the rest. They hadn't got around to shopping for gifts so had picked up a few things at the airport. When Lola chose a red hooded sweatshirt for Kathy, a garish depiction of the Golden Gate Bridge emblazoned across the front, Duncan had grimaced and said something about it frightening the horses. She asked what he thought Alison might like but he had shrugged his shoulders. Lola bought a bottle of Chanel No. 5 and a single malt whisky for Mr Snook. It seemed peculiar now, standing in front of her house, holding a bag of gifts from a country in which she would soon own another house. Unreal somehow, like she had imagined it all.

She took a set of keys from her handbag, unlocked the front door and pushed it open. Two weeks' worth of mail lay on the flagstone floor. Lola gathered it up and put it on the hall table.

'Would you mind if I headed to the livery yard?' she said. 'I want to see Darcy.'

'No, you go ahead,' said Duncan, sorting through the mail.

She walked along the hallway, switching on lights as she went. It was only five o'clock but so gloomy it seemed much later. In the kitchen, she threw open the windows, swapping stale air for fresh. A bluebottle flew in and buzzed an erratic trail from sink to stove and back again. The kitchen was bigger than the whole of the Treehouse.

Coats, jackets and fleeces hung from a long row of hooks in the boot room. She didn't know why they had so many, except that she never got around to throwing any of them out. An array of hats sat on a shelf along the opposite wall. She slipped off her sandals and pulled on her mud-splashed Hunters. The rain had stopped but an opaque mist hung stubbornly in the air. She unlocked the back door and hurried to the stable yard. The cobbled path was slippery and uneven. Flat emerald fields stretched into the distance.

She beamed when she spotted Darcy, racing along the path to greet her. He barked and jumped up, his wet paws leaving dirty smudges on her clothes. She hugged him, said what a good boy he was, how much she had missed him.

'I wondered what all the noise was about,' called Kathy.

Her own dog – a feisty Jack Russell called Beau – stood loyally at heel. He barked too and Kathy said something about a canine choir that Lola didn't quite catch.

'When did you get back?'

'Just now – I couldn't wait to see Darcy.' Lola lifted up his muzzle and lowered her face to kiss him. 'And I wanted to check everything was okay here.'

'Course it is.'

Lola glanced around the freshly swept yard. The stables were empty except for one.

'Why is Polo in?' she asked.

'The grass is a bit rich with all the rain. I was worried about laminitis. I've been turning him out in the small paddock every morning and bringing him in before I leave.'

Lola rubbed the white blaze that ran down the middle of Polo's face. She had bought him for Clarissa's birthday. He was a bit big for a skinny five-year-old but gentle and well mannered – a good first pony. Lola wondered if he missed Clarissa too. She scratched behind his ears and he nodded.

'Did you have a nice time?' asked Kathy.

Lola turned around.

'Really good, actually. Where's Mr Snook?'

'Dentist.'

'The dentist?' said Lola, surprised.

'I know. He said it was hardly worth the bother with just half a dozen teeth left but I said all the more reason to look after them.'

'How is he?'

Kathy hesitated.

'Alright, I suppose. Same as always.'

Mr Snook was part of the collateral damage from Clarissa's accident. He blamed himself, just like Duncan blamed himself. Lola said neither of them was to blame but there was more than enough guilt to go round and they were all greedy for their share.

'The horses are in the lower paddock. Mr Snook took them their hay before he left and I mucked out the shelter this morning. All the tack's been cleaned and the blacksmith's coming on Tuesday.'

Kathy had been just thirteen when she first turned up at the livery yard – a shy, plump girl with a broad West Country accent and braces on her teeth. She asked if she could help out at weekends and since Lola was new to the village and relatively friendless, she welcomed the company. Lola's own childhood was spent in livery yards, exchanging hours of mucking out and tack cleaning for riding lessons and hacks. When Kathy left school at sixteen, Lola took her on full-time. Her teeth were straight by then but the puppy fat had settled into something more solid and permanent. Lola could scarcely believe she would be thirty in a few years.

'I should imagine you could do with a couple of days off,' said Lola.

'If you can spare me?'

'Oh yes. It's the weekend so the owners will be in to ride and Mr Snook is around if I need a hand.'

'While I think of it, Jackie phoned. She's got to work so Hector will need exercising.'

'Perfect,' said Lola. 'I could do with a nice long hack. Now why don't you walk back to the Grange with me – I've got something for you.'

'Really?' said Kathy. 'Okay – just give me a minute.'

Darcy dropped a tennis ball at Lola's feet. She threw it to the other end of the yard and he sprinted after it, scooped it into his mouth and raced back. She took the ball from him – slimy with saliva – and threw it again. It rolled under a stable door, sending Darcy into a tailspin of barking and whining. He tried to crawl under the door, jump over the door, push the door open with his paws. Beau squeezed himself under the gap and appeared triumphant a second later with the tennis ball clamped in his mouth. Darcy chased him around the yard at full pelt and Lola imagined Clarissa right there with her, clapping her hands in delight.

'Ready?' said Kathy.

Her pale gold hair hung lank and loose around her shoulders, flattened by hours under a riding hat. She rubbed Vaseline onto her chapped lips – a side effect of working outside in all weathers.

'Tell me about your holiday,' she said.

'Well, I ate too much food and drank too much wine,' said Lola.

'Of course you did. That's what holidays are for.'

'And San Francisco is a great city, but it was the Napa Valley I fell in love with. It was nothing like I expected. Actually, I don't know what I expected. I certainly didn't expect to buy a house.'

Kathy stopped abruptly. Her raised eyebrows showed the lines she would have when she was older.

'A house?'

'Yes. I know. Utter madness.'

Kathy stood rooted to the spot.

'In America?'

'Yes. Northern California. It's more of a shack really – needs a huge amount of work.'

'I don't believe it.'

'I'm not sure I do either.'

The shrill urgency of distant sirens zipped through the damp air. The motorway was half a dozen miles as the crow flies, but the low rumble of fast traffic carried across the fields. Kathy wanted to know all about the house, but Lola didn't feel like talking about it. In Kathy's astonished face she saw her own doubts reflected, the slow realisation that buying a wreck thousands of miles away – a fixer-upper, McCann had called it – was a ludicrously rash decision.

'First I want to hear everything that's happened while I was away,' she said.

'Not much to tell,' said Kathy, and as she chatted away Lola's mind drifted back to the Curtellas' deck, to Joanne's girlish chatter and Mike's crazy taste in shirts. She pictured the sunlight as it filtered through the trees in slivers and slices, making a dappled pattern on the wood.

'... so I told him that I'd ask you.'

Lola blinked.

'Sorry?'

'Mr Snook. He wondered if he should get on and repair the bits of broken fence in the far paddock, or get the fence people in to replace the whole section.'

Lola struggled to concentrate.

'I'll look at it tomorrow.'

As they walked back to the Grange, Darcy tried to goad Beau into another game of chase. The dogs shot into the boot room as soon as Lola opened the door, then followed her and Kathy into the kitchen where they made straight for Darcy's bed.

'Now where did I put your pressie?' said Lola.

'Doesn't matter,' said Kathy. 'You must be exhausted. How long was the flight?'

'Ten hours,' said Lola. 'Oh, I know. I left it in the hall.'

She retraced her steps to the front door and found the duty-free bag next to a pile of mail, which Duncan had arranged into a neat stack. She fished out Alison's perfume and Mr Snook's whisky, and put them back on the hall table.

'Sorry about the wrapping,' she said, handing Kathy the plastic bag.

Kathy pulled out the sweatshirt and held it in front of her, arms outstretched.

'I love it,' she said.

Duncan came into the kitchen carrying a bottle of wine in each hand. He stopped for a moment, as if surprised to see them. Darcy dashed up to him and barked, his tail in perpetual motion.

'Thanks for the present, Mr Drummond.'

Lola always thought it odd that Kathy called her Lola but called her husband Mr Drummond. He put the wine on the long pine table and patted the frantic dog. She thought Duncan might open one of the bottles and offer Kathy a drink, but he didn't. When Lola walked her out and Kathy thanked her again for the sweatshirt, Lola gave her a quick hug. Kathy looked surprised for the second time that afternoon.

'Something I picked up in the Napa Valley,' said Lola.

They ate supper early. Lola searched the cupboards and found a packet of dried spaghetti and a jar of Bolognese sauce dubiously close to its sell-by date. Duncan opened a bottle of Spring Mountain Cabernet and took a long drink, as though impatient for the alcohol to take effect. Lola poured most of her wine into the sauce as it bubbled away in the pan, even as Duncan grumbled that it was a bit too good for cooking. When she took the spaghetti off the heat and drained it into a colander, a sheet of steam enveloped her face. She tipped the pasta into two bowls and divided the sauce between them. Duncan rummaged around in the fridge and found an old lump of Parmesan.

'What are you smiling about?' he asked.

Lola looked up from setting the table.

'I didn't realise I was.'

Duncan topped up their wine glasses and they sat down to eat.

'Actually, I was thinking about the leaving party the Curtellas threw for us,' she said.

Duncan grated Parmesan over his bowl until all the pasta was covered. He offered the cheese to Lola but she shook her head.

'What about it?' he said.

'Oh, nothing in particular, just how everyone brought food and wine, and how relaxed it all was. The dinner parties we go to are always so formal.'

He took another drink and then started on the spaghetti.

'Are we mad?' said Lola.

'What do you mean?'

'When I told Kathy we'd bought a house in America, she was amazed.'

'You told Kathy?'

'Yes.'

Duncan put his glass on the table, sat back in his chair and looked at her. Lola sensed he was about to embark on one of his pep talks and wished she had kept her mouth shut.

'First of all,' he said, 'Kathy has never been anywhere except Piliton, so of course she was amazed. Secondly, we bought the Treehouse because it made you happy – made you feel more like your old self again.'

Her old self? Her old self was a mother – something she would never be again. He had summoned Clarissa's ghost. She was right there with them at the kitchen table, trying to twirl spaghetti around her fork.

'And you took an instant liking to the Curtellas, and vice versa. You fit in there – you said as much yourself.' He sat forward and touched her hand. 'Look, I don't want you to have buyer's remorse. We made a decision and we're going to follow it through. I've given everyone your email address so you'll need to log on each day instead of once every few weeks. There'll be paperwork, things that need to be done and I'm going to be too busy with work. We'll probably need to pay a visit to the American Embassy at some point to get the paperwork notarised. You can get the train up and meet me – maybe have some lunch, make a day of it.'

He stopped talking for a moment, as if to gauge her reaction. Lola thought how tired he looked. Shadows framed his eyes like week-old bruises. Lead-coloured stubble reinforced the impression of weariness. He was trying to make it all sound like an adventure, but it sounded daunting.

'You can do this, Lola. You need to do this. I feared that as soon as we got home you'd slip back into ...' He held his hands up, palms open, as if hoping for the right word to fall into them. 'Lethargy,' he said. 'But please, Lola – don't. Finding that house is the best thing that's happened in a long time. You loved it straightaway. It doesn't matter if you don't know why – go with your instinct. This is a good thing, Lola. Don't overthink it.'

So typical that he got through the whole lecture without once mentioning Clarissa – the reason they had bought the Treehouse in the first place. Lola poured the last few drops of wine into her glass and when Duncan went to open a second bottle she told him not to bother. Another few drinks and she might be tempted to say how his patronising 'I know best' attitude infuriated her, how belittling it was to be treated like a child, how cruel to expunge Clarissa from their lives as if she had never existed.

'Are you alright?' he asked.

She emptied her glass and set it back on the table.

'Fine.'

They made small talk during the rest of the meal. Everything alright at the livery yard? Anything interesting in the mail? Seems like it rained the whole time we were away.

Duncan went to his study while Lola cleared up. It was only eight-thirty but she didn't think she could stay awake much longer. Duncan said something about jetlag being worse, west to east. She went upstairs to unpack, grateful it was easier to empty a suitcase than to fill one. Ten days earlier she had stared at it, lying empty and open on the bed, her mind blank. When she had confided in Kathy that she didn't have a clue what to pack, Kathy said that was a nice problem to have – I wish I had your life.

One of the Piliton mothers had said that too: *I wish I had your life.* The woman cleaned houses and took in ironing while raising twin boys a year younger than Clarissa. They had bumped into each other in the village shop – the woman refereeing a fight over which comic to buy, Clarissa politely asking Lola if she could have a pony magazine – and the woman turned to her, red-faced and only half joking, and said, I wish I had your life. Lola saw her again a few months after the accident – the boys still scrapping, the woman still red-faced – and this time, instead of wishing for Lola's life, the woman had looked at her with blatant pity.

She unpacked the black silk dress she had worn to the Curtellas and thought how much simpler everything was when people didn't know about Clarissa. The dress smelled of Joanne's lavender soap.

The morning was drizzly and cool. Dew gleamed on the soft grass and the air was thick with the sweet, sickly smell of silage. Lola's riding boots felt tight. Her feet had got used to the freedom of sandals. She pushed her hands into her pockets and told Darcy that she missed the sunshine. A jumble of questions buzzed in her head. How difficult would it be to take him to California? She couldn't bear the idea of quarantine but maybe you didn't need to do that these days. Kathy could look after the yard. She'd done it many times before, when Lola was pregnant or resting on doctor's orders. Too many times. A large house for a large family – that's what Lola said to Duncan when they bought the Grange. They tried for a baby straightaway, and every month, when her period arrived, she was genuinely surprised. Disappointed too, but mostly surprised. They were healthy and happy – it didn't make sense.

The local doctor blamed Lola's stress – *but I'm not stressed* – and Duncan's peripatetic lifestyle, prescribing relaxation and bracing country walks. Idiot, said Duncan after their second visit. He made an appointment with a doctor in London who suggested that because Duncan was away so much, he probably missed those precious few days each month when Lola was fertile. Duncan agreed this made some sense but pointed out that it was difficult to organise his business diary around his wife's menstrual cycle.

They carried on as before, relieved no physical cause had been found and convinced Lola would soon conceive. She didn't. A year later they were back with the London doctor, demanding more tests, more explanations. Good news and bad news, the doctor said with a little too much theatre for Lola's taste. Good news, Duncan's sperm were plentiful and motile, bad news, the irregularity of Lola's cycle made ovulation difficult to predict. The remedy? Give it time; it will happen when you least expect it.

Almost overnight Lola became one of those women who defined themselves by their inability to conceive. She ached for a baby and everything else was subsumed beneath that ache. On the outside she seemed the same but inside it ate away at her. She walked the dog – Rufus, Darcy's predecessor – past the little village school, saw mothers huddled together in motherly gossip and longed to be included in their exclusive club. Some days were worse than others. Innocent comments about starting a family cut her to the bone. The first day of her period was always bad. Their lovemaking was frequent but functional. Lola lost the knack of climax and it never occurred to her to fake it. She could see that Duncan's pride was hurt, his own pleasure diminished. Their pillow talk focused on the mechanics of reproduction, when she was due to ovulate, which positions favoured conception. A calendar hung on the kitchen wall, some dates circled, others marked with big red crosses. Lola studied it constantly, as if trying to crack some mysterious code.

The first morning that she couldn't face breakfast, she thought nothing of it. Kathy had been off with a stomach bug and even Mr Snook, who never complained about anything, hinted at a bit of tummy trouble. It was only after several mornings, and obsessive scrutiny of the calendar, that Lola dared to hope. She bought three pregnancy tests and took them all. Positive, positive, positive. She sat on the bathroom floor, laughing and crying with joy, the plastic urine-soaked sticks scattered around her. Duncan was called out of a meeting because she told his secretary it was urgent.

'I'm pregnant!' Lola shrieked. 'Pregnant.'

Duncan took a moment, then spoke quietly.

'That's wonderful,' he said. 'I'll get the earlier train.'

Lola glowed with satisfaction. Physically she was below par but Doctor Morton insisted this was a good sign. The first three months are always difficult – a rush of hormones, the more the better. The thought of food made her nauseous. Kathy and Mr Snook ran the livery yard and made sure Rufus got two good walks a day. Roll on month four, Lola would say, telling herself she would feel better soon.

Month four never arrived. A dull, cramping pain, spotting, more pain. Lola curled into a ball and refused to acknowledge that anything was wrong. Blood started to flow and she couldn't ignore it anymore. Duncan was in Singapore so Lola called Kathy who called the doctor and an ambulance. When Lola was discharged the next day, she was no longer pregnant.

Duncan was already en route, unaware of the loss. He arrived home with gifts – most of them for the baby – and a bouncy sort of happiness. Lola heard him call her from the hall but didn't answer. He found her in the bedroom. *There you are*. She pulled the covers over her face.

'Lola, what's the matter?'

He sat on the bed and stroked her hair. She sobbed, a pained, purging sound that told him everything he needed to know.

It was eight years before she carried a child to term. Clarissa – their perfect little girl. The pregnancy was horrible, much of it spent in bed on doctor's orders, but then there was the baby and everything else was forgotten. Lola had doubted herself, doubted her purpose, until the moment she held her daughter. That screaming, wriggling scrap of life made sense of everything. Post-natal euphoria – the purest love of all.

Clarissa's life was lived at Piliton Grange and everything about it was also about her. Lola could see her trotting Polo around the small paddock, her legs flapping at his sides like wings. She would try to sweep the yard like Kathy did, and they'd all laugh because the broom was taller than she was. She could tie hay nets by the time she was five and jump cavaletti by the time she was six. Lola closed her eyes and inhaled: silage, wet grass, horse manure and hay. Clarissa asked why horse poo wasn't smelly. It's because they only eat grass, Lola had told her. They eat hay too, Clarissa had said. Hay is dried grass, explained Lola, and gave her a handful to smell.

And now Lola felt guilty, realising she had been happy in California – a place that had nothing to do with Clarissa.

When Lola got to the lower paddock Mr Snook was there inspecting the broken fence. His ancient waxed jacket, tweed flat cap and heavy duty Hunters all looked a size too big, like a new school uniform you had to grow into.

'Morning,' Lola called.

When he didn't turn around she called again, louder this time. He had a hearing aid but never wore it.

'Mrs Drummond,' he said. 'I wasn't expecting to see you.'

She had given up asking him to call her Lola years ago. He was of a different generation. She would always be Mrs Drummond and he would always be Mr Snook. She didn't even know his Christian name. His friends – those that were still around – called him Snooky. That was what Clarissa had called him too.

'We got home yesterday. I gave Kathy the day off.'

'She did a grand job when you were away.'

Lola patted Hector, a frisky young gelding, as he scooped a mouthful of hay and chewed, his jaw moving slowly from side to side.

'You look well,' said Mr Snook. 'The break must have done you good.'

He pulled off his tweed cap and scratched his head. The liver spots and few strands of silver hair made him seem not just old, but elderly. Lola stared at the purple scar on his temple – a physical reminder of that terrible November day. He saw her looking and put the cap back on.

'You riding this morning, Mrs Drummond?'

'Just Hector. The others are being ridden by their owners. Keep an eye on Darcy, would you? I don't want him to follow me again. Oh, and could you turn Polo out into the small paddock for an hour?'

'Right you are.'

Riding was as natural to Lola as walking. In the leafy Surrey village where she grew up, the stables were her refuge, the place she fled to when her parents argued. Later, when her father had left and her mother was drinking, the stables were close enough for Lola to run home and check that everything was okay. Okay was a relative term. If her mother drank and fell asleep, that was okay. She wouldn't hurt herself if she was asleep. But sometimes she tried to do things – cook a meal, drive to the shops, stand on a chair to change a light bulb – and that wasn't okay. That's when she would hurt herself. Lola shook her head. She didn't want to think about her mother.

A gentle squeeze of her heels nudged Hector into a brisk trot. The sky was a murky white, devoid of clouds or sun. She should have asked Cain if he rode. It was easy to picture him on a big Western saddle, sporting a Stetson and cowboy boots. The thought made her chuckle, but she knew it was important to keep the memory of California close and real, that without nurture it would fade to nothing. Perhaps that's why Duncan gave her email address and not his own. He wanted to keep it alive for her.

Lola leaned forward and opened the gate to Five Acre Field while Hector shuffled impatiently from foot to foot. She gathered up the reins, keeping taut contact with his bridled mouth. He shook his head and snorted to convey his objection. Lola took both reins in one hand and reached down to close the gate. He bucked and she grabbed a handful of chestnut mane to stop herself from falling off. His nostrils flared, sucking in oxygen for the steep gallop ahead. Lola felt his muscles tense as he waited for the signal. She shifted her weight forward and released him with the lightest touch of her heels. He thundered across the spongy grass, head and neck outstretched. Lola felt spits of rain against her face. She rose out of the saddle and took the weight in her legs. Adrenalin crackled through her body. The first time she galloped she was terrified – the ground moved so fast – but when it was over she was breathless and exhilarated. During her mother's drunken rants, she summoned that sensation like a genie from a lamp. She would close her eyes and see the ground move, hear hooves pound, feel her heart quicken, and remind herself that she was strong and brave and there was more to the world than this.

After she lost Clarissa, Lola didn't ride for months, and when eventually, after much gentle coaxing from Kathy and Mr Snook, she had got back on a horse, she galloped recklessly, not caring whether she lived or died. Mornings were a torment – those fleeting seconds between sleeping and waking, the blissful lightness before remembering it was real, it did happen, then the crushing pain that made it hard to breathe. Evenings were no better – the prospect of going to bed and either lying awake, thinking about Clarissa, or falling into a fitful sleep and dreaming about her. One night Lola emptied the sleeping pills Doctor Morton had prescribed onto the kitchen table. She wanted it all to go away. For a long time she had stared at the pills – small and white, like Clarissa's coffin. How easily they would slip down her throat. What relief they would bring. When the phone rang she barely noticed, but it kept on ringing, like an alarm. It was Duncan, calling to say he'd got a room at the Carfax. She had thought what it would do to him if he lost her too. One by one she had put the pills back into their child-proof bottle and went upstairs to bed.

Duncan grabbed a tea towel and took a plate of bacon and eggs out of the Aga.

'How was your ride?'

'Good.'

He put the plate on the table and poured two mugs of tea.

'Where's yours?'

'I've already eaten.'

She thought he might keep her company but he folded the newspaper, picked up his tea and mumbled something about catching up with work.

It was wearing at first in California, being around each other day and night, but then she got used to it – enjoyed it even; their tipsy anniversary dinner, their walk around St Helena hand in hand. She looked at the table and six chairs, and wished the other five weren't always empty. Loneliness closed in on all sides. For a moment she thought of phoning Joanne Curtella but then remembered it would be the middle of the night there. She nibbled on a piece of crispy bacon and gave the rest to Darcy. He hesitated at first – he wasn't allowed to beg for food – then gently took it from her hand. The bacon disappeared with a single gulp. He sat there, staring at her with big, hopeful eyes, waiting to see if there were any more treats coming his way.

'You'll love Riley,' said Lola, feeding him another strip of bacon. 'He's not a pedigree like you and Duncan calls him a scruffy mutt, but he's very sweet natured. You can get up to all sorts of mischief together. Joanne and Mike can't wait to meet you. They're our neighbours across the creek. You love water, don't you?' she said, patting his head. 'But it's seasonal, so it will probably be dry when we're there.'

'Who are you talking to?' asked Duncan.

'Darcy,' said Lola. 'I didn't see you there.'

'Can't find my glasses,' he said, looking around. 'Why are you talking to Darcy?'

'He's a good listener.'

Lola glanced at Duncan's weekend clothes – beige corduroys, plaid shirt, brown suede brogues – and an image of Cain McCann popped into her head. Faded jeans and Birkenstocks. He had nice feet – very straight toes. Odd she should remember that.

'Have you seen them?' said Duncan.

'What?'

'My glasses.'

'They're on your head.'

'Pardon?'

She tapped her head.

'Oh,' said Duncan. 'I didn't think to look there.'

'Do you have much work?'

'Afraid so.'

Sitting alone with just the dog for company was suddenly the last thing Lola wanted. She picked up his lead and said, 'Let's take Mr Snook his whisky.'

Duncan pulled a handkerchief from his trouser pocket and wiped his glasses.

'See you later, then,' he said, holding his glasses up to the light.

A steady plume of blue-grey smoke rose from the stone chimney at the far end of the cottage. All the stable buildings had been renovated a few years after work on the

Grange was finished. Lola offered Mr Snook a room in the house until the cottage was ready, but he wouldn't hear of it. She asked how he would manage without heating or a bathroom and he smiled his gummy smile and said he didn't have either of those things as a lad and it didn't do him a bit of harm. Lola knew arguing was pointless.

The slate plaque on the front door was her idea; 'Stable Cottage' in grey lettering, bordered by a row of horseshoes. She knocked twice then let herself in. The planning committee had insisted on keeping the low ceiling and heavy wooden beams. They stipulated the use of reclaimed materials too, with strict adherence to the original design. That was why Lola was surprised by Birdie's ideas for the Treehouse. She said they could do pretty much what they wanted. It certainly wasn't that way in England.

In the wood-burning stove, flames flickered yellow, orange and red. Mr Snook was snoozing in his old leather armchair, a copy of the *Racing Post* open across his lap. Lola was about to make a quiet retreat when Darcy bounded in and woke him.

'I'm sorry,' she said. 'I didn't mean to disturb you.'

For a moment he looked confused.

'Mrs Drummond? What a nice surprise.'

He closed the newspaper and pushed himself out of the chair. The leather was worn and several shades darker where he rested his head. Darcy sniffed the quarry-tiled floor like a bloodhound trailing a scent.

'A present from America,' said Lola, and handed Mr Snook the whisky.

He pulled his thin lips into a smile and said she shouldn't have gone to any trouble. His hands trembled when he took the bottle.

'It wasn't any trouble,' said Lola.

'That's very kind,' he said. 'You'll stay for a cup of tea?'

'If you're sure we're not disturbing you.'

'Not at all.'

Darcy followed him as he shuffled into the kitchen. Lola went over to the stone mantelpiece and picked up a sepia photograph of a dashing young man in World War II uniform. It was hard to imagine that young man was Mr Snook. A pewter tankard stood next to the photograph along with two commemorative plates – one from the Queen's Silver Jubilee and the other from Charles and Diana's wedding – and a gold-plated carriage clock. Channel 4 horse racing blared out from a small television in the corner of the room.

Lola wandered into the kitchen and saw Mr Snook give Darcy a biscuit.

'No wonder he follows you around,' she said.

'It was just the one,' said Mr Snook. 'Isn't that right, young Darcy?'

'Here, let me take that,' said Lola, picking up the tray of tea and biscuits.

She carried it into the sitting room and laid it on the table in front of the fireplace. Mr Snook turned off the television and lowered himself back into his armchair. Lola settled into the other one – a striped cloth recliner that had seen better days – and handed him his tea. The vase of fake flowers surprised her – not the sort of thing she thought an old man would like.

'It's very cosy,' she said.

He looked around, as though trying to see it through her eyes.

'Well, it suits me,' he said.

Lola picked up her teacup – bone china with a dark red rose pattern – and said a mug would have been just fine.

'These belonged to my parents,' he said, holding up his cup and saucer. 'Their wedding china. Wedgwood. Don't make this pattern anymore. I know it's a bit old-fashioned, but I think tea tastes better out of good china. Biscuit?'

Lola took one to be polite and watched Mr Snook dunk his biscuit into his tea. He caught her watching and said, 'Sorry, I forgot my manners.'

Lola dunked her biscuit too and said it tasted much better soggy. The tea was hot and strong – proper builder's tea. Lola put down her teacup and unzipped her fleece.

'It's warm in here,' she said.

'June's late for a fire but the damp gets right into my bones. I can open a window if you like.'

Lola shook her head and took another sip of tea. Mr Snook was dressed more for winter than summer: moleskin trousers, woollen cardigan, his shirt buttoned all the way up to the top. The tweed cap he wore indoors and out, sat slightly back and revealed a craggy forehead, criss-crossed with lines. His eyes had sunk deep into their sockets, his cheeks hollow and bony.

'Are you alright, Mr Snook?' asked Lola.

'What do you mean?'

'I wondered if maybe you were a bit under the weather. You would say if the work was getting too much for you?'

He put down his teacup and sat up straight.

'I'm right as rain,' he said. 'Don't you go worrying about me. It's the work that keeps me going. You and young Kathy, and the horses.' Darcy looked up from his spot in front of the fire.

'You too, Darcy,' he said. 'Mustn't forget about you.'

'But you would let me know, wouldn't you, if you wanted to retire? The cottage is yours; you know that. We think of you as family.'

Strictly speaking, she and Clarissa had thought of him as family. Duncan didn't have much to do with him. Lola joked that Duncan had a 'Lord of the Manor' complex but Duncan said that wasn't true at all – he was simply too busy to get involved with the day-to-day minutiae of running the place. Whenever Mr Snook had a query, it was Lola he came to.

'If there's anything I can do for you, you only have to say,' she said.

He studied his hands for a moment. 'There is.'

'Pardon?'

'Something you can do for me.'

'Oh?'

His eyes stayed fixed on his hands when he said, 'You can let her rest.'

The words hung between them, potent and unexpected.

'We found a house, in America,' Lola said. 'A run-down old thing but in a lovely, peaceful setting. I got this idea in my head that it had been waiting for me to save it. For the first time since Clarissa died I thought maybe, just maybe, I could be happy again. This last two years have been – well, you know how they've been.'

He looked at her and nodded.

'I know you miss her too,' she said.

He wiped his eyes with the heel of his hand.

'So,' he said, 'this house in America? Are you going to live there?'

Lola shook her head.

'No. If we go through with it, then I suppose we'll spend the summers there.'

'If you go through with it?'

'Our offer has been accepted but now that we're home … I don't know – it's a long way away.'

'But you were happy there?'

'Briefly.'

'Well, that's a start.'

They sat in silence for a while and then Lola said, 'I feel guilty about Clarissa, about leaving her behind.'

'She'll always be with you, right here where it matters.'

He made a fist and tapped his chest. 'I hope I haven't spoken out of turn, but I had to say my piece.'

'I'm glad you did,' said Lola. 'The only person I can talk to about Clarissa is Darcy.'

'And me,' said Mr Snook. 'You can talk to me.'

It preyed on Lola's mind. Her husband was sitting at home in his study but it wasn't him she confided in, it was a frail old man who wouldn't even call her by her Christian name. He had been there too, the day Clarissa died. He lay unconscious as her life slipped away. It broke him, knowing he was so close and not able to save her. But he understood that Lola needed to talk about her, however hard it was for him. Lola admired his courage – more courage than Duncan could muster.

Six

The train was twenty minutes late. Duncan strained to hear the announcement – something about a points failure at Reading – and checked his Rolex. He had planned to be in the office early, but that wasn't going to happen now. Sunshine and showers, the weather forecast had said. It started to rain and Duncan realised he had left his brolly in the Land Rover when Lola dropped him off.

Was that dog hair on his jacket? He huffed and brushed at it with his hand. His nice, clean Mercedes was sitting in the garage, yet Lola insisted on driving him to the station in the scruffy Land Rover. She said it was such a bother having to alter the seat position and adjust the mirrors and remember which switch was for the lights and where the windshield wipers were, when the Land Rover was right outside and good to go.

Holidays were supposed to leave you rested and refreshed, yet Duncan was neither. He hadn't slept well for days, worrying about Vasquez and the contract he might lose, the commission he might not get, and how the hell he'd pay for the derelict house he'd promised Lola. When he did finally speak to Vasquez late Sunday afternoon, it was a waste of time – he had refused to discuss business. Duncan discerned a sanctimonious edge to his voice when he declared that in Spain, Sunday was for God and family. Duncan's Sundays used to be for God and family too.

We'll talk tomorrow, said Vasquez, sentencing Duncan to another night of torment.

He paced up and down the platform and told himself to calm down, for Christ's sake. Whatever was on Vasquez's mind, he would deal with it. And if he found out that Hilliard had screwed up, he'd fire his incompetent arse. The whole point of poaching staff from a competitor was to get someone you didn't have to nursemaid, someone who knew what the hell he was doing. There were only two major players in the water business: AquaEco and Dawes. Hilliard had been with Dawes for four years and Duncan had almost doubled his salary when he hired him. He'd better be worth it.

The train was crowded, even in first class. Duncan liked to spread out but a stout, sweaty man sat down next to him and talked incessantly on his mobile about some tedious IT problem. Duncan closed his eyes but couldn't shut out the nasal, droning voice. He tried to ignore the tight coil of pain in his chest but by the time he got to the AquaEco building on London Bridge, the coil had sprung open, squeezing his lungs into a miniscule space. He had to take small, shallow breaths that didn't draw in enough oxygen. Mercifully, the lift was empty. He pushed the button for the nineteenth floor and clenched and unclenched his fists, trying to relieve the tingling sensation crawling up his fingers. Nausea swilled around his stomach. When the lift doors opened he walked briskly along the corridor to the toilets, squinting against the harsh fluorescent light. He dropped his briefcase, turned on a tap and splashed cold water on his face. Hyperventilation. It helped to put a name to it – offer a rational explanation for an irrational event. Slow, deep breaths.

'Everything alright?'

Duncan spun around, dripping water onto his starched white collar, and saw William Hilliard, shirt sleeves rolled up, hands pushed deep into his trouser pockets. His brown leather belt sat below the beginnings of a well-rounded belly.

'Stomach bug,' said Duncan. 'Probably something I ate on the plane.'

He pulled a wad of paper towels from the dispenser on the wall, wiped his hands and face, then straightened his tie.

'Glad I've bumped into you, actually,' he said. 'We need to talk about the Spanish contract. Give me an hour then come along to my office. I want to go through it with you before I speak to Vasquez.'

Duncan picked up his briefcase and swept past Hilliard with a quick nod.

Alison jumped to attention – a reflex Duncan thought more Pavlovian response than considered action. One moment she was sitting and the next she was standing. Not glamorous like some of the other director's secretaries – PAs – but Duncan cared more about her efficiency than her looks. When Lola once asked him what Alison was like, he had to think hard. Nondescript, he said. Loyal, though, and reliable, and knew how he liked things done.

Duncan made the necessary small talk before slipping into his office. Solid reproduction furniture and oil paintings set the right tone, but it was the floor-to-ceiling window overlooking the Thames he treasured most. It soothed him, watching the river slither its way through the capital – helped him to think.

He flicked on his computer and set about scrutinising every detail of the Spanish deal so he would know what to say to Vasquez. At ten exactly Alison came in with a tray of coffee and biscuits. She quietly laid it on the desk and was just about to leave when Duncan remembered the perfume.

'This is for you,' he said, handing her the small white box.

She looked at it, and then at Duncan.

'Chanel is my favourite. How did you know?'

'I didn't. My wife chose it.'

As Alison's smile faltered, he realised the gift would have meant more if he had chosen it himself.

'Please thank her for me,' she said.

When Hilliard arrived, Duncan was pleased to see he had put on a jacket and a tie. 'Feeling better?' asked Hilliard.

'Much,' said Duncan. 'Please . . .'

He pointed to the leather chair on the other side of the desk. Hilliard made himself comfortable and crossed his legs. Duncan picked up the agenda for the board meeting and glanced through the list of items. He pushed it across the desk and said, 'You have a copy of this, I assume?'

'Not with me, but yes. Our Alison is nothing if not efficient.'

The familiarity of Hilliard's tone irked Duncan.

'Have you finished drafting the quarterly sales figures?' he asked.

'Just tidying them up,' replied Hilliard. 'You'll have them this afternoon.'

'Now,' said Duncan. 'Vasquez. Details, please. When did he call and what did he say?'

A deep red blush crept into Hilliard's cheeks. He pushed his hair back off his face and furrowed his brow, as if trying to recollect.

'Middle of last week. Wednesday, I think. He spoke to Alison – asked when you were expected back. I called him back to see if there was anything I could help with, but he said he wanted to speak with you.' Hilliard uncrossed his legs and straightened his back. 'I reassured him that with several years' experience in the industry, I was more than capable of answering his questions.'

Duncan thought how smugness was difficult to pull off when you blushed like a girl, but somehow Hilliard managed it.

'Anyway, I got him to talk. Upshot was, he wanted to review some of the figures and confirm that the filtration system met EU guidelines.'

Duncan stood up and went over to the window. The river was flat and dull today, the colour of sludge. He turned back to Hilliard.

'Of course it meets guidelines – he knows that. And we've been over the figures a dozen times. This has to be about something else.'

Alison buzzed to say Mrs Drummond was on the line. Duncan was about to say he'd call her back but decided to dismiss Hilliard instead.

'I'll expect those figures this afternoon,' said Duncan, opening the door for him.

He hoped Lola was in a good mood – not having one of her moping days.

'How's your morning going?' he asked.

'I've had an email from Joanne Curtella,' she chirped. 'Says she misses us – isn't that sweet? They're having a bit of a heat wave – a hundred and two on Saturday. She saw Birdie over at the Treehouse, taking photographs and making notes. Oh, and Mike says hi – wants to know when we're coming back.'

The excitement in Lola's voice confirmed that buying the house was the right thing to do. And he was glad Joanne Curtella had made the first move. Lola needed someone with Joanne's persistence and enthusiasm to push things along.

Alison appeared at the door and said Vasquez was on the other line. Duncan ran his fingers around the collar of his shirt, as if to loosen it, and told Lola he had to go.

The bar at the Carfax was crowded for lunchtime. Businessmen like Duncan escaping for an hour. He took a seat and ordered tonic water. It wasn't alcohol he needed; it was a place to think. Vasquez had been cagey – evasive even. It was as much as Duncan could do to get him to agree to a meeting. He had asked Alison to book a morning flight from Bristol to Malaga. He finished the tonic water and asked for another, this time with vodka. Maybe he did need alcohol after all.

The girl appeared in his peripheral vision: tall, long blonde hair loosely tied back, well-cut trouser suit, white blouse and heels. She took the high leather stool next to Duncan's and ordered a glass of champagne. He realised he was staring, but didn't look away. Her champagne arrived and she brought the glass to her cherry red lips, pursing them as though for a kiss. She tipped her head back, closed her eyes and drank. Her throat rippled as she swallowed. When she put the glass down, it was half empty. Her phone rang and she answered it, speaking softly in a foreign language. Eastern European, Duncan thought – possibly Russian. She finished the call and then her champagne.

'Can I get you another?' asked Duncan.

He hadn't meant to say that – it just came out. She looked at him with wide, pale eyes and smiled. Her top lip was plumper than the bottom one.

'Thank you,' she said.

She glanced at his wedding ring.

'I'm Saskia.'

She offered her hand and he held it for a moment longer than was appropriate.

'Duncan Drummond.'

Her phone rang again, but she ignored it.

'Where are you from?' he asked.

'Russia. Where are you from?'

'The big building across the street. I'm taking an early lunch.'

'You eat lunch, or drink lunch?'

'Eat, usually.'

'But today is a bad day?'

'It was,' said Duncan. 'It's getting better.'

Until then, paying for sex had been a nocturnal activity – something to offload stress and help him sleep. He wondered if this lunchtime tryst meant his habit had escalated? If so, it had been worth it. As he put on his clothes, and watched her lie there without hers, he felt a sense of calm that bordered on serenity. Effortlessly floating instead of swimming through treacle. She was exquisite – an intoxicating fusion of purity and passion. Wide-eyed innocence and fingernails that gouged the flesh from his back.

She had asked for five hundred pounds – more than he had ever paid – and he said he didn't have that much on him. They were already in the room. The thought that she might leave made him feel sick.

'How much do you have?' she asked.

He opened his wallet and took out five twenties.

'One hundred.'

He started to say, 'I wasn't expecting –' but she took the money.

'You give me the rest later.'

He put her number in his BlackBerry and promised to meet again; settle the debt. He had never done that before either. He abided by a self-imposed code of practice: never divulge personal details; never see the same girl twice.

'Can I trust you?' she said.

He leaned over her naked body and whispered in her ear.

'Absolutely.'

The afternoon went quickly and at five o'clock Duncan called Lola and told her he would catch the early train. She was waiting for him in the station foyer, wearing her usual stable-girl attire: jodhpurs, Hunters, a lightweight navy fleece. Her hair was tied back in a ponytail and her face was fresh and shiny. He pecked her cheek.

'Good day?' she asked.

'Not bad. I have to go to Malaga in the morning.'

She unlocked the Land Rover with a click of the key fob.

'How long will you be away?' she asked, climbing into the driver's seat.

Duncan got in the passenger side and put his briefcase on the floor by his feet.

'I'm not staying. It's just one meeting – I'll get a flight back when it's finished.'

The smell of horse manure and wet dog made him grimace.

'You really should get this car cleaned,' he said. 'My suit was covered in dog hair this morning.'

'Covered?'

'There was definitely dog hair. Anyway, tell me about your day.'

'Well, you know about the email from Joanne Curtella. It was so lovely to hear from her. People sometimes say that they'll keep in touch and then don't. Anyway, I wrote back straightaway – said how much I missed her and Mike and how excited we were about getting started on the Treehouse.'

'Steady on,' said Duncan. 'We don't even own it yet.'

Lola's smile faded.

'What do you mean?'

'Nothing,' he said. 'Just that there's a lot more paperwork before we can start knocking the place about.'

Lola bit her lip and nodded.

'Perhaps I should call Cain McCann,' she said. 'Hurry things along a bit.'

What perfect irony. Duncan had cajoled and conspired to get Lola to want this, and now that she did, he didn't know if he could deliver.

'Why don't you let me do that,' he said. 'Tell you what. I'll handle the finances and you handle the design.'

She thought about it for a moment and said, 'That makes sense. Play to our strengths.'

'Exactly.'

Seeing her like this was a strange kind of torture. For so long she had veered between sadness and indifference – enthusiasm had vanished from her emotional spectrum. He hoped to God he hadn't promised too much.

After dinner Duncan excused himself – said the taxi was booked for six-thirty so he needed an early night.

He undressed in the bathroom with the door locked. Saskia flashed into his head when he saw the scratches on his back. The serenity she had induced had almost worn off. He needed it to last long enough to get to sleep. He put on his pyjamas, got into bed, and replayed every detail of their encounter: the moment he first saw her in the bar, the allure of her accent, booking a room he would only need for an hour, standing next to her in the lift, the thrill of anticipation, watching her undress, letting her undress him, the smooth softness of her skin, her warm, wet mouth, the sweet smell of champagne on her breath, her fingernails in his back, pain and pleasure blurred in the brief bliss of orgasm.

When Duncan shook hands with Vasquez, he knew. He wouldn't look Duncan in the eye. After the small talk was dispensed with there was a lull. Vasquez took a cigarillo from a silver box on his desk then offered one to Duncan, even though he knew Duncan didn't smoke. He shook his head and Vasquez shrugged, lit the cigarillo and drew the smoke deep into his lungs. He held it there for a moment, then exhaled.

'So,' said Vasquez. 'We have a problem.'

Duncan pictured Lola chatting happily about the Treehouse, making plans that might never materialise.

'Perhaps,' said Duncan with more confidence than he felt. 'But I'm sure there is a solution.'

Vasquez took another drag from the cigarillo and shook his head.

'I respect you, so I will be honest with you. A competitor came to me with a better offer – the same product but for less money. At first I was sceptical, but the proposal looked good and they were very persistent. You are a businessman, so I know you will understand.'

No, Duncan didn't understand. It was as though Vasquez was speaking a language he couldn't quite comprehend.

'We can look at the figures again,' said Duncan. 'See what can be done.'

Vasquez put the cigarillo in the overflowing ashtray on his desk. He shook his head.

'I'm sorry. The papers have been signed.'

Despite being stunned, Duncan managed to keep his composure. He couldn't bring himself to admit defeat.

'Alberto, I thought we had an understanding. Why didn't you tell me you were talking to other people?'

Vasquez's tone was apologetic.

'I wasn't. They came to me at the last minute.'

He stood up and walked over to Duncan.

'You're a businessman,' he repeated, perching on the edge of the desk. 'You know how these things work.'

Humiliated, Duncan rose to leave. They shook hands without speaking. Duncan paused at the door, then turned back to face Vasquez.

'Who is it?' he asked.

'Dawes.'

There were three calls Duncan needed to make. The first was to Alison, telling her he would be in the office by five and to make sure Hilliard was waiting for him. The second was to his bank manager. On the taxi ride to Malaga airport, Duncan had formulated a damage limitation strategy. Yes, the commission would have been useful – probably paid for the renovations – but he did have other sources of finance. A good chunk of company shares, for a start, and other investments he could sell. He got a notebook out of his briefcase and played with a few figures. The house cost four hundred thousand dollars – around three hundred thousand pounds. He had at least that much again in other shares, thanks to a generous inheritance from his parents. Then there was his pension fund – maybe he could skim fifty thousand from that. And there was always the overdraft. He needed to keep things in perspective. It was a setback, not a disaster. The bank manager would advise against liquidating his assets, getting into debt, but Duncan would make his own decisions. And there was one debt he relished the thought of paying. Saskia answered at the second ring and agreed to meet him at the Carfax at six.

Duncan spotted Hilliard on the pavement, puffing away with the other nicotine addicts. Filthy habit. Duncan's suit reeked of Vasquez's cigarillo smoke. When Hilliard saw him, he threw the cigarette on the ground and followed him inside.

'How'd it go?' asked Hilliard as they waited for the lift.

Duncan glanced around the foyer and said, 'We'll talk in my office.'

They stood in silence as the lift stopped and started, eventually reaching the nineteenth floor. Duncan told Alison to hold any calls – they weren't to be disturbed. He closed the door behind Hilliard and put his briefcase on the floor.

'We lost the contract,' said Duncan.

A crimson bloom crept across Hilliard's face.

'I didn't realise it was that serious.'

'Apparently someone else pitched for the business at the last minute.'

Duncan watched the bloom spread to Hilliard's neck.

'That's too bad,' he said.

Duncan walked over to the window and looked down at the river. The tide was out, exposing a bank of mud and shingle. He turned back to Hilliard.

'You may want to be a tad more analytical in your report to the board. Get something drafted and over to me tomorrow.'

Hilliard nodded and went to leave. It was only when he'd opened the door that Duncan said, 'You didn't ask who it was.'

Hilliard stopped and turned.

'Sorry?' he said.

'It's just that when Vasquez told me that a competitor had got the contract I wanted to know who it was. You, on the other hand, didn't ask, which makes me wonder if you already knew.'

Hilliard pushed his hands into his trouser pockets.

'What are you suggesting?' he said.

'I'm suggesting that you may have had a word with your friends back at Dawes – told them about a great deal that could be theirs if they got the numbers right.'

Hilliard gasped. As an attempt to convey indignation, it failed miserably. Duncan looked at his hot red face, his shifty eyes, and saw nothing but guilt.

'That's an outrageous accusation,' Hilliard spluttered eventually, but Duncan was unmoved.

'I'm terminating your contract,' he said.

'You can't do that,' said Hilliard, his voice raised.

'I think you'll find that I can. You're still in your probationary period, so I can let you go without notice or compensation.'

'But you have no proof,' said Hilliard.

'Don't need any,' said Duncan. 'The seed of doubt has been sown, which means I can't trust you. And if I can't trust you, I can't work with you. I'll have security help you clear your desk.'

'And what if I won't go quietly?'

'Then you won't get a reference.'

Hilliard undid the top button of his shirt and loosened his tie.

'For the record,' he said, 'you're wrong about the contract, but right about us not being able to work together. I want a good reference and three months pay.'

'And if I refuse?'

'Then I go to Dawes and tell them about the other deals you've got in the pipeline, and everything else I know. Give me what I want and I'll say I resigned because the chemistry wasn't right. That covers a multitude of sins.'

Hilliard's audacity was staggering, but there was a small part of Duncan that almost admired the cocky little shit.

'Very well,' he said evenly. 'Now get out of my sight.'

Duncan wasn't meeting Saskia until six, but he needed a drink. As if things in Malaga hadn't been bad enough, on the plane home he had found himself across the aisle from a young girl and her father. She chatted and giggled and asked a thousand questions, just like Clarissa used to do when she was excited. When turbulence suddenly struck, her father slipped his arm around her narrow shoulders and quietly comforted her. Duncan looked away. He didn't need to be reminded how little girls turn to their fathers for protection, or how small and fragile they feel in your arms.

When Clarissa was born, Lola guarded her possessively. She had waited so long for a child that she didn't want to share her. Duncan saw the rush of love that had swept over Lola and wondered when he would feel it too. Mostly he felt bemused. He knew he loved Clarissa in a dutiful sort of way, but it felt once removed. Then one night Lola was so exhausted that she didn't wake when Clarissa cried. Duncan went to her instead and found her squirming in her cot, all pink and angry. He picked her up and held her to his chest like he'd seen Lola do. It was miraculous, the way she suddenly stopped crying and snuggled into him. He thought about putting her in the cot and going back to bed himself, but at that moment he understood how the language of parenthood – mother, father, child – described more than roles. It described an instinct: something deep-seated and elemental. As he stood there, rocking his baby daughter in his arms, he was consumed by a love so pure and primal, he knew he would give his life for hers.

A tap on the door startled him.

'I'm leaving now,' said Alison. 'Unless there's anything else?'

Duncan shook his head and then remembered.

'Oh, I've let Hilliard go. I'll need you to get on to Human Resources in the morning – sort out the paper-work, et cetera.'

If she was surprised, she didn't show it.

'Of course. Will you be advertising the position?'

The thought of interviewing another tranche of applicants appalled him.

'No.'

Saskia was early too, and just as stunning as Duncan remembered. Her hair was pinned in a loose knot and she wore a simple blue dress and heels. A cocktail glass with an olive sat in front of her on the bar.

'What are you drinking?' he asked.

'Vodka martini.'

The way she pronounced 'vodka' sent a tingle down his spine. He ordered one for himself.

'You have another bad day?' she asked.

Duncan couldn't help but smile.

'That's something of an understatement,' he said.

She put her mouth to his ear.

'I hope you didn't lose too much money,' she whispered. 'You owe me four hundred pounds.'

Her voice dripped over him like warm honey.

'Nine hundred,' he corrected.

The barman brought Duncan's martini. As he raised it to his lips Saskia plucked out the olive and slipped it in her mouth. Her eyes stayed fixed on his as she chewed and swallowed.

'You want me tonight also?' she said softly. 'You must be very rich.'

Duncan shook his head.

'I'm not very rich, but you are very, very desirable.'

She put her mouth to his ear again.

'We go upstairs now?'

So, down to business. He would have happily stayed in the bar for longer, savouring their flirtation, the way she teased and enticed him. How gullible of him to imagine that this gorgeous, fascinating young woman was interested in anything other than the cash in his wallet. He knocked back his drink and stood up. She must have discerned a change in his demeanour because she said, 'I do something wrong?' Duncan put a twenty-pound note on the bar and walked towards the lift, Saskia a few paces behind.

The room was comfortable but corporate: king-size bed, flat-screen TV, desk and chair, botanical prints on pale walls. He sat down on the end of the bed and wondered if it had been a mistake calling her? It was anonymous sex he craved, but this didn't feel anonymous. Never see the same girl twice – hadn't that been his rule? He couldn't shake himself loose from Clarissa. In his tormented mind she was the girl on the plane, he the protective father. Except that he wasn't.

Saskia sat down next to him without speaking. A distant siren sharpened memories he had come here to forget. She rested her hand on his and laced her fingers through his own. An image of her as a young child intruded: thin limbs, braided hair, innocent grin.

'This isn't going to work,' he said, standing up. 'I think you should leave.'

She looked at him but didn't move. He got his wallet and counted nine hundred pounds in crisp new fifties. He held out the money but she didn't take it.

'Tell me what I do wrong,' she said.

He shook his head.

'Nothing. You did nothing wrong.'

'But you want me to leave?'

He didn't know what the hell he wanted, except not to feel like this. His head had begun to ache and he realised he hadn't had a proper meal all day.

'I'm going to order room service,' he said. The thought of eating alone seemed pitiful. 'You're welcome to join me.'

Over steak, salad and a bottle of Stellenbosch Merlot, Duncan began to relax. Saskia told him about Ulyanovsk, her hometown and Lenin's birthplace. She was too young to remember much about life under the communist regime but had vivid memories of freezing winters: snow so deep it packed into your boots, wind so cold it flayed the flesh from your bones. She asked Duncan about his own childhood. Nothing so dramatic, he said. She cut a piece of steak and waited. To Duncan's surprise, he found himself sharing snippets of his early years in Surrey before he headed to public school in North Yorkshire. He pointed out that public school meant private school and Saskia said something about how difficult it was to learn English when one thing meant its own opposite.

'Like earlier,' she said. 'When you say I should leave, but you want me to stay.'

Duncan wiped his mouth with a napkin. He realised that for nearly an hour he hadn't thought about Clarissa. Despite the wine and having been up since five that morning, his head felt remarkably clear. With Saskia maybe it wasn't sex he needed; maybe her company was enough. Still, it seemed a shame to waste the opportunity.

He fell asleep on the train and would have missed his stop if the announcement that they were pulling into Bristol Temple Meads hadn't roused him. It was too late to expect Lola to meet him, so he'd have to get a taxi. He had checked his wallet when he left the Carfax, to make sure he had enough cash. It was the first time he'd felt guilty – not about the sex, but the money.

Lola was sitting at the kitchen table when he got home, staring intently at the screen of her laptop. Darcy was in his basket and didn't get up to greet him.

'He's in the dog house,' said Lola. 'Literally.'

'What's he done now?'

'He killed a rat and dropped it at my feet.'

'You're not squeamish.'

'I'm not, but the prospective client with a couple of children in tow certainly was. The youngest burst into tears. She's probably having nightmares as we speak.'

Duncan filled a tumbler from the tap and took a long drink.

'I hope you explained it's just part and parcel of country life.'

'Mmm. I don't think she saw it that way. Anyway, how was Malaga?'

'Not bad,' he lied. 'What are you doing?'

'Cain sent the contract as an attachment but I can't open it.'

'Let me have a look.'

Duncan put on his spectacles, pressed a few keys, and the contract appeared on the screen.

'Now why couldn't I do that?' said Lola. 'Cain said we need to sign it and send it back with a cheque for thirty thousand dollars. Roger suggested we open a local bank account – said it would make things much more straightforward.'

Duncan massaged his temples with his thumb and middle finger.

'Do you mind if we talk about this tomorrow?' he said.

'Of course not,' said Lola. 'You go up. I'll put Darcy out and lock up.'

Duncan climbed the stairs wearily, his whole body spent and sore. Lola came into the bathroom as he was brushing his teeth and asked if she could interest him in a hot bath.

'Too tired,' he said.

She leaned against his back and folded her arms around his waist. He had longed for her to want him again, but this didn't feel right.

'Are you sure?' she said. 'I could wash your back.'

A vision of Saskia's soapy nakedness floated into his head. They had showered together at the Carfax and the tenderness with which she had washed him brought almost as much pleasure as the passion with which they had made love. Usually he thought of it as fucking, but it had felt more than that.

'Tempting though that is,' he said to Lola, 'I really do need to sleep.'

Lola smiled coquettishly and slid her hands under his pyjama top. He caught his breath and stepped back.

'What's wrong?' she said.

'Nothing.'

He saw the hurt in her face.

'Sorry,' he said. 'It's been a really long day.'

She squeezed toothpaste onto her toothbrush and brushed vigorously. Duncan left her to it and got into bed, even though he didn't expect to sleep. His life felt like a snakes and ladders board – three squares up then four squares down. He deserved it, though – deserved to be punished. He had failed his wife, his daughter, his God. Lola got into bed and curled into a ball, her back to him. He had a sudden urge to recite the Lord's Prayer, to ask for his trespasses to be forgiven, but then he thought about original sin, the perverse belief that babies were born with tainted souls because of some perceived transgression by

Adam and Eve. What utter bullshit. What a terrible blight on innocent children. There was so much to understand and so little he understood. If he put rationality to one side, all that was left was faith, and he had lost that too.

Seven

'There's something I need to talk to you about,' Lola said to Kathy.

The tack room smelled of old leather and coffee. Lola filled the kettle and switched it on to boil.

'What's that, then?' said Kathy.

The saddle she had just cleaned shone like a new conker.

'You know this house we've bought in America,' she said. 'Well, if it all goes to plan, it's going to keep me pretty busy, and I wondered if you would be happy to take care of things here.'

The kettle whistled and Lola popped a tea bag into one mug and a spoon of instant coffee into the other. She poured the boiling water and offered Kathy a biscuit from an open packet by the sink. Kathy took two. She broke one in half, gave a piece each to Darcy and Beau, and ate the other one herself.

'Course I am,' she said. 'I'm going to need some help, though.'

Lola put milk and two spoons of sugar in the coffee, stirred it and handed the mug to Kathy.

'I was thinking about that. What about your cousin, Emma? She's helped out before.'

'In the holidays – she's at university. There's always Mr Snook.'

'I think we need to keep an eye on him,' said Lola. 'He does too much for a man of his age.'

'Yeah, but have you ever tried stopping him?'

Lola discarded the tea bag and poured a splash of milk. She leaned against the sink, one foot crossed in front of the other, and sipped her tea.

'Good point.'

Kathy took a bridle off a hook on the wall and undid the buckles. With a soft cloth and some saddle soap, she began to wipe the long leather straps.

'How soon are we talking about?' she asked.

Lola shrugged her shoulders.

'That's just it – I don't really know. I was wondering if I should hand over the reins to you, so to speak – promote you to manager and take on a junior. We have enough liveries to pay for it and that way I won't feel guilty disappearing off for the summer. What do you think?'

Kathy stopped cleaning the bridle and said, 'Manager?'

'Why not? You've run the place often enough.'

Lola thought of the miscarriages, the months of bed rest when she was carrying Clarissa, the months after Clarissa's death, when she could barely function. Kathy had stepped in without complaint and kept the place going.

'So this is really happening then, this house in America?' said Kathy.

Lola took a biscuit from the packet and dunked it in her tea.

'Do you think we're crazy?' she asked.

'Maybe,' said Kathy, 'but it's nice to see you happy.'

Lola left Kathy in the tack room and jogged back to the house with Darcy. She had made a quick 'to-do' list before she had gone to bed. Top of the list was getting those contracts signed and back to Cain, along with a cheque for thirty thousand dollars. She had wanted to go through it all the previous evening but Duncan said he was too tired to talk, too tired for anything. She shook her head at the irony. Now it was him, rebuffing her. The phone was ringing when she got back. She grabbed it just before it went to voicemail.

'Hello?'

'Darling, it's me.'

Lola saw that her Hunters had dragged mud across the quarry tiles. Darcy slurped noisily from his water bowl, then curled up in his bed by the Aga.

'How's your day going?' she asked.

She heard him sigh.

'Not bad. Yours?'

'Good, actually. I've just been talking to Kathy about managing the yard and taking on some extra help.'

'Oh?'

'Well, I'm going to be busy with the Treehouse and once it's finished we'll want to spend time there, so I need to start planning ahead. I was wondering if I should book a flight.'

'A flight?'

'Yes. Cain's email said we could close in a few weeks' time. The house has been empty for ages so it should all go through pretty quickly. Then we'll need to meet with Birdie so we can get the renovations underway. It wouldn't have to be a long trip – four or five days if that's all you can manage.'

'I see. Right. Well, I'll have a look at my diary – see what I can squeeze in.'

Lola wished Duncan's enthusiasm matched her own. She couldn't understand why it didn't. Buying the house had been his idea, after all.

'Duncan, are you sure you're okay?'

Another sigh: longer and more dismissive.

'I'm fine. Just busy. That's why I was calling, actually, to say I will probably need to stay up here for a few days later in the week – there's a lot going on. But look, well done for getting on top of all this. I'll definitely be home tonight – we'll talk then.'

Lola pulled off her boots and then wiped the floor. She wished Duncan didn't have to work so hard. The incessant travelling exhausted him, and the Carfax must seem like his second home. He was often in the office so late that he couldn't face the commute back to Bristol. Maybe she could persuade him to slow down once the Treehouse was finished. It would be lovely to have somewhere they could relax together.

She switched on her laptop and worked out that it would be early morning in California. Her spirits soared when she saw an email from Cain. She read it out loud to Darcy, attempting an American accent.

Hi Lola. Hope you're doing great and that you got the contract I sent over. Roger reminded me that it needs to be notarised at the American Embassy, which I guess

149

is in London, right? Can't wait to see what you guys are going to do with the place. Birdie has some great ideas. I think you're really going to like them. It's pretty hot here right now and everyone's getting ready for the 4th of July. Give my best to Duncan and come visit us again real soon.

All the best, Cain.

She savoured the flutter of excitement – thought of it as her California high. It made her smile to recall her first impression of Cain: pushy, scruffy, far too confident. As she got to know him better she realised he was none of those things.

She was still buzzed when she collected Duncan from the station and rattled off her news of the day: the vet said Darcy wouldn't need to be quarantined, just microchipped and vaccinated against rabies; Kathy was over the moon to have been promised a promotion, a pay rise, and someone to help out in the yard – oh, and they needed to get the contracts notarised at the American Embassy as soon as possible.

'Goodness,' said Duncan. 'You have been busy.'

'So, the Embassy,' she said. 'I'll catch the train and come to your office.'

'Really?'

Her California high drifted towards a Piliton low.

'I thought you'd be pleased. You're always trying to persuade me to come to London.'

'Yes. Of course I'm pleased. I'll need to check my diary, that's all.'

They sat in silence the rest of the way home and when they got there, Lola went to the kitchen and Duncan went to his study. She prepared dinner – steak and salad – and opened a bottle of Opus One. With any luck, it would cheer Duncan up a bit. She poured a glass of the wine and took it to his study. The door was ajar and she could hear him talking on the phone. She wasn't going to disturb him, but then she thought no, he's been working all day – enough is enough. When he saw her he hung up. She didn't usually notice the age difference, but at that moment he looked almost haggard.

'Is that for me?' he said.

Lola handed him the wine.

'Taste it and tell me what you think,' she said.

He sniffed, swirled and sipped, then after a moment's consideration said, 'It's a blend. Good body, lots of oak, finishes well.'

He took another sip, then tilted the glass and held it up to the light.

'Is it Opus One?'

'Very good,' said Lola. 'Now come and have dinner.'

As the train sped towards London, Lola realised how much her life had contracted over the years, occupying an ever-diminishing space. Clarissa's death shut it down completely, but even before that, she had stopped being adventurous. When she sold the chocolate-box cottage she was born and raised in and bought a tiny flat in Chelsea – that was adventurous. When she went to Goldsmiths to study Art History without knowing much about either art or history – that was adventurous too, like marrying an older man and leaving London to settle in Somerset. Having a baby was her greatest adventure, and then all of a sudden she didn't need any more – she had everything she wanted. Until she didn't. Out of the window, the landscape changed from rural to urban: green to grey, grass to concrete. Buying the Treehouse was adventurous. She needed it again now.

Paddington Station was noisy and crowded. Lola found her way to the taxi rank and joined the end of a very long queue. She was surprised that she wasn't more nervous. All those times Duncan tried to get her to meet him after work, she made excuses, or if she couldn't be bothered with excuses, she just said no. The worst had already happened, so in some ways it made no sense to be timid and shut herself away in Piliton. Maybe that was why Duncan took her to California – to show her that the world was still there and there were good things in it.

No wonder he was exhausted, having to face that journey every day. It had taken Lola an hour and a half, and she wasn't even at the office yet. They hadn't made love since California. He was distracted – wrapped up in worries that he wouldn't share. It would be so easy to slip back into celibacy – go back to how they had been before. Except this time it was different – it was Duncan who made excuses, Duncan who didn't want to be seen naked, Duncan who pretended to be asleep when she could tell from the rhythm of his breathing that he wasn't asleep at all.

It was years since she had visited Duncan here – she had forgotten quite how impressive the AquaEco building was. Revolving doors led into a brightly lit foyer – lifts on one side, escalators on the other – with a row of reception desks and uniformed staff. She took the lift to the nineteenth floor and the prim young woman waiting for her there introduced herself as Alison Davey.

'How lovely to meet you at last,' said Lola.

A tinge of rose pink brightened Alison's pallid cheeks. Lola thought how much prettier she'd look with a bit of make-up.

'Duncan is in a meeting,' she said. 'He asked me to take care of you.'

'That's very kind,' said Lola.

Alison showed her to a chair in the corner of her office. On a low glass coffee table, copies of *Country Life*, *Vogue* and *Tatler* sat in a neat fan arrangement.

'Can I get you anything?' asked Alison.

Lola shook her head.

'I'm fine,' she said, and picked up a copy of *Country Life*.

'I'm sure Duncan won't be long,' said Alison.

When Lola had dropped him at the station that morning, she hadn't noticed he was wearing the cornflower blue shirt that matched his eyes, but when he walked into the office she was reminded of what had attracted her to him all those years ago. He had looks, style and confidence – all good qualities in their own right – but he had something else as well. Presence. It wasn't just women who noticed him; men did too. Not in a sexual way – more in a competitive, survival-of-the-fittest way. Duncan was an alpha male. When he chose Lola, she felt as though she had won first prize.

'You made it,' he said. 'I half expected you to call and cancel.'

She put down *Country Life* and followed him into his office.

'I'm glad I can still surprise you,' she said.

He closed the door and hugged her.

'Well done,' he said.

She walked around the office, refreshing her memory. His desk was neat and organised, just like his desk at home. She went over to the window.

'I don't think I'd get any work done if I had this lovely view.'

'And speaking of lovely views,' said Duncan, admiring her.

She was pleased that her efforts hadn't gone unnoticed: charcoal grey trouser suit, cream blouse and heels. The heels were agony. He opened the door and popped his BlackBerry in his pocket.

'Back around three,' he said to Alison.

Outside, city noise blared: traffic, sirens, a helicopter hovering overhead. Lola looked around and tried to get her bearings. She noticed the smart white building on the other side of the street.

'Oh, so that's the Carfax,' she said. 'It looks nice – why don't we pop in for a drink?'

Duncan whisked her in the opposite direction, saying something about a new Japanese place around the corner that he wanted to try.

Japanese wasn't Lola's favourite, but it did feel nice to be out with Duncan, doing something grown-up like having sushi and sake. She wished he would relax a bit, put his worries to one side and just enjoy the moment. Lola smiled, realising how American it was to think of *enjoying the moment*.

'Something funny?' said Duncan.

She shook her head, and then another thought occurred to her. If he was too tired to make love at home, maybe a hotel would perk him up. It had worked wonders for her in California. She put her hand on his knee and said she'd had enough to eat – maybe they had time to stop by the Car-fax after all? She expected him to be surprised – pleasantly surprised – but she didn't expect him to almost choke. He coughed and spluttered until a waiter rushed over with a glass of water. Other diners glanced in their direction and suddenly Lola felt very foolish. He used to love it when she propositioned him – couldn't wait to take her up on it: in a hotel room, his locked office, the Land Rover on the way back from the station. It didn't matter where as long as he had her. Now, he just seemed embarrassed.

She didn't look at him in the taxi. He busied himself with his BlackBerry for a few minutes and then put it in his pocket.

'Look,' he said. 'I'm sorry about earlier. You caught me by surprise with that whole hotel-room thing.'

'Rather the point,' said Lola, staring out of the window.

Duncan was quiet for a moment.

'There's a lot going on with work,' he said. 'I'm finding it hard to switch off.'

Now she looked at him. His eyebrows were knitted together in that taut, tense way he had.

'Why don't you talk to me?' asked Lola. 'Instead of keeping it all bottled up?'

His face relaxed a little.

'I don't like to worry you,' he said.

'But I worry anyway,' she said. 'It would be easier if I knew what it was I was worrying about.'

Duncan started to say something but they had arrived at the Embassy, the driver needed paying, and the moment passed. After they had gone through security, had their names crossed off a list, taken a ticket with a number on it and found two hard plastic chairs in the noisy, crowded waiting room, Lola tried again.

'You were saying something about work.'

Duncan gave a heavy sigh.

'I sacked William Hilliard, my assistant.'

Lola was stunned.

'Why?'

'We lost a big contract.' Duncan shook his head wearily. 'Long story.'

'I had no idea,' she said. 'So that's why you went to Malaga?'

Duncan nodded.

'Complete waste of time. And I have a board meeting tomorrow – papers to write, figures to prepare.' He massaged his temples.

'Is that why you won't be home tonight?'

'Afraid so. I'm still trying to work out how to explain this contract going belly-up.'

She felt guilty now, thinking everything was about her.

'I wish you'd confided in me,' she said. 'It doesn't seem fair, me being all chirpy about America when you're dealing with this.'

'No,' said Duncan, turning towards her. 'I love that you're chirpy. Seeing you excited about the Treehouse, making plans, it's wonderful. Whatever else is going on, you're wonderful.'

Lola felt a warm tug in her chest. She put her head on his shoulder and was glad that she'd come to London.

The sun, which had been hidden behind fat grey clouds since morning, suddenly made a dramatic entrance. It transformed the dull city gloom into something bright and warm. Lola took a pair of sunglasses from her bag and noticed Duncan check his watch. He offered to put her in a taxi back to Paddington but she declined, said that now she was in the city, she might as well make the most of it. He raised an eyebrow.

'Are you sure?'

'Don't worry about me,' she said. 'You go. I'll see you tomorrow.'

She stood on the pavement in her elegant suit and sunglasses, and knew exactly what she wanted to do.

The last time she had been to the Deanery was before Clarissa was born. It was part of her other life. She hadn't expected to find a job so quickly when she finished at Goldsmiths. The economy was grim – dole queues full of art graduates with big dreams and no prospects. A few of her friends had decided to ride it out – go backpacking around South East Asia until things got better – and asked Lola to tag along. She was still thinking about it when she met Clive by chance at a photographic exhibition at the Serpentine Gallery. He flirted shamelessly all evening, slipped her his card and made her promise to visit his own modest gallery in Soho. The Deanery, he said, as if she should know it. Curiosity got the better of her. It was a shock to walk in and find Clive wearing a flamboyant red dress, his arm draped around his boyfriend *du jour*. He greeted her gushingly, insisted she would make a stunning gallerina and spoke eloquently about taking her under his wing. How could she refuse? And it was fun for a while – meeting artists and collectors, staging exhibitions, learning the practical things not taught in her degree.

It was at an exhibition that she had first met Duncan. He took a glass of champagne from the tray she was holding, and said, 'Poor artist.'

'I'm sorry?' said Lola.

'Having all eyes on you, rather than his paintings.'

She couldn't remember if she had blushed. They arranged to have dinner the following evening.

'Be careful, my sweet,' warned Clive, clearly only half joking. 'That distinguished gentleman has designs on you.'

It gave her great pleasure, on her twenty-second birthday, to announce to Clive that the distinguished gentleman had proposed.

'Naturally you declined,' he said.

Lola laughed.

'Naturally I accepted.'

After the wedding, when she told Clive they intended to decamp to the West Country, he took the news of her departure as one might the death of a loved one. He threw her a small but tasteful leaving party, which he insisted on calling a wake, and wore a black slinky dress and a veiled pillbox hat. He berated Duncan for ruining the career of his most talented gallerina, but Lola had never been interested in a career. She didn't believe that what you did was who you were. She had simply been marking time – keeping busy while she waited for her real life to begin, and then it had, in Piliton with Duncan and Clarissa.

Clive had changed so little she wondered if there was a portrait in the attic, ageing in lieu of his corporeal self. He stared for a moment, then in a flourish of recognition, threw his hands in the air and shrieked. 'It can't be, can it? My beautiful gallerina?'

Lola laughed and said, 'It can. It is. How are you, Clive?'

He rushed over and kissed her on both cheeks.

'Overcome with joy,' he said. 'Let me look at you.'

He took a few steps back and studied her as though she were a work of art.

'Breathtaking,' he said. 'Simply breathtaking.'

An assistant appeared, and Clive dispatched him to get some wine.

'You'll stay for wine?' he said to Lola. 'Of course you'll stay for wine.'

'Just a glass,' she said. 'You know what a lightweight I am.'

The assistant returned with a bottle of Montrachet and two glasses. Clive introduced him to Lola and then sent him on an errand.

'I want you all to myself,' he told her. 'No distractions.'

He poured the wine.

'To the prodigal gallerina, who has at last returned,' he toasted.

Lola raised her glass.

'It's been far too long since you visited,' he said. 'I want you to tell me everything.'

She told him about California and the Treehouse, about Duncan working too hard, about having not been up to London in a very long time. She didn't mention Clarissa – it would only have made them both sad. As she left, Clive made her promise to visit again.

'And next time bring that distinguished gentleman with you.'

Duncan called to make sure she had got home okay.

'How was your afternoon?' he asked.

'Good, actually. I went to the Deanery and saw Clive. He sends his love.'

Duncan laughed.

'I'm sure he didn't. He's never forgiven me for stealing you away.'

Lola could hear Darcy scratching on the back door. She opened it and he padded past her en route to his bed.

'I'm drinking a Russian River Chardonnay,' she said to Duncan.

'Is it good?'

'Very,' she said. 'Have you eaten?'

'I'll get something later. How about you?'

'Cheese. I think I'll take my wine upstairs and have a nice long soak – wash away the city grime.'

'Good idea. Sleep well.'

'You too.'

She hated to think of him alone in the Carfax.

After almost two weeks of hearing virtually nothing from Cain, Lola started to worry. She'd had long, chatty emails from Joanne and Birdie – she told Joanne how Darcy had disgraced himself with the dead rat – but the only thing she gleaned from Cain's non-committal email was that it was *all good*. All good? What did that mean? She was itching to discuss it with Duncan but he was hardly ever home and when he was he looked so tired and tense that she didn't feel she could. The board meeting hadn't gone well, apparently. The contract he lost was worth quite a bit, and it seemed Human Resources weren't too pleased that he fired his assistant without any sort of warning – just told him to clear his desk and go. No, it wouldn't be fair to burden him with this too.

She dialled Cain's number and paced around the kitchen while she waited for him to answer. Silly that she felt so nervous.

'Cain McCann speaking.'

'Oh hello, it's Lola Drummond. I'm calling about –'

'Hey, Lola, how are you doing? It's great to hear from you.'

She took a deep breath.

'Yes, you too. Sorry to bother you –'

'It's no bother.'

'Oh, good. Well, I was just a bit concerned that I hadn't heard anything about when we complete – I mean close – on the Treehouse, and I wondered if there was a problem?'

'Really?' said Cain. He sounded surprised. 'God, Lola – I'm so sorry. I thought Duncan would keep you up to speed. No. There's no problem at all – quite the opposite. I have the signed contracts right here on my desk, and the deposit is in the client account. The balance is due tomorrow, actually. Duncan said he'd have it wired straight over.'

Lola didn't know what to say. Cain must have thought her a complete fool.

'Oh, I see. That's wonderful.' She screwed up her face. 'Sorry, Duncan's been so snowed under at work, I've hardly seen him. Actually, yes, he did mention something the other day, but the phone rang and I got distracted.'

'Sure,' said Cain. 'When are you guys back in town?'

She hesitated. 'Umm ... I'll need to ask Duncan.'

'Of course – he's a busy guy. Well, it's great talking to you Lola. Really miss hearing that cool accent.'

Lola put the phone down and buried her head in her hands. She was cross with Duncan for having kept her in the dark, and embarrassed that Cain knew about it. But hearing him say that he missed her cool accent, she couldn't help but smile. And now that she thought about it, she missed his cool accent too. It didn't stop her being annoyed, though. She called Duncan at the office and asked why he hadn't told her he'd been speaking to Cain. He said sorry, he was about to go into a meeting, could it wait until this evening? The dial tone hummed in her ear.

She left a message with Alison to say that Duncan would have to get a taxi from the station. A horse had thrown a shoe and she needed to wait for the blacksmith. Kathy said she didn't mind staying but Lola sent her home. It wouldn't kill Duncan to make his own way home for once. Anyway, she wanted to have a serious talk with him over dinner, not dilute the message with a half-baked conversation in the car.

She cooked lamb shanks with new potatoes and broccoli. Duncan opened the last bottle of Opus One and poured them both a glass.

'You're quiet,' he said, once they sat down to eat.

She unfolded her napkin and took a drink of wine.

'Why didn't you tell me what was happening with the house? I called Cain, only to be told that you'd dealt with everything. What must he have thought?'

Duncan shrugged.

'What does it matter what McCann thought?'

Lola didn't have an answer, but his condescending tone irritated her so she pressed on.

'I just don't understand why you felt the need to take control. You're always saying how busy you are, and this was supposed to be *my* project, something to keep *me* busy – wasn't that the idea?'

Duncan put down his knife and fork.

'Do you remember a conversation we had, when we agreed that you would deal with the design and I would deal with the finances? Play to our strengths, I think you said.'

The conversation came back to her – in the car on the way home from the station – but she pressed on again.

'That didn't mean you could keep me in the dark. I felt like a fool, not knowing what was going on.'

She couldn't read Duncan's expression.

'Perhaps I took our arrangement rather too literally,' he said, and plucked an envelope from his pocket. He slid it across the kitchen table. 'By way of apology.'

'What's this?'

'Open it.'

Inside were two tickets to San Francisco. Her heart did a bunny-hop.

'We're going to California?'

'Next week,' he said. 'Am I forgiven?'

Lola put her hand to her mouth, but it didn't hide her beaming smile.

The days passed slowly, even though there was a lot to do. Kathy advertised in the local paper for a stable hand and they interviewed three applicants. A friendly, well-spoken girl called Arabella got the job. Kathy said she'd call her Bella, if that was alright. Lola spent an entire morning with the vet, getting Darcy inoculated and chipped, and filling out the reams of paperwork needed for his passport. The thought of Darcy with a passport was hilarious – she couldn't wait to tell Joanne. He wouldn't be travelling with Lola this time, but it excited her to think that soon he would. When she went to Bristol for some shopping and a haircut, she treated herself to lunch at Hotel du Vin. She scrutinised the wine list, looking for something Californian, and ordered a Sauvignon Blanc from Santa Barbara. As she closed her eyes and sipped, she thought of berries and lemon and sunshine. She packed her case two days before they were due to leave. Duncan looked at it sitting on the plum velvet chaise in their bedroom, and said, 'Actually, I need to talk to you about that.'

Something churned in Lola's stomach.

'What is it?'

'I have to go to Mexico. There's a deal I've been working on – a big hotel complex in Puerto Vallarta. Three or four days – five at the most. I'll fly straight from there to San Francisco.'

It was a moment before she could speak.

'You're not serious?'

'I'm sorry, but it can't be helped. You know how difficult things have been at work and I need this deal to happen.' He put his hands on her shoulders, and spoke as though reassuring a child. 'You'll be fine on your own. Actually, you won't be on your own. McCann is going to meet you at the airport. Joanne offered his services. She and Mike are busy getting their guesthouse ready for you. I didn't even know they had one – it's tucked away around the back, apparently. I thought you'd prefer that to a hotel.'

Lola was speechless. She wasn't sure which appalled her more: that Duncan was prepared to abandon her, or that he had gone behind her back again. He planted a quick, dry peck on her forehead. His tone changed from reassuring to cajoling.

'Come on, darling, this will be good for you.'

Lola's throat was tight, but she managed to say, 'Good for me?'

'Yes. Look how well you did in London. I thought you'd get the train straight home but you went to the gallery – had a lovely afternoon.' He smiled to underscore his point. 'It's just a question of pushing yourself, seeing what you're capable of when you try.'

Was that what this was about, testing her to see if she was finally over Clarissa? Wind gusted through an open window and shut the bedroom door with a slam. Lola gasped.

'It's okay,' said Duncan.

He walked over and closed the window. Downstairs, Darcy had started to bark.

'I'd better see to him,' said Duncan.

Lola wished her stomach would stop churning. She sat down on the chaise next to her packed suitcase, and swallowed a very strong urge to cry.

It was like it had been in St Helena, when Duncan handed her the keys of the convertible. She hadn't wanted to drive, but she gave into him, then wondered why she had been so reluctant in the first place.

When she spotted Cain McCann in the arrivals lounge, a surge of relief flooded through her. A familiar face. His hair was longer than she remembered and he was more tanned. Compared to the youngsters with just a backpack and a passport, Lola wasn't exactly intrepid, but she had overcome a debilitating sense of helplessness to make the five-thousand-mile journey alone.

Duncan had flown off to Mexico, just as he said he would. Lola couldn't believe it. *You can't expect me to do this on my own.* He had booked a car to take her to the airport, used air miles to get her a first-class ticket, which meant use of the first-class lounge, and arranged for Cain to meet her at the other end. *You'll be fine, I promise.*

Cain was talking on his mobile – Duncan reminded her to call it a cell, but she thought of it as a mobile – and when he saw her he waved. He made his way towards her, his smile so bright and welcoming, she couldn't help but smile back. When he reached her, she hesitated, unsure of the etiquette. Should they hug or shake hands? Cain looked unsure for a second too, but then put his arms around her and squeezed so hard she felt a little breathless.

'You look great,' he said, and took her suitcase. 'How was your flight?'

'Fine. It seemed long, but that's probably because I'm not used to it. Duncan flies all the time – says there's a knack to switching off and then before you know it, you're there.' She drew breath. 'Sorry – I'm a bit nervous.'

Cain laughed.

'Well, we'll have to see what we can do about that.'

Lola had no idea what he meant, or if he meant anything at all, but she felt she was in good hands and that was enough.

The San Francisco air smelled fresh and salty, just as Lola remembered.

'Golden Gate or Bay?' asked Cain as he put her bags in the car.

'I've never been over the Bay Bridge,' she said.

'Bay it is then,' said Cain.

Sunshine bounced off the rippling ocean. It was almost surreal, sitting in a Prius with Cain at the wheel and Vine on the radio. He chatted easily about himself, like they were old friends. He said he was from Southern California originally and had come north to surf and ski. Lola asked why he couldn't do that in Southern California and he said he could, but he wanted to put some distance between him and his family. No reason; it just felt like time.

'Where do you ski?' asked Lola.

'Tahoe,' said Cain. 'You never been there?'

Lola shook her head. Cain enthused about what a beautiful state California was, how it had everything you could ever want: the ocean, incredible beaches, mountains, sun and snow, great cities, vineyards, and the friendliest people you'll ever meet. Lola couldn't muster up the same enthusiasm when he asked her about England, although she did say Somerset was quite pretty in parts and her village was rather nice.

'So, Duncan couldn't make it this time?' said Cain.

'He had to go to Mexico on business,' said Lola. 'He'll join me in a few days' time.'

'He's a busy guy,' said Cain.

Lola was about to say she was fed up always coming second to his work, but couldn't bring herself to be disloyal. And anyway, it was Duncan's work that made all of this possible.

'How about you?' she said. 'Are you selling lots of houses?'

Cain turned and looked at her.

'As a matter of fact, I'm not selling any houses. Truth is, Roger gave me the job because my dad asked him to. I was never cut out for real estate.'

'I didn't realise,' said Lola. 'So what are you cut out for?'

Cain threw back his head and laughed.

'Beats me,' he said. 'I've tried my hand at most things. Working construction is my favourite, I guess, being outside, doing something physical. I feel I can breathe – you know what I mean?'

'Actually,' said Lola. 'I do.'

'I'm helping out my buddy, Pete, right now. He's the winemaker at a place on Diamond Mountain. It's pretty busy up there this time of year – visitors in the tasting rooms, harvest in a few months' time. After that, who knows?'

Lola found his laid-back attitude strange and refreshing. Duncan had always been so career-driven. In the evenings, when he stepped off the train in his made-to-measure suit, a calf-leather briefcase in his hand, he epitomised the successful businessman. And of course she was grateful that his high-earning job meant she never had to worry about money, but as she glanced at Cain's faded jeans, his pale yellow T-shirt with its Rip Curl logo, the wooden beads around his wrists, she thought how he and Duncan couldn't be more different.

She must have dozed a little because the next thing she knew they were off Highway 29 and headed towards Falcon Drive. That was when a horrible thought occurred to Lola – what if she experienced buyer's remorse? It had all happened so quickly – they saw the house, they bought the house, they went back to England. Any reservations she had along the way, Duncan quickly dismissed.

'Everything okay?' asked Cain.

'Bit nervous, actually,' said Lola. 'Suppose I see the house and don't like it, or wonder why on earth we bought it in the first place?'

Cain looked at her and shrugged.

'Guess we'll find out soon enough.'

When he pulled into the driveway and turned off the engine, they sat for a moment without speaking. Lola stared at the pines, the oaks, the firs, the mountain that rose up behind them, the dry, rocky creek, and the Treehouse.

'So what do you think?' asked Cain.

'I think I'm in love,' said Lola.

The adrenalin that had fuelled her finally waned during dinner on the Curtellas' deck. No sooner had she got out of the Prius than Riley appeared, barking and demanding to be made a fuss of. Mike and Joanne weren't far behind – all hugs and kisses and welcome back. Cain took her bags to the guesthouse, and Joanne showed her around. There were two rooms – a small, cosy sitting room with a couple of armchairs, a low table and a fireplace – and a bedroom, just big enough for a double bed and a wardrobe. A door led into the bathroom – shower room really, said Joanne, since there wasn't a bath – and off the sitting room was a basic galley kitchen. Unlike the main house, the guesthouse was neat and tidy. A vase of yellow day lilies adorned the mantelpiece. Joanne's watercolours brightened the walls while a pair of ceiling fans stirred up a cool breeze.

'I hope you'll be comfortable,' said Joanne. 'But just let me know if there's anything you need.'

'No,' said Lola. 'It's perfect.'

She would have said more, but a wave of emotion sprung up from nowhere and lodged in her throat. Ridiculous, but she really did feel as though she'd come home.

Mike grilled steaks for dinner and poured a Spring Mountain Cabernet. Cain stayed too, and Lola realised how much she liked to listen to them talk, how different American was to English – the accent, the informality, the colloquialisms.

'You're quiet, honey,' said Joanne.

'I haven't been to bed in almost twenty-four hours,' said Lola. 'I think I should call it a night.'

Mike checked his watch.

'It's only eight o'clock. Are you sure you can't stay up a bit longer? You don't want to be wide awake at four in the morning.'

'I know you're right,' said Lola, yawning. 'But if I don't go to bed, I'll fall asleep right here at the table.'

It was nine when she woke; she'd slept for more than twelve hours. She couldn't remember the last time that had happened. The sun was already hot when she took her coffee onto the deck. Joanne and Riley joined her.

'Sleep okay?' said Joanne.

'Like a log,' said Lola. 'Can I get you a coffee?'

Joanne shook her head.

'I've already had mine,' she said. 'Two cups is my limit. You have any plans for today?'

'I'm meeting Birdie,' said Lola. 'We're going to talk about the renovations.'

'I still can't believe the old place is going to get a makeover,' said Joanne.

'Me neither,' said Lola. 'Why don't you come over and join us?'

'I have to run some errands, but sure, maybe when I get back.'

After Joanne had left, Lola sat quietly with her coffee. She took slow, deep breaths and felt at peace. She couldn't remember the last time that had happened either.

Birdie arrived early and greeted Lola like a long-lost friend. They hugged and then laughed when they saw they were both wearing the same wide-brimmed sunhats. Birdie's plans for the Treehouse delighted Lola: lots of glass and light and clean, open spaces.

'Any questions?' said Birdie

'How soon can we get started?' said Lola.

'You're the sort of client I love,' said Birdie. 'But we need to talk numbers first. Isn't Duncan with you?'

'No,' said Lola. 'He had to go to Mexico, but I'm expecting him in a day or two.'

Birdie's mobile rang. She glanced at the caller's name but didn't answer.

'Okay. Well, I've calculated a ballpark figure of a hundred thousand. That includes a pool. If we lose the pool, then it comes down to around seventy-five. How does that sound?'

Lola didn't know what to say. Duncan never discussed money with her – something she was too embarrassed to admit, especially to a confident businesswoman like Birdie.

'Duncan tends to handle the financial side of things. I'm sure there won't be a problem, but I should probably run it by him. So tell me,' she said, changing the subject, 'will you manage everything personally?'

Birdie moved into the shade of a giant oak tree and Lola followed.

'So, this is how it works,' said Birdie. 'I handle the design and the materials, and I have a team of guys that take care of the construction. In the middle is a project manager – someone who oversees the construction guys and reports back to me. Now the person that I usually use is out of town for a few months, so I'm going have to find someone else.'

Lola was just about to say she hoped that wouldn't hold things up, when Joanne and Riley appeared through the clearing.

'There you are,' called Joanne. 'Why are you hiding under a tree?'

She gave Birdie a quick hug and handed her a small bottle of water.

'Shade,' said Birdie. 'It's pretty toasty out here.'

'Tell me about it,' said Joanne, and handed Lola a bottle of water too. 'You need to stay hydrated,' she said. 'So how's it all going?'

'Great,' said Birdie. 'Just talking about who we're going to find to manage the construction guys.'

'What about Cain?' said Joanne.

'Cain McCann?' said Birdie.

'Sure,' said Joanne. 'He's not doing real estate anymore, and he knows his way around a construction site.'

'Oh that's right,' said Lola. 'He told me he worked in construction – said he liked it.'

'He'd be good with the guys too,' said Joanne. 'Everyone gets on with Cain.'

Birdie raised her eyebrows.

'I'm not sure he has the right experience,' she said.

Lola liked the idea of Cain working on the Treehouse. If it wasn't for him, they wouldn't have found it in the first place.

'I think Cain might be good,' she said. 'At least he's someone you know, someone you can trust.'

'Well, I guess I could talk to him about it,' said Birdie. 'See if he might be interested.'

Lola sipped her water and thought how Cain – a man she hardly knew – had had such a profound impact on her life. He had led her to the Treehouse and introduced her to the Curtellas, Roger, Birdie, people she now thought of as friends. She hoped he would work on the house. It seemed fitting somehow.

When the meeting was over, Lola stayed behind. She wanted to spend some time in the Treehouse on her own.

She let herself in and inhaled the smell of warm wood. It took her straight back to that hot June day. Duncan was sceptical at first, put off by how shabby the place was, but when he saw what it might mean to her he had to have it. Duncan was a problem-solver. Lola's enduring grief was the problem and the Treehouse was the solution. She was excited about the renovations, but sad to think it wouldn't be like this for much longer. There would be a different smell, clean and new. She wondered if Birdie was serious about Cain. She hoped that she was.

Lola spent the whole afternoon walking around St Helena. There were three art galleries on Main, a small independent cinema, high-end boutiques, four jewellers and several places that sold beautiful things for the home. She would go back to those when the Treehouse was ready to move into. When she stopped at a coffee shop and took a seat by the window, she watched people walking by and saw what Cain had meant by 'wine country casual': expensive but understated – nothing formal or flash. Perhaps she would treat herself to some new clothes. It was ages since she had done that.

Cocktail hour was already in full swing when she got back to the Curtellas at six-thirty.

'There you are, honey,' said Joanne, handing her a glass of wine. 'Birdie called, said Cain was thrilled about the job and asked if you could meet her at the office tomorrow, around ten?'

'Goodness, things certainly happen quickly around here.'

'But that's a good thing, right?'

Lola thought about it for a moment, about how her life had been on hold.

'Yes,' she said. 'It is.'

Birdie's office was on the ground floor of an old Victorian building on Main. Cain was already there, the obligatory styrofoam cup in his hand, and wearing a smarter version of the jeans and T-shirt he'd worn to meet her at the airport. Lola preferred this to his perennial teenager look, although she cringed to remember how she had compared his casual style so unfavourably to Duncan's preferred formality when they first met. The more she got used to 'wine country casual', the more she liked it.

'Hey, Lola,' he said, brimming with his trademark enthusiasm. 'Isn't it great? We're gonna be working together.'

'It is, but what about your friend's winery?'

'Pete? Yeah, I'll divide my time between the two jobs until we start on your place.'

It sounded funny, Cain calling it *your place*.

Birdie rushed in, dropped a pile of papers onto her desk and apologised profusely for being late.

'No problem,' said Cain. 'Lola and I were just catching up.'

'Guys, I'm so sorry,' she said again. 'I have a client in from Portland – called me half an hour ago – wants to meet up at his ranch out in Browns Valley. It's a huge project and he's hardly ever in town. I really have to go.'

'Of course you do,' said Lola. 'Please don't worry about it.'

Birdie exhaled so emphatically that her whole body shifted gear, tension to relief.

'Thank you,' she said, palms pressed together and fingers pointed up, as though she was about to pray. 'But listen, the reason I asked you here this morning was because I thought Cain could show you some contemporary properties around town, maybe get some ideas for the Treehouse.'

She opened a file, took out a sheet of paper and handed it to Cain.

'I've jotted down some addresses,' she said, checking her watch. 'Sorry, but I really have to go. Lola, great to see you. We'll talk.'

'Wow,' Cain said as Birdie swept out again. 'Guess she's having a bad morning.'

'Or a good one, depending how you look at it.'

Cain took a swig from the styrofoam cup.

'Okay then,' he said. 'So, you ready to go and see some property?'

Lola had never really had any male friends. With no brothers or male cousins, and an all-girls school, boys didn't really feature in her childhood. There were boys at university of course, but they were interested in sex, not friendship. Clive was probably the closest she'd come to friendship with a man, but he was a gay cross-dresser, so she wasn't sure he counted. Mr Snook perhaps, although he was more of a father figure than a friend. It was Cain that got her thinking. They had been in each other's company the whole day and had got on so well that she would certainly describe him as a friend. Duncan went on about men and women never being able to have truly platonic relationships, because if there was even a hint of attraction, sooner or later sex would rear its ugly head.

As they drove back from the final viewing, Lola wondered if he was right. She found herself studying Cain's caramel-coloured forearm, imagining how she would draw it. Even with the downy coating of golden hair and hippy-style wooden beads, it looked sturdy and masculine. His hands were broad, with long fingers and neatly clipped nails. They didn't look like they had seen much manual work and she hoped the Treehouse wouldn't spoil them. He tapped his fingers on the steering wheel in time to a song she didn't know.

'So what do you think?' he said.

'Sorry?' said Lola.

'The houses we've looked at. You still sure you want to go the contemporary route?'

'Oh, yes,' said Lola. 'Quite sure.'

Earlier, when they had stopped for lunch, the waitress – *Hi, I'm Terri* – had flirted with him, right in front of her. She recited the specials in a sing-song voice, running her fingers through short blonde hair. Her nipples pushed hard against her skin-tight T-shirt. Cain appeared oblivious, more interested in whether he should have the grilled chicken or the tuna salad. Why did the girl assume that Cain was available, that they weren't a couple? Was it because he was younger? Not that much younger: eight, maybe ten years? She was fifteen years younger than Duncan. When the waitress left the bill, she left her phone number too.

'I think that's for you,' Lola had said.

Cain slipped it into his pocket without comment. Lola knew it shouldn't have irritated her, but it most definitely did.

He parked in the Curtellas' driveway and jogged around to open Lola's door.

'It's been great working with you today,' he said. 'Best job I ever had.'

'Thanks,' she said. 'I had a lovely time too. I mean, it was useful, you know, seeing those other houses.'

'The pleasure was all mine,' he said.

Was he complimenting her or just being exuberant? Either way she felt girlishy flattered.

'Lola, Cain, come join us for some wine.'

Mike was on the corner of the deck, a bottle of wine and a corkscrew in his hand.

'Sure,' said Cain. 'Just got to make a call.'

Lola walked over to where the Curtellas were sitting, and right there with them was Duncan.

'Surprise,' said Joanne.

It certainly was. For a fraction of a second, Lola felt something less than delight. She dismissed it immediately.

'Darling,' she said, 'why didn't you tell me you were coming?'

'That would have ruined the surprise,' he said.

He put his hands on her shoulders and kissed her on each cheek. His shirt was creased and damp. She was just about to suggest that he take a shower when Cain walked onto the deck.

'Hey, Duncan,' he said. 'Good to see you, sir.'

Lola couldn't believe that Cain called him 'sir.' It emphasised the difference in age and status.

'Cain, you'll stay for supper,' said Joanne.

'Love to, but I just made plans.'

'Plans?' said Lola.

'Yeah, I gave Terri a call.'

Lola wasn't sure which was more startling, that Cain was interested in the vacuous waitress, or that it bothered her. She busied herself with an imaginary burr in Riley's coat. When Cain said bye and left, Lola didn't watch him go. She tried to focus on the conversation, the wine, the food, her husband, but an inconvenient question nagged and distracted her. Why was she so preoccupied with Cain McCann?

Eight

Lola's transformation had astounded Duncan. It was hard to believe this was the same woman he had brought to San Francisco just a few months before, so detached and indifferent he had wondered if it was even worth the bother. She looked radiant when she had bounced onto the Curtellas' deck, hair loose under a wide-brimmed hat, McCann her chauffeur for the day.

Duncan, on the other hand, had felt the opposite of radiant. The three days he had just spent in Puerto Vallarta equalled three days of sleep deprivation. He loathed the place – thought it the American version of the Spanish Costas. Package holidaymakers in search of cheap booze and sunshine. Whatever charm or history it may once have possessed had been erased by the gaudy imperatives of mass tourism: high-rise hotels, seedy bars, shops peddling tacky souvenirs and vulgar mementos – all designed to appeal to the lowest common denominator. The streets were as busy at four in the morning as at four in the afternoon. The hotel Alison had booked was in the centre of the downtown area. Duncan would lie awake on the king-size bed, trying to shut out the noise and relax, but he'd give up around three, order a bottle of Scotch from room service and turn on CNN.

One night he got dressed and went downstairs to the bar. He had only just got his drink when two girls came over and sat either side of him. They wore their sexuality like a badge of honour – waist-length ebony hair, skimpy dresses that exposed breasts and thighs, trashy jewellery, heavy make-up and stiletto heels. He noticed the barman's wry smile when the girls asked him to buy them a drink. Just for a second he had considered it. Two women at the same time – would that be exciting or just exhausting? No, they were too young and too obvious – not his type. He downed his martini and went back to the room.

There was only one woman who could lull him to sleep. He picked up his BlackBerry and called Saskia. When she answered and said his name, he wished he hadn't called, because now that he'd heard her voice he ached for her even more. He had seen her almost every day since he had got back from the abortive Malaga trip. Their lunchtime assignations were brief but intensely satisfying. Sometimes they met after work, before he caught the train home. He liked it best when they managed the whole night together, when he could watch her sleep and make love in the morning, still smelling of each other's bodies. Guilt tugged at him when he thought of Lola sleeping alone in the Grange, especially as she never questioned him or complained when he said he had to work late and wouldn't make it home. That she trusted him completely made his betrayal all the more heinous, but he batted that thought away and turned his attention back to Saskia.

'Where are you?' he asked, and then immediately regretted it.

In a hotel, a bar, waiting for a client? He didn't want to know. *Lie to me, please lie to me.*

'I'm at home.'

Good girl. She knew what he wanted to hear.

'Where are you?' she asked.

'In my hotel room.'

'Alone?'

'Yes, I'm alone.'

'Are you lonely?'

He took a deep breath that caught somewhere between his chest and his throat.

'It would be nice if you were here with me,' he said.

It was as much as he could admit to.

'I see you when you get back to London?' she said.

He hadn't wanted to dwell on how long that would be. Three days in Mexico followed by three days in California with Lola. If he couldn't do without Saskia for a week, he was in real trouble. He hadn't wanted to dwell on that either.

Gonzalez had reminded him a lot of Vasquez – middle-aged, portly, balding but in denial about it. Both swept their few strands of hair across shiny, sun-spotted scalps and both smoked cigarillos. The deal Duncan had gone to negotiate was similar too: a hotel and golf resort that needed an efficient water-recycling system. With Hilliard out of the equation, Duncan was confident he could deliver what Gonzalez wanted. When he checked out of the hotel, the receptionist had asked if he enjoyed his stay. He smiled politely and said that his trip had been successful.

The flight from Puerto Vallarta to San Francisco was five hours. Duncan had spent three hours trying to work and two hours trying to sleep. It irritated him that with all the time he spent on aircraft, he never quite managed to use that time efficiently. He didn't know if it was the recycled air, the constant interruptions from cabin crew, or just being cooped up for so long, but when he saw other passengers tapping away on their laptops, or snoozing under the thin scratchy blanket that was standard issue, even in first class, he didn't understand how they did it.

He had let the Curtellas know he was on his way, but asked them not to tell Lola – said he wanted to surprise her. When he saw how happy she was, how at home in their cutsie little guesthouse, he felt exonerated. He had been right to push her into travelling without him. It had been good for her, just as he had said it would. Between the Curtellas and McCann, she had been well looked after. Duncan hadn't realised that McCann wasn't working for Roger Williamson any longer. Lola said something about it not being *his thing*, whatever that meant, and he appeared to have some role in the renovations instead. Duncan didn't quite see how one minute McCann was selling them a house and the next minute he was renovating it – a jack of all trades, master of none. Lola told him not to worry about it – Birdie knew what she was doing. Really? A hundred thousand dollars for the renovations? It seemed a huge amount to Duncan, although he didn't say that to Lola. He kept reminding himself it was worth it. Lola's renewed enthusiasm for life was all the proof he needed. She couldn't stop talking about all the spectacular houses McCann had taken her to see, how spectacular their house would be. Everything was spectacular, it seemed.

All Duncan had to do was figure out a way to pay for it. By liquidating some of his investments and negotiating an overdraft with the bank, he had just about managed to scrape together enough to complete the purchase. Most of his money was tied up in the Grange. The money from his parents' estate had paid for renovations that had been required, and now he faced more of the same with the Treehouse, but with no inheritance to fall back on. He needed to take control of the budget, understand exactly what it was he had committed to.

While Lola was out having some *quality time* with Joanne Curtella – Duncan failed to comprehend the distinction between quality time and any other time – he paid a visit to Birdie's office. At first she was concerned – had she overlooked an appointment? – but when Duncan said he was passing and wondered if they could have a quick chat, she relaxed and said of course, she was going to call him anyway.

The neatness of her office impressed him: rows of tidy shelves with clearly labelled files and a large, well-organised desk.

'So what did you think of PV?' asked Birdie.

'PV?'

'Puerto Vallarta.'

'Oh, not really my kind of place. A bit too touristy.'

'I went there for spring break when I was at college,' said Birdie with a smile. 'Had a pretty wild time.'

Duncan found it hard to imagine Birdie being wild. She looked so sweet and wholesome with her ginger curls and milk-white skin.

'Anyway,' she said, 'I've drawn up a schedule of staged payments.'

She took a sheet of paper from one of the files and handed it to Duncan. He put on his spectacles and saw that the first payment of thirty thousand dollars was due in a week.

'I'm not sure if Lola mentioned it, but if we don't put in a pool, the cost comes down from a hundred to seventy-five.'

Duncan studied the schedule for a moment.

'As someone in the water business,' he said, 'I'm not sure how I feel about a pool. Water is such a scarce resource, particularly in this state.'

Birdie nodded, her face suddenly serious. Duncan didn't feel at all guilty playing the 'saving the planet' card, although really he was just saving money.

'I can't argue with that,' she said. 'How about we scale things down a bit – a hot tub maybe?'

The notion of him and Lola sipping cocktails in a hot tub seemed so absurd Duncan had to smile.

'Mmm,' he said. 'Not sure we're exactly the hot tub type, but I'll have a chat with Lola, see what she thinks.'

Birdie took a set of plans from one of the shelves and unrolled them across the desk. On the top, in bold black type, was printed 'The Treehouse, Falcon Drive'.

'I sent these over by email,' she said. 'I know Lola loved the design, but I wondered if you had any comments.'

Duncan remembered Lola hadn't been able to print them – something to do with paper size – so he had only seen them on her computer screen.

'It's very contemporary,' he said.

'Is that a problem?' asked Birdie.

Duncan had no strong feelings one way or the other. This was Lola's project and providing he could find the money to pay for it, she could have whatever design she wanted. The fact she was taking the lead proved she was growing in confidence. It also meant he worried about her less, and about being away from home so much.

'Not at all,' he said. 'As long as Lola's happy. When do you intend starting work?'

'We need to clear the site – take out some of the trees – and aim to break ground in a couple of weeks.'

'I was rather surprised to hear that McCann will be working on it.'

'Cain?' said Birdie. 'Yeah, I was a bit surprised myself. It was Joanne who suggested it and Lola was keen to have him on board, so I thought, why not give him a go?'

Lola was keen? She hadn't mentioned that. Duncan thought back to that first dinner on the Curtellas' deck, when he had got it into his head that McCann was attracted to her. She had laughed it off, told him not to be ridiculous. Had he been right all along?

'I'm so sorry, Duncan,' said Birdie, 'but I have to be somewhere. Why don't you take that away with you' – she pointed to the schedule he was holding – 'and let me know if you have any questions?'

She picked up her bag and her phone, then showed Duncan to the door.

'I hear you're leaving tomorrow,' she said. 'It certainly was a quick visit.'

'I have a lot on at the moment,' he said. 'You know how it is.'

She offered her hand and he shook it gently.

'It was great seeing you,' she said. 'Have a safe flight home.'

Once back in England, Duncan spent very little time at home. He had a long list of tasks, top of which was knocking the Mexico contract into shape. Second on his list was sorting out his personal finances. When he instructed his broker to sell all his AquaEco shares, the broker had said, 'So what do you know that you're not telling me? Is the company in trouble?'

'Not at all,' said Duncan. 'I just need to raise some cash.'

He realised too late that he had made an error of judgement. The news spread like Chinese whispers: the Sales Director had lost a big contract, the Sales Director's assistant was escorted from the building by security, the Sales Director had got rid of his company shares. One and one made eleven. Rumour and innuendo swarmed around him. He thought what an honestly worded memo might say – *I bought a house on the West Coast of America to help my wife get over the death of our only child. No mystery, no subterfuge; I just needed the money* – but then he reasoned that the shares were his to do with as he pleased; they could all go to hell.

And that's where Duncan feared he was headed too. He stared out at London Bridge, lit up like a fairground ride, and the Thames below it, black as oil. Saskia dozed in the unmade bed. The room was quiet and dark – a warm cocoon. He looked at her angel hair, fanned out across the plump feather pillow, and thought how unlike him it was, this fascination. Until Saskia, the women had been an antidote to the anxiety that bubbled like lava under his skin. If they despised him because he paid for sex, so be it. It wasn't just sex – it was ownership, control. While they were in that room, they were his. The only thing they could demand was money – all other demands were his prerogative. He couldn't be rejected or required to explain himself. He didn't have to consider their needs.

And then there was Saskia. She opened her eyes, smiled a slow, sleepy smile, rolled onto her back and stretched.

'You have to leave?' she asked.

He thought about that for a moment. Did he have to leave – go home to Lola? The brightness he had discerned when she'd skipped onto the Curtellas' deck didn't fade when they got home. He had feared it would – that she'd slide back into despondency – but when she wasn't busy at the yard, getting to know the new girl (Bella something), she was engrossed in plans for the Treehouse. She spoke to Birdie and McCann almost daily, it seemed, and brought Duncan *up to speed* via detailed progress reports that he feigned interest in. His input was minimal – he nodded, smiled, posed the occasional question – but Lola was excited and that was what counted. It lifted a huge burden off his shoulders, not having to fret about her so much. He turned back to Saskia.

'No,' he said, reaching for his phone. 'I don't have to leave.'

One of Duncan's many reflections on the failure of the Spanish deal was that he had nursed it along too slowly, allowed too much time for deliberation. It was a mistake he wouldn't repeat. He would bring the Mexico deal to fruition quickly.

He left Saskia eating breakfast in bed: a hearty full English that belied her slim figure. Duncan had orange juice and poached eggs – no coffee, no carbs. When he strode into his office, bristling with purpose and vigour, he was surprised to see Alison there, rummaging through the papers on his desk.

'You're early,' he said.

She stood up poker straight.

'Oh, good morning,' she said. 'I didn't hear you come in.'

'I didn't mean to startle you,' he said. 'Are you looking for something?'

She pressed her hands together and shook her head.

'No,' she said. 'Just having a bit of a tidy up.'

Duncan looked at his desk – neat as always – and said, 'I need you to book me a flight back to Mexico. Call Gonzalez, would you – see when he's available? Oh, and find a quieter hotel this time.'

'Certainly.' said Alison. 'I'll do it right away.'

* * * * *

When he told Lola he had to go back to Mexico she said that job would be the death of him. He reminded her that 'that job' provided a very comfortable lifestyle. She took that as her cue to talk about the Treehouse – rapidly becoming her only topic of conversation. Duncan switched off until the word 'budget' cropped up.

'Hang on a minute,' he said. 'What was that?'

Lola stopped loading the dishwasher and gave him her full attention.

'Birdie said that so far, we're coming in a bit under budget.'

'Oh. Well, that's excellent.'

Lola studied him for a moment.

'Is the money a problem?'

'No. Not at all.'

Her tone went from chatty to serious in a breath.

'You're not lying to me, are you?'

What was it the Americans said – *Don't go there*? Duncan kissed her forehead.

'No, Lola. I'm not lying to you.'

This time his hotel was in the Sayulita area of Puerto Val-larta – quieter than the previous hotel, but still not quiet. It would have to do. Hopefully he wouldn't be there too long anyway. It was Saskia's birthday in a week and he wanted to take her out to dinner. *Like a date?* Yes, Duncan had told her, like a date. Usually they just had drinks together before they went to the room and if they were hungry, Duncan ordered room service. They had never had a meal together in public. It would steer their relationship in a different direction, which, he realised, was exactly what he wanted. Could he dare to think of her as his girlfriend? The ambiguity of their relationship confused and concerned him. Prostitute was such an ugly word, not one he associated with Saskia. When he paid for her services, he discreetly slipped the money into her bag. However long she was with him, she charged him for an hour. He took this to mean that his feelings were reciprocated, that she no longer thought of him in strictly business terms either. The rational part of his brain wondered why she charged at all if that was the case, but the irrational part of his brain – the part that was hopelessly besotted – reasoned that she still had to eat and clothe herself and pay rent.

He imagined them sitting opposite each other in a restaurant – a successful middle-aged man and his beautiful young mistress. Other men would glance over at their table with envy. The thought filled him with pride until the Catholic part of his brain insisted on having its say. *But what about Lola – what about your wife*? He didn't have an answer.

Gonzalez kept him waiting for half an hour. Duncan's legs ached after the twelve-hour flight and he paced up and down, trying to get the circulation going. Punctuality meant a great deal to Duncan – he hated the culture of *mañana*.

'Will Señor Gonzalez be much longer?' Duncan asked the receptionist.

She looked at him with a blank expression, so he tried again.

'Señor Gonzalez,' he said, '*Cuánto tiempo será?*'

'*No sé,*' she replied. '*Lo siento.*'

As he paced, Duncan tried not to dwell on how much was as at stake here – not just his commission, but his professional reputation. If he lost another large contract, the board would lose confidence in him.

'Señor Drummond. I'm sorry to have kept you waiting.'

Gonzalez bustled his way towards Duncan, a stubby cigarillo in his mouth, his hand outstretched. Duncan took his hand and shook it firmly.

'Please,' said Gonzalez, opening the door to his office. 'Come in.'

The air was pungent with stale tobacco. Gonzalez gestured for Duncan to sit. He crushed the cigarillo butt in an overflowing ashtray and emptied it into a plastic wastepaper bin. Duncan looked at the paper-strewn desk. He had an uncomfortable sense of déjà vu – Vasquez's office, smelly and disorganised – but forced it to the back of his mind. He took some papers from his briefcase, handed one set to Gonzalez and kept the other for himself. Their conversation alternated between English and Spanish, but whichever angle he approached it Duncan was unable to get Gonzalez to share his sense of urgency about agreeing terms. Gonzalez leafed through the papers with little more than mild curiosity and when he announced after thirty minutes that he had another meeting to go to, Duncan was dismayed. He wanted to protest but he needed to keep

Gonzalez on side. He rose to leave, gathered up his papers and spotted another piece of paper on the desk, one whose logo he instantly recognised: Dawes.

It was early evening but fiercely hot. There was no breeze, just a faint but unmistakeable whiff of sewage. Duncan walked along the pavement hoping to hail a cab. Needles of sweat pricked at his skin. His head throbbed; the flight, the heat – he was probably dehydrated. He stopped by a bar for some water and five minutes rest, but the music was too loud and he left. When he did eventually get a cab, his legs were so shaky he couldn't have walked much further anyway.

He thought he would feel better after a shower and something to eat, but he didn't. If Dawes had approached Gonzalez, he would have to work fast. Panic danced its spiteful little dance in his chest. He poured himself a large Scotch, lay on the bed and called Saskia. He wanted her to tell him what she was wearing, or not wearing. Sometimes he told her to touch herself, describe how it felt – every shiver, every sensation – and listen to her come. She answered on the fifth ring – he always counted.

'It's me,' he said.

She hesitated.

'I can't talk now, Duncan. You call me later?'

She was with someone. It hit him like a punch.

This time Gonzalez didn't keep him waiting. His secretary showed him straight in and after the usual polite preamble, the two men got down to business.

'You have a good proposal here,' said Gonzalez. He picked up the sheaf of papers Duncan had left with him, and waved them to make his point. 'But I need more time.'

Duncan nodded. Negotiation was his forte. Work out what the client wants and give it to them – or let them think you have given it to them. It was all in the phrasing.

'I understand,' he said. 'You are a cautious man and you don't want to make a mistake.'

Gonzalez puffed on his cigarillo and waited for Duncan to continue.

'But I believe the mistake would be to delay. The figures quoted in this proposal include a substantial discount if work begins within the next three months, when our engineers and technical people are available. Also, a five per cent price increase is due in November.' He leaned forward and paused for effect. 'I want you to have the lower price.'

Gonzalez picked a speck of tobacco from his lip and examined it. He would have made a good poker player. Duncan had no idea what he was thinking. Smoke curled in noxious ribbons that drifted in Duncan's direction. His eyes stung. Gonzalez picked up a sheet of paper from underneath a pile on his desk. He looked at the paper and then at Duncan.

'I am in negotiation with another company also,' said Gonzalez.

It was difficult to breathe in that room. Duncan needed air.

'Is it Dawes?' he asked.

Gonzalez nodded. Duncan inhaled as deeply as the crushing sensation in his chest allowed.

'Whatever they have offered,' he said, 'I guarantee to match.'

'But you have just said that your people are only available for a limited time and your prices will soon rise. Was this not true?'

Duncan's head throbbed. Pain pressed against his skull.

'It was true, it is true, but I want us to do business together.'

Gonzalez had his poker face on again. Duncan wished to God he'd open a window.

'If I say yes, how do I know that your terms won't change again? You tell me this –' he waved Duncan's papers again – 'is your best offer, but then you say you can match any offer that your competitor makes. How can I trust you?'

Duncan thought about that for a moment.

'I am an honourable man, a man of my word.'

Gonzalez put his cigarillo in the ashtray.

'I believe that you are, but the other proposal –' he held up a piece of paper bearing the Dawes logo – 'is a better proposal, and that is what matters.'

Fight or flight? Duncan wanted to stay and fight his corner – get Gonzalez to trust him, agree to his terms – but his lungs screamed for air so flight won. He stood but felt so lightheaded he had to steady himself on the desk. Nausea and dizziness coalesced into something stomach-churning and vile.

'Are you alright, Mr Drummond?' asked Gonzalez.

Duncan nodded and left. He didn't mean to be rude, but he couldn't find the breath to speak.

He stood in the street wearing his Savile Row suit, the afternoon sun a furnace above him. A hot dry breeze fanned his face. Sweat from his forehead seeped into his eyes, its wet saltiness blurring his vision. The air stank of stagnant water. Dog excrement baked on the ground beside him. Nausea rose in his throat and he retched. He gulped in the fetid air but it made him feel worse. When he saw Gonzalez, he tried to walk away, but his legs seemed to liquefy.

'Is everything alright, Mr Drummond?' asked Gonzalez.

Duncan could see him forming the words, but they sounded distorted. When he clutched his chest, Gonzalez shouted something to his secretary, watching open-mouthed from the doorway. Gonzalez grabbed him, tried to steady him, but Duncan's legs folded and he slid to the ground. The stench all around made him retch again – an empty, painful spasm that yielded nothing. *Please let this be over* – did he think it or say it out loud? He grabbed Gonzalez's arm and tried to pull himself up but his damn legs refused to cooperate. Gonzalez said something about the hospital but Duncan shook his head. It was probably only a minute or two before he could stand, but it seemed an interminable amount of time. He dusted himself down and straightened his tie.

'I'm so terribly sorry about that,' he said. 'Bout of food poisoning I'm afraid. Profuse apologies.'

Gonzalez looked sceptical, but somehow Duncan managed to walk away. Not stagger, not stumble, but walk; a triumph of sorts.

Duncan would have preferred a heart attack to a panic attack. His father had his first coronary at fifty-eight, and the one that killed him two years later. There was something noble about a heart attack, something masculine. You worked hard, took care of your family, and even though the strain killed you in the end, you died quickly and with dignity. No lingering illness like his mother had to endure. What would his parents think? They had always been so proud of him. Not much to be proud of now. That Gonzalez had witnessed his meltdown made it a hundred times worse. Duncan felt as though his skin had been ripped away, exposing the raw mess underneath.

It didn't matter that exhaustion grabbed and tore at him, Duncan knew there was no prospect of sleep on the long flight home. When he closed his eyes he saw Gonzalez helping him up off the filthy pavement, Saskia naked in a stranger's bed, Clarissa's broken body. He kept his eyes open.

No matter how many times he went over it, he didn't understand how Dawes had stolen another contract from under his nose. How could they have offered better terms without knowing what terms he had offered? He looked out of the window at London below. The captain told the cabin crew to prepare for landing. Duncan wasn't prepared at all.

'Where to, mate?' asked the cab driver.

'London Bridge,' said Duncan.

He called Lola, got her voicemail and left a message saying he wasn't sure if he would be home – he'd let her know later on. He called Alison but got her voicemail too. One o'clock; she'd be at lunch. The traffic got worse as they got nearer to the city, but Duncan wasn't in a hurry. He was grateful for the solitude, the chance to gather his thoughts and regroup. Between Bank and Mansion House, the traffic came to a standstill. That's when he saw Alison walking along the street. She waved at someone and quickened her step.

'Sorry, mate,' said the cabbie. 'Looks gridlocked up ahead – I'll double back.'

The driver made a three-point turn and manoeuvred into the line of traffic on the other side of the road. As the taxi crawled along, Duncan saw Alison again, now arm in arm with a man – a man Duncan recognised. No, it couldn't be. The traffic thinned out and the driver accelerated.

'Stop!' shouted Duncan.

The driver swerved into the kerb.

'Everything alright?' he asked.

'Just a minute,' said Duncan.

He needed to be sure. Yes, it was Hilliard – Alison, arm in arm with Hilliard. She laughed at something he said. Duncan watched them walk away, the magnitude of her betrayal slowly sinking in. No wonder Dawes was always one step ahead – Alison told Hilliard everything he needed to know. Duncan had heard he was back consulting for them – stealing AquaEco contracts by fair means or foul. He had always thought Hilliard a self-serving little prick, but Alison? He considered her loyalty beyond question.

'What do you want to do, mate?' asked the cabbie.

Duncan knew exactly what he wanted to do.

*   *   *   *   *

When Alison got back from lunch, Duncan was sitting at her desk. He had trawled through her emails looking for messages from Hilliard, but she must have deleted them. He opened her deleted file but it was empty.

'Mr Drummond,' she said. 'I wasn't expecting you until tomorrow.'

She looked at her computer screen and then at Duncan. Did he imagine it, or did she seem nervous?

'Is there something I can help you with?' she asked.

Yes, definitely nervous.

'As a matter of fact there is,' said Duncan. 'Step into my office, would you?'

He closed the door and told her to sit down. She tucked her hair behind her ears and folded her hands on her lap, the picture of innocence. Duncan stood at the other side of the desk.

'How long have you been seeing Hilliard?' he asked.

She blinked several times, but other than that her mask of innocence remained intact.

'William Hilliard?' she said.

Duncan smiled. He hadn't given her enough credit all these years, thinking her straightforward and loyal. There was obviously a lot more to Miss Davey than he had realised.

'Yes, William Hilliard. Did it start when he was working here?'

She thought about it for a moment, then said, 'I don't wish to be rude, but is my personal life any of your business?'

'It is if you're passing on confidential information.'

What little colour she had in her face drained away. She shook her head.

'I'm not,' she said.

'And yet I've lost two contracts to Dawes in as many months.'

'You can't blame me for that,' said Alison.

'Oh but I do,' said Duncan. 'You and William Hilliard.'

She looked at her hands for a moment, and then back at Duncan.

'That's pure speculation,' she said. 'You have no proof.'

Duncan smiled, remembering that Hilliard had said exactly the same thing.

'I don't doubt that you've covered your tracks, so no, I don't have any proof, but I will tell you what I told Hilliard – if I can't trust you, I can't work with you.'

'You're firing me?'

'You've left me no choice.'

She stood up and stared at him, her eyes defiant.

'I'll sue for wrongful dismissal.'

'And the company lawyers will keep you tied up in court for years.'

The mask slipped. Tears welled up in her eyes but she didn't wipe them. Duncan felt a moment's compassion but then thought of her and Hilliard, laughing behind his back.

'Clear your desk,' he said.

In some ways it was a good thing. At least now Duncan could explain to the board why the company had lost two lucrative contracts. He thought about the commission he had lost personally and how he needed to sit down with his broker and figure out exactly how much of his remaining share portfolio he would have to sell to raise the rest of the money for the Treehouse. He was relieved that Lola didn't want a pool or a hot tub – she wanted to keep the garden natural. Whenever she raised the subject of cost, which she seemed to do more frequently as the project progressed, Duncan reminded her that was his responsibility. This had satisfied her at the beginning but now she pressed him to *discuss numbers* with her – such an unlikely expression for Lola. She hadn't taken kindly when he chuckled. Her surprisingly testy response was that she wished he would stop treating her like a child. He said he didn't realise that he was, but apparently Birdie had had questions about the budget and Lola was embarrassed that she couldn't answer them. He had placated her with a hastily produced spread-sheet that inflated their liquid assets and his projected bonus. She filed it away in a box marked 'Treehouse' and said she was glad he understood.

Duncan's father had been a stockbroker when it was still a gentleman's profession. Every morning Geoffrey Drummond caught the eight-ten from Godalming to Waterloo, wearing a pinstripe suit and a bowler hat. Duncan's mother was responsible for all domestic matters. She employed a cleaning lady and a gardener and the Drummonds' large Victorian house ran like clockwork. It was considered an equitable division of labour in a time when feminism was about burning bras – something utterly unfathomable to Duncan's genteel mother – and it was perfectly acceptable for women to eschew independence and rely entirely on their husbands. Geoffrey Drummond went to his grave without ever having bothered his wife with financial concerns. Duncan took the same approach in his own marriage. Lola had never been particularly interested in money, so why should he bother her about it? He thought of the livery yard as an extension of her childhood hobby. Some years it broke even and some years it made a small profit, but the accounts were irrelevant as far as he was concerned. Both the livery yard and the Treehouse were about giving Lola a sense of purpose. The livery yard had kept her busy all those years while they waited for a baby, and when Clarissa finally came along, she had loved it as much as Lola. And the Treehouse – well, that had brought joy back into Lola's life. To complain about the cost would be to miss the point entirely.

No, he would keep his worries to himself. It was the right thing to do. He called her to say he would be home after all and could she meet him at the station.

He had thought of calling Saskia, but gave himself a stern talking to and resolved to try to wean himself off her. It scared him that he needed her so much. He had let her into his life, his heart, and no good could come of it. She was costing him a fortune, too. Five hundred pounds every time they met. Sometimes they met three times a week. No, he needed to get this thing under control. He would ration himself to once a week – twice at most.

As he left for the evening and walked past Alison's empty chair, he knew he would miss her. Duplicity aside, she had been an excellent secretary.

Outside it was starting to drizzle. Duncan had just put out his hand to hail a cab when he felt a tap on his shoulder. He turned around and standing right behind him was William Hilliard.

'What the hell do you want?' Duncan asked.

Hilliard had that smug look on his face. He'd had his hair cut short and his suit looked expensive.

'I want you to give Alison a decent pay-off. God knows she's earned it, putting up with your pomposity all these years.'

Duncan couldn't believe the gall of the man.

'Who the hell are you to make demands? She got what she deserved and if you want someone to blame, blame yourself.'

Hilliard actually smiled.

'I don't think you're in a position to take the moral high ground,' he said.

Duncan clenched his hand into a fist and imagined how satisfying it would feel to punch him.

'Meaning?' he said.

'Your little hooker habit.'

For a second Duncan thought he'd misheard, but Hilliard looked so pleased with himself he knew that he hadn't. He had the strangest sensation that his body – its flesh, muscle and bone – had turned from solid into liquid. States of matter: solid, liquid, gas. He remembered it from school. That he could still stand amazed him.

'Don't bother to deny it,' continued Hilliard. 'Alison told me all about your sleepovers at the Carfax – lunchtimes too, from what I understand. Horny old bastard, aren't you?'

'How...?' was all Duncan managed to say.

'Receptionist is a friend of Alison's. Terribly indiscreet. Oh, and don't think you can get her fired too – she's leaving anyway.'

The urge to pummel the smirk off Hilliard's face gave way to an all-consuming sense of shame. He imagined Hilliard and Alison sniggering together, his weakness a source of lewd entertainment. If he had been standing there naked, he couldn't have felt more exposed. What choice did he have but to capitulate?

'I'll agree to a reasonable severance payment,' said Duncan in a voice that didn't sound like his.

'Good decision,' said Hilliard.

He moved as if to walk away, but changed his mind. A self-satisfied grin lit up his chubby face.

'And in the meanwhile, think what a pity it would be if the tragic Mrs Drummond were to find out.'

Nine

It was her own fault for daring to believe that life might be good again. She had arrived at the station, eager to greet Duncan after his Mexico trip, and there he was, eyes wide, like he'd seen something he wished he hadn't, his jaw set firm and solemn. This wasn't jetlag or work stuff, the explanations he usually fobbed her off with. He walked towards her – briefcase in one hand, suitcase in the other – and the cheerfulness she had brought as a welcome home gift, evaporated into the cold night air.

'Rough trip?' she asked.

He nodded. She didn't press him to talk; experience had taught her it was pointless. In the Land Rover, Radio 4 masked the silence and when they got home, he said something about a shower and disappeared upstairs. Darcy, shut in the kitchen, barked his deep, gruff welcome. He tried to bolt past her as she opened the door, but she grabbed his collar and pulled him back.

'He's not in the mood,' she told him. 'He'll say hello later.'

Her laptop sat among a scatter of papers on the kitchen table – emails from Birdie and Cain that she had managed to print so that she could show them to Duncan. She wanted him to feel as excited about the Treehouse as she did, but when she talked about it she could tell he wasn't really listening. He seemed disengaged, his mind elsewhere. Maybe he was concerned about money after all. It wasn't as if they had planned to buy a second home – what if they couldn't afford it? Every time she asked him about it he reminded her that the finances were his responsibility and, if pressed, he produced her a spreadsheet or jotted down a few numbers. However much she sensed she was being humoured or placated, she had never challenged him. It certainly wasn't a subject she would raise tonight. She tidied the papers into a single pile and switched off her laptop.

The lasagne she had made for dinner was overcooked – hard crust around the edges, black-brown splodges marring the cheesy topping. She left it to cool and was about to open some wine when she changed her mind and went to Duncan's study instead. It smelled of his Cartier cologne. She took a bottle of Scotch from the drinks cabinet, half filled a crystal tumbler and brought it upstairs.

His unpacked suitcase was open on the bed. He sat next to it in his dressing gown and slippers, staring blankly at the wall. His hair was wet and dishevelled, as though he'd rubbed it roughly with a towel.

'Here,' she said, handing him the Scotch. 'You look like you could use it.'

He took the tumbler and drank deeply.

'Can I interest you in dinner?' she asked, hopefully. 'It's lasagne – homemade.'

He shook his head.

'Maybe later,' he said.

She didn't want to go but she didn't want to stand there in silence either. When she started to unpack the suitcase Duncan said leave it, he'd do it later. His voice was flat, monotonic. This blatant wretchedness was so unlike him; it filled her with trepidation. Was he sick? Had he lost his job? Was ignorance bliss? No. Whatever it was, she needed to know.

'Has something happened?' she asked.

He took another hit of Scotch. She waited.

'Mexico didn't go well.'

Business was a grey area in terms of permissible topics. It wasn't taboo, like Clarissa or the accident or his loss of faith, and he did bring his work home in the sense that he spent hours in his study, but he didn't discuss business as such, other than to fill her in on his travel arrangements. Perhaps that was the way to coax it out of him.

'Will you have to go back again?' she asked.

He finished the Scotch.

'No,' he said. 'I won't have to go back again.'

Blood from a stone. Again, she waited. Nothing. Eventually she asked, 'Is there something else? It's just you seem –' she thought for a moment – 'forlorn.'

She had no idea know why she used that word, except that it seemed disturbingly apt. For the first time since she'd walked into the bedroom, his eyes met hers.

'You know I love you?' he said.

An unprompted declaration of love? That was unexpected. Duncan was all *show don't tell* when it came to his emotions. Why expose the soft underbelly of his feelings when he could convey the sentiment by proxy: send flowers, proffer compliments, bestow gifts? This was a man whose idea of an anniversary surprise was to buy her a house. Gestures, not words, ruled in Planet Duncan. When she had begged him to talk about Clarissa, he employed the services of a bereavement counsellor. It was the kind of man he was and she knew that when she married him.

Even in the first flush of their romance, he had admitted rather than declared his love. On her twenty-second birthday he whisked her off to the Cotswolds for the weekend. The hotel was old and quaint, with oak-beamed ceilings, inglenook fireplaces and four-poster beds. They still hadn't slept together, something Duncan was surprisingly patient about. Previous suitors had tried to pressure her into sex and took her refusal as evidence she was frigid or gay. The truth was much simpler; until Duncan, she had never met anyone she particularly wanted to sleep with. When she realised Duncan had booked two rooms, she was dismayed. In her mind, this was the night she would surrender her virginity. Several times over dinner she attempted to broach the subject, but couldn't quite find the words. After dinner, Duncan suggested a walk. The evening was still and balmy, bathed in the pale glow of a full yellow moon. He took her hand as they strolled.

'I have something to ask you,' he said.

Of course. Duncan was nothing if not a gentleman – he would never *presume* they would share a room; he would seek her prior consent. She took a deep breath and turned towards him. The fast flutter in her chest was not at all unpleasant.

'Yes?' she said.

He took something from his jacket pocket – a small box. When he opened it, a diamond ring glinted in the moonlight. She looked at the ring and then at Duncan. Words failed her.

'Will you marry me?' he asked.

He looked so serious and so very handsome. She put her hand to her chest, the flutter now so frantic it felt as though a tiny bird was trying to escape.

'Yes,' she said breathlessly. 'I will.'

It was only when he took the ring from the box and slipped it on her finger that he said, almost as an afterthought, 'You know I love you?'

A lifetime had passed since then. She sat down next to him and rested her head on his shoulder. If they had known what the years would bring, would he still have asked? Would she have accepted? All those never-born babies – each loss more heartbreaking than the last. Then the baby that *was* born and grew into their cherished child: the ultimate loss, the ultimate heartbreak. It was as if the others had been a morbid dress rehearsal for that final act. How could they have known their story would be a tragedy? Duncan took the burden of blame upon himself and forsook the God who denied them their happy ending. But in forsaking God, he denied himself succour, the promise of eternal life. Lola didn't believe in eternal life, just this flawed and fleeting life. She looked at the empty tumbler, still in his hand, the thin platinum wedding ring, still on his finger.

'Yes,' she said. 'I know you love me.'

The lasagne was cold and untouched. Lola had no appetite and Duncan still hadn't ventured downstairs. She covered the dish with tin foil and put it in the fridge. On the shelf below the orange juice and skimmed milk was an opened bottle of Viognier. She poured a large glass and sat down wearily at the kitchen table. When she was younger she hated alcohol: the perfumed smell of gin, the chemical smell of vodka. Mummy's tipples, knocked back with a cigarette and a good dose of self-pity. Lola vowed to be teetotal. Those last few years of school, when parties were all about getting drunk and getting laid, she watched from the sidelines, certain she was missing out on nothing but a hangover and regret. It was the same at university, but with drugs thrown into the mix. Lola never saw the appeal. Clive was the one who showed her that good wine was one of life's great pleasures. Moderation is the key, he told her, as if he recognised some defining characteristic borne by the children of alcoholics, some implicit damage, visible to the astute observer. Clive taught her how to taste wine, how to classify and appreciate it. He underscored her education with a gift – *The Rubaiyat of Omar Khayyam*. She hadn't expected a book of poetry. *Ah, not just any poetry, my dear – eleventh-century Persian poetry, celebrating wine in all its glorious splendour*. Clive's inscription gave her as much pleasure as the poems. *To my beautiful gallerina – love art, love wine, love life*. A blueprint for happiness. Duncan's comment had been, *If only it were that simple*. He had a point. She did love art, and she had learned to love wine, but life? That was a work in progress.

Once she had left the gallery, Duncan assumed the role of wine mentor and though she never said as much, she felt he lacked Clive's passion. Duncan was certainly knowledgeable, and his cellar boasted some very collectable vintages, but he viewed them as an investment, not a celebration. For Khayyam, wine was synonymous with celebration. Quietly she recited one of the poems – all of them just four lines long – that she had learned by heart:

Drink wine.
This is life eternal.
This is all that youth will give you.
It is the season for wine, roses and drunken friends.
Be happy for this moment.
This moment is your life.

Lola drank her wine and tried to be happy for the moment. *You know I love you*? A question, not a statement; a question she had been asked before. Seven years old, in bed but not asleep, the covers pulled over her head to muffle the shouts from downstairs. *Please stop, please stop, please stop*. At last it did. She must have fallen asleep, because her father woke her. It was very dark and he sat on her bed. She couldn't really see his face, but she could see he was wearing his coat. He said, *you know I love you*, and kissed her forehead. She never saw him again.

Darcy jumped up when Duncan walked into the kitchen. He patted the dog but looked at Lola.

'Are you hungry?' she asked.

He shook his head.

'Not really.'

She pulled out the chair next to hers.

'Wine?' she asked.

'Please,' he said, and sat down. 'Sorry; a lot on my mind.'

His face had a bit more colour, although that may have been the Scotch.

'Tell me.'

He looked at the pile of papers.

'What are these?'

'Never mind about those; tell me what's going on.'

He massaged his temples with the heel of his hands.

'I had to let Alison go.'

Lola raised her eyebrows.

'Alison? Your secretary? But she's been with you for years.'

Duncan nodded.

'I know.'

'What happened?'

'She was passing confidential information to William Hilliard, the assistant I let go a few months back.'

'Oh, I see,' said Lola, although she didn't. 'How did you find out?'

'Fluke, actually. I saw them walking along the street, arm in arm, and then I confronted her.'

Lola tried to put the pieces together.

'Is that why Mexico didn't go well?'

Duncan nodded again.

'And Spain,' he said. 'They've cost me two contracts and God knows how many months of hard work.'

Was that all? Lola understood why Duncan was upset, but worse scenarios had been going through her head. There would be other secretaries, other contracts. He rubbed his temples again, as though trying to erase something. Unburdening himself didn't seem to have helped. His anguish was almost palpable.

'Is there more?' she asked.

Duncan looked at her.

'Isn't that enough?'

'I suppose. It's just, I haven't seen you this distraught since –'

She didn't have to say it – he would know she meant Clarissa's accident.

'Hilliard made threats.'

'Threats? What sorts of threats?'

Duncan's face was pinched with disgust.

'Vile threats. He said he would tell you things about me – things that aren't true.'

Now she was completely lost.

'I don't understand. What did he threaten to tell me?'

Duncan stood and paced around the kitchen, his hands clenched into fists by his sides.

'It doesn't matter. I refuse to let his poison –' he spat out the word – 'into our life.'

His loss of composure alarmed her. This was as close to angry as she had ever seen him. Her childhood demons stirred, shouting father, sobbing mother. She and Duncan weren't like that – they were polite and civilised and she wouldn't have it any other way.

'I'm sorry,' she said. 'Of course I trust you.'

She wrapped her arms around his neck. His breathing was heavy and deliberate, like he was forcing the anger back inside. Lola felt his breath on her face, his heartbeat against her chest – a strange kind of intimacy, but intimacy nonetheless. Calm returned slowly, in breaths and beats, and she was grateful for it.

Autumn chased away the last of the summer with howling winds and short, cold days. Bare trees and darkness, the ground thick with rotting leaves. Lola slipped back towards her own darkness. Soon there would be another anniversary, but not one they would celebrate.

The letter arrived innocently, hidden among junk mail and bills: an invitation for Clarissa to attend an open day at St Mary's School for Girls. They had put her name down when she was six and forgotten about it. With the letter came a glossy brochure – happy, carefree children in the science lab, on the sports field, playing musical instruments – explaining why St Mary's was the best possible choice for their child's future. Lola gazed at Clarissa's name: strict and formal in black italics. Clarissa Emily Drummond. Clarissa after Lola's grandmother and Emily after Duncan's mother; all of them gone. Lola stroked the lettering with her fingertips – emotional Braille. Her heart felt so heavy she had to sit down. Clarissa used to sit at that table and draw pictures with the fat, waxy crayons she kept in her KitKat tin: stick figures – Mummy, Daddy, Darcy and Polo. Yellow for sun, blue for sky, green for grass.

If only it were that simple. The walls used to be bright with those pictures. Lola closed her eyes and remembered the warm weight of Clarissa on her lap, the way she fidgeted until she got comfortable then snuggled down, thumb in mouth. Her empty bedroom was still pink and cream, with puffy white clouds on the ceiling. Clarissa was everywhere and nowhere.

The emails from California helped a little, although Lola chose not to dwell on her preoccupation with Cain McCann. He was friendly and handsome and she dismissed it as a fleeting, out-of-character anomaly, a symptom of the sadness that engulfed her in Piliton, especially this time of year. He had been such good company that day he drove her around to look at contemporary houses. Time spent with him had been so delightfully effortless. She thought of Duncan's moods, how unapproachable he had become. Was it any wonder Cain seemed like a breath of fresh air? Well, until he had rushed off to meet the silly waitress with the sing-song voice and skin-tight T-shirt. That was the last she had seen of him; the next two days he had worked at his friend's winery and the day after that she and Duncan had flown home. She tried to put him out of her mind, but then, a week later, there was a message on the answering machine.

'Hi guys, it's Cain. Hope you're both doing okay. Just wanted to let you know we've started work over at your place – broke ground last week as a matter of fact and everything's going great. Anyway, you've got my cell so call anytime. Oh, and have a great day!'

Lola's heart swelled at the sound of his smooth Hollywood voice. It was laughable, the way he induced such instant happiness. She thought of all those facile platitudes – act your age, pull yourself together – and once again, tried to put him out of her mind. But as the day wore on her resolve wore down. Duncan had called to say he wouldn't be home so she had another long evening with only Darcy for company. She didn't bother to cook, just had some Brie and an apple, washed down with a delicate Sonoma Chardonnay. After the second glass she replayed the message, closed her eyes and imagined she was in California and Cain was right there with her. This time what she heard was impersonal (she was never mentioned), work-related (a progress report), and non-committal (call me anytime). She felt like a jilted schoolgirl. Pathetic. She reminded herself that the first time they had met she thought him pushy and cocky, but then she had got to know him. The third glass of wine helped rationalise her feelings. Cain, the Treehouse, and everything that went with it was a harmless diversion. When she was thinking about them, she wasn't thinking about Clarissa.

It didn't help that Duncan seemed lost in his own private hell. Lola thought he might feel better once he had confided in her about Alison and the scurrilous Hilliard, but instead he withdrew. She was curious to know more about Hilliard's threats, the lies he had fabricated, but when she hinted at the subject Duncan got that look on his face again – the one she had seen at the station – and refused to talk about it. It was difficult to talk to him about anything at all, since he was hardly ever home. When he did come home it was late – too late to eat together – and he'd go straight to his study or straight to bed. He revealed nothing in conversation beyond the obvious or routine. She thought it best to leave him be. Things were probably still difficult at work and she knew he would be tortured by Clarissa's accident, making all sorts of bargains with a God he claimed not to believe in. She knew this because she did it too – begged a God she didn't believe in to let her relive that day, to do everything differently so that Clarissa would still be alive. God wasn't interested. He had Clarissa and he wasn't giving her back.

Lola tried to keep busy but grief sapped her strength. With Duncan, it was the opposite. He was like a tightly wound spring, always pacing or drumming his fingers, bristling with pent-up energy. In bed he tossed and turned, often giving up on sleep altogether and disappearing downstairs. Lola would have stayed in bed all day but she recognised that depression was trying to creep up on her again, so she forced herself to wash and dress and eat and pretend that everything was normal. It wasn't, of course. Even the short walk to the stable yard seemed like a huge effort, although now that Kathy had Bella to help out, Lola was surplus to requirements anyway. The two girls chatted about YouTube and Facebook, conversations lost on Lola. It was inconceivable to her that a person could have hundreds of friends, virtual or otherwise. She could count her friends on one hand. Quality, not quantity, was what mattered to Lola. Duncan said she was self-contained, which he meant as a compliment. She did tend to keep people at arm's length, a legacy from her chaotic childhood. How could she invite friends home – risk them finding out that her mother was a drunk? Strangely, it was her mother's brief periods of lucidity that she found most difficult to deal with, those sober interludes when Mummy could see all too clearly how useless she was to her daughter. Even then, it was Lola who comforted her; child as parent, parent as child. Lola wondered if one of the reasons she had married Duncan was that he wanted to take care of her. He was old-fashioned like that, which suited Lola just fine until she realised how maddening it was having a husband who kept his feelings bottled up inside – a legacy from his own childhood, no doubt.

From what Lola understood, life *chez Drummond* was formal and reserved. She had never witnessed it first-hand because Duncan's parents had already died by the time they met, but he claimed that he never saw them kiss or hug and that they didn't kiss or hug him, at least not that he could remember. He vaguely remembered sitting on his mother's lap and definitely remembered holding her hand as they crossed the road, but he would have been very young – no more than seven. It was at around seven that his father taught him to shake hands. Lola asked if he felt rejected when he was sent away to school but Duncan said not at all, it was simply how things were done. When his parents dropped him off at St Martin's Ampleforth, a month after his ninth birthday, Duncan watched with horror at the emotional goodbyes some of the other boys were subjected to. His parents would never embarrass him with public displays of affection. Duncan and his father shook hands while his mother watched proudly. It was two months before he saw them again. *And you didn't feel abandoned?* asked Lola. Duncan shrugged his shoulders and said he was too busy to think about it. Keeping busy seemed to be the guiding principle of the boarding-school regime – no time for inconvenient emotions if you were occupied every waking hour. Duncan took a similar approach to her mourning; keep her busy and she'll soon get over it. That was why he bought the Treehouse.

The phone rang and Lola answered just before it went to message.

'Hey, Lola, how you doing?'

Cain McCann. It was weeks since he had called and his voice delivered an instant shot of joy. She took a breath and said she was fine – how lovely to hear from him.

'I was sitting here writing you another one of those long emails and then I thought, hey, why don't I call instead?'

'Well, it's lovely to hear from you.' She giggled. 'I just said that didn't I? Oh, there's nothing wrong is there?'

Cain laughed. The sound zinged all around her.

'Not at all,' he said. 'We're ahead of schedule, actually, so need your input on materials – you know, flooring, bathrooms fittings, kitchen appliances, that sort of thing.'

'Already?'

'Yeah, I know, but the lead time with these things can be weeks, months even, depending on what you decide to go for.'

'Oh, I see. To be honest, I haven't really thought that far ahead.'

'Sure. It must be hard being so far away.'

Lola closed her eyes and tried to see the Treehouse. In the photos Cain had sent, it looked like a building site: felled trees, gaping holes where windows and doors used to be, part of the roof missing. It was difficult to imagine what it would look like when the work was finished.

'Be a lot easier to figure things out from here,' he said. 'When are you planning to be in town? I know it's not long since your last trip, but things are moving pretty quickly. Got a great bunch of guys working for us and the weather's been on our side too. No rain forecast, which is pretty unusual for late fall.'

Lola smiled when Cain said *fall*. In autumn, leaves fall, therefore autumn is fall; such a literal interpretation, elegant in its simplicity. She ached for her California life. A few minutes talking to Cain had reminded her how good she felt there. The bleak days ahead loomed before her – the grim countdown to November 6th, the third anniversary of Clarissa's death. Lola was condemned to spend those days alone and lonely, or with Duncan, the atmosphere taut with strained civility.

'I'll look into some flights,' she said.

She hoped Duncan would be pleased. Yes, it meant more travelling, and he probably did enough of that anyway, and yes, it meant a few days away from the office, but the break would do him good. Apparently not. He looked aghast, as though she'd suggested they fly to the moon.

'You want us to go to California *again*?' he said.

Lola offered a cheery smile and nodded.

'Next week?' he said.

'I know it's short notice, but Cain phoned and explained that we need to get on with ordering stuff for the Treehouse –'

'What stuff?'

'Bathrooms, kitchen, flooring, that sort of thing.'

'Already?'

'That's what I said, but apparently there's a lead time or something. Anyway, I've got a hold on some flights – if we go on Wednesday and come back on Monday, you'll only miss a few days at work.'

He had got home late again and after a quick hello, scuttled off to his study. Lola didn't usually disturb him there, but she needed him to agree to the trip. Her tone was light and as near to casual as she could manage. She thought she'd made a rather good case, but Duncan dismissed it out of hand.

'That's not possible, I'm afraid.'

'Why not?'

'I've got too much on.' He pointed at the carefully organised paperwork on his desk. 'I can't just fly off to California, which doesn't mean to say that you shouldn't go.'

'On my own?'

'You've done it before.'

'That was different.'

'Why was it different?'

He must have realised the moment the words left his mouth, because he made a point of turning back towards his computer screen and tapping away at the keyboard. She took a deep breath.

'It was different, because it wasn't the anniversary of our daughter's death.'

There, she'd said it. Duncan stopped tapping. Lola waited for a reaction but he stayed still as stone. If she pushed too hard he would get up and walk out, but she pushed anyway.

'The thought of living through that again, here, where she died – I just thought it might be easier somewhere else.'

'Then you should go,' he said evenly.

'But I want to go with you.'

'Not possible,' he said again.

His feigned composure was too much for Lola.

'Three years, Duncan,' she said. 'Three years without Clarissa, without talking about Clarissa.'

He didn't look at her.

'Talk to me about her, please. It doesn't have to be a big heart-to-heart, just something small, like how she sucked her thumb, or the way she lisped when her two front teeth fell out.'

He shook his head.

'I can't.'

'Duncan, please –'

He stood up so suddenly that his chair tipped backwards and crashed to the floor.

'I just can't!'

Lola stayed very still and breathed as quietly as she could. Alarm stabbed at her chest. Duncan put his hands on the desk and crumpled forward.

'I'm sorry,' he said, his voice barely audible.

She wanted to go to him, tell him she was sorry too, that she should never have said anything, but she couldn't. She couldn't forgive him for denying her those precious memories – the only thing they had left of their child. Perhaps it was better if she went to California without him after all. It wasn't as if they would be much comfort to each other.

Ten

The days leading up to Lola's departure were marked by an eerie quiet that was almost harder to bear than the confrontation in Duncan's study. His strategy was avoidance. He would come home late, after Lola had gone to bed, or make excuses and not come home at all. It had been the same three years before, after they lost Clarissa. He couldn't bear to look at Lola's stricken face, to see the stunned suffering his negligence had inflicted. She had asked only one thing of him, that they talk about Clarissa in the present tense, as if she was still with them. The loss was too great, Lola said; she needed to ease into it slowly. Duncan couldn't do it. He tried to explain that his memories were different to hers, tainted with guilt and regret and a lacerating sense of failure. He needed to forget, not remember – couldn't she understand? No, she couldn't. This was their undoing. It was the aftermath of the tragedy that separated them in their common grief. And now there was a physical separation too. Lola had gone to California without him.

Duncan knew it was selfish, but he felt relieved. By sending her away, he had spared himself the agony of watching grief claim her all over again. He had never thought himself a cowardly man but the evidence was overwhelming. When he saw himself through Hilliard's devious eyes – *your little hooker habit* – he was mortified, but then he thought, what the hell did Hilliard know about anything? That day – the day Duncan ran through the fields looking for Clarissa – that was when panic had first seized him. He hadn't known what it was until then, had never experienced it. But once it found him, it burrowed under his skin and hid there, waiting to subvert him at will.

He knew he should have asked for help but couldn't. He had sex with strangers instead, until Saskia, and then he didn't need anyone else. His efforts to see less of her had failed abysmally. The hours they spent together were his only respite. It wasn't perfect – he hated that she still saw other men, however discreetly – but he had long given up on the idea of perfection. Once Lola had left for California, Duncan stayed away from the Grange – the rooms where Clarissa had played, the stable where her pony still lived, the paddock where she had died.

Duncan didn't tell Saskia about Hilliard, just that it was no longer convenient to meet at the Carfax. He was touched when she suggested they meet at her apartment instead – a studio on the fourth floor of an Edgware Road mansion block with an elderly porter and unreliable lift. And when she refused to accept money for her services, it confirmed their relationship had deepened and grown. He still enjoyed buying her gifts, though, and insisted on replacing the cheap Ikea bed and sofa that made his lower back hurt like hell. He also paid her fees for the A levels she was studying by correspondence course, and treated her to a new laptop. When she had confided that she wanted to be a doctor, he was astonished. He had no idea she harboured academic ambitions, let alone a wish to study Medicine.

Then he learned she had passed her end-of-year exams with top marks and suddenly it didn't seem such a far-fetched notion after all.

At home she wore jeans and Uggs, or wandered around barefoot. They ate in front of the TV, plates balanced on their laps. She liked reality shows and documentaries and anything about animals. If she could have a pet it would be a dog – something small like a poodle or a Pomeranian. Duncan told her he had a dog – a black Lab called Darcy – although strictly speaking he was Lola's dog.

It was the first time he had mentioned her name. Saskia said that Lola meant 'sorrows'. When Duncan asked how she knew that, she told him she had done a school project about the Virgin Mary, and that Lola derived from the title 'Our Lady Of Sorrows'.

'You're Catholic?' Duncan said, incredulous.

They were in the cramped kitchen area clearing up from the pasta she had cooked for supper.

'My family are Orthodox but I lose my faith.'

She finished drying the large spaghetti saucepan and hung it on a hook over the cooker.

'I lost my faith too,' said Duncan. 'Three years ago to be precise.' He raised his eyebrows. 'Actually, I don't think I've ever said that out loud.'

'What happen three years ago?'

He addressed his answer to the plate he was holding rather than meet Saskia's gaze.

'Something I find very difficult to talk about.'

She took the plate and put it in the sink.

'I think there are many things you find difficult to talk about. English men are like Russian men – they think it weak to show they are troubled, they are hurt.'

She filled a glass with water and handed it to him.

'How heavy does it feel?' she said, pointing to the glass.

'What?'

'The glass. How heavy does it feel?'

Duncan was confused but went along with it.

'Not heavy at all.'

'Exactly. You hold it for a few moments and it is not heavy. But the longer you hold it, the heavier it becomes. In one hour your arm will hurt. You will want to put the glass down. But imagine you hold it for one day, one week, one year? The weight would be unbearable.'

'I'm not sure I follow.'

Saskia cupped his face with her hands and offered a weak smile.

'The longer you hold it, the heavier it becomes.'

How true. He yearned to unburden himself, to purge himself of guilt. Could he really do this, here, now? To his horror, tears scalded his eyes. Duncan had cried only once in his adult life. Not at his parents' funerals, when he was solemn but stoic, his composure as assured as the carefully chosen hymns and readings. Not even at Clarissa's funeral, when he was frozen with shock, numb to the avalanche of pain that was about to engulf him. No, the only time he had cried was when he clutched Clarissa's lifeless body to his chest, begging her to breathe, begging her not to die. The only time until now. He gripped the side of the sink hard, his knuckles white.

'I miss my little girl.'

Saskia stroked his back.

'What happen to her?'

'Clarissa,' said Duncan. He tore a few sheets of kitchen roll and wiped his face. 'Her name was Clarissa.'

She was supposed to go to a horse show with Lola but was getting over a cold so had stayed at home with Duncan. It was hardly ever just the two of them. When he got home from work Clarissa would already be tucked up in bed and at weekends she and Lola spent all day at the stables.

'We took the dog into the village to get bread and a newspaper,' he said. 'Clarissa bought a pony magazine with her pocket money. She was very polite – please and thank you and this incredibly bright smile. I was so proud.'

He tore off another sheet of kitchen roll and blew his nose.

'When we got home I had to do a bit of work but Clarissa pleaded with me to go over to the stable and see Polo.'

'What is Polo?'

'Her pony. Present for her fifth birthday.'

Duncan almost smiled, remembering how she giggled as he and Lola had led her blindfolded into the yard, then her squeals of delight when they took off the blindfold and she saw Polo, a huge red bow on his bridle.

'And you took her?' said Saskia.

It had looked like rain but Duncan couldn't bear to disappoint her.

'Yes, with the dog of course. They were inseparable.'

Snook had been there too, loading bales onto the small tractor he used to ferry hay over to the horses that lived out in the winter. Clarissa jumped up and down on the spot, pleading with Duncan to let her go with him. His eyes burned again and he wiped them roughly.

'I should have said no.'

He was talking to himself rather than Saskia, although she seemed to follow.

'But you say yes?'

Duncan nodded.

'I had work to finish.'

He left her there with Snook, went back to the house, called the new client who had questions about everything, and settled down in his study. It wasn't until he heard the first clap of thunder that Duncan realised it was already lunchtime and he should go and get Clarissa.

The morning's watery sunshine had vanished. Dirty grey clouds had collided and congealed, rendering the sky a dark, leaden mass. Spits of icy rain found their way inside the collar of his Barbour. He shivered, remembering how they slid down the back of his neck.

'I get you a drink?' said Saskia. 'Make you feel better.'

Would he ever feel better? He stared out of the small window over the kitchen sink, its glass opaque with condensation. Yellow lights blurred the graphite darkness. Cars crawled along the Edgware Road: men going home to wives and children. He had taken it all for granted, focused on his career, money, status. Why didn't he see that everything he needed, he already had?

'The stable yard was empty so I headed over to the paddocks. There was no sign of the tractor and then the dog appeared – wet, muddy, frantic, blood on his muzzle.'

Just saying it made Duncan's skin tighten. That had been the moment he knew something was badly wrong. He couldn't get Darcy to calm down. *This is your Lassie moment*, he said, hoping humour might trick the fear into going away. Fat chance. The dog belted towards the furthest paddock, barking, howling almost, Duncan right behind him.

Something was different but he couldn't work out what. This was Lola's domain. Then he realised that a great gash of earth had been ripped from the edge of the slope. It had rained for weeks – the ground must have given way. He raced over and saw the tractor upturned in a ditch. Snook was lying about six feet away, not moving. The old man had been thrown clear but Clarissa was still strapped in her seat, face down. She was whimpering: a faint, soft sound, barely audible over the howl of the wind. Duncan told himself it was a good sign. She was conscious, breathing; she was going to be alright. Water was rising fast in the ditch. Duncan lay down in the mud and could just about reach her arm, but when he tried to pull her out the whimper became a cry and she didn't budge. He repositioned himself, pressing the side of his face up against the cold metal. This time his fingers reached the buckle of the seatbelt. *It's alright, sweetheart*, he said, suddenly elated. *I'm going to get you out*. The seatbelt released with a decisive click and though her upper body slumped forward, her lower body didn't move. He tried to pull her out again but her legs were pinned under the seat. He jumped up and pushed his weight against the side of the tractor, but it was no good; he'd have to get help. He dropped to the ground and shook

Clarissa's arm. *I'll be back in a minute, sweetheart. It's going to be fine, I promise.*

'Duncan?'

Saskia's soft Russian tone brought him back to the present, away from his drowning daughter, from the promise he didn't keep, from the worst decision of his life.

When Saskia handed him his third Scotch, she asked how he was feeling. Lighter, Duncan said. Hollow. His heart felt emptied out. He told her to go to bed, that he needed some time alone. She was reluctant, but he insisted. When she kissed him she murmured something soothing in Russian. He couldn't quite believe that after three years of silence, he had finally spoken about that day. Not to his wife, but to his mistress. Another heinous betrayal.

Lola had implored him to talk. She knew only what she had learned from the inquest. When she asked Duncan for details – had Clarissa said anything, why hadn't he fetched her sooner, why had he run for help rather than jumping in the car? – he couldn't answer. He had resigned himself to a lifetime of guilt and talking wouldn't change that. At night Lola would sit in the rocking chair by the Aga, or climb into Clarissa's bed. Duncan accepted this as punishment for his sins and didn't question it. So when he came home late one night, a year after the accident, and found Lola in their bed, it was as if divine forgiveness had been bestowed upon him. He folded her into his arms, kissed her hair, her face, her mouth, her body. It was the first time they had made love since Clarissa died. Lola cried the whole time.

He had let her down then and was still doing it now. She had begged him to go to California, to spare them another anniversary at the Grange, but he had let her go alone to spare himself.

The room had become so cold he could see his breath. There was a blanket on the sofa – a fringed fluffy thing that Saskia liked to snuggle under; he pulled it around his shoulders and shivered. The brief respite that confession had brought was no match for a lifetime of Catholic guilt. He had shared something with his mistress that he had cruelly withheld from his wife. Shame and remorse returned with a vengeance. Father Michael had said Duncan's Catholicism would help him survive the grief of losing Clarissa, but it was as much as he could do to survive his Catholicism. Forget the confessional, all that 'three Hail Marys and we'll call it quits' nonsense. When his faith was tested, there was nothing to fall back on except punishing, self-destructive tenets. Lip service was paid to love and forgiveness, but really it was all about fire and brimstone and making you feel like a worthless sinner. At least that was how Duncan felt. He had scourged himself after the accident and withdrawn from the one person who needed him. Sin heaped upon sin until he could see no way back to God.

He yearned to climb into Saskia's warm bed and wrap himself around her, but there was something he had to do first. Two a.m. – early evening in California. He dialled the Curtellas' number and waited. When Mike answered, all bright and friendly, Duncan observed the social pleasantries as tersely as good manners allowed, and then asked to speak to Lola. He heard Mike call to Joanne.

'She's over at the cottage, Duncan. Hang on a minute,' he said. 'Okay, Joanne's gone to get her.'

Mike filled in the time nattering about the weather and the Treehouse and the great harvest they'd had. At last, Lola came on the line.

'How are you?' she asked.

Her voice sounded formal, like she was asking out of politeness, not because she wanted to know.

'Fine,' said Duncan, equally formal. 'You?'

'Fine.'

He doubted that very much.

'I'm sorry I'm not there,' he said. Silence. He put his head in his hands. 'I should have gone with you, like you wanted me to.'

'I understand,' she said.

He doubted that very much too.

'I couldn't bear to think of you alone, today of all days.'

Another silence. He could hear her breathing softly. It seemed a long time before she spoke.

'I wasn't alone. I was with Cain.'

Eleven

It was official; the six-month drought was over. A deluge of biblical proportions had started somewhere around 3 a.m. and hadn't let up since. Cain sat in traffic on the Bay Bridge, his windscreen wipers flicking backwards and forwards, and drummed his fingers impatiently on the steering wheel. Lola's flight would land in fifteen minutes and even if it took her half an hour to get through immigration and baggage claim, he still wouldn't make it in time. He hated to think of her coming out of arrivals, scanning the crowd expecting to see him, then realising he wasn't there. She seemed nervous the last time he had met her at the airport, which really surprised him. He'd assumed she travelled a lot, or maybe that was just her husband. Anyway, it was cute the way she spoke quickly, all breathless and excited. He couldn't wait to see her again.

Jesus, would this traffic ever move? A young guy in a beat-up Chevy blared his horn. Cain heard sirens and checked his rear-view mirror. Flashing blue lights: police and ambulance. He tuned into a news station and caught the traffic report: accidents on the Bay Bridge, the Golden Gate and the Benicia – half a dozen more downtown. Had people forgotten how to drive in the rain? He'd give Lola a call but she didn't have a cell. The way she called it a *mobile* sounded real British. He caught himself smiling and shook his head. Lola was a client, a married client; he had to remember that. Trouble was, he liked her. They had a lot of fun that day they spent driving around town together. And he could have imagined it, but she seemed a bit pissed when they had lunch and Terri slipped her number in with the check. Lola didn't say anything, but it got him thinking maybe Lola liked him too. Then Joanne had called on his cell to say Duncan had arrived but don't tell Lola, because he wanted to surprise her. Cain hadn't wanted to hang around for the big husband-and-wife reunion so he called Terri, spur of the moment, and asked her out on a date.

It didn't go well. He couldn't get Lola out of his head. It was like she was on the date with them. Terri talked a lot but he couldn't remember what about. Was she waitressing to pay for a Masters in something? He had no idea, but it didn't matter because he wasn't going to see her again. Pete had a theory. *Look, man, the way I see it, you can pretty much have any woman you want. Mystery to me, but chicks seem to like you. You've never experienced that whole unrequited-love thing. Then along comes Lola – sexy name, by the way – and she's beautiful and older and British and something else. What was it? Oh yeah, married. Unattainable. Seriously, dude, you don't have to be Sigmund Freud to figure it out.*

The traffic inched forward, blue lights still flashing ahead. Lola would have landed now. His cell rang; *Mom* flashed up on the screen. He let it go to voicemail. She'd want to talk about Thanksgiving, make sure he planned to be home that weekend. Josh would be there with his blue-blooded wife. You don't have to be Sigmund Freud to figure that out either. Josh had married a clone of their mother.

Thanksgiving would follow its usual pattern: Dad spending as much time as possible on the golf course, Mom pretending she was too busy to notice and Josh using the visit back home to network with anyone that might be useful to him. They'd assemble in the drawing room for cocktails at six and by six ten, Cain would be the main topic of conversation. When was he going to start thinking about a career? What plans did he have? Was he seeing anyone special? At that point the daughter of a country-club friend would be mentioned, along with phrases like 'settling down' and 'thinking about the future'.

When Roger told his mother that Cain wasn't working with him anymore, she was on the phone immediately, wanting to know what on earth had happened. Cain said it wasn't a big deal; real estate just wasn't for him. An exasperated sigh carried down the line. *But what is for you, darling boy, that's the question?* Well, now he had an answer: construction management. He was good at it – or so Birdie said – and he liked it. It was satisfying to create something, to see it change and form in front of his eyes. The guys on site were cool with him and he loved that the only time he spent in an office was when he and Birdie had their weekly catch-up meetings.

The traffic began to move. A couple of highway-patrol cops directed him around the accident and at last he was on his way. Five thirty-five. He was late.

The arrivals lounge was bustling and he couldn't see Lola anywhere. He walked from one end to the other before he spotted her sitting at the coffee concession, her shiny black suitcase by her side. There was nothing of the summer about her. Those adorable freckles had gone. The sun-kissed glints of honey and gold that brightened her auburn hair – they'd gone too. He rushed up to her, arms wide in apology.

'God, Lola, I'm so sorry. There was an accident on the bridge – the traffic was brutal. Have you been waiting long?'

She offered an unconvincing smile and stood up.

'Not long.'

He hugged her and apologised again, said he felt terrible not being there to meet her.

'Well, you're here now,' she said.

No nerves this time; quite the opposite. She seemed flat, almost subdued. Against her pale skin, the green in her eyes appeared strikingly emerald. She looked tired, though, which he figured was understandable after the long journey. On the ride back she gazed out of the window and let Cain do all the talking.

'See you brought us some of that legendary English weather with you,' he said.

'You're welcome,' she said, still staring out the window.

'The Treehouse is looking great. Got the new roof on just in time.'

She nodded but didn't look at him.

'So, how's Duncan?'

'Fine.'

'Couldn't get away, I suppose.'

'No.'

'Is everything okay, Lola?

Now she turned to face him. She looked beautiful and fragile and out of nowhere he was gripped with a primal instinct to protect her.

'Never mind,' he said. 'You get some rest.'

Joanne had planned a big welcome dinner but Cain doubted Lola would be up for it. They were all waiting – Mike, Joanne, Roger, Birdie – and Lola disappeared into a sea of arms the second they arrived. She was hugged, kissed, hugged some more. The dog barked and whined until he got some attention too. Logs crackled and glowed in the fireplace. Mike poured six glasses of Fischer Chardonnay and made a toast.

'To Lola – our neighbour and our friend.'

'To Lola,' they said in unison.

Lola cleared her throat.

'Thank you. You're so very kind.' She looked at Joanne, a sort of pleading look. 'I'm sorry, you've gone to all this trouble –'

'What's wrong, honey?' asked Joanne.

She stroked Lola's arm, soothing and concerned. Lola seemed overwhelmed. Her voice sounded small when she said, 'I don't think I'm going to be very good company. I'm so sorry.'

'Will you stop saying that,' said Joanne. 'You've got nothing to be sorry about. It's me, getting carried away as usual, thinking you'd want dinner and company, when all you want is some sleep. You must be exhausted.'

Lola nodded.

'I am.'

'Then let's get you settled in the guesthouse and I'll bring you over a tray in a little while.'

'But you've gone to so much trouble,' she said again.

'No trouble at all. The important thing is that you get some rest.'

For a second Lola looked lost. Cain wanted to pick her up and carry her to bed, not out of lust so much as chivalry.

'I'll grab your bags,' he said, and went back out to the car. It was only spitting now, but the creek was full and raging. The air smelled of wet wood and log fires. He pulled Lola's suitcase from the trunk and carried it to the guesthouse. Joanne was showing her where the candles were, just in case the power went out.

'We expecting a storm?' asked Cain.

'Best to be prepared. Let me know if you need anything,' said Joanne, heading towards the door. 'You coming, Cain?'

'Be right there,' he said, still holding the suitcase.

Joanne looked at them for a second and then let herself out. Cain sensed he was expected to follow, but he didn't want to leave.

'I'll put this in the bedroom,' he said.

Lola followed him and sat down wearily on the bed.

'What must they think?' she said, seemingly more to herself than to him.

He sat down next to her.

'They think you've had a long journey and you need some rest.'

She pulled a tissue from her sleeve and wiped her eyes. Was it just tiredness or was she crying? Why would she be crying?

'Lola?' he said softly.

'Take no notice,' she said. 'I'll feel better after a good night's sleep.'

Cain got up to leave but Lola stayed put, staring ahead. The bedroom was clean and neat, but sparsely decorated. Plain wooden shutters on the windows, walls painted nondescript beige. The only splash of colour was a small vase of cut flowers on the nightstand. Cain imagined Lola's home in England to be opulent and grand, and he wondered again what it was that drew her here.

'You're sure there's nothing I can get you?'

Lola looked up at him, her eyes pink-rimmed and weary. She shook her head and he left.

Mike was over by the fire, throwing on some fresh logs and moving things around with a poker.

'How is she?' asked Joanne.

'Exhausted,' said Cain.

'You think that's all it is?' asked Birdie.

Cain shrugged.

'She was pretty quiet on the ride back from the airport, and I did kind of wonder –'

'Wonder what?' said Roger.

'You know, if something was wrong.'

Mike opened another bottle of the Fischer and poured everyone a little more wine. Birdie declined, her glass still half full, and said, 'It's probably nothing, but I got an email from Duncan yesterday, reminding me that Lola wasn't to be bothered with budget considerations – I think that's how he put it.'

Meaningful looks were exchanged in silence. The fire spat out a burning ember. It glowed for a second and then died.

Cain knew how excited Joanne had been about Lola's return and he felt bad for her. Kind of strange to have a party without the guest of honour.

'I think we're reading too much into this,' he said. 'She's had a long flight and she's beat. Now I don't know about anyone else, but I'm starving.'

They ate chicken and sautéed potatoes and reassured each other that Lola would feel much better in the morning. Cain wished dinners with his folks were this easy. There was a formality about dining with his parents that put him on the defensive. Sure, they loved him, but he disappointed them too. When they finally accepted he would never be a doctor or a lawyer or make a name for himself on Wall Street, his mom suggested an acting career – *make the most of those movie-star looks.* Cain found the notion laughable. *You don't think reading all those scripts might be a bit of a problem for someone like me?* Her reply was the same as it always was. *Darling boy – focus on the positive.* He wondered if he could come up with an excuse to avoid going home for Thanksgiving this year. Roger must have read his mind, because he said, 'You heard from your mom?'

'She called today as a matter of fact, but I missed it.'

'So she didn't tell you that she's visiting this weekend?'

'What? Why?'

A wry smile crossed Roger's face.

'Well, I'm sure she'll be pleased to see you too.'

Cain chuckled.

'Yeah, I guess that didn't sound very welcoming. Is Dad coming?'

'No, just Helen. I mentioned something about redecorating and she offered her services.'

'Offered?'

Roger smiled again, broader this time.

'Insisted.'

'She's staying with you, right?'

'Actually, she mentioned something about staying with you.'

'You're not serious?'

Roger laughed.

'No, son, I'm not serious.'

Mike did a circuit of the table, topping up wine glasses and clearing away empty plates.

'What arc you two conspiring about?' he said.

'My mom's coming into town this weekend,' said Cain.

'Well, that's great. Joanne, did you hear this? Helen's visiting.'

'That's wonderful,' she said. 'I haven't seen your mom in what, over a year?'

'Mona's funeral,' said Roger.

After a respectful pause, Joanne announced that there was homemade ice-cream, butterscotch and vanilla. Cain had two helpings and finished off Birdie's as well. He went home with a full stomach and a big dish of leftovers. Joanne walked him to the car.

'Did Lola eat anything?' he asked.

'No. I made her up a tray but I saw the lights were off and didn't want to disturb her.'

'She'll probably feel a whole lot better tomorrow.'

Joanne folded her arms around her bosom.

'I guess we need to get used to the cold again. Feels strange after all the heat we've had.'

'Freshened things up, though. And it's great to hear water in the creek.'

She unfolded her arms and put them around Cain.

'Night, honey,' she said.

He lightly kissed the top of her head.

'Thanks for a great dinner, and the great leftovers.'

'You're welcome. Drive safe.'

There was no denying it – a visit from his mom was the last thing Cain wanted. Just thinking about it propelled him back to the school kid with a diagnosis of dyslexia, something Cain thought would let him off the hook. It wasn't his fault and he wasn't dumb; there was a reason he couldn't read and it had a name. His mother figured if he learned things by heart, then no one need know: Robert Frost poems, the periodic table, an essay on 'My Family' that he had to read out in class. McCanns had to be perfect, or give the impression that they were, and Cain's shortcomings had disabused the world of that particular fiction. His dyslexia, his lack of focus, his struggle with all things academic – hard to put a positive spin on that, however much his mother tried. Sure, he was an athlete, played on just about every team, popular too, but it never seemed enough. She denied it, but Cain couldn't shake the idea that she was ashamed of him. *That's so unfair.* Cain imagined her standing there, a wounded look on her face, pleading with him to believe her. *How can you say such a thing?* Cain wanted to say it was obvious Josh was her favourite, but he always backed down. He hated fighting with his mom – hated fighting, period.

Josh was the opposite: smart, bookish, strategic in his friendships. If Josh befriended you, it was because there was something in it for Josh. Law was a good fit for him. He was adversarial by nature – loved nothing more than a good fight. Thirty-five and made partner already. Their mother adored him. Oprah would have a field day with the dysfunctional McCanns.

November 6th – officially winter, according to the weather guy on Vine. It felt like it too. The rain had stopped but a thick soupy mist shrouded the valley. Cain started the car and turned the heater on full blast. Fall went unnoticed, so warm and dry it tacked seamlessly onto summer. Then winter arrived, cold and abrupt.

Lola perched on a stool by the counter, coffee cup in hand, talking with Joanne. She looked lean and casual in jeans and a black sweater. Her hair hung over her shoulders in gentle waves.

'Morning,' said Cain, unzipping his hoodie.

'Morning,' said Joanne. 'You want some coffee?'

'Sure,' he said. 'Black, no sugar. So, Lola, how'd you sleep?'

'Not bad,' she said with a half smile.

Joanne gave him his coffee and went back to unloading the dishwasher.

'Can I do something?' asked Lola.

'Yes,' said Joanne. 'You can sit there and keep me company.'

'Not for long,' said Cain. 'Got a busy day today.'

Lola gazed at him with those emerald eyes and something stirred deep inside his chest.

'Oh?'

'Well, I thought I'd walk you through the Treehouse –'

'You're gonna love it,' interrupted Joanne. 'They've done a great job.'

'I can't wait,' said Lola with a more convincing smile.

'And then we need to go to Santa Rosa and look at flooring and lights,' he said.

Lola stood up and handed her cup to Joanne.

'Thanks for breakfast,' she said.

'You hardly touched it,' said Joanne.

Lola turned to Cain and said her bag was in the guesthouse; she'd see him outside.

'Something's definitely up,' said Joanne once Lola had left. 'She's been real quiet.'

'Jetlag?'

'Seems more than that.'

'I'll look after her,' he said.

He finished his coffee and as he was leaving, Joanne asked when his mother was arriving.

'Sometime Friday I think.'

'Why don't you bring her and Roger over for dinner on Saturday?'

Neutral territory and Joanne's cooking.

'Sounds good,' he said. 'Catch you later.'

Lola was waiting on the deck, her purse slung over her shoulder. Cain's insides tightened. This was a big moment for him – for both of them. Finally he had found a job he liked, one he believed he was good at, and Lola's validation was crucial to him. He was invested here, personally and professionally. Not only had he sold her the house, he was helping transform her vision of it into reality. And this would be the first time she had seen it since they started pulling it apart and putting it back together again. Maybe she was nervous too and that was why she seemed so quiet. Only one way to find out. He took a sharp breath in and exhaled any negative vibes.

'You ready?' he said.

'I'm ready.'

They crossed the wooden bridge that straddled the creek, and made their way through the clearing. The ground underfoot was soft and wet. When the Treehouse came into sight, Lola stopped.

'First impressions?' said Cain.

Lola stared blankly ahead without uttering a word. He had expected a reaction at least. Guess he got that wrong.

'I know you can't see much with the scaffolding and everything, but that's just because the guys were working on the roof – it's coming down any day now. I emailed you about replacing the roof, right? And the windows – they were pretty rotten. The exterior wood has been stripped back – we'll stain it when it's dried out.'

Was she even listening?

Eduardo, in charge of landscaping, called over and Cain raised his hand in acknowledgement.

'You want to come meet the guys?' he said to Lola, because standing there in silence was killing him.

'Sorry?' she said, like she hadn't heard.

'The guys – thought you might like to meet them.'

She looked towards the Treehouse again.

'I'm not sure I can go inside. Suppose I've made a terrible mistake.'

Was that what was bothering her – a bad case of buyer's remorse? She closed her eyes, like she couldn't bear to see it.

'Look, if there's anything you don't like, we can change it. It's not too late.'

He wasn't sure that was true but he had to say something. She took a long slow breath, as though trying to summon up some courage, and then walked towards the house.

Cain hadn't seen this side of her – morose and closed off – and was at a loss as to how to handle it. When they spoke on the phone she was always so upbeat and her emails positively dripped excitement. He didn't know where this had come from – or what *this* was. Her disappointment sat cold and dense in his chest but no sooner had they stepped inside than her mood visibly brightened. He introduced her to the electrician who talked about Lutron systems and Grafik Eye while Lola listened and nodded like she was really interested. The guys working on the AC didn't speak English so she said hello and left it at that. She walked around, commenting on the sheetrock (Cain had to explain what it was because she had never heard of it before), the bug screens, which apparently they don't have in England but could certainly do with, and how the light – even the dull light of a grey November morning – poured in and made everything clean and fresh. She mentioned how pleased she was with the colour on the walls – a creamy chalky butterscotch – when Danny, the painter, stopped what he was doing to point out that its depth and refraction were due to high levels of pigment and the rich resin binders.

'Here,' he said, handing her the paintbrush. 'See for yourself.'

To Cain's surprise, she put down her purse and took the brush from him. He gave the gallon can of paint a stir and told Lola to dip the brush and then wipe off the excess on the side. She shot Cain a quick smile before following Danny's instructions. As she reached up to paint a long strip of colour where Danny had left off, Cain saw him look admiringly at her ass. Not that he blamed him. Lola turned around, a self-conscious grin on her face, and dipped the brush again.

'Hey,' said Danny, 'don't want you putting me out of a job here.'

'Just one more,' she said. 'It's actually rather therapeutic.'

'Cool accent,' said Danny, clearly smitten. 'I could listen to that all day long.' Lola applied a few more smooth strokes before giving him back the brush.

'Thank you,' she said, admiring her handiwork. 'I enjoyed that.'

Cain made a mental note. If Lola slips towards the dark side, give her something to do.

The afternoon was spent picking out things for the house and Cain was relieved to see more of the Lola he knew, although how well did he know her anyway? They'd met in June, he'd sold her a house, they'd spoken on the phone, exchanged emails, spent a bit of time together a few months later, and now here she was, just as beautiful as he remembered, but quieter, distant, unpredictable. Keeping her occupied seemed to help. She chose solid maple for the floors and contemporary fittings for the wall and ceiling lights. They had a late lunch of coffee and toasted paninis, and a wedge of banana cake that they shared. When he noticed her drifting back to whatever sad place was in her head, he distracted her with the first thing that came into his own. *Those horses keeping you busy? Duncan been anywhere interesting lately? My mom's visiting this weekend – guess you'll meet her at Mike and Joanne's.*

'Your mother?' said Lola, suddenly interested.

They were driving back from Santa Rosa in painfully slow rush-hour traffic. It wasn't quite six but the sun hung low and heavy in a bruised sky. Rain washed down the windshield and Cain flicked on the wipers.

'Yeah. She's helping Roger decorate – probably thinks he won't know where to start without Mona.'

'Oh yes. They were good friends, weren't they?'

'College roommates.'

'Are you looking forward to seeing her?'

Cain raised his eyebrows.

'Interesting question,' he said.

'Does it have an interesting answer?' asked Lola.

The traffic was at a standstill now. Cain noticed a restaurant – grandly called 'La Maison de Cuisine' – its parking lot already filling up with early-evening diners.

'Why don't I tell you about it over a cocktail?' he said. 'It's not like we're going anywhere.'

Lola hesitated, just for a moment, but then said yes, a cocktail sounded good.

The restaurant was decorated in a faux-Western style, which seemed odd considering the pretentious French name. Cain and Lola took a couple of stools at the end of the bar. Cain ordered a beer and Lola had a Sterling Sauvignon Blanc.

'Not exactly cocktails,' she said.

'I don't drink hard liquor when I'm driving,' said Cain. 'Beer's just fine. How about you?'

'I don't like *hard liquor*,' she said, emphasising a phrase that was obviously unfamiliar to her.

'Really?'

'Well, since you raised the subject of mothers, mine was an alcoholic with a penchant for gin and vodka. The smell of them brings back memories I would rather forget.'

Cain didn't know what to say.

'Sorry,' said Lola. 'I'm not sure why I told you that; hardly the stuff of light conversation.'

'Wow,' said Cain. 'I had no idea.'

'Of course you didn't,' she said with a shrug. 'Why would you?'

'What about your dad?'

'Absconded. I'm not sure if that was cause or effect of my mother's drinking. I was young so it's difficult to recall the specifics.'

'Any brothers or sisters?'

'No. Only child. Lonely child.' She drank deeply from her wine glass. 'Enough of my sad story. Tell me yours.'

'Well, my parents have been married forever. My dad worked hard building up the business so he wasn't around very much. My mom is a typical WASP –'

'WASP?'

'White Anglo Saxon Protestant. Our version of an aristocracy. Upper class, socialite, good family, old money.'

'You don't approve?'

He shook his head.

'It's not that. Josh, my older brother, he's always been her favourite.'

'Why?'

'He fitted the mould. Went to Princeton then Harvard Law, partner at a New York law firm, married Melissa the ice-queen and now he's talking about running for political office.'

'And you?'

'None of the above.'

'They have a lot to answer for, these parents of ours.'

Cain raised his glass.

'I'll drink to that.'

He took a long hit of beer.

'If I have kids, they can be whoever or whatever they want. As long as they're happy, I'll be happy. How about you? You and Duncan never want kids?'

What had he said? She looked stunned: eyes wide and wounded, lips parted as though in speech, but with no words. In a single motion she slid off the barstool and walked away. He thought she was going to the bathroom but she headed towards the exit and out of the restaurant. Her jacket and purse still hung on the back of the barstool. He looked around, confused, wondering if he should wait or go out there after her. The barman must have seen her leave because he asked Cain if he wanted the check.

'Sure,' said Cain, fishing his wallet out of his jeans pocket.

The car keys were in there too. He didn't wait for the check, just put a twenty on the bar, grabbed Lola's things and left.

Outside it was raining hard and steady. There, standing by the Prius, was Lola. He ran over, desperate to know what the hell had happened in there, but close up he saw she was shivering and her face was wet – rain or tears, he didn't know which – so he wrapped her jacket around her shoulders and helped her into the car. He got in the other side, started the engine and blasted the heater as high as it would go. The windows steamed up in seconds but she was still shivering so he took off his hoodie and covered her with that too. She stared ahead, blank and oblivious, her hair dripping. He spoke softly.

'If I've done or said anything to upset you, I'm truly sorry.'

'You haven't,' she said, not looking at him. 'It's not your fault.'

'Is there anything I can do?'

She shook her head.

'I shouldn't have come here. I should have stayed at home.'

The car had warmed up and she'd stopped shivering and dried her face with the sleeve of his hoodie.

'Is it the Treehouse?' he asked.

'In a way, but not the way you think.' She swallowed hard and he could see by how she was breathing slowly and deliberately that she was trying to hold it together.

'I had a little girl, Clarissa. She died.'

Her voice was quiet and the heater was loud, so Cain wasn't sure he'd heard right at first.

'There didn't seem to be any point after that. Everything good died with her.' She reached for the sleeve of his hoodie again and used it like a tissue, wiping her eyes and nose. 'I'd got used to feeling numb, disconnected from the world, and then you showed me the Treehouse.'

She stared out of the window in silence. Cain waited.

'It's hard to explain,' she said after a while. 'It was as if all the emotions I'd buried with Clarissa, slowly began to stir. I felt an instant connection to the Treehouse, as though it had been waiting for me.' She shrugged. 'I know it sounds stupid.'

Cain didn't know what to say. What could he say? She had just told him that her kid had died. As personal tragedies go, it didn't get much worse. She cleared her throat.

'And meeting Joanne and Mike reinforced this weird sense that it was meant to be, that I was being given another chance to be happy.'

She turned to look at him, and he could see the hope in her eyes, like she really needed it to be true.

'Not like I was before,' she said. 'I know I'll never have that again, but you and the Treehouse and Mike and Joanne – it feels as though now I can look forward.'

It was as if she was pleading with him to believe it. And he wanted to, but not if it just sounded like he was humouring her.

'Well, that's good isn't it?' he said gently.

Tears rolled down her face but she didn't bother to wipe them.

'Clarissa died three years ago today. I thought if I was here, it wouldn't be so hard.'

Okay, now it made sense. No wonder she seemed down and distracted. Jesus, how could she be anything else? And where the hell was her husband? How could he leave her to face this alone? She looked so sad and fragile, Cain felt an ache deep inside his chest. When he folded his arms around her, she leaned into him, rested her head on his shoulder. They stayed like that for a long time.

On the drive back she seemed calmer, more composed. It was hard to take it all in. They were almost at the Curtellas before she spoke again.

'Nobody here knows about this,' she said.

'Not even Joanne?'

'No. I will tell her, but I haven't yet.'

'I won't say anything.'

'Thank you. And thank you for being so kind.'

'I didn't do anything.'

'Exactly.'

She reached for his hand and squeezed it. This weird desire to protect her rushed to the surface again. He'd never taken care of anyone, not because he was selfish, but because no one had ever needed him that way. It meant something that Lola chose him to confide in, him to comfort her.

'I'm here for you,' he said. 'Anytime you want to talk. I know people say that, but I mean it.'

His reward was a smile – tender, not happy – but a smile nonetheless. She kept hold of his hand.

When they got to the Curtellas, Lola said she wanted to wash her face and change into some dry clothes and went straight to the guesthouse. Cain let himself into the house and interrupted Joanne and Mike having dinner.

'Sorry, guys,' he said.

'We didn't know what time you'd be back,' said Joanne. 'I tried your cell but got voicemail.'

Cain took his phone from his pocket and saw that it was out of juice.

'Forgot to charge it,' he said.

'I kept some food warm for you and Lola,' said Joanne. 'Where is she?'

'Getting changed – she won't be long.'

'Good day?' asked Mike.

Cain wasn't sure how to answer that. Lola did seem a little better now she'd talked about her daughter, but he never imagined that she'd suffered such a terrible loss. When he first met her he thought, now there's a woman who has everything. Guess you can never tell. Although the first time they all had dinner together, he remembered thinking there was something about her, like she'd disappear into her own thoughts. He'd even mentioned it to Joanne and she said she'd seen it too – a kind of loneliness, like something was missing. Turns out they were both right.

The phone rang and Joanne was about to get it when Mike told her to stay put and finish her food.

'Duncan,' he said. 'Great to hear from you. How are things? Lola tells us you're pretty snowed under at work.'

Cain couldn't hear Duncan's response but he wondered what was so important that he couldn't be there for his wife on the anniversary of their child's death.

'She's over at the guesthouse,' said Mike.

Joanne was already on her feet.

'I'll go get her,' she said.

'Okay Duncan, Joanne's gone to get her,' said Mike. 'So, Lola brought some rain with her – been pouring here, although God knows we needed it.'

Cain went to the refrigerator and got himself a beer. Joanne came back with Lola, who had changed into slim black pants and a sweater that matched the green in her eyes. She thanked Mike and took the phone from him. Cain wasn't eavesdropping, but it was hard not to notice how formal she sounded, like she was talking to her bank manager, not her husband. He didn't know what to make of it. She'd poured her heart out to him in the car but could barely manage full sentences with Duncan. He saw a look pass between Mike and Joanne, so he figured they'd noticed too. The call lasted two or three minutes at most.

'Sorry,' she said. 'We've disturbed your meal.'

'Well, you know us by now,' said Mike. 'We don't stand on ceremony around here. Anyway, we're pretty much finished. Let me get you a glass of wine.'

He poured a Pinot Noir and handed it to her.

'You hungry?' asked Joanne.

The look Lola shot Cain conveyed their new intimacy. She was ready to tell Mike and Joanne about her daughter – he could see it in her eyes.

'Why don't we sit down for a minute?' he said.

'Is everything alright?' asked Joanne.

Cain took Lola's hand and led her to the couch. They sat in front of the roaring fire and waited for Mike and Joanne to sit too. Lola took a long, deep breath and began. She explained about the horse show and Clarissa's cold, and how Duncan was looking forward to having his little girl all to himself for the day. She told them about the incessant rain and Mr Snook and the ancient tractor and waterlogged ditch. She told them about the phone call and the hospital and not believing for one second that it was true. When her voice faltered, Cain put his arm around her. Joanne covered her mouth in horror, her eyes wide and wet.

'I wanted you to know,' said Lola. 'You've been so kind – treated me like family.'

Cain buried his face in her hair. It was still damp from the rain.

Helen McCann left a message on Cain's phone early the next morning, telling him to expect her for cocktails at six. Please don't go to any trouble, she said, which made him laugh out loud. He had around twelve hours to transform his house from scruffy crash pad into something his mother would find vaguely acceptable. He washed the dishes, emptied the trash, threw away old newspapers and magazines, tidied the bookshelves, put his laundry in the hamper and made his bed. Better, but still not good enough, so he vacuumed the rugs, mopped the kitchen floor and flicked a duster around. His mother would be appalled to think of any son of hers reduced to doing his own cleaning; the McCanns had maids for that sort of thing. He surveyed his efforts, which would undoubtedly be judged inadequate, and then got on with his day.

Lola was already at the Treehouse when he arrived. She looked delicious in skinny jeans and knee-high leather boots.

'Sorry I'm late,' he said. 'Domestic emergency.'

'Oh?'

'Maternal visitation; cocktails at six. I mentioned my mother was coming, right? I've been trying to make my house look presentable.'

'Perhaps it could benefit from a woman's touch.'

'I'm sure it could. Are you offering?'

'Maybe. What did you have planned for today?'

'Tile shopping. There's a big showroom over in Napa. We could swing by there and be finished by early afternoon.'

'Excellent. That should leave us plenty of time to spruce up your place.'

Cain was relieved to see her mood was lighter. Bottling up all that stuff about her daughter must have weighed heavy on her heart. Now that she'd shared it around a little, it seemed less of a burden. She said choosing things for the Treehouse helped – mopped up some of the sadness. That was the first time either of them had alluded to what happened the day before. He hoped this place would live up to its promise and she really would find some happiness here.

They were back in town by three-thirty.

'Where do you live?' asked Lola.

'Other side of Main. You serious about giving my house a makeover?'

'If you want me to.'

'Sure,' he said. 'But I gotta warn you, you'll have your work cut out.'

'I like a challenge,' she said in a chirpy voice. 'We'll need to stop by the supermarket and pick up a few things.'

Lola chose two bunches of cut flowers and a tall vase to put them in, some scented candles, a set of cocktail glasses, a white damask table cloth with matching napkins, a selection of cheese, crackers, crudités and dips, and rustic-looking dishes to arrange them on.

'Good thing I brought my credit card,' said Cain.

'Have I got carried away?' said Lola.

'Not sure yet,' said Cain.

The total was two hundred and twelve dollars. He slipped his card into the machine and hoped it wouldn't be declined. Since he'd bought Mona's old Prius from Roger, he was on a pretty tight budget. Roger said he didn't have to pay for it all at once but he'd given him such a good price it seemed only fair.

'Any cash back?' asked the checkout girl.

Cain shook his head.

'Oh, what about drink?' asked Lola.

'Now that's one thing I do have at home,' said Cain.

'Approved,' flashed onto the screen and the girl handed him the receipt.

Cain rented his two-bedroom tract house from a friend of a friend. He paid below market value and in return, didn't complain about all the stuff that needed fixing. He didn't notice the noisy plumbing or the rattling windows anymore, or the uneven floorboards, unless he stubbed his toe on them, but he wondered what Lola would think – Lola with her big house in England and her newly remodelled Treehouse. He caught himself apologising for everything until she told him not to be silly, his home was absolutely charming. She got to work straightaway: arranged flowers, lit candles, plumped cushions, set out canapés, polished glasses and laid the table with the crisp new linen.

'Wow,' said Cain. 'It looks amazing.'

Lola stood back and admired her work.

'Thank you,' she said. 'I rather enjoyed it, actually. Does that fireplace work?'

'I guess so, but I don't have any logs.'

'What time does your mother arrive?'

'Six.'

'It's only five-fifteen. Why don't you go and get some? A fire would be a nice finishing touch.'

'You're the boss,' said Cain, picking up his car keys.

He drove back to the supermarket and couldn't help but smile, thinking of Lola Drummond fixing up his house, when she was paying him to fix up hers. She really had transformed the place. The woman certainly had taste. When he picked up the logs, he got her a box of Belgian chocolates, a thank-you for helping him out. Driving back he hummed along to The Beach Boys, happy to think of Lola waiting for him at home, until he turned into his street and realised his mother was waiting for him too. Her Lexus was parked outside; she was half an hour early.

'Darling,' she gushed. 'Your friend has been keeping me amused.'

The way she said *friend* implied something less than wholesome.

'Mom,' he said, pecking her powdered cheek. 'You're early. Sorry I wasn't here – I dashed out to get some logs.' He dropped them in the basket on the hearth, having lost interest in the idea of a cosy fire.

'I see you've met Lola.'

Lola smiled a small, conspiratorial smile.

'Yes,' said his mother. 'Delightful.'

She was wearing one of her signature suits, patent pumps and a string of pearls. His mom modelled herself on Jackie Onassis and pulled it off pretty well. Her hair was sprayed to rigidity and flicked up at the ends in a tube-like wave. She saw the chocolates and said, 'Oh, darling, you know I don't eat chocolate.'

She patted her stomach to emphasise the relationship between her chocolate embargo and her reed-thin figure.

He was about to say the chocolates were for Lola, but why add fuel to the fire? His mother would already have decided that the elegant English woman making herself at home in her son's house could only possibly be his girlfriend. His married girlfriend. What other explanation was there?

'I'm working on Lola's remodel, you remember, the place over by the Curtellas?'

'Of course,' said his mom. 'You did mention it.'

'He's doing a wonderful job,' said Lola brightly, to which his mom replied, 'I'm sure.'

Cain needed a drink.

'Can I freshen anyone's glass?' he asked.

Lola had barely touched her wine but his mother had made good headway into her cocktail. She handed it to him and asked for a splash more Vodka, before turning her attention back to Lola.

'Is your husband not travelling with you?'

'No,' said Lola. 'He couldn't get away.'

'And do you have a family?

Cain shot Lola an apologetic look.

'No,' she said. 'No family.'

Roger's arrival broke the awkward silence. Cain could have kissed him with gratitude.

'Hey, Roger, what can I get you?'

'What are you drinking, Helen?' he asked, pecking her cheek.

'Vodka martini,' she said.

'I'll have the same,' said Roger.

He pecked Lola's cheek too.

'Oh, I forgot,' said Cain's mom theatrically. 'You two know each other.'

Cain handed out the drinks and poured one of Pete's Pinots for himself.

'The place looks pretty spruce,' said Roger. 'Scented candles?'

'Lola's idea,' said Cain. 'She thought it needed a woman's touch.'

He stared at his mother, daring her to comment.

'What do you think of the Treehouse?' Roger asked Lola.

'I can't believe how different it looks,' she said.

'Good different?' said Roger.

'Good different,' said Lola.

She seemed to enjoy playing hostess, handing around the food and napkins. When Cain's mother talked about her charity work, Lola listened attentively. She excused herself at an appropriate pause in the conversation in order to check on everyone's drink. Two cocktails later, Roger said they really should be leaving. He had booked a table at Greystone and didn't want to be late.

'Why don't you and Lola join us?' he said.

'That would be great,' said Cain, 'but we already have plans.'

Lola bought into the lie and said they were going to the cinema.

'Oh?' said Roger. 'What are you going to see?'

'*Vicky Cristina Barcelona*,' said Lola.

Cain coughed and apologised, said his wine went down the wrong way.

'I don't think I've heard of that,' said his mom.

Cain hadn't either but Lola jumped in.

'Woody Allen,' she said. 'I just love his sense of humour.'

They waited until Roger had driven away and then giggled like a couple of kids.

'Woody Allen?' said Cain.

'I noticed it was showing when we drove past that little cinema on Main.'

What a surprise: playful Lola, teasing Lola, not-cowed-by-his-mother Lola.

'Maybe we should go see it,' he said. 'Mommy dearest will probably ask about it tomorrow.'

'Tomorrow?'

'Joanne invited her to dinner. Sorry about that.'

Lola waved a dismissive hand.

'I can handle her,' she said. 'You know she thinks we're a couple.'

'Yeah, sorry about that too.'

'Don't be,' said Lola. 'It was rather fun.'

Sitting next to her in the movie theatre, he had to keep reminding himself it wasn't a date. She was gorgeous and they had popcorn and she touched his arm when something was funny, but it wasn't a date. And after the movie, when they went to Market and bagged two seats at the bar and had mac and cheese and a 2002 Zinfandel, and laughed the whole time because they kept remembering silliness from the movie – *still not a date*.

When he drove her home he turned off the car engine but left the radio playing quietly.

'Mike and Joanne must have gone to bed,' said Lola. 'All the lights are off.'

'It's after eleven,' said Cain. 'That's late around here.'

'I know,' said Lola. 'I'm a country girl too.'

'You tired?' he asked.

'Actually, no,' said Lola. 'I didn't expect it, but I slept well last night.'

A vision of her shivering in the parking lot, crying in the car, telling her sad story in front of the fire, wafted across his mind.

'You must have needed it,' he said gently.

She turned and looked at him, her face illuminated by a thin crescent of silver moon. If it wasn't a date, why was it so hard not to kiss her? She undid her seatbelt with a decisive click.

'Fancy a nightcap?' she said.

He didn't know if he could trust himself, but the words tumbled out anyway.

'A nightcap sounds great.'

The guesthouse was chilly and smelled of Lola's musky perfume. Cain flicked on the light switch but nothing happened.

'Electricity's out,' he said. 'Where did Joanne say those candles were?'

'Kitchen cupboard,' said Lola.

He found the candles and some matches while Lola got a bottle of wine from the fridge. She took a corkscrew from one of the drawers.

'Here, let me do that,' said Cain.

He opened the wine and poured two glasses while Lola fetched a big fluffy blanket from the bedroom. She flopped onto the couch, tucked her legs under her trim ass, and tapped the seat next to her, inviting Cain to sit down too. He complied. She spread the blanket across their laps and relieved him of one of the glasses.

'Cheers,' she said, drinking deeply. 'I think I'm a little bit tipsy.'

She closed her eyes and leaned her head back against the couch. It took all his willpower not to kiss her. When she opened her eyes and caught him looking, she smiled coyly and took another sip of wine.

'I'm all over the place,' she said. 'Down one day, up the next. What must you think?'

'I think that yesterday was really tough for you and today you're relieved that it's over.'

She adjusted her position and turned sideways to face him.

'Yes. You see, you get it. Duncan doesn't.'

Cain realised she was just this side of drunk.

'Like tonight, at the cinema. The last time I was at the cinema was with Clarissa. We went to see *Pocahontas*. She loved it. I had to buy the doll and the T-shirt and the poster for her bedroom wall. And I can tell you that, and it feels so good to tell you, to say her name and talk about something we did together that was ordinary and normal and fun. But Duncan won't let me talk about her. I don't blame him for the accident but I do blame him for that – for not letting me talk about her. It's like she never existed.'

She took another slurp of wine. Cain knew that what she'd gone through, what she was still going through, was way beyond him. She was hurt and he wanted to help her heal. He wondered what Freud would say about that?

'I think we should call it a night,' he said.

She looked up at him.

'I'm sorry,' she said. 'I've embarrassed you.'

'You haven't embarrassed me. Anytime you want to talk about Clarissa, talk away. I'm here for you. And listen, you saved me from my mother this evening – that makes you a hero in my book.'

'She's not that bad. And she clearly adores you.' Lola ruffled his hair. 'Her darling boy.'

They giggled like they'd been doing earlier, and he thought okay, we're good here, I should leave. He stood up, helped Lola up and walked to the door.

'Goodnight,' he said, and leaned forward to kiss her cheek.

He didn't know how it happened, but he kissed her mouth instead. It was nothing – a peck – but she didn't pull away and then they were really kissing, properly kissing. She tasted soft and sweet, like ripe fruit. A deep ache passed from his chest to his groin and back again. Her fingers were in his hair, pulling him closer. He pressed her against the door and she caught her breath. There was a moment – a fraction of a moment – when they stopped, assessed, consented. Then there was no going back.

He wanted to take it slow but the heat in his blood fired all his senses into overdrive. They kissed for a long time – tender, passionate, tender again. When she slid her fingers to his chest and started to unbutton his shirt, he watched, unable to believe what was happening. Why a woman like her wanted a guy like him, he had no idea, but she did, and it felt better than anything he had ever felt. Then he noticed that her fingers were trembling. He told himself it was because she was as aroused as he was, but an inconvenient voice in his head, almost drowned out by lust and longing, asked if maybe she wasn't sure. It took all his willpower to pull back, take her hands in his and hold them still.

'We don't have to do this,' he said.

In the dim light it was hard to read her expression.

'Don't you want to?' she asked.

He groaned.

'Oh God. You have no idea how much I want to.' He took a deep breath. 'But only if it's right for you.'

She nodded and for a terrible moment he thought she was going to thank him for being so understanding, peck him on the cheek and say goodnight.

'I don't do this,' she said.

'Do what?' he said, and then realised how stupid he sounded.

'Infidelity. I've never been unfaithful.'

Crazy, but it was just what he needed to hear. Knowing that Lola was a faithful wife made him feel all the more special, like he'd been chosen.

'Never?' he said.

She shook her head.

'I've been a good girl all my life, but here, now, with you – it feels right.'

'Why me?' he asked.

She didn't answer with words.

He slipped out like a thief in the night. Strictly speaking it was dawn, and he hadn't stolen anything, except maybe Lola's trust, but he felt dishonourable, so the analogy seemed apt. A fine dusting of frost coated his car. Something moved in the clearing – a coyote? – then disappeared into the thicket. He didn't want to leave like that, with Lola still asleep, but he didn't know what he would say to her, how he would explain himself. It wouldn't go away – this nagging sense that he had taken advantage of the situation. Alcohol, a movie, dinner, more alcohol, candlelight too – of course they had ended up in bed together. But she said she had never been unfaithful. Had he pressured her, made her feel she couldn't say no? God, he hoped not.

Back at his house, everything screamed of Lola: the flowers, the jasmine scent of the candles, the unopened box of chocolates. He made some coffee and turned on the TV. The news was depressing so he turned it off again. He took a half-eaten chicken from the refrigerator and pulled bits of meat from the carcass. It tasted of nothing. He needed advice, not food. Maybe Mike wasn't the right person – he and Joanne were very protective of Lola – but he was the only person Cain felt he could talk to about this. He didn't just know Lola, but her history too.

Cain waited until nine to call the Curtella house, but no one picked up so he drove over there anyway. An unfamiliar sensation seemed lodged inside of him: heavy and light at the same time. Thirty-three and he'd never had a serious relationship. Girls were easy come, easy go. He wasn't husband material; not steady enough for the demands of marriage. The way his friends described being in love, it sounded like an alien invasion of body and mind. He had no prior frame of reference, nothing to measure against, but he was as sure as he could be that he was in love with Lola.

Mike was on the deck, covering planters with sheets of plastic.

'Should've been prepared,' he said. 'Hope the frost didn't kill them.'

'Yeah, it was pretty cold last night,' said Cain.

'You want a cup of coffee?' asked Mike.

'Sure,' said Cain, and followed him into the house.

His heart lurched, thinking Lola might be in there, but apart from Riley, curled lazily in his bed, the kitchen was empty.

'Joanne's taken Lola shopping to Corte Madera,' said Mike. 'Sit down.'

Cain took a seat at the counter and Mike handed him a strong black coffee.

'You want to talk about it?' he said.

Cain looked at him, trying to figure out what he did or didn't know.

'About what?'

'About your car being here all night.'

Okay, he knew. Cain nodded a *mea culpa* sort of nod.

'I was with Lola.'

The garish red cuckoo clock ticked really loud. He only noticed it now because the place was so quiet.

'I figured,' said Mike.

'I could do with some advice here,' said Cain.

The cuckoo popped out of its house and made a shrill cuckoo sound. Nine-thirty. He wished Mike would say something, and then he did.

'I want to see this from your point of view. Young guy, beautiful woman – not exactly difficult to work it out. But here's the thing – this isn't just about you. After what Lola told us the other night, after what she's been through, you know how vulnerable she is and you took advantage of that. Maybe not deliberately, but still. And then there's Duncan. They've been married twenty years. That might not mean much to you but, believe me, it binds two people together in ways you can't even imagine, and you've stepped on that and damaged it.'

Cain wanted to defend himself, but didn't know how he could.

'I'm not exactly neutral here, son,' continued Mike. 'I've been in Duncan's position.'

'Joanne?' Cain raised his eyebrows in astonishment.

Mike shook his head. 'Ellie, my first wife. While I was over in Vietnam getting my leg blown off, she was carrying on with the estate manager up at Fischer. Single guy, good-looking, not sure how he managed to beat the draft but he did. Ellie was on her own, taking care of the twins, and I guess I could see how it happened, so we tried to put it behind us and move on. Couldn't do it. Things were never the same between us. I felt I didn't really know her – not deep down. The woman I married, the mother of my children, couldn't possibly have done what she did. I'd look at her and think, who is this person?' He poured sludgy coffee into his mug and stared at it a while. Cain could see it hurt him to talk about this stuff, but he carried on. 'I'd catch her looking at me too,' he said. 'Probably asking herself the same question. Point is, the trust was broken and that's not something you can fix. Woke up one morning and she was gone.'

Cain poured some coffee too. He needed a moment to figure out what to say. Mike's and Ellie's story wasn't his and Lola's story, and he needed to make Mike understand that.

'Look,' he said. 'I see where you're going with this –'

'I don't think you do,' said Mike. 'I know it's not the same – Lola and Duncan don't have a family and Duncan seems like a cold fish – but ask yourself, do you want to be that guy, the guy who steps on the bond between husband and wife and damages it beyond repair?'

Cain shook his head. He saw himself through Mike's eyes and felt ashamed. He *was* that guy.

It plagued him the rest of the day. Mike was a good person – a war hero, for Christ's sake, wounded in action. If Cain had known about his first wife cheating on him and dumping the kids, he would never have confided in him about Lola and dragged up all those bad memories. But despite everything Mike said, Cain didn't feel guilty about Duncan. He left Lola on her own to deal with all that stuff about their kid – won't even let her talk about her. What sort of husband does that make him? No, what Cain did wasn't the same as what happened to Mike, but he hated that Mike might think him no better than the home wrecking draft-dodger up at Fischer.

Cain's mother arrived for dinner on Roger's arm, her Jackie Onassis look preened to perfection. Joanne had decorated the table with candles and flowers, and it was the first time since Mona's funeral that Cain had seen her in a dress; a colourful cotton thing with puffed sleeves and a pinched waist. Next to his mom's contrived elegance, Joanne looked small and homely. Mike wore a shirt – not of the Hawaiian variety – and had brushed his frizzy white curls into something improbably flat. Cain kept looking over to the door, waiting for Lola to arrive. His heart skipped and jumped like a kid in a schoolyard. His mother held court, sharing her decorating strategy for Roger's condo: French country chic with Tuscan overtones. Cain had no idea what she was talking about and he was pretty sure no one else did either. He got a beer from the refrigerator and was about to take a drink when he noticed his mother raise an eyebrow. Duly noted. He poured it into a glass rather than sipping from the bottle like he usually did.

That was the crazy thing – after all these years, he couldn't bear to disappoint her. He'd already disappointed Mike, which seemed even worse because Mike expected better of him. Cain hadn't seen Lola since he'd snuck out of her bed and he kept thinking about what Mike had said.

Do you want to be that guy? As if she'd read his mind, his mother spoke.

'Is your friend not joining us for dinner?'

Joanne looked at him – oh God, she must know too – and he was figuring out how to answer when Lola walked in. She wore a grey dress and heels. Her hair was arranged in a loose knot, her lips pale and shiny. He felt it again – that ache connecting chest and groin – even stronger than before.

'Sorry to keep you all waiting,' she said.

'Don't you look lovely,' said his mother graciously.

She pecked Lola on both cheeks, European style.

'Chardonnay for you, Lola?' said Mike, handing her a glass.

'Perfect,' she said.

Cain wanted her to look at him but she wouldn't meet his eyes. She made small talk with his mom and Roger, got shooed out of the kitchen when she tried to help Joanne, and offered Mike advice about protecting plants against frost. Mike's own advice kept repeating in Cain's head. Seemed like it would be a very long evening.

It can't have been easy, but Lola managed to get through a three-course dinner without looking at, or speaking to him. Even when Roger asked about the movie, Lola answered politely with no reference to Cain at all. If anybody noticed, they didn't comment, until his mother was leaving and asked, very discreetly, if she could speak with him outside. A swirl of cold air enveloped them as they stepped onto the rain-soaked deck.

'I don't know what's going on with you and the English woman –'

'Lola.'

'I am correct in thinking that she's married? Not separated, not divorced – married?'

'Yes, Mother, Lola is married.'

'Are there not enough single girls in the world, Cain? And isn't she a client, for goodness' sake? What about your reputation? This is a small town and if you want to be taken seriously . . .' She looked up at the stars as though searching for guidance. 'I just don't know what to do with you,' she said, shaking her head.

'I'm a grown man, Mother. You don't have to do anything with me.'

It was as if he hadn't spoken.

'I worry about you,' she pleaded. 'Your father and I just want you to be happy and settled.'

'I am.'

'But how can you be? You're obviously infatuated –'

'Look, not everyone can be like you and Dad. Sometimes it's more complicated.'

His mom cast her eyes up to the heavens, but Cain pressed on regardless.

'I know you want me to be more like Dad and Josh –'

She cut him off.

'Not this again. If I have ever given you the impression I favour Josh, then I am truly sorry. And for the record, you're more like your father than you think.'

'How?' Cain asked, genuinely interested to hear her answer.

She turned away, a look on her face Cain hadn't seen before. He was about to ask if she was okay when Roger came onto the deck.

'Ready to go?' he asked.

Cain wasn't sure if she was genuinely upset or feigning it to make him feel guilty, but she swept past and went back inside.

'What's wrong?' asked Roger. 'Has something happened?'

'Mom was just telling me how I'm more like Dad than I think.'

Roger looked surprised.

'She told you about that?'

Cain suspected he had stumbled onto something and nodded. Roger moved closer and lowered his voice.

'It's seeing you and Lola – it's opened old wounds. Now I'm not saying that there's anything going on with you and Lola, but when Helen found out about Skip's affair, her whole world collapsed.'

Cain was too stunned to speak.

'I've got to tell you,' continued Roger. 'I never thought the marriage would survive and if Helen hadn't been pregnant with you, it might not have.'

Everything Cain knew about how his family – their idiosyncrasies, their tacit understandings, the complex weave of their relationships – shattered in that moment. He felt as if something deep and important had been sucked from inside him. Nothing was how he thought it was. He had questions, a lot of questions, but his mother returned, flanked by Joanne and Mike, and there wasn't time to ask them.

'Thank you once again for a wonderful evening,' she said. 'Roger?'

'Coming, Helen,' he said, and hung back for a moment while she made her way to the car. 'I'll call you,' he said quietly to Cain. 'Soon.'

Cain watched them drive away, reeling from Roger's revelation. His mind was both bursting and blank. Even as he shivered, he didn't register the cold.

'Cain?'

Lola was behind him, the fluffy blanket they had shared on the couch draped around her.

'Can we talk?'

'Of course,' he said, although he wasn't sure how much more he could take in.

She hadn't spoken to him all night – hadn't even looked at him. If that didn't signify regret, he didn't know what did. All he could hope for now was damage limitation. He made a pre-emptive strike.

'It was my fault,' he said. 'You were vulnerable and I shouldn't –'

She pressed her fingers to his lips. The intimacy of the gesture gave him hope that his guilt and doubts were misplaced.

'Shhh. I knew what I was doing,' she said.

Really? Had she been just as sure as he had? He sighed a long, grateful sigh, then leaned in to kiss her. It felt like a slap when she stepped back.

'But it shouldn't have happened. I've had all day to think about this, and I believe it was a mistake. We got carried away in the moment . . .' She lightly touched his cheek, and as she took her hand away it was as much as Cain could do not to grab it back.

'I know, and I understand,' he said. 'But...'

She interrupted him, her tone soft but firm. 'It was beautiful, and I'm not saying I regret it, but it can't happen again.'

He wouldn't have thought it possible, but he felt physical pain at that moment. They had shared something beautiful – she said so herself – and to be told they would never share that again seemed cruel and unusual punishment.

'I'm a married woman,' she said, bringing his conversation with Mike flooding back. 'I know my marriage isn't perfect – far from it – but Duncan would never be unfaithful to me.'

She paused, as if giving Cain the chance to object. His mom probably thought his dad would never be unfaithful either, but she sure as hell got that wrong. Lola could be wrong about Duncan too, but Cain didn't want to be the one to tell her. A sharp breeze gusted around them and Lola pulled the blanket tight over her shoulders.

'Last night was an aberration,' she said. 'A wonderful, tender aberration.'

The breeze had whipped her hair off her face and her eyes shone with emotions he couldn't read.

'You do understand, don't you?' she said, and it seemed pointless to say no. It wasn't so much a question as an ending. Cain had waited so long to fall in love – it wasn't supposed to be this way. He should be walking off into the sunset with the girl, but the girl wasn't his and her sun set on a different continent, half a world away. Suddenly he felt bone-weary. Lola, his dad, Mike – too much information in too short a space of time. He needed to let it all sink in, drip by heart-wrenching drip.

Twelve

Saturday's *Financial Times* was usually a pleasure to read, with its glossy supplement and clever arts reviews. Not today. It focused on '*Everyday Victims of The Global Economic Meltdown*', families whose homes had been snatched from them because they'd been sold a bad loan, men and women who had lost their jobs and any real prospect of finding another, all those diligent savers who could never retire because their pensions had been wiped out by plummeting stock markets and the poor judgement of investors.

Duncan folded the newspaper and put the kettle on the Aga to boil. His own descent into debt was rather more complicated. In addition to Alison's severance pay, Hilliard had demanded ten thousand pounds for his silence. On a rational level he understood that you should never give in to blackmail, but on an emotional level he had to protect Lola: blameless, trusting, faithful Lola. He couldn't risk her finding out about his coping mechanism – his *little hooker habit*. No, the loathsome prick had to be paid off and if there was any justice in the world, which of course there wasn't, he would die a painful and imminent death.

More disturbing was that Hilliard's ten thousand paled against the spiralling cost of the American folly. The renovations to the Treehouse – God, how tired he was of hearing about it – had cost him more than five times that and it still wasn't finished. And his Midas sales touch had deserted him, or so it seemed. He hadn't closed a deal in almost a year, which meant professional embarrassment and slashed personal income. No deal, no commission. He was fifty-seven years old and the prospect of financial ruin was frighteningly real. There was a solution, but it seemed unthinkable until he had a meeting at the bank to review his accounts, after which it seemed not only thinkable, but essential. He would have to sell the Grange.

Once he had got used to the idea, he actually felt relieved. They had bought it as newlyweds, full of love and hope – a beautiful home where they could raise their family – but it stopped being a home when Clarissa died. Saskia's little Edgware Road apartment felt more like home than the Grange did. He could relax there, be himself. Not so with Lola. As if it hadn't been bad enough before, she had returned from California distant and moody. He knew it was wrong not being with her on the anniversary of Clarissa's death. Saskia had comforted him but Lola had to face it alone. Perhaps it was a transgression too far and there was no more forgiveness in her heart. He would find out soon enough, when he told her about the Grange.

The dreaded weekend stretched before them, barren and empty, their emotional estrangement laid bare. Earlier, when Duncan had walked into the village with Darcy, he had thought about Clarissa's last morning, how she jumped in and out of puddles, giggling with delight at every splash: a good memory, a happy memory until the final memory stormed in like an invading army and trampled all over it.

Someone drove past in a muddy Land Rover – one of the men who had helped to shift the tractor. They didn't make eye contact. What was left for him and Lola here anyway? Kathy and the new girl managed the livery yard. Snook was a frail old man – he wouldn't be around forever. They knew people in the village but had no real friends to speak of. That was how he would put it to Lola. Not the money side of things – he wouldn't worry her with that.

The kettle boiled and Duncan made two mugs of tea. Lola had been home for four days but her sleep pattern was still on California time. He carried the mugs upstairs, the newspaper under his arm, and was surprised to see that she wasn't asleep, but sitting up in bed talking on the phone. She finished the call when Duncan walked in.

'Who was that?' he asked.

She took a sip of tea and rearranged the duvet.

'Cain McCann,' she said.

'What did he want? Nothing wrong at the house, is there?'

'No. He just had a few questions about the kitchen.'

Duncan checked his watch.

'It's the middle of the night there.'

Lola looked at him, wide eyed.

'Is it?'

'Why would he call at midnight to talk about kitchens? At the weekend too?'

Lola shrugged her shoulders.

'I've absolutely no idea. Does it matter?'

Duncan switched on Sky News.

'Just seems odd, that's all.'

A pretty female presenter talked over footage of staff leaving Lehman Brothers with their belongings in cardboard boxes; the universal symbol for 'you're fired'.

'We need to have a chat,' he said.

'Oh?' said Lola.

In his head he'd been over it a dozen times but now that he had to say the words out loud – *we need to sell the Grange* – he felt sick to his stomach. She looked so innocent sitting there with her mug of tea, her hair dishevelled from sleep.

'I think we need a fresh start,' he said.

She raised her eyebrows.

'Do we?'

'Yes. Away from here. London perhaps?' He hadn't meant to say that. London was for work and for Saskia. Lola didn't fit there. 'Or not. It can be anywhere you want.'

Surprise gave way to confusion.

'I don't understand,' she said.

'The house felt so big and empty while you were away. It made me wonder if maybe it wasn't time to think about selling, getting somewhere smaller, more manageable.'

Lies. He had spent every night with Saskia – hadn't been home at all.

'This is very sudden,' she said, glancing at the TV – the stock market depicted by a stark downward line. 'Is it anything to do with that?' she asked, pointing to the screen.

Duncan shook his head.

'Not at all. I just feel it might be time to move.'

A braver man would have said it was a family home without a family, that all those empty rooms mocked them, taunted them with their failure. He didn't say that. Instead, he reasoned that as she would be spending more time at the Treehouse, it didn't make sense to keep the Grange. Lola didn't respond at first, just fixed him with a perplexed stare.

'I need time to process this,' she said finally.

Delivered with an English accent, the Americanism sounded ridiculous. But she didn't say no or cry or start talking about how she could never leave the place where Clarissa had lived her short life. She seemed calm and reflective, which he took to be a very good sign. At least she was prepared to consider it.

The weekend followed its usual pattern, Duncan in his study and Lola either at the kitchen table, typing feverishly on her laptop, or over at the livery yard. Having planted the idea of selling the Grange, he left her alone to mull it over. He had much to mull over too. Try as he might, it was impossible to deny the truth of his situation. He loved Lola, but was in love with Saskia. He had never taken a mistress before – never wanted one. The prostitutes didn't count. They were a vice, certainly, a necessary form of escapism, but there was no emotional attachment, nothing that detracted from his feelings for Lola. But now there was Saskia. That first time with her he knew this was something different. Not about her as such, but about him with her. What did that say about his marriage? Surely if he was in love with Lola he would have been immune to Saskia. Instead, he became obsessed with her. When they were apart, he missed her – pined for her like a lovesick teenager. He didn't miss Lola.

On the contrary, he looked forward to her spending time in America. What bound him to Lola was history and guilt. Their marriage had no exit strategy. She had already lost her only child – how could he cut her loose into the world, alone and unprepared?

He thought back to their whirlwind courtship – how shocked he was to discover that someone so beautiful could be a virgin at twenty-two. Even then Lola's life was sheltered and insular. Despite working at a smart London gallery, she had no interest in the parties, the free-flowing champagne and cocktails, the endless supply of cocaine. It was her extraordinary mix of innocence and elegance that had captivated him, and once they were married she couldn't wait to leave the city and make a life for them in the country. All she wanted was a home and a family and despite all the heartbreak she had never quite lost that innocence. He was the only man she had ever slept with. No, whatever accommodation he made, whatever shape his future took, there would have to be a place for Lola.

A message from Saskia on his BlackBerry asked him to call her. She was working on the personal statement for her university application and wanted his advice on what she should say she had been doing these eight years in London. He didn't want to think about what she had been doing. It was an anomaly, something inconsistent with his view of her.

'Public Relations in the hospitality industry,' he suggested.

'And if I need a reference?'

'We'll work something out.'

King's was her first choice, then Manchester, Southampton and Leeds. The thought of her moving to a different city was too distressing to contemplate. Perhaps she wouldn't get the grades – four As was the standard entry requirement for Medicine – or King's would accept her and she could stay in London. He told himself it was a long way off – a lot could happen between winter and summer.

The Grange had five bedrooms and four receptions rooms if you included his study. Such a large house was a liability, especially in the winter when the oil-fired central heating blasted out from six in the morning until eleven o'clock at night, but it did at least allow its residents to avoid each other if they chose to. It was suppertime before Duncan saw Lola again, over a rack of lamb and a bottle of Argentinean Malbec. All the Napa wines had been drunk and Lola didn't bring any back with her. Duncan thought it rather remiss, although he didn't say so. She knew he was particularly fond of Opus One and expected her to produce a bottle or two from her suitcase. Still, given the circumstances she probably wasn't feeling particularly fond of him so he *cut her some slack*, to use another dreadful Americanism.

They exchanged small talk about their respective days – did he get much work done, was everything alright over at the yard? – and agreed that the lamb was very tender but the wine had lost some of its fruit. It was only when Duncan poured the last dregs into Lola's empty glass that he broached the subject of the house again.

'I wondered if you had any more thoughts about selling?' he asked bluntly, too bluntly if the look on Lola's face was anything to go by. She seemed startled – caught off guard.

'Mmm,' she said. 'Yes, I have thought about it.'

He waited expectantly, but that appeared to be it. He got up from the table and fetched a second bottle of wine.

'Not for me,' said Lola.

'Are you sure?' said Duncan. 'It's better than the last one. Just a small glass?'

She shook her head.

'No, really.'

Fine. He poured himself a generous glass and sat back down again.

'And what did you think?' he said.

'About what?'

Was she being deliberately obtuse? He wanted it to sound appealing – a positive not a negative.

'About a fresh start somewhere new.'

She looked around the kitchen – about the same size as Saskia's entire apartment – and sighed.

'I think you're right,' she said.

Tantalised by the prospect of a return to solvency, he offered a grateful smile.

'In a year or two,' she continued. 'I mean, if I'm in California for months at a time and you're in London, then it doesn't really make any sense to keep this.'

Right direction, wrong timescale. He drank some wine.

'Why wait?' he said as brightly as he could manage.

Her brow furrowed into a delicate crease. Oh God, was she going to talk about Clarissa?

'I'm not ready,' she said quietly. 'Too many memories to walk away from. I need to get used to the idea.'

'Of course,' he said, relieved that she had only alluded to their daughter's omnipresence. 'But I don't imagine it will ever be easy – perhaps the best approach is simply to do it.'

Again he waited.

'Why now?' she asked.

It was a reasonable question with many unreasonable answers: because I felt so guilty I bought a house I couldn't afford, because I was blackmailed and had to pay my tormentor, because if I can financially support my mistress she won't have to sell sex to strangers.

'The Treehouse will be finished soon and you're so much happier there,' he said.

She bit her lip like she used to. He hadn't seen her do that in a long time. It reminded him of the virginal gallerina who offered him champagne and her undying love. He wasn't worthy of the latter.

'I told them about Clarissa,' she said.

He knew immediately that she was referring to her California coterie. So now they saw his true colours – Duncan Drummond, the man who let his little girl die. He couldn't blame Lola. The Curtellas treated her like a long-lost daughter – it was only natural she would confide in them.

'I'm sorry you had to deal with it all on your own,' he said. 'I should have been there.'

She shrugged.

'Well, you weren't.' Her tone was resigned, not accusatory. 'Perhaps I will have some more wine after all.'

Duncan filled her glass and topped up his own. His instinct was to change the subject, but maybe if he showed contrition she might relent and agree to sell the house.

'It must have been very difficult,' he said.

Lola sipped thoughtfully.

'Yes, at first,' she said. 'But Cain was so understanding –'

'Cain? You mean McCann?'

She blinked in the same fast, fluttery way that Alison had done when he challenged her about Hilliard.

'Yes.'

'I thought you meant that you told the Curtellas.'

'I did. I told them too.'

'Why McCann?'

She sipped some more.

'I mentioned to you that we spent the day together sorting out stuff for the Treehouse. Well, we got talking over a drink and he asked if we'd ever wanted children –'

'He's the bloody builder. What gives him the right to delve into our personal life?'

Yes, Duncan was well aware of his hypocrisy but this was Lola, for God's sake. He had his doubts about McCann from the very beginning.

'He's not the *builder*, as such, and anyway, it wasn't like that,' she said weakly. 'I was upset and he was kind.'

I bet he was. So naive – didn't she realise what men were like? Duncan blamed himself for having cosseted her too much. And why did she feel the need to jump to McCann's defence? All very tiresome.

'Look, I'm sorry,' he said. 'But I don't like to think of McCann –'

'You're making too much of it,' she said. 'Can we talk about something else, please?'

Could they? Their usual topics were the Treehouse, what to have for dinner, what to drink with dinner, the weather and – only occasionally – anecdotes from the livery yard. So now they whiled away half an hour discussing a young gelding, new to the yard and so ill mannered it couldn't be turned out in the same paddock as the other horses. Kathy had offered some much needed schooling but the owner didn't want to pay for it so the poor animal grazed on his own while the other horses had company.

'Such a pity,' Lola said. 'Horses aren't solitary creatures – they're herd animals, happiest in groups.'

Duncan affected the appropriate degree of inter-est before revisiting the question of moving, but Lola's eyes glassed over as he made his case. It was obvious her thoughts were elsewhere – California, no doubt. There was nothing to be gained by prolonging the discussion. He suggested she have an early night while he cleared away the dishes. Such a rare offer should have aroused vigorous protest, but instead Lola left with a full glass of wine and a grateful nod in his general direction.

Mondays brought pleasure and pain, although in reverse order. Life at AquaEco had become an ordeal for Duncan. A succession of temps had replaced the duplicitous Alison, none of whom had proved satisfactory. And with so few sales leads, and no actual sales, morale in his department was at an all-time low. Those who had managed to find alternative employment jumped ship with ill-concealed glee, and those that stayed did so, he suspected, not out of loyalty or commitment, but out of fear.

The sceptre of a long and deep recession loomed large and real, predicted by every pundit on the planet. Only a fool would tender their resignation in such a hostile climate. Except that was exactly what Duncan longed to do. He believed that each huddle by the photocopier, each snigger or sideways look, was aimed at him. It was only paranoia if it wasn't true, but Alison had told Hilliard about his Carfax assignations – how many other people had she told? Was Duncan now the butt of office jokes – a sad old pervert, derided and mocked behind his back? Bad enough that his professional failings were common knowledge – AquaEco losing two major contracts to industry competitor Dawes had made a few column inches in the *Financial Times* – but to have his personal failings the subject of gossip and innuendo was the finishing blow. A mere stroll along the corridor rendered him rigid with apprehension. He was convinced that the temps reviled him. He had to psych himself up to go into meetings, sure that everyone was judging him from a position of ridicule or disgust.

Against all his stiff-upper-lip principles, and at Saskia's insistence, he finally agreed to see a doctor. With impeccable insight she reasoned that suffering in silence was like self-flagellation – very Catholic but not very helpful. We're all sinners, she reminded him, and you think your sins are so bad that you deserve to suffer. But who does it help, Duncan? Who does it help?

The anti-depressants he was prescribed took the edge off, but didn't do much more. Paranoia still stalked him, if that was what it was. How could he possibly tell? When he dropped into a colleague's leaving party, did he imagine a sudden hush in conversation, or was there *actually* a sudden hush in conversation? And when he searched out a friendly smile, the smallest gesture inviting him to join that group, come sit at that table, did he imagine being ignored, or was he *actually* ignored? A man could slip into insanity trying to unravel the nuances and subtexts, the subjective absurdity of it all. So he took the anti-depressants and sent his CV to an executive search agency, letting them know that for the right sort of package, Duncan Drummond, Sales Director with thirty years' experience in the water-recycling business, could be tempted away from AquaEco. *Nothing at present* was the lacklustre response, *but we'll keep you in mind if we hear of anything.* Duncan told himself it was the economy, the recession, the understandable wariness of the moment, because the alternative – that he was too old or too mediocre to get another high-flying position – only added to his anguish.

So, as if each strained weekend in deepest Somerset wasn't enough to break his ailing spirit, Mondays at the office threatened to finish the job. Pleasure and pain, he reminded himself. Now for the pleasure. Instead of the slow cab ride to Paddington and the long train ride to Bristol, on Mondays he made the short and pleasant journey to Edgware Road, where his mistress waited with a warm heart and a cold Scotch. Clever, worldly, understanding Saskia, with whom he could be his true self.

Since early afternoon he had been watching the clock, counting down the hours until he could hold her, smell the apricot shampoo in her hair, kiss her soft welcoming lips. He had only known her six months but couldn't imagine his life without her. That was what he thought of as he jogged up the stairs, his heart pounding as much with anticipation as aerobic effort. And when he knocked on her door – she hadn't offered a key and he didn't feel he could request one – he recalled the exhilarating keenness of a child on Christmas morning. The memory brought a tingle of anticipation but when the door opened he saw her perfect, porcelain face, marred by a vivid purple bruise. It began over her right eye and bled down towards her cheekbone. Her top lip had another bruise – smaller, like an angry blood blister – and a cut about a centimetre in length. Shock rooted him to the spot. She pulled him inside and closed the door. He dropped his briefcase with a thud.

'What happened?' he said.

She tried to turn away but he took hold of her and turned her back to face him.

'Saskia, talk to me. What the hell happened?'

She shrugged and tried to turn away again.

'Did someone hit you?'

She lowered her eyes but didn't deny it. A painful spasm gripped his gut and he thought he might retch. He asked again.

'Did someone hit you?'

'Please don't shout at me, Duncan.'

'I'm not shouting *at* you. I'm just shouting. Who did this?'

Duncan despised them all – the one-nighters who fucked her and fucked off and the regulars who asked for her by name. But the thought that one of them had hit her erupted in a compulsion to find the bastard and kill him. He squeezed Saskia's shoulders so hard that she shook herself free from his grasp.

'I'm sorry,' he said, trying to regain control.

He reached for her, gently this time. She hid her face against his suit while she sobbed and all he could do was stroke her hair. What else had the monster done to her? Were there other bruises Duncan was yet to see? He needed a drink. Yes, anti-depressants and alcohol didn't mix, but these were exceptional circumstances. It took three large Scotches before his heart slowed from a sprint to a jog, and despite her pleas to let it drop, he badgered her to name her attacker or, at the very least, explain why she was protecting him.

'I'm not protecting him,' she cried. 'But you can't undo it. Please, Duncan, I don't want to talk about this.'

They had never argued and he didn't want to upset her even more, but how could he forget about it when it was written, quite literally, all over her face? He asked her one more time, his voice as calm and measured as he could manage.

'I need to know what happened.'

She took the tumbler from his hands and sipped some Scotch.

'He wear suit and wedding ring, like you.'

Was she trying to hurt him with the comparison because she was hurt?

'He spoke with good accent, like you.'

She took another sip.

'But he is not like you. He want to beat me before he fuck me.'

This time Duncan did retch. A sour cocktail of bile and Scotch scalded his throat.

'No more,' he shouted, on his feet now. 'It stops here, Saskia. I won't let you do this anymore!'

She sprang to her feet as well, every bit as angry.

'You think I want this?' she screamed. 'You think when I was little girl I dream of being whore to rich men? No. I dream of being doctor.' She picked her textbooks off the table and flung them to the floor. 'I work hard to make my dream come true but I have no family to help me, no husband to help me, no one to help me.'

Stunned, Duncan tried to say that she had him but that only enraged her more.

'I do not have you,' she yelled. The cut on her lip split open and blood trickled into her mouth. 'You come here to get what you can't get from your wife, then you go back to her, your big house, your rich man's life. You leave me here, in this small cold apartment, and you think you can tell me what to do?' She opened the door. 'You are no different to the other men that use me. Get out. Get out and don't come back.'

Duncan walked along Brick Street, numb with shock. It wasn't only what she had said – every word sickeningly true – but the way she said it. Screamed it. He was completely at a loss. How was he supposed to react? Lola never screamed – never even raised her voice. Her parents' furious rows taught her that shouting did nothing to resolve disputes, it only made them louder. She brought that knowledge to her marriage like a dowry. Saskia's anger was raw and authentic and he was hopelessly unprepared to deal with it.

He needed somewhere to sit and think, and the dimly lit jazz bar on the corner seemed as good a place as any. A single saxophonist stood on the small raised stage playing a low, melancholy tune. The sour taste of Scotch still lingered in Duncan's mouth so he ordered water and a martini. Like some sad old loner in a black-and-white film, he slouched at the bar and stared into his drink. He had let Saskia down, just as he had Lola and Clarissa. No amount of booze or anti-depressants would change that. He didn't deserve to feel better anyway. Did Saskia mean it when she told him not to come back? The thought of life without her was unbearable. Two martinis later he convinced himself she had been lashing out, that her anger was really aimed at the pervert who beat her. He paid for his drinks and left.

She answered the door in her pink dressing gown, her hair wrapped up in a towel. He had braced himself this time but her face looked even worse. The bruise seemed to have deepened in colour and spread further down her cheek, and her lip – her beautiful rosebud lip – was swollen and scabbed. When she saw him her eyes filled with tears. She said something in Russian that he didn't understand and he threw his arms around her and held her while she cried. He said he was sorry so many times that she attempted a lopsided smile and said yes, yes, you're a very sorry man. She poured them both some brandy and they sat down on the sofa. The textbooks were back in a neat pile on the table. He hadn't known what he was going to say until the moment came to say it, and then it seemed the only solution. He would give her enough money so that she could concentrate on her studies and didn't have to work. Then, after the Grange was sold, he would buy her an apartment of her own. When she asked if he would live there too he said yes, when his wife was in America, he would live there too.

'So everybody is happy,' said Saskia, and he thought of verisimilitude – the appearance of truth. It would have to do.

To make a promise was one thing – to keep it was another. Before Duncan could keep his promise to Saskia, he had to get Lola to agree to sell the Grange. How to resolve that problem was what occupied him, filling the space that ought to have been occupied with how to devise an aggressive sales strategy to bring in desperately needed new business. The fallout from the economic crisis – it had gone from a downturn to a full-blown crisis – contaminated every industry. If he had ever doubted the theory of globalisation, he didn't now. No one was building luxury hotels – the lifeblood of his new business sales. And with the world looking to oil as the planet's sacred elixir, water was not forgotten, but it was taken for granted.

At the end of the month, Duncan paid two thousand pounds into Saskia's bank account. Her rent alone was fifteen hundred so two thousand wasn't enough, but the bank refused to increase his overdraft, citing their newfound duty to 'lend responsibly'. Well, at least he knew where he stood. He told Saskia he would deposit another thousand in a few days and she kissed him and thanked him and told him how happy he had made her.

The bruises hadn't completely faded – a visceral reminder of what could happen if she carried on working, and the pressure he was under to ensure that she didn't. She concealed them under make-up but when they were alone in the apartment, she kept her face bare. She liked her skin to be clean and fresh, and he liked it that way too. How could he disappoint her when she trusted him completely? No, all he had to do was move some money around – sell what was left of his share portfolio and juggle his credit-card limits. He approached it as one might a Sudoku puzzle, the task being to get the correct numbers in the correct places. Just like Sudoku, it was harder than it looked.

That was what he was doing when the temp buzzed through to say he had been summoned by the chairman. Had he forgotten to produce a report, a set of figures? He asked the temp but she was clueless so when he walked along the corridor to the other end of the building, and was ushered into the chairman's spacious, wood-panelled office, he had no idea what to expect. Panic crouched like a predator waiting to pounce. Fear of an attack was almost as bad as an attack itself, not knowing when or where it would seize him, always having to be on his guard. The chairman stood up – a year younger than Duncan, but balding and rotund – and offered his hand.

'Robert,' said Duncan. 'Good to see you.'

'Yes, you too. Please,' he said, gesturing towards the deep leather chair at the visitor's side of the desk.

Duncan sat and before he had a chance to speak – enquiring after his golf game was usually a good opener – the chairman came straight to the point.

'Dawes has proposed a takeover bid. It's generous and early signs put the shareholders on board so we intend to make an announcement before close of business.'

Duncan was dumbfounded.

'Out of the blue?' he asked.

'Yes and no,' said the Chairman. 'We were aware of their interest but the timing was a bit of a surprise. No matter – the deal is a good one and of course the share price will jump, so that's a bit of a windfall.'

Was he being facetious? He must know that Duncan had sold all his AquaEco shares so would miss out.

'Anyway,' said the chairman. 'There will be some changes, a bit of restructuring, some voluntary redundancies, and I wondered if that might be of interest to you?'

The predator unfurled inside Duncan's chest and punched out fast, irregular heartbeats, so that all he could manage were tight shallow breaths. Something kicked inside his head and it was difficult not to squint against the light that streamed in through the windows.

'I'll certainly give it some thought,' he said, although he knew that he wouldn't.

He had already tested the market and not been invited for a single interview. And however much he relished the idea of escaping his now tainted office life, it would plunge him even deeper into debt, something he couldn't possibly allow.

'Perhaps voluntary wasn't the right word,' said the chairman, his hand under his chin in a thoughtful, almost philosophical pose.

The cramping pains in Duncan's legs were his cue to leave. Déjà vu – Gonzalez's office, or more accurately, the street outside his office, the scene of his humiliating grand mal of panic attacks.

'I'll give it some thought,' he said again, pushing himself up out of the chair.

To his great relief, his legs appeared fully functional. The chairman stood too.

'I don't think you understand, Duncan,' he said. 'It wasn't a request. Your department has had very disappointing results of late.' He paused as if to observe a minute's silence for the dead. 'Dawes, on the other hand, show very robust sales.'

Hilliard. Just the thought of his paunchy pink face made Duncan seethe with loathing. So the little shit really had got his revenge, twice over.

'I'm sorry, Duncan, but you know how these things are.'

It felt crucial at that moment for Duncan to walk away with dignity, his self-respect intact. No scene, no drama – just two professionals doing what had to be done.

'Of course,' he said, and offered his hand. 'I'll clear my desk.'

Perhaps he hadn't given the anti-depressants enough credit. A few weeks ago, that scene would have triggered an explosion of blind panic but here he was, in his office – soon to be his ex-office – coolly packing his personal effects into a cardboard box. The TV image of staff leaving Lehman Brothers popped into his head. He had wondered how they felt and now he knew. Stunned, like an animal in the seconds before it was slaughtered. Lola looked up at him from a mother-of-pearl frame, smiling and serene in a white floaty dress, a beach sunset in the background. He put the photograph in the cardboard box, face down. She shouldn't have to witness this.

The box was full in less than half an hour. Not much to show for a career. It was when he went over to the window that sadness and fear joined forces and it was as much as he could do not to cover his face in despair. This was the last time he would admire his privileged view from the nineteenth floor: the Thames, the bridges, the vibrant cityscape, the sense of being at the centre of things. No more. He was unemployed, possibly unemployable. In corporate years, fifty-seven was old. He would be fifty-eight in just over a month. A motorboat roared by, churning up the water as it bounced along its surface. It split the river in two and left a frothy, foamy wake. When the water was flat and glassy again, Duncan turned away, picked up the box and left. With a cursory nod to the indifferent temp, he headed along the corridor to the lift. No one came to say goodbye. It was as if he were leaving for lunch, not forever. So this was what failure felt like. In a moment of unwelcome self-awareness, he realised he was a weak man, a man destined to disappoint. He lacked the courage to tell his wife or his mistress the truth about his finances and made promises to both he was in no position to keep. He told himself that his motives were pure; he wanted to protect them, spare them undue worry. In truth, it was his own ego he wanted to protect, himself he wanted to spare.

The lift stopped at almost every floor. People got in and out, careful not to acknowledge the man holding the cardboard box for fear of contagion. They stood in silence, eyes cast upwards, intensely interested in the digital display that counted down the floors. On the ground floor they spilled out and scattered. Only twenty yards to the revolving doors but Duncan knew he wouldn't make it. The panic had tricked him – it had been there all along, waiting to unleash its malevolence to maximum effect in the busy foyer for all to see. He didn't remember falling to the floor or the commotion that followed, just faces peering down at him and then spinning out of focus. A dull pain clawed at his chest. It wasn't until he was in the ambulance that he registered what was going on. He tried to sit up but was strapped onto a stretcher, an oxygen mask over his mouth. The siren couldn't be for him, surely? When he tried to pull off the mask and tell the paramedic that he felt much better, she held it in place and told him not to talk.

They were at the hospital within minutes, his stretcher unloaded and hurried along a corridor that smelled of disinfectant and urine. The last time he was in a hospital was when Clarissa died. He closed his eyes and tried to imagine he was somewhere else. It was difficult with two nurses removing his jacket and tie and undoing his shirt buttons. The paramedics lifted him from the stretcher to a bed and pulled a faded floral curtain around it. One of them referred to it as a cubicle but that was an overstatement. The flimsy cloth did nothing to shield him from the din – screaming babies, an old drunk yelling 'fuck off' to no one in particular – or afford him any real privacy. The nurses wired him up to a monitor and asked if there was somebody he would like them to contact. Without a second thought, he gave Saskia's number. The fuzzy, loose feeling in his head, he put down to some sort of sedative. Even in his university days he had been more of a drink man than a drugs man, but now he realised he'd missed a trick. It was as if he was floating, light and unencumbered. Time passed – seconds, minutes, hours – he wasn't sure. An Indian woman in a white coat examined the print-out from the monitor and declared his heart was fine, although his blood pressure was slightly elevated.

'Severe anxiety can mimic the early signs of a heart attack,' she said. 'You should make an appointment to see your GP.'

My GP's an idiot, thought Duncan, but he said yes, he would do that.

'Your daughter's here,' she said. 'Would you like me to send her in?'

'Clarissa? Clarissa's here?'

His heart rate spiked, triggering an alarm on the monitor.

'Mr Drummond?' said the doctor. 'Try to stay calm.'

Disorientated, he pulled at the wires attached to his chest and tried to stand up.

'Where is she? Where's Clarissa?'

The curtain swished open and a second doctor appeared with two more nurses. As they grappled with Duncan and forced him back onto the bed, he felt sharp sting in his arm, then oblivion.

When he came around, Saskia was holding his hand. She had the look of a student – casual, preppy, heartbreakingly young, and as the fog cleared he realised the doctor's mistake. He remembered calling for Clarissa and experienced a fresh stab of loss that hurt more than any physical pain he could imagine.

'How are you feeling?' asked Saskia.

Her eyes were full of concern. In the stark fluorescent light he thought he could still make out a faint mark on her top lip.

'Foolish,' he said.

He wanted to go home. Not to Piliton, but to Edgware Road.

If he had believed in such things he would have sworn that malicious forces were at work, dismantling his life piece by piece. He even considered throwing himself at God's mercy, denouncing his sins and begging for forgiveness, but God hadn't listened to him before; why should he listen to him now? No, he needed to get a grip and think clearly, which wasn't easy with all the drugs swilling around in his system: Diazepam to stave off anxiety, a stronger anti-depressant, and Zopiclone to help him sleep. He had been given a prescription for more of the same when he was discharged a few hours later. Saskia had treated him like an invalid, helping him into a cab, even buckling up his seatbelt. She made him take the stairs slowly and insisted on carrying the box he had filled before leaving the office. Lola's picture was on the top, but Saskia said nothing.

By his third day on the unemployment scrapheap, he had made some decisions. Firstly, he would have to go back to the Grange. He had phoned Lola once the hospital had discharged him, and told her he would be staying in town to prepare for a board meeting. She didn't sound unduly bothered so he stretched it out for another day, but now he really did have to leave the sanctity of his Edgware Road refuge, where his mistress tended to his every need, and face his wife. Even through a haze of pharmaceuticals, the thought of telling her he had lost his job made him agitated and anxious. It wasn't just the money – although with the final payment on the Treehouse due, that was a large part of it – it was the loss of face. Lola looked up to him. Older, successful, self-assured – that was the man she married. What would she think of him now that he was unemployed, drowning in debt, medicated and pathetic? And it wasn't just his job he had lost, it was his confidence, his place in the world.

Which was why his second decision was that it would be kinder not to tell Lola about the whole redundancy thing. Perhaps the drugs were clouding his judgement, and yes, it was another lie by omission, but why burden her? It wasn't as if it was a problem she could fix. He would get his usual train in the mornings but instead of going to the office, he would come here, to Saskia's. And it was perfectly possible he had overreacted and his finances weren't even that dire. After all those years with the company he was bound to get a generous pay-off and even if he couldn't find another job, with his contacts and experience he could always pick up some lucrative consultancy work.

He might have believed his own bullshit if the memory of Lola imploring a lifeless Clarissa to wake up hadn't returned to torture him. That image had been his mental screensaver since her death, but had faded with Lola's blossoming happiness. And now it was back. If Duncan told her about Saskia he would tear her world to shreds all over again, but the strain of keeping his two lives separate propelled him towards a terrifying, heart-bursting panic that no amount of deep breaths could allay.

Saskia still stood over him like a vigilant nurse as he washed down the anti-depressants with a quick gulp of water, but she needn't have worried. His aversion to medication was a thing of the past, like his career and his dignity and the delusion that he was a decent human being. By the time he had gathered his things together and checked his BlackBerry (more out of habit than hope), the sedatives had begun to flood him with their numbing magic.

The train journey to Bristol had a surreal quality to it. Duncan sat in his usual seat, read his usual newspaper and recognised the usual commuters engrossed in their various electronic devices – everything the same but different. Work had given structure and purpose to his entire existence and without it he was lost. Five milligrams of Diazepam assuaged the incipient panic; the thick fuzziness in his head seemed a small price to pay. Part of him wanted Lola to see that something was very wrong, that something fundamental had changed. If she coaxed him, he would tell her. She didn't coax him, though – she didn't even notice. They spoke little in the car and when she asked about work he said it was fine.

The phone never rang in the evening. All Duncan's calls came through on his BlackBerry, and who would call Lola? When Duncan heard a man's voice, an American accent, he looked over at Lola and mouthed that it was McCann. She took the phone from him even though McCann hadn't asked to speak to her, but Duncan didn't object since he had no interest in hearing about the Treehouse or anything to do with it. He remembered his indignation when Lola told him she had confided in McCann about Clarissa, but really it was shame and jealousy he had felt (exposed as a negligent father, his wife comforted by another man). Watching her on the phone to McCann now, Duncan was too medicated to feel very much at all. Lola's responses were brief and matter-of-fact and when she replaced the receiver, he felt obliged to ask if everything was alright.

'Good,' she said. 'Very good, actually. It was going to be a surprise, but the Treehouse will be ready for us to have Christmas there.'

'Christmas?' said Duncan.

'Yes, why not?' said Lola.

Because the thought of Saskia on her own in that cold apartment was horrible. Because the thought of not seeing her for what – a week, two weeks? – was even more horrible. He knew he wasn't supposed to drink with his medication, but he poured a large glass of wine anyway – an acidic Viognier that Lola had picked up at the supermarket.

'I just hadn't thought about it,' said Duncan.

'It's only a few weeks away,' said Lola.

This wasn't the conversation he had planned. The only thing on his agenda had been putting the Grange up for sale, but that had been hijacked by the Treehouse and Christmas and Lola's request for another expensive trip to the West Coast of America. He tried to form a coherent response but was thinking in slow motion. Everything in his head felt vague, not fully formed. Lola wore that far-away look he was all too familiar with. A good husband would have asked what was wrong, but he wasn't a good husband. Besides, he already knew. Christmas without their child was what was wrong. It was almost as bad as the anniversary of her death, which, he needed no reminding, he had made Lola face without him. No, she had the upper hand here – the best he could do was be gracious in defeat. And he could probably scramble enough air miles for a round trip in business class. Ten hours in an economy seat was not an option.

'If that's what you want,' he said. 'Why don't you go ahead and I'll join you on Christmas Eve?'

That was how he would put it to Saskia. She could have him all to herself for the next few weeks but Christmas he would have to spend with his wife. And while Lola was away, he would get an estate agent around to value the Grange. He expected her to protest about having to make the journey on her own again, but she didn't.

'That's a good idea,' she said. 'There'll be a lot to do – furnishings, buying things for the kitchen, that sort of stuff. I can have everything ready when you arrive.'

Duncan saw his severance pay being sucked into the bottomless pit of his Californian folly. The Treehouse was supposed to make things better but it had made them worse. He was still a stranger in his own marriage but now he was broke too. No, he would have to come clean and tell Lola he had lost his job. If he could just find a way to break it to her that didn't sound so terminal – fabricate a few interviews, some consultancy – but trying to think was like wading through mud. Tomorrow. He didn't have the energy to do this now. What difference would one more day make? And besides, maybe tomorrow would bring some good news.

He finished his wine and stood up.

'So that's settled then?' she said. He had lost the thread of their conversation and was practically incoherent with fatigue.

'I'll sort out some flights,' she said.

'Fine, yes. Sorry, but I'm going to have to turn in.'

He was almost too tired to register it, and certainly too tired to ponder it, but he didn't understand Lola's reaction. She had got what she wanted – Christmas with the Curtellas *et al.* – and yet she remained distracted. But in the seconds before sleep claimed him, a single thought cut through the blurred haziness with searing clarity. It had all been a huge mistake – their wedding anniversary in California, the Treehouse – grand gestures to show Lola he was truly sorry, that he would do anything to make her happy again. How hopelessly misguided he had been. Lola's happiness was no longer within his gift.

Every moment of every day he deceived her and no amount of houses or holidays could cancel that out. It would be easier if he didn't love her, but he did, just not in the same urgent way he loved Saskia. His love for Lola was quiet and suffused with duty, his instinct to protect her, to provide for her. She was the innocent victim in a mess of Duncan's making, and the thought of destroying her nascent happiness paralysed him with guilt.

Lately he wished they had been able to fight – shout, smash things, exorcise their grievances. Lola's aversion to confrontation was something he had always respected, but that was before Saskia flung her textbooks on the floor and threw him out of her flat. It was shocking at the time but it deepened their commitment to each other and brought them closer together. It made him see how stifling Lola's long-suffering saintliness was. When he thought of growing old with her in the strained civility of their marriage, passion and laughter a far distant memory, it felt like crawling towards death.

He heard the back door open and close as she put Darcy out. Duncan turned onto his side, frustrated that he could be this tired and still not able to sleep. Soon Lola would come to bed and they would lie back to back in the darkness. He thought of taking another Zopiclone but couldn't summon the energy to get up and fetch his toilet bag from the bathroom. He kept his stash of pills there so that Lola wouldn't find them. Part of him hoped she would. It would force him to tell her everything and say, *look what it's doing to me – look how bad I feel.* At least then it would be over.

Sometimes he daydreamed that they sold the Grange for a good price, Lola started a new life in California, he started a new life in London with Saskia and everyone was happy ever after. Other times he imagined finding Lola hanging by the neck, unable to face the future alone.

More than once he wished he had never met Saskia. She had made his life both better and worse, and the fiction that he could compartmentalise – wife in Somerset, mistress in London – was laughable. The strain was literally killing him and he didn't know how long he could keep up the charade of going to work every day. If they didn't sell the Grange soon, he would run out of money.

The back door opened again and he heard Lola call Darcy. Duncan turned onto his other side and sighed with relief that she was going to America. He could be with Saskia, who always held him as he drifted into a drugged and dreamless sleep. Being apart from her felt like his skin didn't fit.

Thirteen

Lola gazed down on Great Salt Lake, thirty-five thousand feet below. She hadn't realised that Salt Lake City actually had a salt lake. It looked dirty white, like trodden snow, and vast. America was vast. In an hour or so they would fly over the Rockies, over another unique and dramatic landscape. Maybe some day she would travel across the whole of America in one of those huge camper vans. What an adventure that would be. For now, though, she was happy to stay put in the Napa Valley, with its mountains and vineyards and forests and friends.

Joanne was like the mother she never had. Addicts think only of themselves, their needs driving every relationship until there are no relationships left. Alcohol had robbed Lola of a mother – a father too, perhaps, if that was why he deserted them. When Lola had cleared out the cottage after her mother's death, she found a photograph of her father tucked away in the bottom of the ugly mahogany sideboard where her mother stashed bottles of gin and vodka. No wedding album, no random family snapshots, just this one, unremarkable picture. He stood with his hands in his trouser pockets wearing a self-conscious smile and a knitted pullover. There were flowers and grass, something concrete in the background. The resemblance surprised her, the realisation that she looked like him: wild auburn waves, high cheekbones, toothy smile.

The indelible mark of genetics. She wondered what Clarissa would look like now.

The seatbelt sign lit up and the captain warned of turbulence ahead. Lola closed her eyes and saw Cain's smooth chest, the way his torso broadened out from the waist like Michelangelo's Vitruvian Man, his strong arms and thick beaded wrists. He smelled of sawdust and the sea.

It was difficult to believe she had slept with him – completely out of character, although there were extenuating circumstances. She wasn't sure if it was because she was sad about Clarissa, or happy to finally be able to talk about her. Cain had held her as she shivered and cried, but more than that – he had *listened*. Lola remembered being lightheaded with relief. She had wrapped her sorrow in a bubble of words and let it float away.

The next evening, when they stood on the Curtellas' deck and she told him it should never have happened, it wasn't because she regretted it. On the contrary – sex with Cain was beautiful and sensual and passionate. But she was married and however imperfect her relationship with Duncan, he was her husband and she was still seeing things in black and white.

The grey haze of uncertainty descended gradually in the few days that followed. Reluctantly, Cain had accepted there could be nothing physical between them, but the time they spent collaborating on the Treehouse, furniture shopping in San Francisco, walking Riley together, had been intimate in so many other ways. If she objected when he held her hand, he would smile, one eyebrow raised, and say, 'Really?' He'd let her hand go and then take it again a little while later, as if she hadn't said anything at all. Sometimes he'd plant a chaste kiss on her cheek, or slip his arm around her waist. She had forgotten what it was like to relax and be herself. With Duncan she had learned to be guarded to the point where it was second nature. When the time came to return to her barren life in England, Cain drove her to the airport and she insisted he drop her outside. He pulled her suitcase from the boot, set it down on the pavement, and hesitated a moment before he put his mouth on hers. Her mind emptied of everything except how wrong it felt to leave him.

Back at the Grange, Lola's existence revolved around the torrent of emails she exchanged with Cain and their long, frequent telephone calls. Intimate late-night conversations were her favourite, just before she fell asleep. They spoke about everything. Cain was so open – emotionally available, he called it – she felt she knew him better than she knew Duncan. Often, when she had finished talking to Cain, the glow of intimacy still warm on her skin, she would think of Duncan alone at the Carfax and feel ashamed. She had Cain and Duncan had no one. Cain said she couldn't be sure of that, but Duncan's moods veered between tense and tormented, interspersed with occasional bouts of eerie calm. If he did have someone, she certainly didn't make him happy.

It suited her that he was hardly ever home, although the Grange wouldn't be home for much longer. To assuage her guilt she had agreed to sell it. They hadn't talked about where they would go afterwards.

Cain urged her to come clean with Duncan. For him it was simple – *tell him you want the Treehouse and then you'll walk away.* Cain was right of course, and Lola had no intention of insisting on a large settlement. As long as she had enough to live a quiet life in St Helena, Duncan could have the rest. She was the guilty party, after all, and he was the one who had earned the money. It was only right he should keep most of it.

Several times she had waited anxiously for Duncan to come home from work, determined to confess, but lost her nerve when she saw how tired he looked, how weighed down with worry. It wasn't just that she wanted to avoid a terrible scene (although the thought of it rendered her weak with dread), she wanted to hold on to the swell of joy she felt now that Cain was in her life. She knew it was selfish and cowardly, but what could she say to Duncan anyway – how could she explain herself? Duncan would never cheat on her; he was far too moral and principled. Too Catholic. When they married, it meant everything to him that she had never been with another man. He said it made her rare and precious, and he would cherish her forever. Knowing she had been with Cain would devastate him. Duncan had no family to speak of. He had acquaintances and colleagues but no close friends, no one to turn to. How would he cope without her? He couldn't cook or do laundry and a pitiful image of him sitting with a tray of microwaved food on his lap crippled her with guilt. When she confided this to Cain he said Duncan would probably move into the hotel he spent so much time at, then he wouldn't have to worry about any of that domestic stuff. He was trying to make her feel better, so Lola couldn't bring herself to explain that the mental image was a metaphor for Duncan being abandoned and alone, and room service at the Carfax was largely beside the point.

She hated that Duncan might think she was punishing him for not being with her on the anniversary of Clarissa's death. She had begged him to go to California, he refused, she slept with Cain. Cause and effect. That wasn't how it was but Lola could see that was how it might look. But why torture herself trying to second-guess what Duncan might think or do? On an intuitive level he must know the marriage had run its course. They hadn't talked properly in months, hadn't kissed or hugged or made love. Even when Duncan was at home, they were only in the same room for the purposes of eating or sleeping. When the time was right, that was how she would put it to him. The marriage was already over – she would never have entered into a relationship with Cain if she thought otherwise. Sleeping with Cain was a beginning and an end.

The plane rolled and dropped and someone let out a cry. Lola gripped the armrests and waited for it to be over. How sad to think she might plummet to her death and miss out on the second chance she had been given. It was messy and complicated with so much still to resolve, but now she knew for certain what before she hardly dared to hope: she could be happy again.

Her heart tapped out a quick, staccato beat as she pulled her suitcase into the arrivals hall. The sea of faces blurred into one – an indistinct collage with no Cain. The lights and noise and busyness spun around her at a dizzying pace. She turned three hundred and sixty degrees but still couldn't see him. Fatigue and the stinging fluorescent light marred her vision. She fumbled in her bag for a tissue and as she dabbed her eyes, Cain's beaming face came into focus.

'Sorry,' he said. 'I went to get these.'

He handed her a bunch of shop-bought flowers; wilted yellow tulips, pink carnations past their best and an incongruous sprig of holly, all crammed together inside a limp sheaf of cellophane.

'Pretty lame, huh?' he said.

Lola looked at the flowers.

'They're lovely,' she said, and they both laughed because they really weren't.

He pulled her towards him and they kissed deeply. Lola knew how shameful it must look – the age gap, the public display of intimacy – but she was too happy to care. Shame was overrated anyway.

Downtown San Francisco sparkled with Christmas lights. Lola had taken Clarissa up to London one year to see the lights switched on at Harrods. She told Cain how they had queued for over an hour to see Santa and when they finally got their turn, Clarissa refused to sit on his lap.

'Smart kid,' said Cain. 'You gotta wonder about those guys.'

Lola expected to stay in the Curtellas' guesthouse like she usually did, but they had family visiting over Christmas and wanted to spruce the place up a bit. Mike had spoken to Danny, the painter at the Treehouse, who said he was just about finished there anyway. He had already started work at the Curtellas when Lola phoned Joanne, and she was so apologetic Lola felt awful for asking. In a fluster, Joanne suggested she take the spare bedroom in the house but Mike reminded her that was where they had put all the furniture from the guesthouse so Danny didn't have to work around it. No problem at all, Lola had said cheerfully so that Joanne wouldn't feel bad. It was only for a night or two anyway.

Several times Cain had asked Lola to stay with him and now she didn't have a reason not to, but until she had been honest with Duncan she felt she wasn't being fair. And of course she wasn't being fair to Cain either. He assumed Lola coming to California on her own again signified a separation, and she hadn't exactly corrected him. She would have to, though, and soon. Much easier face to face.

Being back in Cain's house reminded her of the afternoon she had helped him prepare for his mother's visit. She smiled, remembering how much fun they had had.

'I'll get this going,' said Cain, crouching down at the log-filled grate with a box of matches.

Lola thought of the drawing room at the Grange, with its grand Adam fireplace and the fire they didn't bother to light anymore.

Cain waited until the flames took hold, then stood up and turned to Lola.

'You hungry?'

Her stomach felt peculiar; empty and full at the same time. She put it down to nerves and wondered if Cain was nervous too.

'I'm not sure,' she said.

'How about a drink while you figure it out?'

'Actually, I don't feel much like drinking.'

'No food, no wine – you're a cheap date.'

'No one's ever called me cheap before,' said Lola, thrilled at the thought of being his 'date'.

While he went to the kitchen to see what he could tempt her with, Lola excused herself and went to the bathroom. A stack of surfing magazines filled a wicker basket by the toilet. The shower curtain over the bath was patterned with starfish. She brushed her hair, splashed water on her face, pinched her cheeks to give them a bit of colour and smeared a dab of Vaseline over her lips. Back in the kitchen, Cain had his mobile in his hand.

'That was Joanne,' he said. 'Duncan called – wanted to know you got there okay. You told him you were staying with the Curtellas?'

Not this conversation – not now.

'He assumed.'

'And you didn't put him straight?'

'Not as such.'

'What does that mean? Seriously, Lola – what's going on here?'

Good question.

'What's going on here is that I've been up for almost twenty-four hours, I'm tired, my stomach's doing back flips and it's a very difficult situation that I wish we didn't have to talk about right now.'

They locked eyes across the food-strewn counter – a couple of steaks, a large bag of salad leaves, some plump red tomatoes – and it was Cain who spoke first.

'Well, okay I guess. But only because you're tired and it's your first night here.' He pointed his index finger at her to emphasise how serious he was. 'Tomorrow we're gonna sit down and talk this thing out.'

So that was Cain being firm. How unaccustomed she was to a man insisting they sit and talk. The last remnants of doubt about being unfaithful to Duncan vanished into nothing. She wanted Cain so badly, a raw heat spread over face, neck and chest. If she didn't do something she would combust. She skirted around the counter until there was barely an inch between them, and said, 'Now can we please go to bed?'

When Cain didn't immediately reply, Lola wondered if she had got it wrong, if this wasn't how things were done. What did she know anyway? Before Cain, the only man she'd slept with was Duncan and he was inclined to take the initiative. Maybe there were different rules for Americans, for lovers, for younger men? She was about to draw back when, with a single gesture worthy of a Mills and Boon romance, Cain picked her up and swept her into the bedroom. Even if it all went horribly wrong and she was left heartbroken and alone, it would have been worth it for the ecstasy of that one soaring moment.

* * * * *

It was impossible not to make comparisons. With Duncan, sex was a serious business, intense, earnest, laden with meaning. If she were to compare it to a conversation, it would be deep and philosophical – Duncan wouldn't rest until his point was made. Cain was a very different lover. His conversation was witty and nuanced – more debate than monologue. He gave himself without inhibition, revealed himself through tenderness and passion. His hair was longer now and fashionably untidy. She loved the different shades of blonde: flaxen, wet sand, gold. She loved his warm, smooth skin and the tattoo between his shoulder blades. In the early-morning light, it looked like a large bird or some sort of flying dragon.

Duncan associated tattoos with jailbirds and sailors – she remembered him saying so when he noted, somewhat pejoratively, that a young man fixing the stable roof was covered in them. She wished she could stop Duncan intruding into her thoughts, but the moment when she would have to tell him she wanted to separate was drawing suffocatingly close. She felt nauseous merely thinking about it and had to make a conscious effort to breathe slow and deep.

Cain rolled over and smiled sleepily.

'You're not going to bail on me again, are you?' he said, reaching for her.

She tried hard to banish Duncan from her mind and focus all her attention on Cain.

'Um, I seem to remember it was you who slipped out at first light.'

He ran his hand down her back and rested it on the curve of her hip.

'Yeah, but you gave me the whole "we can only be friends" speech.'

'I felt guilty about Duncan. I still do.'

Cain propped himself up on one elbow and looked down at her. The way his hair fell forward made her think of heart-throbs and rock-stars and posters on bedroom walls.

'Look, you didn't want to talk about him last night and I don't want to talk about him now. Deal?'

She pushed his hair back so she could see his eyes.

'Deal.'

As he worked his way down her body with licks and kisses, she allowed herself to drown in sensual pleasure. They fell back to sleep again afterwards and it was gone nine before they were up and dressed and ready to go to the Treehouse.

'I've got butterflies,' said Lola, arms wrapped around her stomach.

This was her new life – a life without Duncan. It was really happening.

Cain picked up his car keys.

'It's gonna be fine.'

Wispy threads of morning mist wafted around the hilltops. The bare vines looked stark and woody in the bright winter sun. It wasn't until they were in the car, Cain talking so quickly he barely drew breath, that Lola realised he was nervous too: something about this being his first project, wanting to feel proud of it, wanting to impress his favourite client. He winked at her when he said that and she giggled like a teenager.

When they reached the clearing to the Treehouse, a new driveway of herringbone brick had been laid. Cain drove slowly so that when the house came into view, it had all the drama of a curtain rising. Lola caught her breath.

'Oh,' she said, bringing her hands to her face.

Cain switched off the engine.

'Well, what do you think? I mean, it was covered in scaffolding the last time you saw it so you couldn't really see it at all but I think now that it's finished –'

'It's perfect,' she said.

It was touching how relieved Cain looked, like he'd got top marks in a test. He got out of the car and rushed around to open the door for her. She drew the cool air deep into her lungs and thought of that hot June day when she had first seen the abandoned wooden shack. Three of the original walls remained but the wall of glass to the front had transformed the place – old to new. All the wood had been stained a rich, deep brown that blended perfectly with the hillside's earthy palette. The curiosity and hope that had stirred in her all those months before stirred again, only this time it was Cain who took her hand as she stepped tentatively inside.

The front door – glass with a sleek metal frame – was unlocked. On the hall table were a bottle of champagne from Mike and Joanne, a white orchid from Birdie and a book about Napa vineyards from Roger. The tightness in

Lola's throat took her by surprise. It was their kindness that touched her. There were cards too – not Christmas cards, but 'welcome to your new home' cards. Lola read them through misty eyes, caught off guard by the up-swell of emotion.

Cain took a set of keys from his jacket pocket and handed them to her.

'You'll need these,' he said.

She closed her hand around the keys and buried her face in his shoulder.

'Hey,' he said. 'Don't get all weepy on me. You haven't had the tour yet.'

He led her into the sitting room where natural light poured in and bounced off the walls. She remembered the day she put paint on one of those walls – the anniversary of Clarissa's death. The grief was still there, but its sharp edges were smoother now.

A constellation of tiny spotlights studded the sloping ceiling like stars. The fireplace was neatly stacked with logs and the thick oak lintel above held a row of tall church candles.

'Did you do that?' asked Lola.

'Uh-huh,' said Cain proudly.

Deep burgundy cushions, which Cain insisted were called pillows, brought a splash of colour to the chic beige sofa. At the far end was the kitchen, separated from the sitting room by a breakfast bar with two black-leather stools pushed underneath. The work surfaces were shiny black marble flecked with silver – a cool contrast to the warm sitting-room tones. Lola looked inside the distressed oak cupboards, the giant-sized American fridge, the range cooker with its six gas burners, and declared that it felt like Christmas.

'It is Christmas,' said Cain. 'Or pretty much.'

He opened the sliding door and they stepped out onto the elevated deck. Some of the trees had been felled but others had been planted in their place. Lola thought how secluded it seemed, even though Mike and Joanne's house was just a few hundred yards away. Privacy and neighbours; the best of both worlds. She could hear the creek and something scurrying in the undergrowth, but nothing else. The last time she had stood on that deck was with Duncan, trying to explain the strange feeling that restoring this neglected old house was in some way linked to restoring her own happiness. From the very first moment she sensed she had stumbled on to something significant, although she could never have imagined this: new love, new friends, new home, new life. All Duncan had wanted was to make her happy.

'You want to see the rest?' asked Cain, and Lola nodded, because she was happy and sad and too choked to speak.

Both the bedrooms had identical queen-sized beds, thick-pile carpet the colour of putty, built-in wardrobes and matching bedside tables.

'What do you think?' he said.

Lola forced all thoughts of Duncan out of her head and focused on Cain, so eager for her approval.

'I think you've done an excellent job,' she said. 'It needs a few finishing touches, but Joanne and I are shopping later so that's easily sorted.'

'What do you have in mind?'

'Bed linen, obviously, as we're sleeping here tonight.'

'Are we?'

'Sorry, I assumed…'

Cain laughed.

'I'm kidding. Try stopping me.'

He grabbed her roughly and they only just heard Joanne's voice over Lola's delighted squeals.

'Can I come in?'

'We're in the bedroom,' called Cain, releasing Lola with a regretful sigh.

Joanne wore loose fitting jeans, a 'Chardonnay Princess' sweatshirt and pristine white sneakers. Her hair was brushed in a pageboy style that framed her pretty round face.

'Welcome back, honey,' she said, planting a kiss on Lola's cheek. 'You look even more beautiful than usual. What's your secret?'

Lola shot Cain a glance and thought how all the wonderful sex must have brought a satisfied glow to her skin, but she shrugged her shoulders and said it was probably the clean valley air.

'The place looks great, doesn't it?' said Joanne.

'Fabulous,' said Lola.

'I'm gonna leave you gals to it,' said Cain. 'Enjoy your retail therapy.'

Shopping with a friend was such a simple pleasure – the sort of thing most people took for granted. Not Lola. As she strolled around the outdoor mall at Corte Madera, listening to Joanne chat about this and that, it brought into sharp focus just how isolated a life she had lived. Her solitude began in childhood, a sort of self-preservation mechanism, but over time it had become second nature. The few shopping trips she took with her mother didn't go well. Particularly harrowing was the afternoon they had spent getting a new uniform for senior school. Her mother had been restrained enough not to drink beforehand – Lola could always tell – but she must have underestimated how long the whole arduous exercise would take because her enforced sobriety made her edgy and tense. There had been several other customers in the small, airless shop – mothers and daughters, the odd younger sibling bored and misbehaving – and only two harried sales assistants. Lola's mother made no attempt to conceal her impatience. She stepped outside several times to smoke, leaving Lola to work through the long list of requirements on her own: dresses for summer, skirts, shirts and jumpers for winter, a complicated games kit with different coloured socks for different sports, a hockey stick and tennis racquet, plimsolls, a swimsuit, a scarf, several pairs of non-sports related socks, also in various lengths and colours.

Keen to move things along, Lola hadn't objected when the pleated navy skirt was so large on the waist that it flopped onto her narrow hips, or asked for a smaller blazer, one that didn't swamp her skinny frame. It was pure good fortune that she had shot up in that first term and the ill-fitting clothes weren't so ill fitting anymore. She sewed her own nametapes too. The lesson was clear: shopping was a pursuit best undertaken alone – more expedient and a lot less stressful that way. But now she was happy to be proved wrong, happy to be guided from Pottery Barn to Restoration Hardware via Starbucks and Banana Republic by Joanne, until they had so many bags that twice they had to walk back to her Jeep to drop them off.

'Duncan okay with you spending all his money?' asked Joanne casually, then she squeezed Lola's hand and added, 'I didn't mean anything by that.'

'I know you didn't,' said Lola. 'And yes, I told him there were things I needed for the house.'

'How's he doing?' asked Joanne.

Lola thought about that for a moment. The sun was high now and she wished she hadn't worn a winter jacket.

'Actually, I'm just about ready for a break. Is there somewhere we could have lunch?' she asked.

Joanne suggested the Cheesecake Factory – one of a dozen or so restaurants at the end of the mall.

'I didn't expect it to be so warm,' said Lola as they took a table by the window.

Joanne slipped off her own jacket – a lightweight bomber-style thing with elastic around the wrists and waist – and said they could talk about the weather if she wanted, but she was more interested to hear about how she and Duncan were doing.

'Tell me to mind my own business if you like, but does he know about you and Cain?'

Lola shook her head.

'He's been under so much pressure with work I could never find the right moment.

'You think there will ever be a right moment?'

Lola picked up a menu and stared at it without reading a word.

'Probably not. I've been putting it off for weeks, telling myself I'll do it tomorrow or the next day or the day after that.'

Joanne must have heard the despair in her voice because she reached over and patted her hand.

'Don't get upset, honey. I know it seems bad right now, but marriages break up all the time. It happens.'

'But he's been so stressed and unhappy lately and I'm going to make that a thousand times worse.'

'People survive,' said Joanne softly. 'Duncan will survive.'

Lola nodded, badly needing it to be true.

'I thought if we could have one last Christmas together – a peaceful one to make up for the awful ones since Clarissa died, maybe it would give us some kind of closure.'

'How does Cain feel about Duncan being here for Christmas?'

Lola's stomach churned – a cross between nausea and apprehension.

'He doesn't know. It came up last night but we got side tracked. He made me promise we'd talk but the opportunity hasn't presented itself.'

Joanne sat back in her chair, eyebrows raised.

'Wow, you've got a lot of talking to do.'

For a few seconds Lola thought she might be sick, but the sensation passed.

'You feeling okay, honey?' asked Joanne. 'You look a little pale.'

'I do feel a bit strange,' said Lola. 'It's nothing – probably jetlag.'

'Let's get you some water,' said Joanne, raising her hand towards a waiter.

He brought a jug of iced water, poured two glasses, then asked if they were ready to order.

'Give us a few minutes,' said Joanne, picking up a menu.

'That feels better,' said Lola, sipping the water.

'You hungry?' asked Joanne.

'I'm not sure. I thought I was. Maybe a doughnut might settle my stomach.'

'Really? A doughnut? For lunch?'

'Don't judge me.'

'Hey, no judgement on my part. You don't mind if I have pizza? I've worked up quite an appetite with all that shopping.'

'Not at all,' said Lola, feeling calmer now.

She took another sip of water. The restaurant was bustling and bright, the sort of place Clarissa would have loved. Each time Lola saw mothers with their little girls, she felt the loss of her own little girl like a dull ache that she knew would never leave her, but now there was stillness too, and that made it easier to bear. Joanne reached out and touched her hand again.

'You sure you're okay, honey?' she asked.

'I was just thinking about Clarissa,' said Lola

Of all the ways in which her California life was better than her Somerset life, being able to talk about Clarissa was one of the most important – not having to keep her memories hidden away like some guilty secret. Holding them inside had weighed her down and now that she could set them free, she was free too. And having a friend to confide in was another kind of freedom. She asked Joanne about her own children – Sandy and Luke – and the twins, Tony and Carla, from Mike's first marriage to Ellie. Joanne told her about Ellie's affair and how she just up and left Mike to raise the twins on his own. They were two years old and into everything. Mike was still recovering from Vietnam and struggling to learn to walk again. The whole neighbourhood rallied around – set up a kind of rota to help with the cooking and cleaning and the kids, so he didn't feel like he was alone. Joanne used to bake bread and cookies for them. She'd find herself staying for longer and longer visits, giving the twins their bath, reading them a story, tucking them into bed and then cooking a meal for Mike. When he invited her to stay and eat with him, she thought he was just being polite, or maybe he was just plain lonely, but then one night he kissed her and she didn't leave.

'How romantic,' said Lola.

'It really was,' said Joanne. 'You know, even after all these years, it still makes me tingle a little to think about it.'

'Duncan and I lost that a long time ago. I was too consumed mourning the death of our child to notice I was mourning the death of our marriage too.'

'That's sad,' said Joanne. 'But you know, if you compare Mike's situation when his first wife left, with Duncan's situation …' She shrugged. 'I'm just saying.'

Joanne was right.

'I'm going to talk to him on Boxing Day,' announced Lola. 'Without fail.'

'Boxing Day?'

'Oh, don't you have that here? It's the day after Christmas Day.'

Joanne nodded, amused. 'And speaking of Christmas Day, why don't you come over to our place? I mentioned Luke and his girlfriend are coming, and Sandy too. Tony and his wife are staying at home in Pasadena this year because they've got three little ones under five and they don't want to travel. We're going down there for New Year's. Carla's going try to make it but she's not sure if she can get the time. The ER gets pretty busy over the holidays.'

'But you've already got a houseful,' said Lola.

'Exactly,' said Joanne. 'Two more won't make any difference and there's safety in numbers – gotta be better than just you and Duncan and all those awkward silences.'

Lola bit into her doughnut and let the thick raspberry jam ooze into her mouth, sweet and delicious. She licked the sugar from her lips and then wiped them with a paper napkin.

'Look, are you sure about Christmas? I don't want to impose.'

Joanne shook her head.

'I'm only gonna say this once, so listen up. You are not imposing, you have never imposed, you could never impose. Got it?'

'Got it,' said Lola.

* * * * *

Back at Joanne's, Mike and Cain were watching baseball and drinking beer.

'Anything left in the stores?' asked Mike, looking at the quantity of shopping bags Lola and Joanne had arrived home with. He insisted that after a long day's shopping, the girls – Lola thought it cute to be referred to as 'the girls' – put their feet up. Cain poured them each a glass of Chenin Blanc but Lola said she'd really prefer a cup of tea if it wasn't too much trouble? The tea was dreadful – watery, weak, with a slightly floral fragrance – but Lola thanked him and drank it anyway. She relaxed in front of the roaring fire, content to hear life buzzing amiably in the background. It was only when Christmas Day came up in conversation that she roused herself. Cain was saying something about how Josh and the ice-queen were going to her family on the East Coast and when Cain had told his parents he could only spare a couple of days, they sort of invited themselves to him.

'I don't know how it happened,' he said, 'but I think I agreed.'

'Well, that's lovely,' said Joanne.

'Is it?' said Cain.

'Why don't the three of you come here for Christmas Day?' said Mike. 'You know Roger's coming, right?'

Lola shot Joanne a pleading look, but she seemed too excited by the prospect of swelling the numbers around what would already be a crowded dining table to notice.

'That's a wonderful idea,' she said.

'Um, aren't you forgetting something?' said Lola.

Joanne looked at her quizzically and then brought her hand to her mouth.

'Oh,' she said.

'Oh what?' said Mike. 'Would someone mind telling me what's going on?'

'I've already invited Lola and Duncan,' she said.

'What?' said Cain. 'Duncan's coming *here*?'

His disbelief was directed at Lola.

'I was going to tell you,' she said weakly.

'When were you going to tell me?'

Mike placed a firm hand on Cain's shoulder.

'I think you two need to talk. Why don't you go over to the Treehouse and come back for dinner in an hour or so if you feel like it.'

Cain nodded and walked over to the door, where Lola's shopping bags lay in a neat cluster. He didn't pick them up, but stepped outside and waited for her to join him.

She hadn't seen her new house in the dark. Subtle uplighters marked the path to the front door and with a single flick of a switch, the whole building was illuminated. Cain dimmed the light and walked into the sitting room, although he didn't sit. She could tell by his brisk walk, five paces ahead of her, that there would be a confrontation, but she felt unnaturally calm. She even walked over to the fireplace and set about the logs with a lighter that looked like a little rifle, but she couldn't work it properly so Cain took it from her, lit the fire and then the candles.

'It looks beautiful,' said Lola, watching the flames spring to life.

'What's going on with us?' asked Cain.

Direct and to the point. Lola was grateful, given how hard she had to work to get Duncan to talk about anything of consequence.

'I haven't told Duncan about us yet, or that I'm leaving him. I know it sounds pathetic but he's had so many problems at work, he often doesn't come home at all. And we're selling the Grange.'

'But he's coming here for Christmas. You two are gonna play happy families together, right?'

Lola lowered herself wearily onto the sofa.

'Hardly happy families. We haven't been a happy family since Clarissa died. I wanted to have one last Christmas together that wasn't all about what we've lost. And Joanne invited us and I thought, safety in numbers. I'll talk to Duncan the day after.'

Cain looked down at her in disbelief.

'That's crazy. You can't let him think he has a wife and a marriage one day and the next day tell him it was all a lie.'

'I've been waiting for the right moment but Joanne made me realise there is no right moment. He deserves to know the truth. And I can't keep putting it off just because I'm frightened of hurting him, or worried about how he'll manage on his own. It's sad, but relationships end and people move on. Duncan will move on.'

She paused for Cain to say something, preferably to agree with her, and when he didn't, she carried on.

'Our house is on the market and we haven't made any plans for when it's sold. I think on some level that signifies Duncan understands we don't have a future together.'

Lola didn't know if that was true, but it made her feel better to think it might be.

'What about this place?' said Cain. 'Will you have to sell that too?'

The possibility had never occurred to her. Would Duncan insist on selling the Treehouse to get back at her? He wasn't a vindictive man but he bought it to mark twenty years of marriage – a marriage she was ending.

'I don't know. I hope not.'

Her eyes welled up at the thought of losing her beautiful Treehouse – the catalyst for so much promise and joy. When she envisaged her future it was here, Mike and Joanne across the creek, Riley and Darcy getting into mischief together, Cain coming home to her each evening after work.

'Hey,' he said. 'Don't cry.'

He sat down and put his arms around her, his head resting against hers. She watched the flames flicker and dance, hoping she had the strength for what lay ahead.

'Okay,' said Cain. 'We'll do this your way. Duncan comes here for Christmas but you tell him straight after. Deal?'

Lola sniffed and wiped her eyes.

'Deal.'

Cycling was Cain's idea. He got up before Lola awoke, borrowed two mountain bikes from the Curtellas, drove to the coffee shop to get breakfast, and got back before she had even realised he was gone. She hadn't got around to buying food but it didn't matter. Her first night in the Treehouse – despite having had the 'Duncan' conversation with Cain – was everything she hoped it would be.

They had gone back to Joanne and Mike's for dinner but not stayed long afterwards. Beds to make, rooms to christen, Cain had muttered under his breath. She was relieved he had accepted her way of handling things with Duncan, but preoccupied with the thought that she might lose the Treehouse. Cain suggested she 'lawyer up', but Lola prayed it wouldn't come to that. If he hadn't worn her out (three times *in one night*?) she probably wouldn't have been able to sleep at all. She woke at eight-thirty to find him sitting on the edge of the bed, watching her.

'Morning,' she said, stretching.

'Am I too much for you?' he asked, blatantly pleased with himself.

He handed her a frothy coffee and cream cheese bagel. She didn't mention she would have preferred tea and a plain croissant.

'Yes,' said Lola. 'You're utterly insatiable.'

'I thought we could do with some fresh air,' said Cain. 'It's a beautiful morning and there's a couple of bikes outside, so when we've finished breakfast, pull on some sweats and we'll head up the mountain trail.'

Lola wasn't sure she had the energy for a mountain trail since Cain had kept her awake until the early hours, but he looked so excited by the prospect that she said it sounded fun.

Surprisingly, it was. The mountain road was steep and narrow by American standards – reminiscent of an English country lane. Traffic was mainly of the human variety: joggers, walkers, other cyclists. Her muscles burned from the exertion but the cool valley air felt good on her skin and she was determined to keep up with Cain. It thrilled her how young and fit he looked in his hoodie and combat shorts, but worried her too. Would he tire of her once the novelty wore off? If she were asked what they had in common, she would struggle to answer. He glanced over his shoulder and treated her to one of his toothpaste-ad smiles. She smiled back and pedalled harder.

The road ahead looked steeper still. Lola flicked down to a lower gear for the climb and passed a pair of turkey vultures snacking lazily on road kill. They glanced in her direction as she rose out of the saddle and headed towards the row of redwoods that bordered the top of the pass. She pushed down hard on the pedals, establishing a strong steady rhythm. Then, out of nowhere, came a low rumble that sounded like a crescendo of express trains. She barely had time to register it before the ground shifted with a sudden, violent shudder, sending her and the bicycle in opposite directions. Her hip and elbow hit the road first, her head protected by the helmet Mike had insisted Cain take for her. Pain shot through her whole body. She groaned but instinctively remained still. When Cain saw what had happened he jumped off his own bike, let it fall to the ground, and ran to her.

'Lola, are you okay?'

He scanned her body for blood or obvious injury and told her not to move.

'Where does it hurt?' he asked.

'My side,' she said, wincing. 'What happened?'

'A tremor,' he said. 'Probably a four or five.'

A mini-earthquake. She remembered reading about the San Andreas Fault and the mega-quake that was overdue in California. When she tried to sit up, a hot, sharp sensation radiated from her hip down the whole length of her leg and she moaned in pain.

'I'm calling 911,' said Cain, reaching into his pocket for his phone.

Disinfectant, floor polish, something medical she couldn't name. Did hospitals the world over smell the same? And the light, so bright you had to see everything more clearly than you wanted to. Clarissa laid out in white: wet hair, cold skin. A bruise like a thumbprint on her right temple. Not dead, sleeping. The doctor was lying. *Wake up, darling, it's time to go home.* Duncan's face so ravaged he looked like a different man. Clarissa's hair was parted on the wrong side. *Wake up, darling. Please.*

The fine layer of dirt on Lola's face was streaked with tears. Cain asked the nurse to give her something for the pain but what could take away the agony of losing your child? The nurse fitted a neck brace – just a precaution, she reassured Cain – and gave him an ice pack to hold against Lola's bruised arm. A young, prematurely balding man pulled the curtain aside and introduced himself as Doctor Gleeson. He shook Cain's hand and asked Lola how she was feeling.

'A little sore,' she said.

He shone a light in her eyes then flicked through her notes.

'You fell off your bicycle onto the road. Did you lose consciousness?'

'No,' Cain answered for her.

'Where does it hurt?'

'My left side – hip and elbow mostly.'

'What about her neck?' asked Cain. 'Why does she need a collar?'

'Standard procedure with a fall injury. Her neck seems fine but we'll know more when we've taken some x-rays. I need to examine her first, assess any soft-tissue damage.'

Doctor Gleeson took hold of her arm and cautiously tested its range of motion.

'Does that hurt?' he asked.

'A little,' she said.

'Can you wiggle your fingers for me?'

Lola moved her fingers and wrist, which meant a fracture was unlikely. Doctor Gleeson said he needed to lower her shorts so he could examine her hip. Lola closed her eyes, feeling more naked than when she and Cain were in bed together. Doctor Gleeson manipulated her pelvis and palpated her abdomen, then checked her notes again.

'Is there any chance you could be pregnant?'

Lola opened her eyes and glanced down at her belly.

'What? No.'

'When was your last period?'

Her mind was too scrambled to remember.

'I'm not sure.'

'What birth control are you using?'

She looked at Cain, his eyebrows raised as though waiting for the answer too.

'Umm, I'm not actually using birth control,' she said.

Doctor Gleeson flicked through her notes and asked the nurse to go get the portable ultrasound.

'We can't do x-rays until we're sure you're not pregnant,' he told Lola. 'It'll only take a few minutes.'

The nurse left and Doctor Gleeson scribbled some notes until she trundled back with the ultrasound machine. He put cold gel on Lola's belly and moved the probe around in silence. They were all captivated by the fuzzy black-and-white screen and when Doctor Gleeson pointed out an ectoplasmic blob the size of a kidney bean and announced it was a six-week-old foetus, Lola said there must be some mistake. She was amazed she could form a coherent sentence given the maelstrom of emotions assaulting her.

'No mistake' said Doctor Gleeson, pointing again to the blob. 'It's right there.'

He waited a moment, studying the screen, before asking, 'Do you have any children?'

Cain squeezed her hand, his eyes transfixed on the blurry image.

'I had a daughter,' said Lola. 'She died in an accident when she was eight.'

She qualified Clarissa's death in case there was any question of stillbirth or hereditary disease – medically relevant points, she felt.

'I've had seven miscarriages, all of them in the first trimester. And I'm forty-two, so I imagine my chances of carrying a baby full-term are virtually nil.'

Doctor Gleeson put down the probe and pushed his hands into the pockets of his crisp white coat.

'Look,' he said. 'Given your history and age, the pregnancy should be considered high risk. But every pregnancy is different and the outcome really can't be predicted at such an early stage.'

The nurse handed Lola a wodge of tissues to wipe away the gel.

Cain laid his free hand so gently on her belly, she barely felt its weight.

'This is unreal,' he said, wide-eyed with delight. 'We're pregnant.'

His voice registered a mix of shock and excitement.

'Can I take her home?' he asked Doctor Gleeson.

'Sure. She doesn't need to be admitted, although she will have to take it easy with those bruises. Doesn't look like anything's broken so my advice would be to rest and I'll prescribe a mild analgesic for the pain.'

Lola shook her head.

'No painkillers. Nothing that might hurt the baby.'

'They won't, but if you don't want to take them, that's up to you.'

The nurse left with the ultrasound machine, and Doctor Gleeson asked Cain to go with him so they could get the paperwork done. Alone in the cubicle, Lola tried to comprehend the news. A baby. It existed. It was real. She crossed her hands over her belly, protecting the precious life inside. Losing it would tear her apart, just as she had begun put herself back together.

Cain arrived back with two cups of machine-dispensed coffee and put one down on the table next to Lola.

'I've called Joanne to come pick us up,' he said.

Lola looked at him, her eyes pink-rimmed from crying.

'I don't know how this could have happened,' she said.

'Well, we didn't use any protection. I sort of assumed you had that covered.' He took a sip of coffee and grimaced.

'Jesus, that's awful.'

He put down the coffee and took Lola's hand.

'Did you think you couldn't have any more kids?'

She shrugged.

'Duncan and I tried for years. We must have gone to half a dozen doctors.'

'Did they ever find a reason?'

'No.'

'Maybe the chemistry wasn't right.'

Lola thought about that for a moment. Could it be that simple? Were she and Duncan not a good match and that's why it had been so difficult to conceive?

'But the miscarriages – there must have been something wrong with me.'

'Or the babies – it might not have been you at all.'

She had never considered that either. Had nature weeded out the weakest embryos, the defective ones, so that only the strongest made it through those nine months to birth?

'I'm sorry,' said Lola, welling up again. 'I've ruined everything, haven't I?'

'Hey,' said Cain. 'Are you kidding? This is the most incredible thing that's ever happened to me. I mean, I wasn't expecting it, obviously, but do you know how I felt when I saw our baby – what my gut told me?'

Lola shook her head.

'It told me this was the reason the universe flung us together – two people from two whole different continents. It wanted us to make this little person growing inside you.'

Lola's eyes filled and stung. She wiped them with the gel-sodden tissues, still clutched in her hand.

'That sounds so Californian,' she said, laughing and crying and absurdly in love.

Cain's phone pinged.

'Our ride's here,' he said. 'Joanne's in the parking lot.'

As he slowly helped Lola to her feet, she asked him to say nothing about the baby.

'Not yet,' she said, her face now tight with pain. 'It's too soon.'

'You're the boss,' said Cain, supporting her as she hobbled lopsidedly.

Doctor Gleeson was outside, smoking a cigarette.

'I'm gonna quit,' he said sheepishly and threw the smouldering butt to the ground.

'Actually, I was just thinking about you,' he continued, 'thinking that you got pregnant without trying at an age when it's really tough to get pregnant, and that the baby held on despite your fall. I guess what I'm saying is that this little one seems like a fighter.'

Joanne made a fuss about getting her into the jeep and doing up her seatbelt and driving slowly so she wouldn't feel any bumps or jolts. Lola sat mute with shock, staring into the middle distance. The memory of all those miscarriages flooded back – the terrible toll they took. Maybe

Doctor Gleeson was right and this baby would fight for its life. Could she dare to hope? Joanne asked questions about what happened exactly, what the doctor said, did it hurt very much, how long would she have to rest for? Cain answered them all. Lola's mind was saturated with thoughts of the baby she had conceived exactly three years after she lost Clarissa. She wasn't sure what that meant, but she was sure it meant something.

Despite Joanne's protests, Lola went back to the Treehouse to rest. Joanne wanted to look after her but Lola needed solitude, time to think. Cain helped her get changed into a dressing gown and onto the bed they had christened so athletically the previous night, and then he lay down beside her. She thought she had wanted to be alone with her thoughts but Cain being there felt right. When he asked if she was ready to talk, she shook her head.

'Not yet,' she said quietly, and he didn't press her.

To her amazement, she slept. The first few months when she was expecting Clarissa, she could hardly stay awake. No matter how much sleep she got, it never seemed enough. Duncan worried about her driving in case she nodded off behind the wheel.

Duncan. He would arrive in less than a week. She had been trying to cling to a version of events in which, once he got over the shock, they could be civilised and part on good terms. And she had decided to tell him she wanted the Treehouse, that she intended to make it her permanent home. In her fantasy he was decent and charitable enough to agree, but how charitable would he feel now that she was pregnant by her virile young lover?

Nausea swelled inside her and she put her hand to her mouth. Was it the baby or trepidation about the conversation she had to have with Duncan? The sickness passed and she lay there, hardly daring to think how he would react. Her hope had been to cause him as little pain as possible, to explain that she cared deeply for him and always would, but neither of them were happy and they both deserved to be. She would give him her blessing to find that happiness with someone else, like she had done. And now she was pregnant. Lola closed her eyes and tried to stave off the next wave of sickness as it rose up into her throat. She wouldn't blame Duncan if he hated her.

Cain peeked his head around the door.

'You're awake,' he said. 'How you feeling?'

'Sick,' she said. 'Can you help me up?'

He put an arm around her waist and raised her up slowly, moving her legs over the side of the bed until she was in a sitting position.

'You okay?' he asked.

Her left side felt stiff and tender but she didn't want to make a fuss so she nodded and attempted a smile. He helped her to stand and then supported her as she limped gingerly to the bathroom.

'I can take it from here,' she said, and shut the door.

The nausea had passed again but she needed to pee and was terrified there would be blood. That was how it happened – sometimes there was cramping and sometimes not, but there was always blood. Just a few spots to begin with, then more and heavier as the baby was flushed out of her inadequate womb. She sat, peed and wiped herself. Not this time; not yet.

A cup of tea was waiting for her on the bedside table. Even though Cain's tea was watery and fragrant and tasted of nothing much at all, it was hot and comforting and she liked the ritual of drinking it. A good cup of tea was the only thing she really missed about England. In time there would probably be other things too, but for now that was it.

Cain helped her back onto the bed and rearranged the pillows so that she could sit up. He'd put some cookies on a plate, but Lola wasn't hungry.

'There's something I have to ask you,' he said.

Lola waited for the question.

'The baby – is it mine?'

It hurt that he had to ask, not because he doubted her, but because she had caused this doubt.

'It's yours. Duncan and I – the last time was on our trip here in the summer.'

'I'm sorry, I shouldn't have said anything. I feel terrible.'

'No,' said Lola, putting her hand to his cheek. 'I feel terrible that you had to.'

He kissed her gently.

'Wow,' he said. 'I can't believe I'm gonna be a father!'

Lola demurred.

'You mustn't assume that because I'm pregnant you're going to be a father. I've had so many miscarriages…'

'I know,' he said, letting his eyes drift towards her belly. 'But Doctor Gleeson said –'

She tilted his face so that his eyes met hers.

'He was being kind. It would be wrong of me to let you believe this is likely to have a happy ending.'

Cain looked troubled and she wasn't sure if it was for himself, for her, the baby, or all three. They had known each other such a short time and their courtship had been so unconventional, she had no idea how he felt about children. Too giddy with the newness of it all, they hadn't talked about what a future together might look like. The honeymoon phase had come to an abrupt end.

'If you really want children, Cain, then you need to be with someone who can give them to you.'

He shook his head.

'That's not what I meant. I'd never even thought about having children, but I'd happily have them with you. Being with you is what I want – with or without children.'

She wanted to believe it and she had no doubt he believed it at that moment, but how could either of them be sure he wouldn't change his mind? It was a pointless conversation anyway, one that meant speculating about the future. Lola knew all too well, the future was something over which no one had any control.

Duncan's arrival disturbed the fragile equilibrium Lola and Cain established after the baby bombshell. Cain had removed his things from the Treehouse to eradicate any evidence of his presence. He objected, reasoning that now she was carrying his child, he couldn't be expected to simply stand aside. That was exactly what Lola expected. She hadn't let him tell anyone about the baby, not even Mike and Joanne. The thought of telling Duncan made her sick with dread. No, Cain would have to do this her way.

She had used his mobile to call Duncan and tell him about the fall, suggesting that as she couldn't do very much, perhaps it wasn't worth him making the journey. He hesitated for a moment – was he actually considering it? – before he said no, of course he must come.

Cain's parents arrived on the morning of Christmas Eve, keen to see this Treehouse they'd heard so much about. Do you mind, he'd asked Lola awkwardly – just a quick look around? The prospect of seeing Helen again, and meeting Skip for the first time, was a daunting one, but she understood how much it meant to Cain.

He had confided how shocked he was to discover his dad had had an affair while his mom was pregnant. How they got through it, he couldn't imagine. We'll be great parents, he told Lola, and though his excitement was touching, she wished he would accept that the tiny embryo, still hanging on in the seventh week, was highly unlikely to make them parents. She tried not to think of it as a baby because then she imagined cradling it in her arms, the powdered smell of its warm, pink skin, its mewling cry for milk or comfort. Bittersweet memories that made her ache with longing.

Skip and Helen were a handsome couple – his tall, military bearing and her carefully groomed elegance. In Skip, Lola could see Cain thirty years on. Lola asked if Cain harboured any resentment towards his father in light of his infidelity? Guess that would make me something of a hypocrite, was Cain's pragmatic reply.

Seeing Cain show his parents around the Treehouse brought it home to Lola how much he wanted their approval. They ooh-ed and aah-ed as Cain walked them from room to room with a running commentary on how run-down the place had been when Lola first bought it. Technical details about materials and utilities he directed at Skip, who seemed happily impressed with his son's newfound expertise. He asked questions, listened keenly to Cain's answers, nodded a good deal. Helen complimented him on the colour schemes, the lighting, the soft furnishings.

'Lola chose those, Mom,' he said. 'She's got great taste.'

'You've done a fine job, son,' said Skip, placing a broad hand on Cain's shoulder. 'I'm proud of you.'

Cain beamed. Lola knew he had waited his whole life to hear that.

Joanne had invited the McCanns to dinner so that when Duncan got there, he and Lola would have some privacy. It seemed wrong, Lola not telling her she was pregnant, but she wasn't ready yet. She sat on the sofa and stared into the fire, waiting for Duncan to arrive. The sun had disappeared behind Spring Mountain and with it the warmth of the day. Cain had lit the fire before he left, and shyly proffered a well-wrapped Christmas present.

'Open it,' he said, brimming with childlike impatience.

'Now?' said Lola.

She looked at the shiny silver paper and matching gossamer bow.

'Well, you can't open it tomorrow in front of your husband.'

'I suppose not,' she said.

She pulled at the bow and undid the paper. In a rectangular white box lay a mobile phone.

'I've put my number in, so you can call me anytime,' he said.

'I'm not sure I know how,' said Lola. 'I've never had one before.'

'Never?'

'I haven't needed one. So thank you – my very first mobile. Only about twenty years behind the rest of the world.'

'I've put Joanne and Birdie's numbers in there too.'

'That's so thoughtful. Now I feel terrible. I haven't got you anything.'

'Everything I want is right here in front of me.'

Since the fall he had treated her like a fragile doll but now, when she put her mouth to his, she felt him stir.

'How long before those bruises heal?' he whispered.

'Soon,' she said, unzipping him, reaching for him, moving her hand in firm, rhythmic strokes. 'And in the meanwhile –'

His eyes stayed fixed on hers until his breathing became hard and fast and then he closed them. That was the image in Lola's mind when the car headlights approached. She took a deep breath, stood up and went outside to greet her husband.

Polite. When Joanne asked how Duncan was, that was how Lola replied. He looked tired, gaunt. They kissed each other on the cheek and made small talk about the flight, the weather, how wonderful the house looked.

He enquired after her health and in her addled, anxious mind she thought he meant the baby. Even as her heart raced she reminded herself he didn't know she was pregnant and the terrible task of telling him still lay ahead. She swallowed and attempted a small smile as she reassured him that she had been well taken care of and the bruises were fading nicely. She offered to reheat the casserole Joanne had dropped by earlier but he said he'd eaten on the plane – some bread and cheese would be fine. The pungency of the Stilton and the pus-like runniness of the Camembert turned her stomach. She poured a glass of Opus One from Mike's cellar for Duncan and a glass of milk for herself.

'Milk?' said Duncan.

'Helps with the healing,' said Lola.

When he admitted to being shattered and suggested an early night, Lola was relieved. The effort of keeping her grenade of a secret had made her so edgy and guarded, she felt Duncan was bound to notice and ask what was wrong. She showed him to the guest room rather than the master bedroom, with some excuse about her bruises.

'You don't mind?' she said.

'Not at all.'

Nine o'clock and they had already retired to their separate bedrooms – courteous strangers in a twenty-year marriage. Lola sat down, breathless with relief that the evening was over. Her phone beeped with a text from Cain: *Love you xx.*

*   *   *   *   *

Christmas morning was very un-Christmassy. Lola slept late and they hadn't had a tree since Clarissa died. Cain had sent four text messages declaring his love. That sentiment sustained her through a formal breakfast with her husband, a stilted exchange of gifts – Cartier cologne for him and a Gucci scarf for her – and an uncomfortable retreat to their respective bedrooms to dress for turkey and all the trimmings at the Curtellas' lunch party.

So many people; so much noise. The contrast to the quiet of the Treehouse took a moment to adjust to. Lola saw Cain chatting to a couple she didn't know and it was hard not to go to him. Joanne rushed over with a glass of bubbly, which Lola couldn't drink, but she took it anyway. Duncan slipped into the role of charming guest, greeting people he knew and introducing himself to those he didn't. Lola handled things less well. Twelve hours' sleep was no longer enough, it seemed. Helen made a beeline for her, resplendent in a pale blue Chanel style two-piece.

'So this is your husband,' she said, offering Duncan an expensively jewelled hand. 'Helen McCann. Cain's mother.'

'Not possible,' said Duncan smoothly. 'You're far too young.'

Helen emitted a girlish giggle and her cheeks coloured slightly.

'It's such a pleasure to meet you at last,' she said. 'How do you like the Treehouse?'

'I like it very much,' said Duncan. 'Cain and Birdie have done an excellent job.'

Helen took a sip from her champagne flute.

'We're simply delighted he's found his calling at last. And of course Lola has been very supportive of him.' She looked at Lola for a moment longer than was comfortable. 'I hope she hasn't spoiled him. I'm sure all his clients won't be so attentive.'

If Helen was hinting at the true nature of their relationship – did she know the true nature of their relationship or just suspect? – it was lost on Duncan. Lola excused herself and went to see if Joanne needed any help.

'The table looks beautiful,' said Lola.

'Doesn't it? Sandy's work – Sandy, come over here and meet Lola.'

Sandy Curtella was a cross between her parents: Mike's wide, fleshy smile and Joanne's shiny dark bob and rosy complexion. Pretty too, and surprisingly slight given how stout Mike and Joanne were.

'Hi,' she said with a big Curtella hug. 'I've heard a lot about you. Mom's so excited that you're neighbours. Is that your husband?'

She looked over to where Duncan was nodding in agreement to something Helen was saying.

'Yes,' she said. 'Why don't I introduce you?'

'Can you spare me, Mom?' asked Sandy.

'Sure,' said Joanne. 'You go have fun.'

Did talking to Duncan constitute fun? Helen seemed to think so – leaning in as he spoke, touching his arm in response. Was she flirting with him?

'Darling,' said Lola, 'this is Sandy Curtella, Mike and Joanne's daughter.'

Duncan's handshake seemed very formal.

'And do you know Helen McCann?'

'Cain's mom, right?' said Sandy.

'That's right, dear,' said Helen. 'Now, am I correct in thinking you and he used to date?'

News to Lola. Cain had never mentioned anything about that, and come to think of it, Joanne hadn't either. An image of Cain and Sandy together sparked an uncharacteristic flash of possessiveness. Lola told herself not to be so silly, but it felt good to glance over at him, laughing at something Skip had said, and know that it was her he wanted, her he loved.

'No,' said Sandy casually. 'Although I think my mom tried to fix us up a few times last summer. He's a great guy.'

A spontaneous round of applause erupted as Mike produced a ten-pound turkey from the oven. He looked comical in a chef's hat, apron and oven gloves. The applause got louder when he held up the roasting tray like a winner's trophy.

'I better go help Mom,' said Sandy. 'Lovely to meet you, Duncan, and nice to see you again, Helen.'

A single bleep from Lola's clutch bag signalled the arrival of another text message. She excused herself saying something about needing fresh air, and went onto the deck. *Next Christmas it's just me, you and Junior, right?* Why hadn't she asked Cain to show her how to text back? She tried to write *Roll on next Christmas* but couldn't get the spelling right. Perhaps she should settle for a simple *Miss you.*

'Is that a mobile?'

Lola turned and there was Duncan, right behind her. She should have lied. If she had said that she'd finally got around to buying one, or that it was a present from Joanne and Mike, Duncan would have believed her. He had no reason not to. Instead, her mind went blank.

'Yes,' was all she could think to say.

'May I?' said Duncan, taking it from her. 'An iPhone,' he said. 'Very smart.'

Cain's text was on the screen. At first Duncan seemed confused. He looked from the phone to Lola and back to the phone. When he read the message out loud, it was in the tone of someone trying to solve a particularly difficult crossword clue.

'*Next Christmas it's just me, you and Junior.* I don't understand.'

Lola's mind was still blank. She could offer no plausible explanation, but this was neither the time nor place to tell him about Cain. She watched helplessly as Duncan read the other texts – declarations of love, every one. His eyes widened in disbelief.

'Lola, what the hell is this? Who are these messages from?'

Cain's initials were at the top of the screen but Duncan didn't appeared to have made the connection.

'Can we talk about it later?' she pleaded. 'Joanne and Mike have gone to so much trouble. Let's not spoil Christmas.'

'I don't give a damn about Christmas. I want to know who sent you those messages.'

'You guys okay?' Joanne called from the doorway. 'We're about to sit down and eat.'

'We'll be in in a moment,' said Lola, her tone so unconvincing that rather than go back inside, Joanne came over to see what was going on.

'Do you know who sent these?' Duncan asked Joanne, holding up the phone.

She looked at Lola, her face creased with concern.

'Honey?' she said gently.

'So you do know,' said Duncan. 'Wonderful. Well, perhaps you could enlighten me.'

Joanne touched Lola's arm but said nothing.

'What does this mean – *me, you and Junior*?' demanded Duncan. 'Who the hell is *Junior*?'

Now it was Joanne who looked shocked. In that moment Lola felt more guilty about concealing her pregnancy from her friend than from her husband.

'I think I need to sit down,' she said, suddenly nauseous and lightheaded.

'You can sit down over at the Treehouse,' said Duncan firmly. 'Come on, we're leaving.'

Lola steadied herself against the railing that bordered the deck. When Cain appeared at the door she willed him to stay there, but he headed straight over.

'Is everything okay? Lola? What's going on?'

'Good question,' said Duncan.

Cain ignored him and put a proprietorial arm around her shoulders. She envisaged some hideous showdown, destroying what should have been a wonderful Curtella Christmas. She had already hurt Joanne. And Skip and Helen were inside – what would they think?

'I can't do this now,' she said quietly to Cain, and to Duncan, 'Can we please go.'

Neither man moved. Duncan glared at McCann, his arm still around Lola, and the colour leeched from his face. He had solved the crossword clue. He visibly tensed and for a split second, Lola thought he might lunge at them. Instead, he turned on his heel and marched towards the Treehouse.

No one spoke for a moment. What could they say? Lola realised she was shaking and wished she could stay there, Cain's arm around her, comforting and strong. But she had to go to her husband. It was the least he deserved.

The Treehouse was chilly and silent. She thought about lighting a fire but Duncan's agitated pacing put her off the idea.

'You and McCann?'

'I'm sorry you found out like that.'

'Good God, Lola.'

His face was still ashen.

'And the reference to *Junior*?'

She wished she could stop shaking.

'You can't be pregnant. Please tell me you're not pregnant.'

'I need to get a blanket,' she said, and disappeared into the bedroom.

She pulled a cashmere throw from the foot of the bed and draped it over her shoulders. Armed with a box of tissues grabbed from the bedside table, she went back out to face Duncan.

He was still pacing, his jaw clenched.

'Do you have anything to drink – Scotch?'

'There's some champagne in the fridge.'

'I don't think this calls for a celebration, do you?'

She assumed the question was rhetorical. There was half a bottle of Opus One from their strained supper the previous evening. She poured him a glass and put the bottle on the coffee table in front of the sofa, hoping he might calm down and sit. He drank the entire glass in one gulp and poured another.

'You and McCann?' He started on the second glass. 'How long has it been going on?'

Lola took a deep breath.

'November – Clarissa's anniversary.'

Duncan nodded, his lips tight and frowning.

'Ah. Well then, I suppose I only have myself to blame.'

'I was worried that was what you would think.'

'What else am I supposed to think?'

'That I was lonely and grieving and we hadn't been really happy together for such a long time. I'm not making excuses – I want you to try to understand.'

Duncan went over to the window and looked out in silence, his back to Lola.

'So it was my fault,' he said, turning around to face her. 'If I had come with you like you wanted me to, this never would have happened?'

Lola opened her mouth to speak but struggled to find the right words. While he waited for an answer, Duncan grabbed his glass from the coffee table and drained it.

'Probably not, no,' said Lola, but then remembered Cain's theory about the universe throwing them together to make a child. 'Although in a strange way,' she continued, 'I wonder if it was meant to happen?'

'What do you mean, *meant to happen*?'

She furrowed her brow, trying to piece together a coherent explanation from the jumble of thoughts in head.

'When I found out I was pregnant...'

'How can you possibly be pregnant? It's insane. You're over forty. All those years we tried, all those doctors –'

'Believe me, I was as surprised as you are.'

'I doubt that very much.'

She cast her eyes down in contrition.

'Sorry. Stupid thing to say.'

'When were you going to tell me?'

'Tomorrow,' she said. 'I wanted us to have a nice Christmas together.' She laughed at the irony. 'Rather ruined that, didn't I?'

He emptied the dregs from the bottle into his wine glass and drank.

'Why didn't you talk to me, tell me how unhappy you were?'

'Oh, Duncan,' she said. 'How many times did I try to talk to you?'

There was no reproach in her voice, only regret. He hung his head, eyes closed, as if anger had given way to defeat. Lola wanted to comfort him but she wasn't sure he would let her. To conceive a child by another man is the worst betrayal a wife can inflict on her husband, so what Duncan said next really threw her.

'How are you feeling?'

A trick question? No, that wasn't Duncan's style. Still, could she trust that his concern was genuine? The way he looked at her suggested it was.

'Nauseous,' she said, tentatively. 'Sleepy, expecting to lose it every minute.'

'I remember,' he said. 'Craving doughnuts again?'

She nodded and smiled and felt the hot sting of tears. Duncan's eyes had a sad, haunted look about them – probably thinking back to all those blighted pregnancies and the emotional devastation that followed. She sat next to him, her head resting hesitantly on his shoulder. He allowed it, or at least he didn't pull away.

'I'm so sorry,' she said, letting the tears run down her face. 'We've made such a mess of things, haven't we?'

Duncan stared into his empty wine glass.

'Indeed we have.'

For a while neither of them spoke, but the silence didn't feel awkward. If anything, it felt oddly companionable.

'I went to hospital when I fell off my bike.'

'Interesting non sequitur.'

'They all smell the same, don't they? It made me think of Clarissa laid out in that white gown.'

He nodded gravely.

'I had the same thing,' he said. 'Panic attack, thought it was a heart attack, sirens, the lot, very embarrassing, but whatever drugs they gave me had a strange, disorientating effect and I kept asking for Clarissa.'

Lola was confused.

'When did you have a panic attack?'

'Attacks – plural. They started after the accident and got worse when I lost my job.'

'You lost your job?'

'Yes.'

'When?'

'Three, four weeks ago.'

None of this made sense. She didn't know he suffered from panic attacks, let alone that they were severe enough to put him in hospital. And he'd lost his job? For some reason, that seemed more shocking.

'Why?' she asked.

'Takeover bid from another company – restructuring – out with the old and in with the new.'

'No, I mean, why didn't you tell me about all of this?'

He turned his wedding ring around and around.

'Haven't I given you enough bad news?'

A deep twisting pain in her chest accompanied the memory of that phone call from the hospital. *You need to come now.* He didn't tell her Clarissa was dead but the moment she saw him, she knew. Lola folded her arms over her belly, protecting the scrap of life growing inside.

'What are you going to do?' she asked.

'Regroup. Get the Grange sold.'

He looked around.

'I daresay you'll want to keep this place.'

'Yes. I was going to ask you but thought you might want to punish me by insisting we sell this too.'

'No, it's yours. I bought it for you. I wanted you to be happy.'

'I'm sorry,' she said. 'This wasn't quite what you had in mind, was it?'

He almost smiled.

'Hardly.'

'But what about you? I can't bear to think of you being alone and –'

He cut her off.

'I'll be fine,' he said. 'Once we get rid of the Grange I'll buy a place in London, put out some feelers for a bit of consultancy.'

'I wish you'd talked to me.'

'As you pointed out earlier, talking isn't my strong suit. And trust me, you wouldn't have wanted to hear what I had to say.'

The statement was heavy with undisclosed meaning but she didn't press him to elaborate. Experience told her it was futile.

'Do you love him?' he asked.

Another question Lola hadn't expected.

'Yes,' she said softly. 'I do.'

'And do you love me?'

'Yes,' she said again, firmer this time. 'But it hasn't been the same since Clarissa died. It ripped us apart. I hoped we might find our way back to each other, but we didn't. You said it was time for a fresh start.'

'This wasn't exactly what I had in mind. A baby? I'm sorry, I just can't take it in.'

'Me neither,' said Lola.

'You know he's not good enough for you.'

He meant it as a compliment. She placed her hand over his and gently squeezed.

'Are you sure you don't have any Scotch?' he said, on his feet again.

'Quite sure.'

'Champagne it is then,' he said, opening the bottle with a loud pop.

'And I can't tempt you?' he asked. 'A small one won't do any harm.'

Lola shook her head. He sat down next to her and drank his first glass in silence. Halfway through the second he spoke.

'I'm sorry too,' he said. 'We wouldn't be in this position if I had been a better husband.'

'You were a good husband.'

He shook his head.

'You can add hypocrisy to my list of sins,' he said.

'Hypocrisy?'

'My outrage over you and McCann.' He put down his glass. His voice was softer when he said, 'There's someone in London. It's been going on a while.'

'I see,' said Lola.

So Duncan had a lover after all. She took a moment to let it sink in, waiting for a flare of jealousy that never came. All she felt was disappointment. He wasn't the man she thought he was.

'You didn't suspect?' he said.

'Occasionally, I suppose. You were hardly ever home and when you were you were so distant. But I didn't think you would ever do that to me. I was sure of it, actually.'

Lola thought of all those nights she spent alone in the Grange, worrying about Duncan alone at the Carfax, too worn out to make the journey home. How naive she had been. How little they really knew each other. She was about to ask when it started but thought better of it. Their marriage was over so what did it matter? Instead she asked, 'Does she make you happy?'

'I don't deserve to be happy.'

Lola sighed.

'It was an accident, Duncan. You have to stop punishing yourself.'

'I punished you too, though, didn't I? You needed to talk about Clarissa and I wouldn't let you.'

He drained his glass and poured another. Lola stayed still and silent, shocked that he had actually said Clarissa's name.

'You thought I was trying to erase her from our lives, but that wasn't it. I simply couldn't bear the pain.'

Was he finally ready to talk? Lola had waited over three years for this, yet felt frighteningly unprepared. Maybe it was his parting gift to her, his way of giving her closure. It would bring them such sorrow in the telling, but it had to be done.

'Go on,' she said gently.

'We were having a lovely day together. She wore that red quilted jacket with the hood and those new pink Hunters you had bought her, and we walked into the village with the dog. The shopkeeper – what was his name? – Ruddy, Ruddle? – he remarked on how much she'd grown. Snook said the same thing later on and I wondered why I hadn't noticed. I missed out on so much.'

He refilled his glass. Lola didn't say a word, fearing that if she interrupted he might change his mind and retreat.

'When we got home I made hot chocolate while Clarissa played fetch with the dog. We sat at the kitchen table with that big KitKat tin she kept her crayons in, and did some drawing. I think about that often – me, Clarissa, the dog curled up in his basket, so ordinary, so perfect.'

He took a deep breath that faltered as he exhaled. For a moment Lola thought he might cry.

'I checked my emails. Big mistake. Some problem with a new client – I spent half an hour on the phone. Clarissa got restless and kept on at me to take her to the yard. It was nearly lunchtime but she was determined – you know when she used to make that face, the one that meant she wouldn't give up until she got what she wanted?'

Lola wiped the tears and nodded.

'All the stables were empty except for Polo's. Clarissa fed him a few carrots and then Snook appeared from the cottage. She ran up to him, arms wide open, that slightly wonky smile because her front teeth hadn't quite grown in properly yet. I was actually a bit peeved, seeing how close they were. She hugged him and he kissed the top of her head. Ridiculous, being envious of Snook. I needed to get back, sort out this thing with the client, but she wanted to stay at the yard with Snook and the dog. He said he had to take hay up to the paddocks in that little old tractor, that Clarissa could help if she wanted. Her face lit up. What could I do? I didn't want to seem harsh by insisting she came back to the house. I didn't even know if she was allowed on the tractor.' He shook his head. 'What does that say about me?'

Lola didn't have an answer. She reached for the tissues and blew her nose.

'I went back on my own,' said Duncan, and then fell silent for such a long while that Lola wondered if that was it. He seemed lost in his own thoughts, his own nightmare. She was about to get up and go to the bathroom when he spoke again.

'There was a clap of thunder. I looked out of the window and saw it had started to rain. I went to fetch Clarissa but she wasn't in the yard. The tractor wasn't there either but then the dog appeared, barking, frantic. I knew something was wrong so I followed him towards the paddocks. It was pouring now. He led me to the upturned tractor. I saw Snook first – he was lying on the ground – but I went straight over to the tractor. Clarissa was trapped inside, face down. You know all this from the inquest.'

'Tell me anyway.'

'Are you sure?'

'I'm sure.'

'She was crying – more of a whimper, really. The field was a quagmire, water rising in the ditch. I knew I had to get her out of there but her legs were pinned under the seat. It was useless – I had to get help.'

He covered his face with his hands.

'If I'd known –'

He pulled a handful of tissues from the box.

'I told her everything was going to be alright, promised I'd be back soon. It was difficult to hear, but I think she was asking me not to leave her.'

He wiped his eyes.

'I should have stayed with her, held her hand, told her not to be frightened. I should have told her how much I loved her, over and over, so it was the last thing she heard. I shouldn't have left her to die alone in a ditch.'

Great heaving sobs racked his body. Lola held him so tight her arms hurt. He kept repeating one phrase: *I'm so sorry*.

Duncan left the following morning. Lola told him he didn't have to but he was eager to get back. She meant it when she said she was glad he wouldn't be alone, that he deserved some happiness after everything he'd been through.

When she walked him to the car to say goodbye, they held each for a long time. It was a good ending. Later, when she recounted the story to Cain and the Curtellas – the showdown, Joanne called it – she was asked how they had remained so dispassionate, so civil. Where was the anger, the hurt, the recrimination? We were letting each other go, explained Lola, and we wanted to do it gently.

Epilogue

Freshers' week – pub crawls, disco parties, an inflatable fun day – new students' inauguration into university life. Saskia had worked hard for her place at King's; she wouldn't squander her time on such silly nonsense. When she called her mother to say she was to study Medicine in London, her mother cried, said how proud she was, how proud her father would have been. Saskia thought that would make it easier to tell her about Duncan but no, her mother didn't understand. *Why are you wasting yourself on an old man when you have your whole future ahead of you?* Duncan wasn't old. He seemed younger now than when they first met. His new lease on life, he called it. They both had their own study in the Notting Hill apartment and there was a small garden for Lara, their Pomeranian puppy. Saskia chose the name from *Doctor Zhivago*.

Duncan was taking her back to Ulyanovsk for Christmas – back to her home and her mother. It would be the first time in nine years. Saskia knew that when her mother met Duncan she would understand; she would see that he was good for her. Saskia liked the expression about having butterflies; that was how she felt when she thought of going back to Russia.

He said her joy brought him joy. She remembered how he was at the beginning, like his soul was frozen. He said she saved him, but she couldn't take all the credit. It was

Lola who made him confront the thing that was destroying him, Lola who released him. He had dreaded going to California last Christmas – having to act as if nothing was wrong when everything was wrong. But Lola had sent him back to her and Saskia would always be grateful.

He often talked about Clarissa – took pleasure in the mention of her name. Lola had called her little boy Skip Junior. Duncan said it was American. Saskia asked if it hurt him to think of Lola with another man, another child.

'No,' he said. 'It has brought me absolution.'

Acknowledgements

I would like to thank Elsa Dixon, who taught me how to speak American, Wanda Whiteley for her invaluable advice, and for introducing me to the wonderful Robert Kirby at United Agents. My heartfelt thanks to Robert for encouraging me to think of myself as a professional author, even when that was more aspiration than reality.

I would also like to thank my editor, Joel Richardson at Twenty7 Books, whose patience and gentle expertise coaxed me through the final drafts. And a word of acknowledgement to all the authors at Twenty7 Books, who banded together to support each other through the publication of our debut novels.

A special mention must go to my book group – Angela Hoey, Christine Kitchen, Kate Larard, Nina Flynn and Fiona Richardson – who read an early draft and were kinder than it probably deserved. And thanks to my dear friend Amanda Muir, who listened without complaint as I talked endlessly about the ups and downs of writing a novel and getting it published.

My final words of thanks go to my family – my children, who are quietly proud of me, and my husband, who is less quiet about it.